Hope's Daughter

by

Joani Ascher

Hope's Daughter

Cover Art by *Tina Lynn Stout*

The Wild Rose Press, Inc.
PO Box 708
Adams Basin, NY 14410-0708
Visit us at www.thewildrosepress.com

Publishing History
First Mainstream Historical Edition, 2019
Print ISBN 978-1-5092-2495-1
Digital ISBN 978-1-5092-2496-8

Published in the United States of America

From the time she entered the crowded room, Jane was unable to tear her eyes away from the speaker. He stood on the podium, above the noisy crowd, imploring them to be quiet. Lloyd Hammer, the man pictured on the flyer, held up his hands and waited for silence.

"It is vital to our country," he shouted, "that we insist there be no involvement of either our men or our resources in this trouble in Europe." His accent, with absent Rs, sounded strange to Jane's New York ears, but she had no time to think about it as a roar of protest rose from the crowd.

"I have family there," shouted one man. "We can't ignore them." Several people echoed his protest.

Lloyd Hammer held up his hands. "We must," he said, as the assembled people quieted. "We have just struggled through an era of terrible poverty. We cannot and we must not risk losing what we have worked so hard to rebuild."

Jane watched people turn to each other, questioning what they heard. She questioned it herself. The thought of ignoring the dreadful trouble in Europe went against her principles and her upbringing. Her father, while too old to have fought in the Great War, had several younger cousins who had, of whom he was exceptionally proud. It was at the wedding of one of them that he had met Hope, a woman who, even though much younger than he, shared his concern for the downtrodden of the world. From everything her father had told her, Jane could not imagine either of her parents agreeing with the man on the stage.

Yet he held her riveted, as he did so many others standing beside her.

Dedication

To my mother, who inspired this book

Acknowledgements

My most grateful thanks to the writers in my authors' group, Deborah Nolan and Kim Zito, for all their help and insights in shaping this novel.

Much appreciation is due to Nan Swanson, whose editorial efforts improved the flow of this book.

To my daughter, Shonna, who was always ready to read and reread for continuity, as well as cheerlead my efforts, I send all my love.

Thanks also to my son Ari, who could help me find my way out of any sentence I had boxed myself into.

And to my husband, David, who can redline with the best of them, there are no words for how much I love and adore you.

Chapter One

February 1941

Jane Baldwin hurried into her room right after work and closed the door, then leaned back against it in wonder. Her vain attempts to keep her lips from rounding into a satisfied smile soon erupted in a laugh, but she had to keep quiet.

It had been easier than expected to persuade her boss, Prescott Weaver, to formally teach her about his business, the trading of stocks. All she had to do was promise never to tell anyone.

Truthfully, Jane was surprised at his willingness. Always so proper and mindful of decorum, he did not seem like someone likely to go against the narrow-minded men of commerce who dictated that a woman could be a wife, secretary, nurse, or teacher, but could not be in business.

Although Mr. Weaver had said he had his reasons, Jane did not know what they were. She knew some things about his dealings, enough to know it was exhilarating and sometimes risky. She wanted to know how to do it well and someday make it her career. All the struggling she had done was over and nothing could stop her now.

Jane was still bubbling with excitement when she dressed for work in the morning. She ironed her blouse with extra care and took the time to brush her wool skirt and jacket thoroughly. As she finished applying lip pomade, her sister, Olivia, came to stand beside her.

"Is something special happening today?" Olivia asked, gazing into the mirror. "You look beautiful."

Jane looked at her own reflection and knew she did not. No one thought she was beautiful. Olivia was the beautiful one. She was lovely, with her eyes the color of liquid chocolate and equally dark brown hair, which was long, straight and gleaming. When she twisted it into a chignon it emphasized her long neck and sat on her head like a crown. Her creamy skin was flawless, not like Jane's freckled complexion. Olivia's buxom, curvy shape had men looking at her from the time she was thirteen. Now, at seventeen, she had callers daily.

Jane, a little too tall and too thin, had acorn-colored hair that kinked and curled, making it nearly impossible to keep in a proper bun. Her eyes were of no particular color, neither brown, blue, nor green, but some middling shade, which seemed to change with what she wore. She was twenty-one and had been out of college for two years already, due to rapid advancement in school, and she had never had a single date.

"I'm only trying to look like a proper secretary," Jane told her sister. "Nothing more."

Olivia seemed puzzled. "You never worry about what you look like. You always say it won't matter one bit, because you are going to be a career girl."

Jane turned away from the mirror and her sister. "Don't be silly. I never said that. It does matter."

"But if you aren't trying to attract a suitor…"

"Now stop," said Jane. "I am being especially careful with my clothes because an important client will

2

be coming to the office today."

"So Mr. Weaver should dress well," Olivia said. "That has nothing to do with you."

Jane reminded her sister about Mr. Weaver's rules for proper dress. *And if I want my own stock brokerage someday,* she told herself, *I have to learn from the best and follow his instructions.* She picked up her purse and walked into the narrow hallway that separated her room from Olivia's. "Shouldn't you be getting ready for your first class?"

"I suppose." Olivia pulled at her robe belt and went slowly into her room. Jane shook her head. Her sister's whole outlook, and even her posture, changed when the subject of college came up.

Olivia had started with so much promise. She was a typical bobbysoxer with a fun-seeking outlook to match, yet over the months she attended Brooklyn College she had become increasingly less enthusiastic about school. Jane wondered why, especially since Olivia had pulled straight A's in the fall term, but did not ask. Olivia was moody enough without her big sister prying into her personal business. Jane would try to find out later what was wrong. For now, she had to get to work.

Jane left the walkup apartment, descending the worn marble stairs and going outside to the street. The cold winter light did little to provide warmth, and the wind tore through Jane's good wool coat, a legacy of her stepmother, Pearl. She pulled the fox-trimmed collar close around her throat and hurried to the trolley, pushing thoughts of Olivia's strange behavior out of her mind. There was too much to do today.

When she got to work she struggled to tuck the

escaping ends of her unruly hair back into her tight bun. Mr. Weaver would be in soon, and she did not want to see another look of disappointment on his face when he saw her recalcitrant curls.

"Good morning, Miss Baldwin," Mr. Weaver said, when he arrived at the office. He took a look at the ticker tape as he came in, even before he hung his overcoat and hat on the tree.

"Good morning, Mr. Weaver," Jane responded, knowing that the Dow Jones Average hovered near 133. She saw him smile, making his brown mustache seem even bigger.

When she first came to work for him Jane was surprised such a young man would wear such a big mustache. She soon decided his round face would look childlike without it. His baby blue eyes added to the youthful image he tried so hard to hide. He also had several unfortunately placed cowlicks in his light brown hair, which no amount of hair dressing seemed able to conquer. At twenty-six, his face could pass for that of a twelve-year-old, except for that mustache.

Yet somehow, with his tall form in his loose-fitting tailored suits, the mustache did not look silly. From what Jane had heard, he had dozens of young society ladies clamoring for his attention. While she held him in the highest esteem, she had done everything she could, since getting her job, to guard herself against personal feelings for him. She knew she would only be hurt in the long run, because a man like him would never think of her that way.

****

Prescott Weaver noticed as soon as he arrived at work that Jane looked different. Her honey-colored

4

hair, usually unruly, was neatly tucked into its bun. Although he had often experienced a strange urge to touch her escaping curls, this looked more businesslike.

She seemed different this morning, with more color in her cheeks, more sparkle in her hazel eyes, and he thought, a touch of lip pomade. She disdained putting makeup on her pretty face, as far as he knew, saying it was not for serious career-minded ladies such as she but for upper-class society women with time on their hands.

He could not help remembering, though, as he looked at the ticker tape, that she had come from an upper-class background, and if not for the crash of the stock market, her life might have been more like that of those other girls.

Yet somehow he doubted that. One of the things he admired most about Jane was how she took care of not only herself but others as well. She was so kind that she even took care of that poor gangly boy Horace, her sister Olivia's friend, when he was left orphaned and alone. She had gone so far as to find some delivery work the boy could do here on Wall Street to help make ends meet.

She was also thoughtful of her employer. She never missed an opportunity to do something nice for Prescott, from finding a new nib for his favorite fountain pen to bringing him an autographed baseball her father had once caught at Ebbets Field, just because he mentioned his childhood idolization of some of the players.

"Good morning, Miss Baldwin," he said, hanging up his hat and coat.

"Good morning, Mr. Weaver," she responded, in her soft, melodious voice.

Prescott went into his inner office. Jane had truly been a find, when she came to work for him two years before, and he appreciated her interest and enthusiasm for his business. Jane was quite astute, and if he let his imagination roam and ignored the tradition of men only in the field, he could foresee the day when he attained his seat on the New York Stock Exchange and she would be the one to manage the office, counseling clients and calling in buy and sell orders. She was eager to learn everything, and he was willing to teach her. If the truth were known, she had not had to work very hard to persuade him to be her teacher.

She would probably never be in the position to need the knowledge he was so happy to impart. He knew that someday someone would come along and convince Jane to leave the business and marry. That man would be one lucky fellow.

Meanwhile, since Prescott had no family money to fall back on to help him with the payment for his seat, not since his father had cut him off, it would be some time before he could afford to buy it and require an associate.

****

At ten past eleven, Mr. Weaver's client, Hugh Canfield, arrived. As usual, he was accompanied by his wife, a woman many years younger than himself, swathed in furs. Mr. Canfield had been one of the few lucky ones who avoided the crash of '29. He had taken his money out of the market and bought real estate, precious metals, and some oil wells. Since then he'd lived an extravagant lifestyle, with several homes, and a country club membership in each locale.

He belonged to one where Mr. Weaver's father, a

prominent attorney and longtime friend of Mr. Canfield, was also a member. That was where he first met Prescott Weaver.

"It's good to see you, my boy," said Mr. Canfield. "I hope you're ready to make some more money for me."

Mr. Weaver smiled. "Of course. I have some paperwork I'd like to show you." He turned to Jane. "Has it come in yet?"

"No, sir. I'll go get it."

"Stay here," said Mr. Weaver. "I'll get it. Make sure my clients are comfortable." He went out, closing the door behind him.

"He's a real pistol," said Mr. Canfield as Jane led him and his wife into the inner office and indicated where they should sit. "His own man." Although Jane had heard the story several times, she did not interrupt.

"Did you know that he defied his father's recommendation, to go into law, in favor of a business career?" Without waiting for an answer, he continued, "and he lost his father's tuition support. His father is a fool for not seeing how capable and hardworking Prescott is. Why, if I had a son like that…" He did not finish his sentence but looked quickly at his wife.

She gave him a frosty look.

He took out his pipe, filled it, tamped down the tobacco, and lit a match. "I wanted to help Prescott out," he said, between pulls on the pipe to light it, "so when he opened his office, I decided to invest a small portion of my money with him. He's done well with it."

Mr. Canfield was a decent man, Jane knew, yet his cold-as-ice wife was another story.

Mrs. Canfield was elegant, with carefully coifed

hair and manicured nails on fingers that displayed diamonds and rubies. Just one of her earrings would have been enough to pay the rent on Jane's apartment for six months, though she seemed unconcerned by their value. She pulled off the heavy earrings and rubbed her lobes before dropping the jewelry into her purse.

Mr. Canfield seemed momentarily annoyed about his wife's carelessness with the earrings. He did not look like a man to regard investments lightly. There was a lot Jane could learn, she knew, from studying the transactions Mr. Canfield made.

Jane could get lost in the subject of stock trading for hours. Mr. Canfield had on several occasions remarked that she had a knack for the market. "Too bad you aren't a man," he had said. "You could have had a bright career."

Jane smiled. "Can I get either of you anything?"

Mrs. Canfield, who had slung her mink-collared Persian lamb coat over one of the office chairs, revealing a bright red wool dress from Saks Fifth Avenue, narrowed her eyes. "I think Miss Baldwin has more important things to think about than our little investments," she said. "Perhaps a young man?"

Jane felt her face get hot, and suddenly the drafty room seemed to have a warm breeze running through it. Nothing could have been further from the truth, nor in all likelihood, would it ever be. "C-coffee or tea?" she stammered.

"Nothing for me," said Mr. Canfield, attempting again to light his pipe. He succeeded, exhaled slowly, and turned to his wife. "For you, darling?"

She finished touching up her red lipstick and,

snapping her compact shut, smiled. "I'd love a cup of tea," she said. "It is so cold outside. When will spring ever come?"

A short discussion of the weather followed, amid speculation about when the golf course would open at the club to which the Canfields, and now Mr. Weaver, belonged. When Mr. Weaver returned, Jane left to go get the tea. After she delivered the hot beverage to Mrs. Canfield, she was alone with the ticker tape machine.

They were closeted for almost an hour, and it was after noon when they re-emerged. "I am concerned about the news from Europe," said Mr. Canfield as he readied himself to leave. "I know Roosevelt says we're neutral, but can we count on that?"

Mr. Weaver frowned. "I think we're going to have to get involved. Look at Canada. They've been in this war since '39, and here we sit, twiddling our principles."

"You'd make a profit if we went to war," Mrs. Canfield said to her husband, with some scorn. Turning back to Mr. Weaver, she said, "Have you considered the people involved?"

Mr. Weaver looked serious, and for once his youthful face did not undermine him. "If this country goes to war," he told Mrs. Canfield, "we will have to fight to win. Whatever it takes."

Mrs. Canfield arched her painted-on eyebrows. "And would you join the effort?" she asked.

"Yes." Mr. Weaver left no opening for further discussion.

Mr. Canfield nodded at Mr. Weaver. "That's why you're taking those courses, isn't it? Yet it may not come to that."

Jane did not know what Mr. Canfield meant. Mr. Weaver had never said anything to her about any courses. She knew there were some being offered to prepare for possible military duty, but she would not have thought they were for her employer.

"If you'd only get married, Prescott," Mr. Canfield continued, as if Mr. Weaver's feelings were trivial, "you'd get over this silly idea of wanting to fight in the war. You should find yourself a nice girl, like Regina, Lee Marsh's daughter. Then you could start a family, and forget about going overseas."

The ticker tape machine clattered in the uncomfortable silence. Mrs. Canfield, who had been checking the seams of her stockings, straightened up and frowned. She pulled on her gloves, while keeping her eyes on Mr. Weaver.

Mr. Canfield seemed not to have noticed his wife's discomfort at his tone. "We won't enter the war," he predicted confidently. "There are too many people in this country opposed to our involvement."

"I hope we don't go to war," said Mrs. Canfield, looking at Mr. Weaver. Turning to her husband, specifically, she said, "Prescott is capable of deciding for himself whom to marry, darling." Then she reached for his arm and propelled him out of the office.

Left alone, Jane thought about the difference between herself and Mrs. Canfield, the kind of person who went to society balls and decorated her husband's arm at the theater. It made her feel even taller and less attractive than usual.

Chapter Two

It was well past dark when Jane stepped out of the office building at 55 Wall Street, but little light could have penetrated to the ground where she stood even if it had been high noon. The buildings were too tall and close together, looming like giants over the narrow pavement below. When she turned into the wind, grit and soot stung her eyes, making them tear. She blinked and pulled her veil farther down to help protect her face.

Jane did not look forward to the subway ride to the President Street station in Brooklyn, after which she still had to board a crowded trolley car and ride it to her Rogers Avenue neighborhood. The subway cars always rocked and stopped short, constantly throwing her against her fellow passengers, while she hung onto the leather straps for dear life. She had to straighten her hat several times each trip, pushing her hatpin farther in to keep her hat from going askew. When she reached her stop, she then had to push her way onto the trolley, hoping to find a place to put her feet without stepping on someone else's.

She was in no particular rush tonight, though, once she got onto Broad Street and out of the wind, since no one was waiting. In a way, she supposed, it was a portent of her future.

In the past, Olivia was always home before her, but

this evening, as with so many evenings recently, she would be out with one of her friends. Tonight it was Horace, Olivia's favorite, the one who used to come to dinner at their apartment four nights a week until he finally learned to cook for himself. Now that they were in college, they spent most evenings at the library, studying for their bright futures.

In a few years, Jane knew, Olivia would marry and start a family of her own. But Jane's intention to become a well-respected leader in her field someday was all the future she expected or wanted. A career was something that her mother, Hope, had dreamed of for Jane, who was born the same year as women got the right to vote.

Toward that end, Jane planned to learn whatever she could from Mr. Weaver. But while she still had the responsibility for taking care of her sister, which she had done singlehandedly for several years, she would not take any risks.

When Jane emerged from the subway station in Brooklyn, a crowd standing outside a meeting hall drew her attention. Someone handed her a leaflet with the heading "America First Committee." It said, "If we permit our country to become involved in the war now raging in Europe, Asia, and Africa, we face disastrous sacrifices—human, social, and material. We risk the liberties of the United States in a conflict from which no nation can emerge truly victorious. Let us spare America from such an act of national folly."

Reading it, Jane found her interest piqued, if only because she disagreed. She pushed her way inside, wondering how anyone could feel that way. What she found was even more puzzling to her.

From the time she entered the crowded room, Jane was unable to tear her eyes away from the speaker. He stood on the podium, above the noisy crowd, imploring them to be quiet. Lloyd Hammer, the man pictured on the flyer, held up his hands and waited for silence.

"It is vital to our country," he shouted, "that we insist there be no involvement of either our men or our resources in this trouble in Europe." His accent, with absent Rs, sounded strange to Jane's New York ears, but she had no time to think about it as a roar of protest rose from the crowd.

"I have family there," shouted one man. "We can't ignore them." Several people echoed his protest.

Lloyd Hammer held up his hands. "We must," he said, as the assembled people quieted. "We have just struggled through an era of terrible poverty. We cannot and we must not risk losing what we have worked so hard to rebuild."

Jane watched people turn to each other, questioning what they heard. She questioned it herself. The thought of ignoring the dreadful trouble in Europe went against her principles and her upbringing. Her father, while too old to have fought in the Great War, had several younger cousins who had, of whom he was exceptionally proud. It was at the wedding of one of them that he had met Hope, a woman who, even though much younger than he, shared his concern for the downtrodden of the world. From everything her father had told her, Jane could not imagine either of her parents agreeing with the man on the stage.

Yet he held her riveted, as he did so many others standing beside her.

"Let them fight their own battles," he continued.

"We must not go up against the German power again. We must gird our shores against the threat…" He spoke for several more minutes, invoking the words of America First's leader, Charles A. Lindbergh, and one of its financial sponsors, Henry Ford. At the conclusion, he handed out more leaflets, inviting everyone present to the rally that was to be held on May 29th in Madison Square Garden.

As the crowd dispersed, Jane turned to go. It was getting quite late, and by now Olivia would be home and waiting. She would worry if Jane did not get home soon.

Olivia worried so much, about so many things. She worried about the people in Europe, and she worried about going to college. Jane swore she would see Olivia make it through without having to drop out and work full time. Olivia depended on her, but Jane felt she must learn to support herself, at least until she was married.

Yet Jane would not push her. Olivia was very sensitive, and she had been through too much already. Jane kept from her the details of her struggle to pay the rent and allowed her to keep half of what she made babysitting for the neighbors, where she was very much in demand. She was wonderful with children. Jane thought she would make a good teacher, and certainly would be a good mother. For herself, she would be content to be Aunt Jane someday.

She waited while several people passed and then made her way to the lobby of the hall. At the other end, she saw Mr. Hammer standing near the door, greeting people who seemed to want to talk to him, some to argue, some to agree.

Even through billows of cigarette smoke, she could

tell he had the darkest eyes she had ever seen, and his hair was blue-black. He wore a suit, with a starched white shirt, and his tie, even though the room had become warm, was tight to his neck.

Jane searched for a path through the throng so she could leave. She edged toward the double doors, excusing herself as she pushed past a group of men whose hand-rolled cigarettes dropped ash on the floor. They did not move aside, as she had expected. One raised his eyebrows and leered at her.

Unaccustomed as she was to that kind of attention, Jane felt her face burn and renewed her attempts to find an exit.

She looked at her watch as she finally got near the door and tried to figure out how soon the next trolley would come. But once there, she was unable to leave, and barely able to move. It was as if she was rooted to the spot, and she could not take her eyes off the charismatic man in the doorway.

At that moment Lloyd Hammer turned his gaze toward her. She was startled by his intensity, and felt herself drawn to him. Only the interruption of another well-wisher broke the connection. She rushed outside.

Taking a deep breath, she walked down the street outside the meeting hall to the corner. She pulled her coat closer around her, and hurried through a light rain toward the streetcar stop.

Someone touched her shoulder. Turning, she gasped. The hand belonged to Lloyd Hammer.

"Please wait," he implored. "I, uh, wondered if I could talk to you."

Unable to speak, Jane stood her ground. She watched as the streetcar pulled in, discharged a few passengers, and loaded up with more, then pulled away. There would not be another for a while.

"Thanks," said Lloyd. "I was afraid you would get on that streetcar and I'd never see you again." He looked around, and pulled his own overcoat closer. "It's gotten colder. Do you want to go for a cup of coffee?"

Jane shivered, even though she was standing close enough to feel his warmth. She did not know how to respond, since this was the first cup of coffee anyone had ever invited her to have. But it was so late, and Olivia would worry. "My sister is waiting," Jane said.

"Surely she can wait for just a little while," he said, his husky voice resonating. "The streetcar is gone. We won't take long, and you can catch the next one." He smiled, waiting for her reply.

She was dazzled by his bright, white, even teeth and by the way his eyes, on a level with her own, crinkled at the edges. When she nodded, he took her gently by the arm and led her down the block to a coffee shop.

It was warm inside, and crowded. The odor of wet wool and cigarettes surrounded her as Lloyd led her to a table near the window. He helped her take off her coat and slung it and his own over the back of an empty chair. She was captivated, seeing her coat touching his, with his hat resting on top.

"I don't even know your name," he said. "But I just had to meet you."

"It's Jane Baldwin."

"I'm Lloyd Hammer."

"I know."

He furrowed his brow. "Have we met before? I'm sure I would have remembered someone so beautiful."

Jane felt herself blushing. "No. I was at the rally tonight." She looked him directly in the eyes, searching for a sign that he had seen her there. Why else would he have stopped her on the street?

"So it was you. I saw you, you know, and I wanted to meet you, but when I turned you were gone. I'm so glad I found you."

Jane suddenly felt very uncomfortable. Why would he say such a thing? She was no one whom men wanted to meet. It did not make sense. But since she had his attention, she decided to speak her mind.

"I can't say I agree with the isolationists and with what you said," she told him. "I don't think we should gird our shores against the threat of pillaging by the unfortunates abroad, as you put it. How can we turn our backs when we are needed? What would have happened if we had not fought in the Great War?"

"You didn't fight in the Great War, and you didn't have to risk dying. You didn't have to give up your goals or dreams because of it."

Jane noticed Lloyd's left hand was balled into a fist. "Did you?" she asked. "You're a bit too young."

"I am not that young," he said, angrily. "I'm thirty."

"So in 1917 you were six," she replied, bristling. "What regiment were you with?"

His angry expression vanished into a smile. "You're right. Sometimes I think I take myself too seriously. Of course I wasn't in the war."

Jane's breath was taken away when he smiled. He had the most wonderful grin, totally charming and warm. Her own anger dispersed like a puff of smoke. She sipped the coffee the waitress had put in front of her, wondering what to say.

Lloyd leaned forward, so close to Jane she could feel his breath on her cheek. "But I do know we shouldn't be in this war. It is not for the United States of America. Why do you think we should enter the war?"

"I don't. I don't want anyone killed any more than you do. But I believe there is a moral…"

He put his hand on hers, effectively stopping her speech in its tracks. "Let's not talk about that right now. I want to get to know you."

"Me? I'm no one. Why…?" Unable to finish, Jane dabbed at her mouth with her napkin.

Lloyd cocked his head. "You are an interesting woman," he said. "And different from the empty-headed girls I so often meet. Why wouldn't anyone want to get to know you?" He took her hand in his. "I know this may seem too forward, but the moment I saw you, I had to talk to you." Releasing her hand, he stayed close. "Tell me about yourself."

Looking away from his eyes, Jane tried to quell her trembling. "There isn't very much to tell. I live with my sister and I work as a secretary in a stock brokerage." She swallowed. "What about you? What do you do when you aren't giving speeches?"

"I also work on Wall Street. But I'd much rather talk about you. Is it just the two of you? You and…?"

"Olivia. Yes. Ever since Father died."

"When?"

Jane blinked back a tear. "Five years ago." Her father had never recovered what he lost in the stock market crash, and his health had declined steadily since that black day. He had taken any job he could, in those times when jobs were so scarce, and had somehow managed to leave just enough money for Jane to finish college, although she'd had to work nights and weekends in Macy's to be able to afford clothes for herself and her sister.

"And your mother?"

"She passed away when I was two. It was a riding accident."

Lloyd had a surprised look on his face, and he glanced at her coat, one far more expensive than any Jane could now afford. She did not explain the change that had occurred in the family circumstances.

"I'm sorry," he said. "But you said you had a sister. Is she older?"

"No, Olivia is younger. My father remarried a year later. She was Olivia's mother." If she concentrated very hard, Jane could almost remember Vanessa, a young woman whom her father had met at the home of a friend when he was barely through grieving his first wife. She had been younger than Jane was now when she married Jane's father, and had looked very much like Olivia. The resemblance in the only picture they had of her was striking.

"A few months after Olivia was born, Vanessa died," Jane explained. She did not remember why, and no one ever spoke of it. "Then, a few years later, Father married Pearl." She was a woman he'd known his whole life, who had secretly loved him since she was a young woman, she had once confessed to Jane and Olivia.

"I had set my cap for him when we were very young," Pearl had told the girls. "He was so busy with his wine importing business then, constantly traveling to Europe, and in no way ready to settle down. When he saw the writing on the wall and the coming of prohibition, he sold out all his interests and came back to the States. He met Hope, fell instantly in love, and married her. Then there was Vanessa. One day, though, there was only me and I could finally be with my life's love." Pearl was a good woman, never bitter about it, and Jane still missed her.

"In 1934, Pearl got TB and died," Jane told Lloyd. That had been devastating. They had tried everything for a cure, including trips to the clean air of the country and a sanitarium in Saranac Lake. When she passed away, leaving the girls motherless again, their father, a great baseball fan, said that three strikes rendered him out and he would not remarry. He swore he would raise his daughters on his own. He had almost made it.

Lloyd's face was filled with sympathy. "That must have been so hard."

Jane chanced another look into those black eyes. "It's all right. Father left us able to fend for ourselves. We manage." She clenched her fists and looked away. She would manage to take care of her sister, no matter what.

"You're very brave."

"Enough about me," said Jane, who was becoming uncomfortable with Lloyd's praise. "Do you have a family?"

"No. I'm alone. I don't have time for a family. Maybe someday I'll find a woman who can take care of me." His wistful gaze made Jane a bit uncomfortable.

"It's getting so late," she said. "I must go home."

"Please let me escort you."

"Oh, no, that isn't necessary."

He smiled broadly. "But it would be my pleasure." He held her coat for her. "Let's go."

All the way to her home they talked about the city, and the opera, which Jane loved. "I saw every opera I could last season," Jane told him. She did not mention that she saw all of them standing, as she had never been able to pay for a seat.

Lloyd's eyes took on another look of surprise, but then he laughed. "I haven't ever seen one," he admitted. "But I'm sure they must be wonderful if you like them so much."

Jane had trouble finding words for a while and let Lloyd chatter on. Eventually, he spoke about what was going on in Europe. She realized he was not as opposed to giving aid as he sounded, but he was unwilling to commit troops. His father was buried in Flanders Field. "No little boy should have to grow up without his father," Lloyd said, and Jane's heart went out to him.

They arrived at the steps of the walk-up she lived in with Olivia. It was hard to pay the rent in that building, since it was more expensive than they could afford, but Jane had insisted they could not live somewhere cheaper, since it was just too dangerous for two girls on their own.

Jane noticed the heavy living room drapes in their front apartment on the second floor sway as her sister let them go. Seconds later the front door opened.

"Thank God," said Olivia, rushing down the steps to the street. "I was so worried."

"You'll catch your death," Jane chided, putting her coat around her sister's shoulders. "I'm sorry if I frightened you."

Olivia smiled, wiping a tear from her eye. "It's all

right, you're here now." She turned to Lloyd, a question on her face.

Jane introduced them. But she could not help noticing that both Olivia and Lloyd kept their eyes on her. It was unusual for her to be the center of attention. And wonderful.

****

The next day Jane's mind was far away, remembering the time she'd spent with Lloyd. She had never been paid so much attention by a man. She did not know what to make of it. When Mr. Weaver said she could go to lunch, she was happy to hurry off to be alone with her thoughts.

She had only walked a half block to the luncheonette when her path was blocked. Looking at the man standing in front of her, Jane felt her face flush.

Lloyd Hammer smiled, gazing into her eyes. "I was hoping to see you. I was just on my way to your office. Might I invite you to lunch?"

It was a lucky thing he took her by the arm, she observed, because there was a distinct possibility she would have passed out from shock. His suit may not have been of the quality of Mr. Weaver's or that of his client, Mr. Canfield, and his collar might have needed turning, but he held her arm as elegantly as Mr. Canfield had held his wife's, and guided her along the street.

They went to the delicatessen and talked so much Jane did not finish her lunch. She was fascinated by Lloyd's stories of growing up in a poor section of Boston, and she could barely tear her eyes away from his. When he told her they had been there nearly an hour, it came as a total surprise.

"I must get back," she said, almost upsetting her wooden chair as she stood. It bumped into another diner, who glared at her as she grabbed at it. Mumbling apologies, she rushed toward the door.

Lloyd hurried to pay the check and catch up with her. "Will you meet me for lunch tomorrow?"

Jane was still unsure about this man with the strange politics, but she agreed. They met every day for lunch after that, sometimes taking their sandwiches to a park, and sometimes, on warmer days, walking over to the river to watch the boats. After two weeks, Jane felt comfortable with him. He was charming, and such a good conversationalist.

"I earned a bonus today and I want to celebrate." he said, turning away from the river and looking into her eyes. "May I see you tonight?"

Jane could not think. But she had to say something. He looked at her with such hope she could not disappoint him. "Yes."

"Wonderful. I'll pick you up at seven, and we'll paint the town."

Chapter Three

Olivia fluttered around Jane, helping her dress for her date. Lloyd had said they would go to Peter Luger's for supper, and hinted that they might even go dancing afterward. Olivia let her imagination run freely, as well as her tongue, and filled the time talking of how wonderful it would be tonight with Lloyd, how romantic, and how someday she hoped she and Horace would have that kind of evening. Jane chuckled at the thought of that beanpole, with his lopsided grin and chipped front tooth, dressing up to go to a place like that. It would probably be years before he made enough money for such an excursion. She also knew Olivia would gladly wait.

The only problem was that Jane had nothing to wear suitable for the occasion. Neither she nor Olivia had ever had a fancy dress.

In the end, they shared their problem with Mrs. McGill, their landlady, who came upstairs a half hour later with one borrowed from her niece.

She held it up proudly for them to inspect. Olivia took it and twirled it around, making it flare.

Mrs. McGill turned to go, reaching into the pocket of her housecoat to take out the soft rag she carried to polish her beloved brass rail. The banister ran from the first floor of the walk-up midway to the second, acting, along with the marble stairs, as the focal point for the large front hallway. Mrs. McGill thought the marble-floored lobby made her building the envy of all the similar ones nearby, a notch above its peers. She never failed to wipe the railing on her way up or down the stairs.

"I'll be right back with an evening bag," she promised Jane, who stood in the doorway watching her rub the rail. "And a stole." Smiling with excitement, she hurried down.

The pale Pacific-blue ankle-length gown made Jane's changeable eyes look the same shade of blue. Unfortunately, when she put it on, the neckline formed a deep V, which gapped, due to Jane's lack of natural endowment. Something would have to be done about it.

Mrs. McGill returned with the accessories and assessed the problem. "My niece fills it out better than you do, dear. I'd recommend using some type of brooch to hold it closed." She and her polishing rag went back downstairs.

Olivia went to her own room to hunt for a pin.

Jane struggled with her corkscrew hair, lamenting its independence. The latest style, a bob with bangs, was totally out of her reach. Her hair was all wrong. No matter how much dressing she put on it, it would never curl under at her neck. If she had her hair cut short enough for the bob, it would surround her head like a bad hat.

Her only defense was to keep it longer; the weight alone helped to keep it down. Ideally, she could put it up, although every attempt she had made so far this evening had failed miserably.

Finally, she allowed Olivia to twist the mess into a low chignon, not as elegant as Olivia could make her own dark hair, but presentable.

"Your hair looks fine," her sister assured her. "But I still haven't found a suitable pin for you. And something else is missing." Suddenly she smiled. "I have just the thing!" She ran out of Jane's room and returned a moment later, carrying a bottle of perfume. "You probably don't remember this," she said. "I know I wouldn't, if I hadn't found that letter with it."

Jane looked at the beautifully shaped bottle. It was still sealed. She could not recall ever seeing it before. "Where did you get that?" she asked.

Olivia held the bottle reverently. "Father had put it away. After he—" She swallowed. "When we cleared out his things, I found the bottle. Father had left a note with it. I guess he wanted to give it to me when I turned eighteen."

She blinked back tears before continuing. "The perfume was my mother's. He said in the letter that he hoped this unopened bottle, one he bought for her when her other one was getting low, would last until I'm old enough to wear it." She opened it, and a long forgotten scent filled Jane's nostrils.

It was as if she were four years old again, on a summer afternoon, walking down the long front lawn of the big house in Westchester to the creek. Little Jane reached up to take the hand of the beautiful lady who had come to marry Father after Mama died. Jane remembered nothing of her own mother and knew only what her father and Pearl had told her about Hope, the woman who had given birth to her. But she vividly recalled those days with Vanessa, whom she was told to call Mother.

Her hair was so dark, and she wore a beautiful

white sundress, which protruded in the middle. She said that soon Jane would have a baby brother or sister. Jane loved that thought, and loved sitting under the weeping willow tree beside Mother while she read to her. Sometimes she fell asleep sitting there, surrounded by the scent of Mother's perfume.

It took effort on Jane's part not to cry now, as the vapors of the long-stoppered perfume wafted in the air. The pain of losing Mother had come so quickly after the joy of Olivia's arrival, and it had hurt so much.

"What shall we name your sister?" Mother had asked, when her baby was born. When Jane did not have an answer, she said, "Your mother chose Jane for you, and it is a nice enough name, but I think your sister will be Olivia. Doesn't that sound lovely?"

Mother had been so happy. But then she was not happy anymore, and it frightened Jane. One day she was gone. Father said she had died, like Hope. Jane thought it might be her fault her mothers went away. But Father said that was silly. He also said that Jane and Olivia would always have him. They moved to the big apartment overlooking Central Park after he married Pearl, and some of Jane's pain went away.

When Father succumbed to cancer, Jane knew how much he hated leaving them, and what a sense of failure he had because he could not be with them anymore. She had tried to relieve his guilt by promising she would take care of everything. But he shook his head. "Don't forget to live your own life," he had said.

"I will," she had replied, through the tears. She would live up to that promise, someday, and she would have her career.

"Put some on," said Olivia, snapping Jane back to

the present and the matter at hand. "Your date will be here in a few minutes."

That sounded so peculiar to Jane. She had never really considered dating. Now she was actually preparing for it.

Jane remembered with clarity the preparations Pearl had made for any evening out. She would spend the morning in the beauty parlor, having her hair done elaborately. She also had a manicure, choosing whatever shade of pink the girls suggested. Then she would come home and soak in a bubble bath. The girls always sat with her, listening to her imagine all the people who would be wherever she was going that night, and which singers would sing and which bands would play. Olivia was too young to understand what their stepmother was saying, and she usually just repeated the funnier-sounding words, making both Jane and Pearl laugh till tears ran.

That was all before the stock market crash. Afterward, many people, among them their parents, no longer had the money or desire to celebrate as they once did.

But Jane had loved those evenings before, when after her bath Pearl would put on her beautiful corsets and most delicate crinolines. She would dab perfume, a very different scent than Vanessa's, behind her ears and on her breastbone, and her dressing room would smell delicious. Then, slipping into her gorgeous clothes and pulling on her gloves and fur stole, she would wait in the front hall for their father. His Chesterfield overcoat made him look so handsome, Jane had often thought her heart would burst.

The memories did not help with Jane's

preparations for her own evening out. The perfume Olivia wanted her to wear only brought uncomfortable recollections of… She shook her head, trying to clear it.

"What's wrong?" Olivia asked.

"I don't want to wear that perfume."

"Why not?"

"I think you should be the one to wear it. She was your mother."

"She was your mother, too. You always told me how much you loved her."

Another wave of shivers passed over Jane. It was true that she told Olivia how wonderful her mother had been, since as a baby she could not have any recollection of her. But Jane had some unpleasant memories. After Olivia was born, it was all kind of dark and foggy, with muffled sounds and strange people trooping through the house until, one day, Vanessa was no longer there. Jane learned quickly not to ask about her.

"No," said Jane. The memories were too painful, and she did not want pain tonight. "I'd rather you be the first one to wear it."

"But I am not going out tonight, and besides, I'm too young for this scent."

"Then we'll keep it for later. It won't be long." Vanessa had been only eighteen when she married their father and had worn the scent. "Now, where is my watch?"

Olivia handed Jane her watch, which she intended, since she had nothing else, to pin to her dress. She had opened the double clasp when her sister stopped her. "Wouldn't you rather wear the cameo?"

Jane had not thought of the cameo in years. It was

a legacy from Father's mother. Pearl was very fond of it and had often said that one day Jane would own it. "You are your father's eldest daughter," she said, "and it will be yours someday, when I am gone." Inspired, Jane pulled out the old velvet box she had kept hidden in her dresser. Inside, the cameo nestled on cotton. It was lovely, with a delicate carving of an ancient Greek scene of long-haired maidens filling urns with water. It was surrounded by gold, with a little fleur-de-lis-shaped top, and tiny diamonds and pearls. The background was of a lovely shade of pinkish brown, and the detail was exquisite.

Jane pinned it to the bodice of her dress, tightening the fabric so it did not gap, and stopped to look at herself in the mirror. What she saw pleased her, even with her slenderness. Her complexion glowed, and for the first time, Jane felt beautiful.

"You look wonderful," said Olivia. "Like a princess."

When Lloyd arrived, he seemed dazzled. He himself looked dapper in his overcoat with a flowing white scarf. It was all Jane could do to remember to keep breathing, seeing him here, in their small living room. Lloyd helped her into Mrs. McGill's stole, took her gently by the arm, and promised Olivia, who seemed unable to stop smiling, that they would not be late. Then he led her down to the street, where he had a cab waiting.

The evening was magical, everything Jane had imagined her parents doing, with the addition of Champagne, which had been against the law during Prohibition. It tickled Jane's nose. After dinner they went to Twenty-One, for an hour or so, and then to the

Rainbow Room. She had never talked so much in her life, but she felt as if she would never run out of things to discuss with this man in the white dinner jacket. She made an effort, however, to avoid talking about Lloyd's advocacy of America First, feeling she had made herself clear that she did not agree. For his part, he did not push his view.

It was in the doorway of the Rainbow Room, while their wraps and Lloyd's hat were being checked, that she saw the Canfields. At first, Jane was embarrassed, feeling oddly shy to be seen in the same establishment as her employer's biggest clients. In the hope of not being recognized, Jane turned to Lloyd and asked if they could leave. His disappointed face convinced her to retract her request, and after a few turns on the dance floor she felt more comfortable. She was grateful to her sister for insisting they practice dancing, for hours at a time, when Olivia was fifteen. As it was, Jane still felt her technique left something to be desired.

They were almost ready to leave when Jane saw Mrs. Canfield staring at her. She seemed to be measuring Lloyd. Jane was convinced the assessment had not been positive. Mr. Canfield turned to look in the direction of his wife's gaze and spotted Jane. Before she could blink, the couple was standing next to her.

"Good evening, Miss Baldwin," said Mr. Canfield. "It's lovely to see you."

Jane made the necessary introductions, all the while feeling Mrs. Canfield's eyes on her. It occurred to her that Lloyd might possibly start to talk about American involvement overseas. She held her breath, hoping he would keep his opinions to himself.

But they discussed the stock market. While Mr.

Canfield and Lloyd chatted about business, Jane turned to Mrs. Canfield, wondering what kind of small talk she could make.

The matter was out of her hands as soon as Mrs. Canfield opened her mouth. "That is a lovely cameo."

Jane's hand touched her brooch. "Thank you."

"It looks very old."

"Yes. It belonged to my grandmother. It was her mother's."

Mrs. Canfield narrowed her eyes, giving Jane the impression that she was a cat, gauging the distance to her prey. "I have always wanted one like that," said Mrs. Canfield. "If you should ever decide to sell it, come to me first."

It was odd, that she, Jane, had something that Mrs. Canfield wanted. She was just as sure, though, that the woman could find one for herself. She knew that while her own was exceptionally high in quality, and different from the more common portrait of a woman's head, it was not rare.

She was saved from having to reply by Lloyd. "Would you like to go home now?" he asked.

She nodded. "Will you excuse us?" she asked the Canfields.

Mr. Canfield's eyes moved from Lloyd to Jane, and his puzzled expression vanished. "Good night, my dear. Take good care of yourself." His sincere warmth almost made up for Mrs. Canfield's chilly dismissal.

Lloyd was charming and sweet all the way back to Brooklyn. He thanked Jane for allowing him to meet Hugh Canfield. His enthusiasm was contagious, and by the time they got back to Jane's street, she was giddy with excitement.

"I wish I didn't have to go away tomorrow," he said, leaning close to her. "I will miss you so much."

This was the first Jane had heard that he was going away. She did not know what to say.

"Please promise me," said Lloyd, holding her at arm's length, and looking directly into her eyes, "that you will still be here when I return."

"I was planning on going inside when you leave," Jane said, forcing a smile to hide her disappointment about his departure. "I don't think it would be practical for me to remain on the street for any length of time."

Lloyd looked up at the star-filled sky and laughed. "That sense of humor of yours is so special. I won't be gone more than a week. May I call on you when I return?"

Jane was relieved. She did not want too much time to pass before she saw Lloyd again. "Yes, you may."

"Would it be all right if I embrace you?" he asked, surprising her with the sudden huskiness his voice. She nodded, unable to speak. He reached his arms around her completely, holding her close. "It will need to last for a week," he warned. "Won't it?"

She looked up at his face, trying to figure out what to say about that. His lips on hers cut short the need for an answer.

****

Prescott studied late into the evening, as he had every night for months. His intention to become an officer if there was a war hung in the balance. As much as he hated the prospect of losing his business, his country was more important, and he had to be prepared.

He fervently hoped the problems in Europe would be solved and war would not come. He still had to repay the loans he had taken out to finish college after his father cut him off and to start his business. Instead of working for someone else, which would have been a safer way to begin his career, he had opted to begin from scratch on his own. He knew he was being headstrong, but that had not stopped him. Consequently, there had been many days when he was not sure he would be able to pay the rent on his office, and quite a few occasions when he had skipped dinner in order to avoid the risk of giving up Jane. That was the last thing he ever wanted to happen, especially since, on days when things were the most difficult, her quiet confidence in him was what kept him going.

His meals were more predictable now, since his client list was building, even including some of his father's legal clients. Still, he spent as little of his income as possible, saving every spare penny for his seat on the stock exchange. Without it, he could never trade on the floor of the stock market.

While seeing men who knew his father did a lot for his business, it did little to ease his mind about the break. The men often reminded him of his father's disapproval. There was nothing he could do about that, however. He intended to live his life on his own terms. But if war came, he could lose everything he had left.

Intent on blocking that worry from his mind, he dropped to the floor and began doing pushups.

Chapter Four

The week Lloyd was away was the longest Jane had ever endured. Normally, the rise and fall of the stocks, the clamor of the ticker tape, and the abundance of information Mr. Weaver taught her daily made Jane's day seem full. She more often than not was surprised when the work day ended. But the week Lloyd was gone seemed interminable.

Olivia kept the date alive, chirping about how wonderful it was that Jane had found someone and endlessly asking for details of that evening. "Tell me about the band," she said, patting the pink brocade couch so Jane would sit beside her. It was one of the few good pieces of furniture they had been able to keep from their old home. She leaned dreamily back against a white lace antimacassar. "Were they the cat's meow?" Before Jane could tell her, she would ask another question. "Was the restaurant really ritzy? Tell me more about the food."

Jane told her everything she could remember about the dinner. She described the shrimp cocktail, the salad, and the prime ribs. Olivia lamented that Jane had not ordered dessert. "I just couldn't eat another bite," Jane reminded her. "But I saw the pastry cart." She described that in detail, even exaggerating the size of the chocolate shavings on the Black Forest Torte.

"That Lloyd is so swell!" Olivia said, jumping up

and spinning around. "And he really likes you. Did you see his eyes pop out when he saw you in that dress?"

Jane felt her face flush, and turned away so Olivia would not see. It did not help that Mrs. McGill kept asking her similar questions about the evening. She had come up the next morning to retrieve her niece's dress and sat in the burgundy lady's chair, expectantly, until Jane told her where she and Lloyd had gone and what they did. "He seems like a decent fellow," Mrs. McGill had said, "but you must be careful. Don't let him break your heart."

Lloyd would never do that, Jane was sure. Every night, when she should have been sleeping, she relived her date, thinking about how Lloyd had held her hand while they walked on the sidewalk, and how gently he had taken her elbow when they stepped into the street. The memory of their kiss lingered on her lips, and she caught herself staring at them in her mirror several times a day. They looked the same, although until now she had never had occasion to study them. But she could not help wondering why he had kissed her, or taken her out. He could have had any girl he wanted, yet he seemed to want to spend time with her.

Sunday night of the following week arrived without word from Lloyd. By the end of the evening, Jane was a mass of goose bumps and considering the possibility that he might not return. She began to re-examine that evening in her mind, looking for signs he did not like her, or maybe did not find her appealing. He had certainly had the chance to get to know her during their date, and maybe he was disappointed. She feared he would not be back.

Jane was crestfallen. Olivia, who had been so

excited on Friday night in anticipation of the return of her sister's beau, had lost her fizz. Now she sat quietly, as if thinking the same thoughts as Jane. Lloyd seemed to have gone out of her life as quickly as he came in. They had been so foolish, thinking something would come of the date.

Jane went through the motions of her life feeling gloomy. Olivia tried to cheer her up on Monday evening, but by Tuesday had moved to a new theme. She told Jane what a fool Lloyd was to stay away. "Pearl was wrong, you know, when she said you were like her, not destined to marry for passion. I think you're beautiful. There is someone out there for you, waiting to sweep you off your feet. And if Lloyd is so stupid he doesn't know how great you are, he's all wet."

Jane appreciated how Olivia stood up for her, but she could not deny the truth. What she had thought was the beginning of passion, with Lloyd, was nothing more than a flirtation. If that were the case, and true passion was an impossibility, she would not bother seeking love. It hardly seemed worth the effort to seek out the suitable but uninspired match Pearl had thought Jane might one day make. She would rather be alone. But the pain was still raw.

The next day Mr. Weaver asked her if something was wrong. "You've been so quiet this week," he said. "Is something bothering you?"

Jane was touched by his concern and assured him she was fine. She asked if he would like her to bring anything back for him for lunch, but he said he had to go out anyway. He left shortly before she did.

All the way down the street to the luncheonette,

Jane thought about Lloyd. It was surprisingly painful, and she chided herself for being so silly. She had to forget about him and about the prospect of falling in love. It was not her destiny.

A strange sweetness filled the air on Jane's return to the office. She was puzzled by it, until she saw the yellow roses on her desk. Her heart fluttered, and she rushed toward them, looking for a card. She knew they were from Lloyd. He had not forgotten her.

"I hope they cheered you up," said Mr. Weaver, from the doorway to his office.

For a second Jane was totally confused. Then she realized Lloyd had not sent the flowers to show his love. Mr. Weaver had bought them out of pity. Her face got hot at her stupidity and tears of disappointment filled her eyes. She could not look at Mr. Weaver as she rushed out of the office to the washroom. There, the sobs that had been building up exploded, and Jane curled up on the floor and wept.

When she returned, she forced a smile to her lips and thanked her employer for his thoughtfulness. But he looked quite annoyed. Who could blame him? The roses were so thoughtful, and she had been unforgivably rude. The hours stretched endlessly until five o'clock, and her embarrassment hung heavy in the air, making her miserable.

****

Prescott chastised himself. What had seemed such a good idea earlier—roses to cheer Jane up, since she had seemed so distracted last week, and positively sad since Monday, was a rousing failure. He had succeeded only in upsetting her more and driving her to tears.

He tried to rid himself of the image of her reaction,

the way her eyes had looked when she ran out. How could he have hurt her like that? He realized he had better learn more about women if he did not want to distress Jane again. It was not as if she were the kind of woman to feign upset in order to garner attention. It was almost the opposite, that she was embarrassed because he had sent those flowers. He would never do that again.

*****

Jane had her head down as she walked through the door to the street because she was so upset with herself, and she almost ran the feather on her hat into Lloyd, who was waiting for her outside her office building.

She was not sure what to do or say. She was not even certain she should acknowledge him, but felt she had no choice when he stepped into her path. She looked into his eyes, searching for some clue as to how to respond.

"Hello, Jane," he said, doffing his fedora and bending forward. "I'm so glad I was able to find you. I've been going crazy not seeing you for such a long time."

He seemed so happy to see her she felt her anger at not hearing from him melt away. It was soon replaced by such a tightness in her chest at his earnestness she thought she would faint. That she had never once fainted in her life did not matter. She had never had a man show her such attention.

But where was he all this time? Why hadn't he called when he said he would?

Her silence seemed to trouble him. He looked at her closely. "Have I done something to offend you?" he asked.

What could she say? That her feelings were hurt because he failed to see or even call her when she expected he would? That she had embarrassed herself with Mr. Weaver, when she was disappointed his roses were not from Lloyd? What rights did she have? Reason told her to answer in the negative.

He took her response as if she had welcomed him with a big hug. "I've missed you so much," he said, falling into step beside her. "I sat through all those meetings and all that traveling wishing you were beside me."

Jane was unable to tell if he was joking. But she turned to him, where he nearly skipped beside her on the sidewalk, and asked, "What kind of meetings?"

For a moment, it seemed as if Lloyd was considering what to say. And his response, that he was in Washington, D.C. to talk about some aspects of the New Deal and the banking commission, was so rudimentary it might have been the explanation of a father to a five-year-old.

Jane turned to him and narrowed her eyes. "I have some knowledge of the subject. Could you be more specific?"

Lloyd stood stock still with his mouth slightly agape. Then he threw his head back, nearly losing his hat in the process, and laughed out loud. Dozens of passersby turned to stare at him, and a few hurried past as if he were in need of psychiatric assistance. After a moment, he recovered himself, and as he wiped his eyes with his handkerchief, he apologized. "Oh, yes, of course," he said. "You work for a stock broker. You know something about the new regulatory agencies."

Jane nodded her head slightly, barely deigning to

accept his apology. "I started working for Mr. Weaver in November of '39. Since then, I have briefed each new regulation, as well as familiarized myself with every regulation since the establishment of the Securities and Exchange Commission."

Lloyd's eyes widened. "I suspected you were smart as well as beautiful," he said appreciatively.

His unexpected and, in her opinion, undeserved, remark took all the wind out of Jane's sails, and caused her to feel uncomfortable. Olivia was the beautiful one.

That thought reminded her that her sister would be waiting, and she did not want to be late. She also did not want to get involved with Lloyd again. She had never felt such pain as when he did not call. It would not do to get her hopes up like that again.

"I have to go home," she said, attempting to go around Lloyd, who was blocking her path. "My sister…"

He cut her off. "Olivia. A lovely child. Yes, you should go home to her. But, if I may, could I possibly accompany you? I would so like to spend the time with you."

With some persuasion, Jane agreed. After an initial moment of discomfort, they chatted amiably on the subway about Lloyd's trip and its several unexpected extensions. While they rode the streetcar Lloyd told Jane about some of the characters he had met.

When they got off on Rogers Avenue, they walked past all the shops Jane so often frequented. The fruit and vegetable stand was still open, and the vendor smiled at Jane while giving Lloyd the once-over. It was the same at the butcher shop. It gave Jane chills, mostly pleasant, to be seen with Lloyd.

Joani Ascher

When they got to Jane's corner, Olivia was coming down the side street. She looked in surprise at the two of them, and frowned.

"You should come home, Jane," she said. "There are too many bums on the street."

Jane was horrified. "Olivia, apologize."

"I will not." She turned to Lloyd. "You were not very nice to my sister, going away like that and not calling. Mrs. McGill said we should give you the brush-off."

Jane put her hand up. "Olivia! Enough. Go inside. I'll be right up." She watched as Olivia turned on her heel and went up the steps.

Her face burning, she wished Olivia had followed her own advice to Jane. She had said, "If you see Lloyd again, you must cut him dead." That would have been a lot better than giving him her opinion, which in some respects, Jane shared.

"Don't be embarrassed," Lloyd said. "She's just looking out for you. I understand completely. But I won't give you up. You mean too much to me."

He scowled, pondering the problem. "Maybe we should let her think we're not seeing each other. At least for a while, until she cools down."

Jane did not like the idea of hiding something from her sister. At the same time, she was moved by Lloyd's having said how much he wanted to be with her. He took her hands in his own and said, "I can't let you go. Could this just be our little secret?"

Chapter Five

"I'll be working late again tonight," Jane told Olivia. "Don't wait dinner for me."

Olivia, who lay prone on the couch with her textbook propped open on the coffee table and her slippered feet in the air, pouted. "Mr. Weaver works you too hard. You haven't been home more than two nights in three weeks. I know he's helping you learn about being a broker, but do you have to have lessons so often?"

Mr. Weaver had lately begun taking Jane to dinner on Wednesday evenings, the one night a week he did not have a standing engagement. He spent the time telling her about the history and intricacies of the stock exchange, and Jane found it absorbing, catching some of her employer's enthusiasm for the complexity of the market. They had interesting discussions about other subjects as well, at those dinners, which were always at modest but lovely restaurants. Jane came to appreciate just how thoughtful and insightful he was. At the same time, she saw how hard it was for him to be patient sometimes, waiting for his opportunities to materialize. She had to admire his self-control.

Jane felt honored that Mr. Weaver took so much time out of his social schedule to work with her. And she loved hearing about the opera and symphony. Twice he took her to an opera at the Met, and once to a concert, when his parents were unable to use the tickets. She had been so surprised he asked her to accompany him, and very grateful, but she knew it was only because the rich society young ladies he saw were not likely to be available on short notice.

"I would never have guessed how different it looks close up," she said breathlessly one evening when the curtains parted, revealing a glittering set for *Die Zäuberflote*.

"Someday you'll see the whole season," he predicted, with his mustache close to her ear. She hoped he was right.

During those evenings, they talked of their families, of her sister, and his parents and married sister. Mr. Weaver always accompanied her home after one of those evenings, which seemed to race by. She came home with her head filled with information and often music, feeling pleasant and serene.

Jane reached for her purse and turned to her sister, who was still in her bathrobe. "It isn't only work, you know. Several of those evenings I was at meetings of the club."

"I don't see why a book group would meet every week. How do you have time to read so many books?"

"I'm a fast reader."

Jane hated lying to her sister about those other evenings she went out. They were quite different from those with Mr. Weaver. She and Lloyd went to dark jazz clubs, where they nursed their drinks until the end of the set. They walked a lot, and window shopped, and Lloyd told her about all the things he would have someday when his ship came in. "You probably think I'm silly," he said. "Wishing for things you take for granted every day."

"What do you mean?" she asked.

"You don't know what it's like to have so little means," he told her. "I long for the day when I don't have to wonder if I'll be able to pay next month's rent."

"I'll tell you a secret," Jane said, leaning close and feeling his warmth. "I long for that day, too."

Lloyd got the strangest look on his face. "I don't understand. Didn't you say your father had left you money to get along on?"

Jane suddenly realized she had somehow misled Lloyd. "I may have overstated it. But we get by."

"I'm sorry," he said, his voice full of sorrow, "I didn't know."

Sometimes he said things that were so funny, and it nearly killed Jane to not repeat them to Olivia. But she could never breathe a word.

It was not as if there was anything wrong with what she and Lloyd did, but Jane thought it best that her sister not know. Olivia had made it perfectly clear how she felt about Lloyd, and Jane was not sure enough about him to tell her she was wrong. Several times Jane was tempted to tell her sister, because Lloyd had been mostly reliable, but for some reason she held her tongue. Each subsequent date made her lie feel much bigger. That kept her quiet.

She and Lloyd never saw each other on Saturday night, so Olivia would not become suspicious. But it seemed one day that all they had tried to accomplish by hiding their relationship from Olivia was about to come out into the open.

She looked at Jane and wondered aloud, "What has changed you so? You seem so happy!" Tears of joy formed in her beautiful eyes when she gazed at Jane.

For her part, Jane had barely noticed the change in herself. But now, as she looked into the mirror, she saw Olivia was right. There was a considerable amount of color in her cheeks, and her hair seemed to have more style. She had found a cut that worked with her hair, and Lloyd's pleased reaction as well as her sister's and even Mr. Weaver's had made her happy to have done it.

Life fell into a smooth, pleasant pattern until Olivia's good spirits appeared to completely evaporate in late April. She became quite moody, often sat quietly staring at nothing, and seemed to cry at the slightest thing.

As the days went by, Olivia sulked more, and her appetite faded. It was different from the times when she was small, when she fought with a friend or when a little girl on the next block claimed to have a prettier dress. Then a new hair bow could bring a smile to her face. It was almost the same as it had been those weeks before Father died and for about a year afterward. She seemed to be grieving, but Jane could not figure out why.

"What's wrong with you?" Jane asked her on several occasions.

She usually responded with stony silence or simply, "Nothing."

One morning Jane questioned her sister as delicately as possible, hoping to avoid another round of tears.

"A young man is bothering me," Olivia admitted. Her voice was very low, and she did not look Jane in the eye.

Shivers ran down Jane's spine at her tone. "Who?"

"It doesn't matter."

Jane didn't press her for the name. Instead she sat down next to her sister on the sofa and took her hand. "How does he upset you?"

"He wants to go out with me and he won't take no for an answer."

Something about the fear in Olivia's eyes made Jane very uncomfortable. "What has he done to you?"

"He got insulting when I refused him for the seventh time. He told me that I act like a child."

"He didn't touch you, did he?"

"No. And I make sure to stay out of his way. I've been pretty successful this week, at least."

There was little relief in that. His words had obviously struck deep. "You should have told me sooner," said Jane. "School is nearly over for the semester. But if he does that again in the fall, please tell me right away. And stay close to Horace. He won't let anyone bother you."

Olivia smiled when Jane said Horace's name. "You're right. I promise." Jane intended to mention it to Horace as well, and ask him to see if he could find out about the fellow. Horace would handle it in a gentlemanly fashion, as he did everything else.

While Jane knew that Horace would protect Olivia, she still found herself imagining what would happen if she told Lloyd about this boy. She could see him leaping to Olivia's defense, and acting as her protector. He would help, and she, for once, would not have to bear the entire burden.

But that would not do at all, now, since she supposedly had no contact with Lloyd.

****

Jane had gotten her hair styled differently, and Prescott supposed it was becoming, but he missed the soft way it had fallen to her shoulders after it worked its way out of her bun.

He enjoyed their evenings out immensely, and was surprised to realize what good company she was. Several times during the week he found himself anxiously looking at his watch, waiting for their time together. She was like a breath of fresh air after the other women he so often saw.

Prescott knew Jane's time was precious, since Olivia was still in college and dependent upon her, and he was impressed at how much importance she placed on developing a career for herself. If any woman could do it, she could.

He had finally finished paying off his college loan and started saving in earnest for his goal. He had also done well on his military tests. While he was satisfied with his progress, it still seemed as if he would have to wait for too long to get what he wanted. But there was some good news. His mother told him his father was softening, just a bit, about the career path he had chosen. It gave him room to hope to heal the rift between his father and himself.

When he had first heard about Prescott's career goals, the senior Mr. Weaver had turned livid, citing scores of his friends and acquaintances who had been wiped out by the crash. "Anyone who dabbles should have his head examined," he had said. "But someone who intends to make his living that way, preying on the tendency to gamble that many men have, is a criminal. I won't have it."

All his own arguments, as well as those of his

mother, did not change his father's mind. Even now, several years later, the wound was still fresh. Prescott knew that while his father had revised his views, he was still not pleased with his son's choices.

The best way to heal the rift would be to settle down with the daughter of one of his father's cronies and give his father grandchildren. As much as Prescott wanted to be in his father's good graces, however, he had not yet found a young lady to court. None of them were one tenth as interesting, compassionate, or genuine as Jane Baldwin.

And with the news from Europe, he had more pressing things to do than look for a girlfriend.

****

In late May, Jane considered telling Olivia about her relationship with Lloyd, because she was positive he was in love with her. Somehow it seemed so underhanded, all the sneaking around they had done, and Jane resolved to talk to Lloyd and ask for his help in making it seem they had just become reacquainted.

She missed two opportunities. They had been scheduled to meet on those occasions, and Jane had rehearsed what she wanted to say several times. But Lloyd failed to appear both times, leaving Jane wishing he could be more reliable, like Mr. Weaver.

On the third scheduled date, Lloyd showed up. As usual, he had a perfectly good explanation of what had kept him away, and lamented that he could not contact her to advise her of his absence. He told her again that if she would only stop having those dinners with Mr. Weaver, they would be able to spend more time together. Then he pulled a bouquet of carnations from behind his back as an apology, and listened closely while she outlined her position.

"I don't think that is such a good idea," he said, after she listed the obvious advantages, in particular that they would be able to go out on weekends and see much more of each other if Olivia knew of the relationship.

His reluctance surprised her, but she assumed he knew what he was doing. "If anything," he said, "we should take it slow. We'll have plenty of time to be together once we're married. But we have to wait until the time is right."

The very mention of the word marriage, in connection with herself, so surprised and delighted Jane that she immediately agreed to Lloyd's request. She did not mention the subject of telling Olivia about them again. But he brought up one of his own, a few days later, that shook her world.

They were sitting in a banquette in a candlelit restaurant in Little Italy. Lloyd's finances did not permit another night out like the one they'd had on their first date. These more reasonable dinners were fine with Jane, who only cared about the company. Lloyd took her in his arms.

"There is something I want to ask you," said Lloyd, holding her close. A violinist who had been playing nearby smiled and edged away.

Jane bit her lip to keep from blurting anything out. But she had no doubt Lloyd was about to ask her to marry him.

"I know that because of my circumstances," he continued, "we can't formalize our relationship yet, but I love you so much that waiting is killing me."

Puzzled, Jane remained silent. She doubted she

could have said anything anyway, since she was so disappointed Lloyd had said they still had to wait to become engaged. Searching his eyes for some indication of what he was about to say, Jane struggled to keep her own from filling with tears.

Lloyd took her hand in his own. "I want to show you how much I love you. It hurts so much when we don't see each other, but even more when we do and I can't hold you in my arms all night."

Jane knew what he was asking her but could not bring herself to look at him. She reached for her glass of Chianti and took a big gulp. She kept her face turned away, not letting him see it burn.

"I know this goes against your upbringing," Lloyd murmured into her hair. "And I wouldn't want you to go all the way. If only I could look at you, all of you, and touch you. I'll stop when you tell me to. I promise."

She turned back, looked into his eyes, and knew he was telling the truth. Maybe she could let him do more than just kiss and fondle her through her blouse. She certainly wanted that. She could still be a virgin on her wedding night. "All right," she whispered.

"We can go to my apartment," he said.

All the way there, Jane felt as if every person on the street knew what she was about to do. Everyone seemed to stare at her, as they walked through the neighborhoods to a rundown area near the river. She was so embarrassed she could barely utter a word.

Lloyd took her to his little flat above a laundry. Leading her by the hand, he opened the door. Involuntarily, she shuddered.

The wallpaper peeled in places, and there was such humidity in the air that Jane had no doubt the steam regularly found its way up through the floor. She felt clammy herself, as if she had wilted on the spot.

Lloyd guided her over to the single bed and sat her down on its damp yellow sheets. He sat beside her for a moment, then slid off the edge of the bed onto his knees. In a breathless moment that astounded her, Jane found him undoing her garters and removing her stockings. Soon he had removed the rest of her clothes as well as his own. She was afraid to look at him yet could not tear her eyes away, even though the dim bulb cast long shadows on them, making it difficult to see. Her face burned even more, especially when he began to touch her breasts. She gasped.

"Don't worry," he murmured. He stroked and suckled both breasts, which stimulated and embarrassed Jane, but Lloyd assured her everything was all right. He did not violate her wishes, and did not touch her anywhere else, seeming to be content with satisfying himself privately in just a few minutes.

They continued in this manner for a few weeks until one night they lay together, naked, with Lloyd kissing her passionately. Jane felt as if she were floating. Lloyd's hands drifted over her breasts, down her stomach, and along her legs. Then suddenly he lay atop her and, holding her very close, entered her. It was incredibly painful. She screamed, and he pulled out.

"I'm so sorry," he said a minute later, when he could talk. "I didn't mean to do that. I didn't go all the way in, I swear."

For several minutes afterward, Jane lay curled up and sobbing.

"I don't think I—" He broke off, and started again. "You're still a—" He swallowed. "Don't worry. It was only for a second. I apologize. It will never happen again, not until we're married."

He showed much more restraint on subsequent occasions, leading her to admire him even more. Alone at night in her own bed, she relived those moments together, sensing that the feelings she had would be even better when they were married. He was so sincerely in love with her, she was tempted to tell Olivia about his return to her life. How could he object now?

"Lloyd," she said, one evening when she finished washing up after the dinner she had made for him in his apartment. Since they had gotten close, he had suggested they eat in, to have more time alone together. That night she had bought thick steaks to cook, and sour cream to go in the baked potatoes, using money saved from skipping her lunch. "I think we should tell Olivia about us."

"I don't think that's such a good idea," he said. "She's probably still man-shy because of that boy who was bothering her. She would probably worry, for nothing. You wouldn't want to do that to her, would you?"

Jane had to admire his thoughtfulness. "I should have realized that," she said. "Thank goodness you did."

****

Jane seemed so different to Prescott lately. She still smiled and laughed, but sometimes she seemed so far away. He wished he could say something to lift her spirits at those times, but was constantly mindful of the incident with the flowers.

It seemed as if everyone was becoming somewhat

moody. The news from Europe was worse. Each day, new accounts of further advances by Hitler's armies filled the newspapers. Germany invaded the Soviet Union on June 22nd, continuing its takeover of that part of the world. It seemed incredible, but Germany now occupied Denmark, Norway, Luxembourg, Belgium, The Netherlands, and France, while actively attacking Great Britain. Italy's and Japan's hostility had people talking in hushed tones, wondering where this would all lead. Some even told of relatives who were suffering from the occupations, or running from oppression.

Prescott could not help wondering how long the U.S. could stay uninvolved. It looked like all his hopes and plans would have to be abandoned. Yet he was not ready to admit defeat, and he continued on his course in the face of the increasingly obvious obstacles.

One Wednesday evening in a restaurant, when Jane had excused herself to powder her nose, Prescott overheard a conversation at a dinner table near theirs which left him feeling uneasy. The couple, whose relatives had recently taken in some refugees, were discussing the need to open their own home.

"I know it will mean extra work for you," the man had said. "But my cousins tell me they are hiding from authorities, and their lives depend on getting out of the country. They need some place to go."

"Do you promise it will only be for a few weeks?" said the wife.

"I can't say for sure," the man admitted, "but I heard they are—" His voice was drowned out by the band starting up again. But Prescott saw the wife daub her eyes with her handkerchief, and nod.

****

One night in mid-July, Lloyd seemed to rethink his "don't tell Olivia" policy. "I would like to take you and Olivia on a little trip," he told Jane. "I've borrowed a car. We'll picnic and enjoy the sunshine."

"That sounds lovely," she said. "I will just tell Olivia I ran into you and you invited us. We will have to be careful," she added, "and not let her see how much we love each other." Their declarations of love were like messages from heaven, when Lloyd uttered them.

On the morning of their trip, Olivia, who seemed not to have guessed the truth, was up very early. "It's wonderful that you ran into Lloyd again," she said. "It was sweet of him to invite us for a picnic. But what does he know about picnics? I made a big breakfast for us, just in case there isn't enough food."

It must have been nerves, but eating anything for breakfast was the last thing Jane wanted to do. She waved Olivia away. "Maybe we should call Lloyd," she said, although she had no idea how to reach him. He did not have a phone. "I think I'm ill."

Olivia looked so sad, Jane was forced to change her mind. She got out of bed, and by the time she was done bathing felt somewhat better. She told herself she should not be so nervous about Olivia seeing them together, that everything would work out. When she went into the kitchen, she managed to take a few bites of the breakfast Olivia had prepared, and assured her sister that their day would not be spoiled.

Lloyd arrived on time, driving up to the front of their house in a shiny black Nash. He held the door gallantly for each of the ladies and dashed back around to his own side. "It's almost a shame it's such a nice day," he said. "This car has the Weather Eye, the finest climate control system." He proudly showed them the other features of the car, as if he owned it.

"Father owned a Stutz," said Olivia. "But this is prettier."

It occurred to Jane that Olivia was flirting, just a bit, with Lloyd. She was like that with many of the men she saw, those who walked her home from her classes at the college and those whom she knew from high school who came to visit in their parlor occasionally. Jane knew it was harmless but was surprised to find herself annoyed when Lloyd was the target. For his part, however, he treated Olivia almost like a child.

They drove along the West Side Highway onto the Henry Hudson Parkway and crossed over into the Bronx. Then they drove along the Grand Concourse, looking at all the luxury apartment buildings.

Lloyd pulled into the Botanical Gardens, and they strolled around, looking at all the flowers and trees. They sat under one and feasted on cold chicken and peaches, relaxing in the sun, and attempted to fly a kite Lloyd had brought along.

But when it was time to leave, Jane noticed they were not headed back the way they came. They went to Westchester. When she asked Lloyd, his face got somewhat grim. "I have to make one stop," he said.

They drove to Valhalla, where Lloyd pulled into a parking lot. The building before them was a mansion, with manicured sprawling grounds, and the sign on it said Garden Acres Insane Asylum. Lloyd put the emergency brake on. "I would like you to come with me to visit my sister," he said softly. The look in his eyes was one Jane could not refuse, and even though she had never heard Lloyd speak of a sister, she asked no questions.

But Olivia seemed distressed. "May I stay out here?"

Lloyd patted her hand. "Of course. We won't be long."

He took a package out of the trunk of the car and led Jane into the dim exterior, where her eyes took a few moments to adjust after the bright sun outside. A nurse came toward them, and said, "Good afternoon, Mr. Hammer. She is in the day room."

Thousands of questions formed in Jane's mind, but she remained silent. Most of them were answered when she saw the girl who was Lloyd's sister.

Chapter Six

She was plump, Jane could tell, even sitting down. But far more noticeable was her face. She had a small head, although her forehead was broad, and upward-slanting eyes. Her bottom lids bulged out on either side of her small, flat nose. She looked more like the other people in the room than like her brother Lloyd.

It was hard to say how old she was. She was dressed neatly in a skirt and blouse, but Jane noticed by the way it draped on the floor that her hemline was much longer than was fashionable. Her hair was as black as Lloyd's but thin, and was pulled back at her short neck into a straggly braid, making her small ears seem to stick out.

She was what Jane had heard called mongoloid.

"Hello, Emma," Lloyd said, softly. He took off his jacket and covered the package with it, setting both on a chair before going to stand beside the young woman and wait for her to recognize him.

Her face brightened when she saw her brother. "Loy!" she shouted, her open mouth revealing several lost teeth, and she stood up awkwardly.

She waddled to her brother and threw her arms around him, which required her to stretch, since she was several inches below five feet. She pulled Lloyd's face close to her own with her tiny hands and planted a sloppy kiss on his nose.

Then she saw Jane. A puzzled look came across her face. "Emma," said Lloyd. "This is my friend Jane. She would like to meet you."

Emma smiled back at Jane. "Outside," she said.

Lloyd laughed. "You always want one thing." He linked elbows with his sister and headed for the door. Reaching back with his free hand, he took hold of Jane's.

Jane admired the tender way Lloyd took care of Emma's feelings and realized it was similar to the way he regarded Olivia's. It warmed Jane's heart. But she was puzzled by the fact that, until this day, he had never mentioned a sister.

Emma led them along a sunny path behind the old mansion, among beds of flowers and several fountains. Lloyd explained that he had, after much searching and disappointment, finally found this place for his sister, which was the very best facility of its kind in the Northeast. He had moved down from Boston to be closer to her, giving up a good job in a large accounting firm.

"But now I'm so glad I did," he added, looking over at Jane as she walked among the flowers bordering the path. "Not only is Emma well cared for, clean and properly fed, but she is also stimulated." A look of grief passed over his face. "Some of those other places were worse than a zoo. She was tied to her bed in one, living in her own filth. I couldn't stand it. So I searched and searched. I couldn't let my mother and stepfather down."

He told Jane about his parents, their joy when one day, unexpectedly, years after they married and had Lloyd, they found out that Lloyd's thirty-six-year-old mother was expecting. But that was followed by despair when the doctors told them they must institutionalize Emma. "Can you imagine?" Lloyd asked. "On the day their daughter was born they were told to put her away. My mother was devastated." He frowned. "I still remember her crying. One of the doctors who came to see her even suggested they withhold food. He wanted to let my baby sister die."

Jane had heard of such things. One of the woman down the block had given birth to a baby like that. The midwife had told her to put it in a home, and the woman had done so.

"My mother refused," Lloyd continued. "She kept Emma with her always, until she died. My stepfather couldn't handle her alone, and my search began. But he died before I found this place."

There were many people like Emma on the grounds. They seemed happy, walking in the sun, some with nurses pushing them in wheelchairs, and a few with canes.

"This must be so expensive," said Jane. She felt uncomfortable mentioning it, but could not help wondering.

Lloyd sighed. "It is. That's why I can't afford my own car, or a house, or, at this time, a wife." He turned to her. "And that truly breaks my heart."

Emma stopped, and they caught up with her. She seemed to be breathing heavily. "Do you want to go back?" Lloyd asked, his voice full of concern.

The girl nodded. Lloyd let her lean against him as he guided her back to the building. They took her to her room and got her settled. While Lloyd went back to the day room for his jacket and the package, Emma lay down and rested. Jane looked around and noticed pictures of Lloyd and two older people, possibly their parents, on the nightstand.

"Those people in the picture look very happy," said Jane.

Following her gaze, Emma turned and picked up the picture frame. "Our parents. But they died."

"Mine died too," said Jane.

Emma's breathing seemed to be better when Lloyd came back. "We have to leave now," he said. "But first, I wanted to give you your birthday present."

Emma's eyes lit up. "Happy birthday to me?"

"Yes," said Lloyd. "Happy nineteenth birthday, Emma."

Nineteen. Jane realized that this little girl, wearing Mary Janes and ankle socks, was older than Olivia.

Lloyd uncovered a brightly wrapped package and handed it to Emma. She tore into it, leaving bits of paper all over the floor, and pulled out a new hairbrush and tortoiseshell comb.

"They're beautiful," said Emma. "Thank you so much."

"You're welcome."

"Jane, will you comb my hair for me?"

"I'd be happy to," said Jane. Lloyd beamed, and Jane felt she had passed an important test. His sister liked and accepted her.

When Jane was finished, Lloyd laid the brush and comb on Emma's nightstand. "You look beautiful, Emma," he said. "But we have to go now. I'll come see you again in a few weeks."

Emma's eyes filled with tears, and a nurse had to hold her hand while Jane and Lloyd left. They turned to wave, and after a few seconds, Emma gave a halfhearted wave. Then she ran her hand over her newly combed hair and smiled.

Jane's mind reeled on their way back to the parking lot. Had Lloyd said marriage was out of the question? What about their confessions of love? Or did it just mean they would have to wait a long time? That was all right with her. She wanted to wait until after Olivia finished college anyway.

When they got back to the car, they found Olivia surrounded by a group of young men. They were the brothers of patients, they explained, and were letting their parents, who had strong-armed them into coming, visit with their siblings alone. If Olivia was going to visit regularly, they said, their own attendance would undoubtedly improve. Jane laughed all the way down the long driveway to the main road.

She suddenly felt euphoric. Even the surprise and sadness she would have expected to feel on finding out about Lloyd's poor sister and parents made her feel more love for him. She wanted to keep that feeling in her heart forever.

Turning, she stole a glance at Olivia. She truly was breathtaking. Before long she would fall in love and marry. Someday, Jane thought, she and Olivia would be the mothers of beautiful children and they would live near each other and their children would be friends. Warmth and love would fill their lives. Pearl's predictions notwithstanding, Jane would also have her own great love. She would never settle for less.

Luckily, she had already found him.

She was so busy imagining her life, one she would share with Lloyd, she didn't realize he was speaking to her until he tapped her on her arm and asked if she had heard him.

"I'm sorry," she said. "I guess my mind was wandering."

"I'm glad you like my sister," said Lloyd. "Some people might not."

"She's very sweet. I'm sure the next time we visit, Olivia will enjoy meeting her."

Lloyd was silent for a bit. His mind seemed to be elsewhere.

"It seems you have a lot on your mind," Jane observed.

"I have some things pending," said Lloyd, his eyes riveted on the road in front of him. "I'm just wondering how they'll work out. And how I'll feel about it."

"Can you tell me about it?"

Lloyd turned to her for a moment. "Not yet. When I can." His serious expression was soon displaced by a jovial grin and he broke out into a song, which he sang at the top of his lungs as he drove them home. "When you wish upon a star…"

****

Jane was surprised when Lloyd phoned that evening. He spoke so fast, she had trouble understanding him.

"Could you repeat that?" she asked.

"I said I have to go away."

"For how long?"

"I didn't really expect it," he said, sounding very excited. "I mean it didn't look like it would happen, not for a while. I had practically given up…"

"Lloyd," said Jane, catching his enthusiasm. "Tell me what you're talking about."

He did not answer her.

"Lloyd? Can you hear me?"

"Yes. I can't explain. Look, I'm sorry, but I have to pack. I just wanted you to understand. I'll be gone for a while, but I will find a way to get back, as soon as possible, so we can be together."

Jane was too upset to speak. She gripped the phone, unable to think. "When will you get back?"

"It won't be that long. I promise. But I had to let you know the moment I heard. I wouldn't want you or Olivia," Lloyd added softly, "to worry about me."

Jane loved him even more for his consideration. "I'm going to miss you," she said, fighting tears.

His voice was husky when he responded. "I'll miss you too."

****

Two weeks passed, during which Jane heard nothing from Lloyd, not even a postcard. That was so like him, to go away and not write, that she did not think much of it at first. She barely noticed at all, because she was so sick, at least early in the day. It was difficult for her to get out of bed in the mornings, nearly impossible to get to work on time.

She told herself it was nothing. But she went to see a doctor, not Dr. Mann, the family physician, but one in Greenwich Village.

"I'm not your usual doctor, Mrs. Peters," said Dr. James.

"I, uh, my doctor is away," Jane stammered, flustered that she had claimed she was married and had given her mother's maiden name as her own.

"I see. Well, let's get on with your examination." Jane thought she would die of pain and embarrassment while she lay on the examining table. "How long have you been married?"

Jane bit her lip. "What do you mean?"

"Your hymen has not been fully broken," the doctor said. "But I think I can see why you are feeling sick. We'll just do a test to confirm."

On Friday afternoon, after work, she went back to the doctor and he told her she was with child. She could expect her baby to arrive with spring, the next year.

Jane wept at the news. "I take it your husband won't be happy to hear about this," Dr. James said.

"It's not possible," she argued. "We didn't…"

"If I could tell you how often I've heard that," said the doctor kindly. "But the fact remains, you are pregnant, and you aren't married, are you?"

Jane shook her head. "But we will be, when he comes back to town."

Dr. James sighed. "I can't in good conscience recommend an abortion," he said, "although I may know of a colleague who could help you. It's dangerous, though. Maybe you should consider giving the baby up for adoption."

"No, Doctor," Jane said firmly. "My fiancé will be back soon, and we'll be married. He loves me." She stood up to go. "Don't worry about me, I'll be fine."

He smiled. "I'm sure you will. Take care of yourself until our next visit. Good luck."

Although she put up a brave front, Jane stumbled out of the doctor's office and onto the street. It seemed to have suddenly changed, becoming more dirty, more frightening. The people she passed seemed to be staring, to know her secret, her shame.

She felt an enormous pressure building inside her.

What had she done? What kind of situation was this for a respectable person? She had to get in touch with Lloyd, she knew, but she had no way to do it. More questions filled her head. What if someone found out? What if Mr. Weaver found out? What if she told Lloyd and he still said they could not marry? What then? What on earth was she going to do? And how would she tell Olivia?

Making a supreme effort not to collapse in the street and weep, she kept walking downtown.

She knew she couldn't do what the doctor had mentioned. She would not try to find someone to give her an abortion. She'd heard about it once from a waitress. The woman had been crying one day, and confided in Jane that her sister had found herself in the family way without a husband, and had gone to a doctor who said he could fix her up. But something had gone wrong, and her sister had died. Even if Jane hadn't heard that story, she knew she could not go to a person like that. She knew she could never kill her baby. Even though she had just learned of the baby's existence, it seemed as if she had known for a while. Maybe that was why she didn't go to see Doctor Mann when she was unwell. It was time for honesty, at least with herself. She had known. And this baby was a part of her.

More memories came to her as she walked. One of Mrs. McGill's nieces had been sent away one year. When she returned, she told Jane she had been to visit another aunt in Maine. Jane noticed she had lost a bit of weight while she was away and surmised she had gone to have a baby and had given it up.

That was another option Jane immediately rejected.

So it was all up to her. She chastised herself for worrying that Lloyd would not come back to marry her. Where was her faith and trust? But remembering Lloyd's problem with marrying, that he did not have enough money because of having to pay for his sister's care, she knew she had to find a way for them to be able to afford to be together, with benefit of clergy.

Over the next week, she studied the stock portfolios and projections closely, more than ever before and certainly more than was required by her secretarial duties, looking for wise investments to help maximize her own worth. She wanted to be able to show Lloyd, when she broke the news to him, that marrying her would not be such a sacrifice. Even though it went against everything she had been told, and the lessons of the stock market crash, Jane bought on wide margin. The stock market had been rising in May, June, and July, and there seemed to be no reason for that to change. But in order to hide her problem, she bought through another brokerage. She did not want Mr. Weaver asking her any questions.

Yet he often astonished her with his thoughtfulness. Several times, when Jane was feeling ill, he had offered to let her go home, but each time she refused.

The first time, he had gone out of the office and returned with a paper bag. "Open it," he said.

Jane found a thick paper cup with hot tea in it. "Drink it," he urged. "It'll make you feel better."

She had dutifully swallowed the tea. "It really helped," she told him. "Thank you. My influenza symptoms aren't bothering me now."

The next day he brought her chicken soup. "One of

my Jewish clients recommended it," he said. "I hope it helps."

She found him staring at her thoughtfully, even after she started feeling better. She had to refuse his suggestion to resume their Wednesday dinners, though, claiming Olivia needed her at home, because she was just too tired after work to go out. Luckily, he never asked her any questions, since she did not have any answers to give him. He would never think she could have become pregnant, and she would never tell him. It was so embarrassing, because she was not married yet. So she kept to herself, even more than before, especially when Mr. Weaver was in her part of the office. Sometimes, when she had turned away, she peeked back and saw him frowning. That puzzled her, but she had so much on her mind she didn't dwell on it.

****

Prescott worried about Jane. The girl who had been so open a few months ago had withdrawn into herself. She never met his eye, and she seemed pale. He constantly worried about her, although she kept saying everything was fine, and he wished there was something he could do to cheer her up. He could not be sure of her reaction, though, and that kept him from trying.

The situation saddened him so that he spent less time in his office, choosing instead to meet clients at his club or theirs. Their dinners and evenings out stopped in early September when Jane claimed she could not spend the time away from her sister. Prescott told himself that was reasonable, but he was quite unhappy about it. The pain only deepened when, each time he returned to the office, she barely raised her head to acknowledge him.

One day, when he could not hold back anymore, he decided to broach the subject. He came out of his office and made sure no one was waiting in the hall to see him, then asked Jane if he could speak to her. She agreed, picking up her steno pad. "You won't need that," he said, causing her to look at him in alarm.

"Is something wrong?" she asked.

"No. It's just that there's something I would like to discuss with you, but I'm not sure how to go about it."

Jane sat silently and waited for him to speak. He stroked his mustache, finding himself completely tongue-tied, but managed to stutter out that he regarded her highly.

"I try to do a good job," she said.

"You do. But it's more than that. I think you are a wonderful person."

Jane burst into tears and asked to be excused. He was left perplexed.

For business reasons, Prescott had to accept invitations to various social gatherings. Anne Canfield sought him out on several of those occasions, and he found himself enjoying his conversations with her more than any of the other people who so often attended those functions. There was an underlying sadness to her, he realized, which did not match her spendthrift and carefree reputation. One night she asked him about Jane, whom he often spoke of with her.

"Oh, she's fine," Prescott replied. "Although I worry about her sometimes."

Mrs. Canfield had raised her lovely arched eyebrows and frowned.

"Is there something I should know?" he asked,

while doubting this society woman would know anything about Jane.

"I'm not sure. I saw her once with a young man at the Rainbow Room. It made me wonder if he was her beau."

Inexplicably, Prescott felt as if he had been punched in the stomach. "She's seeing someone?"

"I don't know," Anne Canfield said. "But I've noticed the last few times I was at your office that she seems different." She paused, frowning. "Not like someone in love," she added.

Relief washed over Prescott, although he would not have been able to say why he felt it. "I've seen it, too," he said. "It's got me worried."

Prescott felt as if her eyes were looking inside him. "Maybe it's just the news from overseas," she said. "Everyone is feeling so sad for the people in Europe. Does she have family there?"

"I don't think so," said Prescott. "But I'm afraid to ask her. If I ever mention anything sad she starts to cry and runs out of the office. It's better if I don't talk to her at all." He took another drink off the tray.

"Hugh would say you should find a young lady and forget your troubles."

"You sound like you don't believe that's a cure for what ails the world."

"I'm not sure Hugh has all the answers."

Prescott nodded. "Even if I found someone tomorrow, I would not enter into a courtship."

"Oh? Why not?"

"If we do go to war, I'm going. And I couldn't saddle a woman with a relationship with me when I might be killed—or worse, injured. I couldn't have her taking care of me for the rest of her life, tying herself to an invalid. It wouldn't be fair."

Mrs. Canfield looked down. "We can't go to war," she whispered. "It would be so awful."

Prescott shook his head. "We probably should have months ago. Then those damnable Nazis would leave everyone else alone." He looked up as Hugh Canfield came to stand beside his young wife.

The man seemed annoyed. "We can't have you monopolizing my wife, Weaver," he said, and told Anne, "We must be off, darling." He steered her toward a gap in the crowd, but turned back to Prescott. "It isn't our business. We give enough aid with our weapons. We don't need to get involved." He turned back toward the door.

Anne Canfield looked around at Prescott as if to apologize, and they were gone.

****

Jane's thoughts were always with Lloyd. She went over how she would tell him, in her mind, hundreds of times, each time imagining his reaction. He would fall to his knees and beg her to marry him immediately, saying all the obstacles could be overcome. Olivia would be her maid of honor, and maybe Emma could even attend. They would have a little girl, born just a few months sooner than expected, and they would name her Spring.

Lloyd's business trip stretched to three weeks and then four. She did not expect him to write, because she knew he probably thought each day of the trip would be his last, and he would arrive home before any postcard could. Olivia, who had talked of the day of their picnic for a week at least, seemed to have found other diversions, and rarely spoke of Lloyd. When she did, it was clear to Jane she did not expect much of the relationship. After all, as far as she knew, Jane had only seen him twice, and there had been a gap of several months between those occasions.

But by the end of September, Jane herself was getting nervous. The stock market seemed to be in a steady decline, and she was sure that any minute her margin would be called. She had no way of covering it. Every day she stared at the ticker tape machine, willing it to show a turnaround.

She knew Mr. Weaver would never have let her take such a risk. For a while, she thought about confiding in him and seeking his help. But she decided against it, since he was increasingly wrapped up in preparing for the possibility of war.

If only Lloyd would come back, she thought. He would know what to do.

A new fear replaced her hopes. What if something happened to him? She did not even know where his office was. She realized no one would know she was waiting for him and so she would not be notified if he were detained. Once they were married, everyone would know, and she hung onto that thought throughout the mornings of nausea and the subsequent tightening of her skirts. Until then, though, she would not be informed of an emergency.

Finally she could not wait any longer. Her thoughts were increasingly filled with trepidation for Lloyd. The feeling got so strong that one Saturday she went to his apartment and knocked on the door, hoping he had come back. A woman from down the hall opened her own door.

"What do you want?" she asked, with her arms folded over her housecoat. "I'm the landlady. Are you looking for a room?"

"No," said Jane. "I wanted to talk to Mr. Hammer."

"Oh, him," said the woman. "He moved out."

That made no sense to Jane. He was only away on a business trip, after all. How would he have had time to move? "Where did he go?"

"I don't know. He just took all his stuff in the middle of the night and left. He didn't even pay me what he owed on the room."

"When?"

"Back in July."

Jane's stomach clenched in panic. She turned to go, struggling to stanch the tears which threatened to flow.

There had to be an explanation. Maybe Lloyd had found a better place to live and had not paid what he owed because he forgot or something. He certainly was not the type to shortchange anyone.

She wracked her brain on her way home, trying to figure out how to find out where he had gone. And by the time she got to her own neighborhood, her overwhelming need to find him finally yielded an idea of how to do it.

She went to a public phone in the Rexall Drug store near her home and closed the door of the booth. Taking a deep breath, she called the one place she knew someone would have to call if anything happened to him—the Garden Acres Insane Asylum.

"I'm calling," she explained, "about Emma Hammer's brother. Have you heard from him?"

"May I ask who is calling?" said the officious voice on the other end of the line.

"My name is Jane Baldwin. I'm a friend of Lloyd Hammer, and I've been worried about him. I know this is peculiar, but I was wondering if you had heard from him."

She did not really expect an answer, but she had been so desperate for news, she was willing to try anything. She knew this must sound ridiculous.

But it turned out she was wrong, about a lot of things.

"Emma was discharged," the woman replied. "Her brother took her down to a residential hospital in Virginia, to be near him and his new wife."

Chapter Seven

Jane felt pressure on her wrist and realized someone was holding it and rubbing her hand. Her head throbbed. "Are you hurt?" asked a male voice.

When her vision cleared she saw a middle-aged, gray-haired man kneeling next to her as she lay on the floor outside the phone booth in the drugstore. How she had come to be in that position was unclear to her.

The man wore an outdated suit with threadbare elbows, but he held himself with a demeanor of gentility. His battered shoes were polished. Jane recognized him as the man who sometimes filled in for the clerk.

She looked into his eyes and was reminded of her father.

The man helped her into a sitting position. His kind face, with its bushy eyebrows and the compassionate concern in his eyes, combined with her predicament, led to an outpouring of embarrassing tears. Without hesitation, he handed her his handkerchief.

When she was able to pull herself together, she saw that the worn fabric was embroidered with a D. She also noticed there was a small crowd of people standing around, staring at her. Someone handed her a glass of water.

"Are you feeling better now?" asked the man.

"What's going on here, Dobbin?" asked the

pharmacist.

Jane looked from one to the other of the men, then took a second to assess the situation. She did not think she was hurt, and she was embarrassed at having fainted in this crowded place. "I'm all right." She made an effort to get up but found she was still somewhat lightheaded. "I just need a minute."

"She is well," said the man, motioning for the crowd to disperse. "May I ask what happened?" he whispered.

"I'm not sure," said Jane. But that was not true. She knew what had happened. She, four months pregnant, had just discovered that the father of her baby had abandoned her and married someone else. She could not possibly tell this kind gentleman that, particularly as he reminded her so much of her father. Instead, she explained that she had not eaten all day.

"I have had days like that, too," said the man sadly. "Some of us have not recovered fully from the hard times. I'm lucky I can occasionally get some work here. Since I did this morning, can I buy you a meal?"

Jane felt even worse. Here the man was, still suffering the aftereffects of the Depression, yet he was willing to help a total stranger. She bit her lip to keep from crying again.

With an effort, and his help, she struggled to her feet. When she was standing, she realized he was only a little taller than she, possibly because he stood a bit stooped over. But he held his chin high.

"It isn't that," she said. "Truly. I didn't eat because I just forgot." Embarrassed again, she told him her first name and thanked him for helping her.

The man smiled, again reminding Jane of her

father. "It was my pleasure." He took her by the elbow.
"I would like to see that you get home without further
incident." Jane thought of demurring, but did not. She
felt safe with Mr. Dobbin and allowed him to
accompany her out of the building, away from the wide
eyes of the crowd. If she had to admit it, she was
grateful he was there, just to keep her upright, since her
head was reeling.

But once she was outside, she pulled away. "I
would rather be alone now."

She could feel his eyes staring at her back, and she
felt worse, having so abruptly rejected that sweet man's
help. But she couldn't talk to him, or anyone. She had
to get away.

Jane walked for hours, going over and over the
phone call. This was a nightmare. Why would Lloyd
marry someone else? She turned a corner, realizing she
was in downtown Brooklyn. She walked over to the
promenade overlooking the East River and Manhattan.

Had he just been using her? No, it was not
possible. He would come back. It was a mistake, it just
had to be. He loved her and hated every minute they
were apart.

Or did he? Hadn't he been unreliable? Hadn't he
been happy to keep their meetings secret? He didn't
want anyone to know about them. It was not just Olivia.
Had he been courting that woman while he was seeing
her?

She had to find him. She had to make him do the
right thing. If he knew she was pregnant, he would
leave that other woman.

But maybe she had been wrong the whole time.
Maybe she was such a pathetic creature Lloyd realized

he could have his way with her and give nothing in return.

She looked down at the water in the river. Lloyd would not even care if she jumped in, killing herself and his baby. The realization hit her so sharply that she doubled over.

Olivia would care. Olivia would be devastated. And this baby inside her, whom she loved, would never have a chance at life. The one person who now mattered the least, Lloyd, would be the only one to benefit from her death.

Turning away from the river, Jane knew she would get through this. She would have to do it alone, but somehow she would work it out.

****

Jane's head still reeled, when she thought of her own foolishness and what it had cost her, a week later when she ran into Mr. Dobbin on the street. He had just carried a very old lady's box of groceries to her door, and he refused her offer of a nickel. "You always refuse me," said the old woman. "It's the least I can do when you help me so much."

He smiled back at her and, turning, came upon Jane. He asked how she was doing, and seemed sad at her curt response.

She felt guilty watching him walk away. She had not noticed, when she had first met him, how his suit hung around him as if it were made for someone much larger. Despite his own apparent run of bad luck he had reached out to her. He was in no way responsible for her problems, yet she had treated him as if he were. She went after him.

Touching his arm, she said, "I must apologize."

He turned his watery blue eyes toward her and smoothed back his gray hair. "It's unnecessary."

Jane felt tears coming on, but refused to let them fall. "If only everyone were as nice as you."

Mr. Dobbin appraised her. "I wish there were something I could say to cheer you up. You remind me so much of my daughter, Caroline. It broke my heart when she was unhappy." He averted his eyes. "That was too often."

While there was nothing to smile about, Jane did not want to hurt this good man again. "Would you like to come for tea?" she asked.

Mr. Dobbin smiled. "I would be honored." He straightened up, and linked elbows with Jane. She was shocked at how thin his arms were.

They walked along the sunny street. Mr. Dobbin chatted about the lovely weather, the Brooklyn Dodgers, and other things, never mentioning her faint nor prying into it.

Before long, they arrived at Jane's door. "Are you sure?" he asked.

Jane nodded. "On one condition. We can't tell my sister the exact circumstances of how we met."

He smiled that warm smile again, but added a conspiratorial wink.

Jane led him inside and introduced him to her sister. "You've seen Mr. Dobbin at the Rexall, haven't you? I've invited him for tea."

Olivia nodded. "Please come in." She seemed puzzled, especially since it had been a while since they had invited anyone to tea, but accepted Jane's explanation.

For several years after their father died, Jane had

invited some of his remaining friends to visit them, even after they moved to their small apartment. It was a way to remember their father, and both Olivia and Jane had looked forward to those afternoons. But there had been no visitors of that kind in years, not since Mr. Wingate moved to Florida

Olivia went to get the tea. Mr. Dobbin, who had been seated in the gentleman's chair, the one that had been their father's, leaned closer to Jane, and in a quiet voice asked, "Will you tell me what is wrong?"

Jane could not tell him about her predicament. "It isn't important. Tell me about yourself." She cleared the coffee table for the tray Olivia was just bringing in.

Mr. Dobbin took the cup of tea and the plate of biscuits and pears from Olivia, setting them down before he started to speak. Jane waited patiently, glad she could give this man some food, since he so obviously did not get enough on a regular basis. But he took just one biscuit, and she had to urge him to take more.

After some encouragement, he spoke of himself. "My wife died several years ago, in early '31."

"Our father lost three wives," Olivia proclaimed.

Mr. Dobbin was so taken back by the revelation that it took quite a few moments for him to begin speaking again.

"Go on," Jane prodded.

He had been hurt hard, as Jane thought, by the crash of '29. He had lost his business and struggled to support his family for ten years. His children had all grown and moved away to start families of their own. "They are doing well, even though I failed them."

Jane was well aware that many men felt the

impoverished times were their fault. From the apple vendors on every street corner to every resident of Hooverville, it had been hard on so many people.

Some had coasted through, somehow making ends meet and avoiding eviction. That was their father. He had even managed to hold on to a few valuables, such as Jane's mother's cameo. But he had never been the same man.

Mr. Dobbin's experiences were similar, but he had not found a new niche. Jane wondered if she could help him. Some sound investments, even in tiny sums, might someday help him out of his predicament. But she knew her own investments would not do that for her. She brought up the subject in a general way, alluding to investing on margin.

"Buying on margin is risky," he said. "That was what caused all those amateur investors, myself included, to lose so much in the crash." His face showed concern.

"I am aware of that," said Jane. But she had needed the money to provide a nest egg for herself and Lloyd, so she had taken the risk. For what? She would have to raise her child alone, as well as see her sister through college, and she was deeply in debt.

Mr. Dobbin smiled. "I'm happy to hear that. I wouldn't want to see you and your sister out on the street."

"The market was doing so well at the end of July," Jane said. "But it has been going down steadily since."

Mr. Dobbin put down his tea cup. "I hope you didn't put any money of yours at risk in this market."

Jane managed a weak smile. "Only a little. We'll be fine."

She was spared having to reassure him further when Horace, Olivia's friend, came to take Olivia to the library. While Olivia got her books, Jane introduced the boy to the man.

Horace, still gangly, seeming all arms and legs at six-four, extended his hand politely. His grandmother had raised him to be well-mannered, and he remembered his training, even though the old woman was gone. He swept his other hand across his unruly sand-colored hair, getting it off his freckled face.

"Pleased to meet you, Horace," said Mr. Dobbin. "You are lucky to have such congenial friends."

"Oh," said Horace, his smile revealing his chipped tooth. "I'm the lucky one. Without Jane and Olivia, I would be a lost cause."

"Horace is studying to be a physician," said Jane, proudly. "I know he'll be a fine one."

Olivia came back into the room, carrying several books and notepads. "Are you ready, Horace?"

He said goodbye to Jane and Mr. Dobbin, and carried Olivia's books for her. They could be heard chatting happily all the way down the stairs.

"He seems like such an amicable young man," said Mr. Dobbin.

Jane beamed. "My sister will be very happy with him, when they are old enough to marry."

Mr. Dobbin's eyes twinkled. "Oh, so you have her life all planned out, do you?" He did not wait for a reply. "But what about your own?"

"I'm working on it," said Jane. But she knew it was spinning out of control.

****

Three weeks later, Jane was in deep financial

trouble. Her money to pay for the long shot she'd taken was due. But the stocks were down and she had no way to pay. There was only one thing to do. Tearfully, she took her heirloom cameo and went to a jewelry store.

Her fingers shook as she carefully unwrapped her treasure. The jeweler used his loupe to examine it carefully, then laid it down beside the brooch.

"It's of outstanding quality," he said. "It was made with exquisite workmanship. But I cannot buy it. We don't need that kind of merchandise." He shook his head. "We still have too much in inventory. Not many people are buying quality jewelry these days."

Several other stores said the same thing. While it was rewarding to know how good her grandmother's cameo was, it only deepened her regret.

So Jane went to a pawn shop.

The price the pawnbroker offered her was less than one tenth the value of the cameo, even without the emotional price it was to Jane. Worse, it would not cover the debt. Six other prices were equally as bad, and Jane's last shred of hope was gone.

She would have to tell Olivia, and they would have to find a smaller place to live. If she did not end up bankrupt, it would still take them a long time to rebuild. And how she would do that once the baby came was beyond her comprehension.

The small thought in the back of her mind, the one she had tried so hard to push away, surfaced. She could swallow her pride and go to Mrs. Canfield, to sell her the cameo, since she had admired it so much that evening at the Rainbow Room.

She dreaded it, not knowing how to approach the caustic wife of her employer's biggest client.

****

"Come in," said Mrs. Canfield. "It's lovely of you to visit." She led the way into the foyer of her huge Manhattan apartment. The opulent furnishings of the living room were visible beyond, as was the dining room that also led off the foyer. But Mrs. Canfield did not lead Jane into either of those rooms. She brought her instead to a small sitting room. In other apartments it might have been the nursery, but Jane understood the Canfields had no children.

Jane chose her words carefully, since she could not just blurt out that she needed money desperately and had to sell the cameo. Mrs. Canfield would wonder why, and might even suggest discussing it with Mr. Weaver. And Jane could never do that. He respected her. If he knew the truth, he would be disgusted.

"I've been thinking about you," said Jane, barely able to get her voice above a whisper. Mrs. Canfield's cordial tone, while warmer than Jane had expected, made her very nervous. "Remember that night at the club? You admired my cameo."

Mrs. Canfield's brow furrowed. "Yes. It was like one my favorite auntie owned."

"I was wondering if you really wanted to purchase it."

A sparkle replaced Mrs. Canfield's puzzlement. "You would sell it?"

"I've been thinking about it." Jane did not add *agonizing over it*. "It seems wrong to hold something I don't care about, when someone who loves it could be appreciating it."

Mrs. Canfield licked her lips. "I would give you a very good price for it." She stood up and left the room, returning almost immediately with a check ledger.

So this was it, Jane realized. She had sunk to selling a piece of her heritage. The check was fair, but just barely covered the debt.

Mrs. Canfield pinned her new cameo to her bodice. "It was good of you to stop by," she said. Her eyebrows knit for a moment, giving her a look of concern Jane had never seen before. "I hope whatever you needed the money for is important."

"It is," Jane admitted, thinking of her baby's, her sister's, and her own future. She had all that paper to cover, worth so much less than when she bought it, or they would be out on the street. She would probably hold on to the stock forever, and it still would not be worth the price of a good steak.

Chapter Eight

Jane found Indian summer nearly unbearable. She always felt overheated, and often faint. Her clothes felt constrictive, and she feared, since she was not covered by a coat, someone would guess her condition.

One Monday morning in mid-October, she found she could not close her skirt. "I seem to be putting on weight," she told Olivia. "It must be from your wonderful cooking. Would you lend me one of your skirts?"

Olivia studied her critically, making Jane worry she would guess the truth.

But Olivia said, "Certainly. I only hope I have something suitable for the office."

Her openness, her faith and trust in her sister, almost caused Jane to burst into tears, but then nearly everything did. She had become highly emotional. Once, when Mr. Weaver started to pay her a compliment, tears flowed. But she knew why that was. She was not the good person he seemed to think. Jane also cried at movies now, especially love stories. It was unlike her, and Olivia, upon seeing Jane's face, was alarmed.

"I wish Lloyd would come back," Olivia said. "You laughed so much that day he took us on the picnic. He would have you happy in a minute."

"He won't be coming around again," said Jane. "I

heard he moved to Washington, D.C., or somewhere near there." She struggled to keep a tremor out of her voice.

"Why did he do that?"

"I'm not sure, because I haven't spoken to him directly, but I guess that's where his wife is from."

Olivia looked at her in horror. "But what about your baby?"

Suddenly the room tipped sideways. Olivia ran toward Jane, and caught her as she fell.

A moment later Jane found herself lying on the sofa, with Olivia staring into her eyes. "You shouldn't be standing so much," her sister said, fluttering around Jane like a maid in waiting. "Stay here. I'm going to get you a glass of water."

When Olivia returned, there was an interminable silence while Jane drank the water. Finally, she couldn't stand it anymore. "How did you know?"

Olivia made a face. "I hope you don't really think I am so stupid I wouldn't have guessed."

"You guessed your sister had relations with a man she is not married to?" Talking about herself as if she were someone else only added to Jane's sense of being off-balance.

"Is there any other way for you to be pregnant?" Olivia asked, not quite suppressing a smile. "Or have you been deified without my knowledge?"

Jane had to laugh. It almost seemed so, since her hymen had not even been broken. But the mirth was short-lived. "What must you think of me?"

"I was shocked, at first. But I've heard of people who have done that, especially now, since there are so many people who aren't sure what will happen in the next few months. All those boys, those friends of mine who had to register for selective service, speak of it."

Jane narrowed her eyes and stared at her sister. "You haven't…?"

Olivia's eyes widened. "Certainly not. I'm only eighteen. But I have been asked."

That made Jane feel worse, and more foolish. Her sister, whom she regarded as naive, had not been persuaded to engage in premarital sex. But she, older and supposedly wiser, had done just that, with full consequences.

Olivia sat down next to Jane. "When is the baby due?"

"March." Jane was barely able to say it, knowing after that they would have no income.

"I'll quit school," said Olivia, as if reading Jane's mind.

"No, you won't."

Olivia's brown eyes regarded her sister. "We will work it out." She left the room, and Jane.

Jane sat, immobilized. As long as Olivia had not known about the baby, or at least as long as Jane thought her sister ignorant of it, Jane had been able to distance herself from the problem. But now it was so close. What could she possibly do? When the time came, how could she work?

The thought of being unemployed had never seriously crossed her mind. They would not be able to survive.

Tears again threatened to fall when Olivia returned. Jane hastily wiped her eyes and attempted a reassuring smile. "We'll manage," she said. She stood up and stepped toward her sister. "I'll think of something."

Olivia brought what she held in her hands into full view. There were four skirts, ones Jane had encouraged Olivia to buy for the times when she felt more adult, more serious. "These will fit you for a while," said Olivia. "I always knew it would come in handy that we were different sizes."

"But you need those for school," said Jane.

"I can wear them sometimes, when you aren't. Besides, I'm not sure how long they will fit you. Try one on."

Jane went into the bedroom and pulled off her own much-too-tight skirt. She slipped Olivia's over her head and smoothed it down. It was a little short on her, but she could not be picky. She could let down the hem if she had to. They did not have money to waste on new clothes.

Once she had the skirt fastened, she looked in the full-length mirror. The skirt was too big on her in every place but the abdomen. There it proved comfortable, except she could not close the button.

She turned to go back to the other room to show Olivia and saw that her sister had followed her. "If you wear one of my blouses," Olivia said, holding one on a hanger out to Jane, "over the skirt, I think you can cover the waistband." She hid a smile.

"You think this is funny?"

Olivia sobered. "Not the baby. But your attempts to hide it." She paused. "In another few weeks, you could start wearing a coat. The baby will be here before spring, so you will be completely covered on the street until then."

"But what about when I am inside?"

Olivia's eyes widened. "I have just the thing." She

ran from the room. Within seconds she was back. "I saved this," she said, bashfully. "I know you said we shouldn't, that there were so many people who needed his clothes…"

Jane understood. She took the cardigan from Olivia and held it in front of herself. "Father's favorite sweater. Yes. I think that will be fine." She hugged her sister.

Olivia wiped her eyes with her handkerchief and smiled. "Well, that's all taken care of, at least for a while."

But it was clear to Jane that although her clothing needs would be met for the time being, there were other, bigger problems to deal with. "What will we tell people?"

Olivia frowned.

Jane ran over the list of concerned people they knew. They had no relatives beside each other, and the only people who regularly checked on them were Horace, who was unlikely to notice anything that did not have to do with Olivia, and their landlady, Mrs. McGill. She only did that, Jane thought, to make sure they kept their respectability. She did not like single girls living alone. What she would say when she found out Jane was no longer respectable was not worth thinking about. They might find themselves out on the street.

"We have to come up with a husband," said Jane.

"Where will we say he is?" asked Olivia.

Jane looked at her watch and bit her lip. Mr. Dobbin was coming to see them soon. They had become quite close with the man, and saw him regularly, usually for Sunday dinner, the one time a week they dragged the dining room table away from its spot in the corner of the living room and put the dining chairs that were usually kept in their bedrooms around it. The thought that she would have to tell him something soon made her breathless. "I wouldn't want him to think I am a fallen woman."

"I think he may have guessed already," said Olivia.

The thought scared Jane. "How many people do you think know?"

"I would say only him. Mrs. McGill is still visiting her sister."

"We have to come up with a story before she comes back," said Jane.

"If we come up with a good one, will you tell everyone?"

Jane thought about that. How many people did she want to lie to? Would she tell Mr. Weaver? She knew as soon as she considered it that she could not possibly tell him any lies.

The resolution was an old one, implemented when their landlady returned. They told Mrs. McGill Jane had married in secret, because the young man's Boston family had not approved of him marrying a nobody from New York. Jane wore her mother's plain gold wedding ring, claiming it was her own, and said they were waiting for the family to accept her before announcing that they had already married. Until then, he would stay in Boston. The baby was a surprise, but one that both of them were thrilled about.

"I can't tell that to Mr. Weaver, though," Jane said.

"Why not?"

Without explaining that she did not have the heart to lie to such a wonderful boss, she said, "If I did, he'd tell me to stop working at once, that I belong at home."

"That's what any man would do," said Olivia.

"But I can't stay home. We'll starve."

"Well, I hope he doesn't notice," Olivia said. "Stay at your desk as much as you can."

Jane promised she would, and they told everyone they knew that she was now Jane Peters, her mother's maiden name.

But that did not keep her from spending endless nights unable to sleep. She was in constant fear of forgetting to put her ring on out of the office, or leaving it on when Mr. Weaver might see it. She had to tell so many people the lie, and worried that she was mixing up her details. It especially hurt to try to pretend to be in love with the father of her child, when her heart was so completely broken.

One night she conceived a plan that she would tell Mr. Weaver that a cousin who lived out of town was ill and she had to go take care of her. She could have her baby, and when it was time to go back to work, she would "return to town." That way she would not lose her job and he would never have to hear the lie.

But the thought of lying to him about a cousin, on top of what she had told everyone else, turned her stomach. And even if that worked, she did not know how she could get through those weeks without income, and how she could pay for someone to take care of the baby while she was at work, and how she would keep Mr. Weaver from ever finding out about the child after it was born. Would more lies be necessary? It was enough to keep her tossing and turning all night.

"You look like you haven't slept a wink," Olivia said one morning.

Jane told her what kept her awake.

"We'll get by," Olivia promised. "And when you go back to work, I'll quit school."

"No!"

"We don't have a choice. Unless you can get one of the nearby ladies who have small children to take care of the baby."

The idea was worth a chance. "I could try."

That weekend, she went to several of her neighbors and humbled herself. She told them about her fictional husband, Louis Peters, and explained he was a student in graduate school, and that they would continue to need her income even after the baby came. One or two of them looked at her in disbelief. She apologized for wasting their time and left. But another lady, Sonia, with two children in diapers and expecting a third, said she would be happy to watch Jane's child for her. She and her husband needed the money.

Jane decided to wait to announce the death of her imaginary husband. As she considered the possibilities of his demise, she realized that her love for Lloyd was dead. She questioned herself. Had she ever really loved him? Or was she just so thrilled someone wanted to be with her that she had imagined it into love?

She had thought he was a man of character, like Mr. Weaver, who would make someone a wonderful, thoughtful husband. For a moment Jane wished she were the kind of woman a man like that would marry, but she quickly put that ridiculous thought out of her mind. She was the type of woman a man like Lloyd would take advantage of. If only she had realized that sooner, she would not have had to develop a pack of lies to cover up for her stupidity.

Mr. Dobbin took the news of her marriage, which she had never mentioned, quite well. But the look in his eyes, while not one of disappointment, was one of disbelief. He offered to help in any way he could. Horace came by to congratulate her. Mrs. McGill, who clucked around saying that if she had been in town, she would have managed to get the family to accept Jane before the secret wedding, kept pressing Jane to introduce her to her husband. She promised not to breathe a word, and kept saying how romantic it was. And on December 4th, when Jane broke the news that her husband had been killed on a business trip, Mrs. McGill broke down in sobs. She was so sad that Jane and Olivia had no trouble shedding tears of their own. Horace came to extend his condolences. His youthful smile was gone, this once, and he spoke in hushed tones. He was so sad, and Jane felt guilty making him suffer for her. But she knew it would hurt him more if he knew the truth. Jane tearfully told everyone she would go back to her maiden name, since her husband's family would now never accept her, and she had her dignity to maintain, after all.

And it was all forgotten a few days later, when America entered the war.

****

Prescott sat with his head in his hands after hearing the news. He had no choice now, not since the moment the story broke of the attack on Pearl Harbor.

He worried how Jane would take his decision. She was so often preoccupied lately. She did not look well, especially since her face had become puffy. Her lovely hazel eyes seemed permanently sad. Although she was still pretty, he thought her slender form had filled out a bit. It was difficult to be sure, since she had started wearing a large sweater, claiming she was cold. She often huddled behind her desk, and no attempt to close the windows and door seemed to warm her. Yet she claimed everything was fine, just that she was worried about the problems in the world.

He missed the old Jane. What if she was sick? He would not be there to see that she took care of herself.

That thought reminded him of his own problem. What would he do about his business? Would it just fold up while he was gone? He could not ask another broker to handle the clients and not take the fees, and without income he could consider himself out of business. Yet there seemed to be no other choice.

He sighed. Everything he had built would be lost. He would have to start over after the war. If he came back.

But his bleak outlook changed on his way to the bathroom. He suddenly realized a solution that propelled him forward to take the next big step. He picked up his shaving mug and started a good lather. His razor had already been stropped, and his large mustached trimmed. With a few quick strokes, he removed it.

Chapter Nine

Everything changed overnight.

Mr. Weaver arrived at the office just after the New York Stock Exchange halted trading to listen to President Roosevelt's December eighth address. "Jane," he said, without preamble, looking at her where she stood next to the ticker tape machine, "I must talk to you."

She had to take a moment to collect herself. Mr. Weaver had shaved his mustache, and he looked very different. Surprisingly, he did not look baby-faced without it. His cheeks had thinned since that old picture of him was taken, and his jaw had become a chiseled line. For the first time, she saw his mouth. Something about his lips pulled at her. But her gaze was drawn to the blue intensity of his eyes. At that moment she could not have refused any request. "Yes?"

"I've been watching you these last few months," he said.

Had he noticed? Could he see the bulge in her middle? Jane felt faint.

"We are going to have to make changes around here. I'm sorry, but it's just the way it has to be."

Jane went to her desk and sank into her chair. Tears stung her eyes as she tried to find the words to explain. But she didn't have a chance.

"I need your help," Mr. Weaver said. "If you'll

agree, I want to leave you in charge of my business. I can't afford to let all of my clients go, and neither can I afford to stay here and let others fight this war." He rushed on, seeming to be trying to convince himself as much as her. "I know you're smart. Your analyses and intuitions have been right on the mark. And you'll do the best you can for my clients."

Once she understood what he was talking about, she felt a sense of relief. But it was short-lived. She could only imagine how hard this was for him, and she had huge admiration for his resolve. She suddenly realized how much she would miss this man. Fighting tears, she asked, "Do you have to go?"

He set his lips together. "William McChesney Martin, the Big Board president, has resigned and will enter the army as a private. Do you really think I'm any more valuable here than he is?"

The tone of his voice, so definite and determined, left no room for doubt in Jane's mind. "When are you leaving?"

"January second. I'm going to teach you everything I know by then."

"But," Jane protested, "I don't have the necessary licenses."

"You can use mine. This is temporary, because of the war. I know it will be a lot of work, because I can't afford to hire someone to do your job, but don't worry, you will adjust. I have faith in you." He moved closer. Jane felt drawn toward him, but because she had to keep her distance so he wouldn't discover her condition, she walked around behind her desk. Now, more than ever, she could not let him find out about the baby. She saw his face had changed when she turned back toward him, ready for his instructions. With his mustache gone, she could see he was gritting his teeth.

****

It was a tense time for the entire country.

The Baldwin girls were plunged, along with everyone else, into the world of blackout curtains and air-raid drills. New York City had its first air-raid alert on December 9 at 1:25 in the afternoon. Olivia was sent home from college, and she worried for hours until Jane came home. The scare was repeated the next day. The people of the United States began to learn some of the lessons the people in England had been practicing for years.

Mr. Johnson, one of the older men in the neighborhood, had served in the Great War, and he painted his old helmet white and became an air raid warden, joining many others around the country. Their presence reminded people daily of what they now faced.

At her request, Mr. Dobbin came to see Jane at her office. It was only the second time he had ever been there. The first time, she'd invited him out to lunch and had him meet her there, so she could introduce him to Mr. Weaver. They had heard so much about each other that it only made sense for them to meet.

This time was different. Jane had noticed how frustrated her friend had become because he was too old to enlist and had not found something he could do to help the war effort. She had figured out a plan that would be good for everyone involved. But she needed help with it, and that had to be handled with care.

Jane had worked on it for two weeks. Things were moving so quickly after America entered the war that two weeks seemed a lifetime. She had all the elements thought out but none of the deals closed, and there was little time left.

Mr. Weaver smiled when Mr. Dobbin came into the office. "It's good to see you," he said, extending his hand.

Mr. Dobbin shook hands, smiling in return. "I think Jane has something on her mind."

Both men looked at Jane, who sat behind her desk, consciously hiding her pregnancy. She took a deep breath. "I found a factory."

Mr. Weaver's right eyebrow went up.

"It's closed. I'm not sure how long it has been, but it's for sale, very cheap."

"What kind of factory, Jane?" Mr. Dobbin's eyes were riveted on her.

"It was a clothing factory. All the sewing machines are still there."

Mr. Weaver looked at Jane. "Are you interested in buying a factory?"

"Not for me. I have a job. But this war is going to require a lot of supplies, and I think someone," she looked straight at Mr. Dobbin, "should buy that factory and make whatever is needed. It could be parachutes or uniforms or bedding."

"Jane," said Mr. Dobbin. "I can't."

Jane wished she could go over to him and put her hand on his shoulder, but she had to stay where she was. "I think you can."

Mr. Weaver looked at Jane and at her friend. "Can you afford it, Dobbin?"

He shook his head. "No."

"We can help you find financing," said Jane, "can't

we, Mr. Weaver? And you have some clients in the fabric business who could help with supplies."

"I see you've thought this all out," said Mr. Weaver. "Would I be right in concluding that you have a file with all the information?"

Jane handed it to him. She looked at Mr. Dobbin to see if she could guess what he was thinking. He was paying attention, she was certain.

They sat quietly while Mr. Weaver read the file. When he was done, he smiled. "You've done an excellent job, Jane. Are you interested, Dobbin? I think this is worth investigating."

Mr. Dobbin just nodded.

While Mr. Weaver returned to his office, Mr. Dobbin pulled his chair close to Jane's desk. "This is impossible. I ran a haberdashery before. I know about fabric in yards, not bolts. Where would I get the fabric? How would I even find out about orders? Who would I hire?"

"You will be able to do it, Mr. Dobbin. I've made several inquiries. There are two factories in Long Island City that are swamped. You can start by taking up some of their overflow orders, while you get the hang of things. They could also get the materials for you, at first."

Mr. Dobbin's cheeks were pink. "Maybe I could. But where will I find the seamstresses?"

"We can place an ad. There are so many men going overseas, and their wives will be looking for jobs to put food on the table. Every woman can sew."

"Would you be there? I need you if I'm going to be able to do this."

"No, my place is here. Mr. Weaver needs me. But

I'll be happy to help you set up your books."

Mr. Weaver had come out of his office, and it was obvious he'd heard Jane's promise of help. He smiled at her appreciatively. "I talked to a few people. They think this would be a good idea."

Mr. Dobbin stood up. "Do you think it's possible?"

"Yes. But if there is anyone who could help you raise the money, you should ask them. The financing will be tight, at best. It'll depend what price you end up getting the building for."

"Would you mind if I took Mr. Dobbin over there right now?" Jane asked. "I can come back later and finish my work here."

"Go ahead. Let me know how it turns out."

****

Jane did not return until late. Her face said it all. Their best offer had been refused. She sat at her desk adding the numbers again and again, and swore she had them right. "He must be trying to recoup the losses he's had over the last ten years," she said.

Prescott though it more likely that the landlord, a Mr. Brick, was trying to take advantage of the war and Jane and Dobbin's inexperience. "Go home, Jane," he said. "You've had a long day. Whatever is here can wait for tomorrow."

When she was gone, he picked up the phone angrily and got Mr. Brick on the line.

Twenty minutes later he had arranged for the man to partially finance the deal himself. Both parties would benefit. At the end of the conversation, Prescott had Brick call Jane himself and suggest the deal.

****

"You want me to what?" Mrs. McGill stood

dumbfounded while Jane explained a second time why she wanted the woman to invest in Mr. Dobbin's factory.

Jane was still amazed at the phone call she had received not ten minutes earlier. Mr. Brick had sounded vastly different from the man she and Mr. Dobbin had visited earlier that day. The deal he put forward would work out well, provided Mr. Dobbin came up with five thousand dollars. "If you invest in the factory, you'll be a part owner. I've already lined up orders, and you should be repaid within the year. You will be first to be repaid."

"I would have to mortgage this building," Mrs. McGill said. "If people don't pay their rents, I could lose everything."

"The people in this building always pay their rent," Jane reminded her. "You told me so yourself. Olivia and I are putting in as much as we can." Jane did not tell her that there was nothing in her own bank account because of her bad investment, but that Olivia had promised two hundred dollars. "And Mr. Weaver told me he would help."

He had said, "I am investing in you as much as in Dobbin. I know you will find a way to make this work." His faith in her nearly made Jane cry.

Jane smiled at Mrs. McGill. "I really didn't think Mr. Brick would do it, but then he did."

"Jerry Dobbin will be able to make a go of it?" Mrs. McGill asked, obviously relenting.

"I promise."

"Well, then," Mrs. McGill said, puffing out her chest. "If it'll help win the war, I'll do it."

****

Until the week before Mr. Weaver's departure, Jane was busy helping Mr. Dobbin open his factory, and she had little time to think or worry. But that final day, as Jane watched her boss hug each of the secretaries on their floor goodbye, she was filled with fear for him, and trepidation for herself, handling his business. Yet, in some strange way, it was a relief. She had hated hiding her pregnancy, lying to him by her silence. But it was necessary. It was important to her that he respected her and had faith in her ability to take care of his business. She could not risk changing that.

She told herself she would explain it all to him when he came back.

"Please take care of yourself," she begged him. He stood straight and proud in his uniform. She realized he had become thinner and wondered why she had not noticed before. His lean form fitted the lines of his jacket perfectly, and he looked more handsome than she had ever seen him. His light brown hair had been trimmed short and he had that determined look in his blue eyes that Jane admired. Her breath caught at the sight of him standing there, ready to walk out of her life, and she was flooded with regrets.

****

He was startled by the way she looked at him. It was as if the changes that had come over her in the last few months were reversed and he saw her as she had been. The somber clouds fell away from her eyes and she was beautiful. Her concern for him was evident, more so than he would ever have imagined. In fact, it was the way he had dreamed a woman would someday look at him, not predatorily, as if wondering what he could do for her, but in admiration and—love?

Was it the prospect of war making him realize that he might have wasted his chances for something that now seemed like such a good idea? With clarity, he realized he would very much have liked to see Jane in that way and wondered how she might feel. How much time he had wasted being blind! But this was not the time to explore those possibilities. He had a job to do. Now more than ever, he was anxious to get on with it.

****

Jane struggled to regain her composure.

"I will," he said, huskily. "And promise me you will take care of yourself, too. I..." His face clouded. "We'll talk when I get back." He moved to embrace her.

Jane hastily stepped behind her desk. While she wanted to hug him goodbye more than anything in the world, if he did he would find out about the baby. She watched him leave, fighting tears and knowing he was hurt at her rebuff.

The office was so quiet after he left that it nearly broke Jane's heart. She missed him, and feared for his safety.

It was the same at home. A parade of uniformed young men, all friends of Olivia's, came to say goodbye. In uniform, each one looked so different from his former self, standing so straight, bragging about how he was going to help win the war, yet wide-eyed with fear.

Mr. Dobbin vanished in a sea of work. He had managed to get his own contract from the government for uniforms, necessitating his factory operate day and night. Olivia and several of her friends spent time after their classes working shifts. It took their minds off their loneliness, especially as so many of their male friends were getting ready to leave. The extra money Olivia earned served to help Jane relax a bit about the family's future.

But now Jane's sleepless nights were filled with fear for Mr. Weaver, Horace, and others off fighting in Europe, Africa, and the Pacific. And a new worry started to niggle at Jane's fragile story of legitimacy.

She would have to put a name down as the father of her baby. She could not use the imaginary married name she had adopted for a while, because she would need a death certificate to prove that Louis Peters, her "husband," was gone. She could not put down Lloyd's name; she would never admit he was the father of her child. She could not write "Unknown," because how would her child be looked at when he started school and had to show his birth certificate?

The endless worrying took a toll on her. While she maintained her professionalism in the office, answering the phone and expediting requests for stock trades made by Mr. Weaver's customers, she was nervous and restless at home. Olivia tried to cheer her up by scouting the neighborhood for a crib and bathinette for the baby, and moving the furniture in Jane's bedroom to make room for the little nursery.

Jane had discarded the phony wedding ring weeks earlier, claiming that her fingers were swollen. She wished she could as easily dispose of the name Peters. She was grateful not to have to use it in the office, where she was still Miss Baldwin. Since no clients ever came in after Mr. Weaver left, and the people in the surrounding offices never saw her without her coat, she had no need to explain. But she was still filled with fears for the future.

On Saturday, March 14th, though, she began to feel better. Much of her tension seemed to disappear, and she decided to give the apartment a good cleaning. She told Olivia to go out for the day, maybe to a movie, or to see one of her friends.

Olivia protested. "You shouldn't be doing all this yourself," she said, reaching for the bucket Jane was filling.

"I'm fine," Jane told her. She turned to look her sister in the eyes. Olivia worked so hard, first in her classes in school, then in the evening in Mr. Dobbin's factory. She worked nine-hour shifts three days a week and deserved this day off.

"Maybe you should come with me," Olivia suggested. "You don't get any time for fun yourself. Your coat covers your stomach."

"I'd rather stay here. I'd only be thinking about how much this place needs to be cleaned, the whole time I was out."

"What if I promise to help you later?" Olivia suggested.

"I'd rather you stay out all afternoon and evening, having fun. That will be the best thing you can do for me. And I promise I won't work too hard."

"If you insist," Olivia said, as she picked up her coat. "I'll see you later."

Jane spent the day cleaning, polishing, and waxing. At four o'clock, she went to make herself a cup of tea, and picked up a magazine to read while she relaxed. She got as far as putting water in the pot and lighting the gas.

A pain gripped her abdomen, stronger than any she

had ever felt in her life, and it knocked the breath out of her. She doubled over and had to hold on to the edge of the sink just to keep herself standing.

When the pain passed, she turned off the gas. Tea seemed less appealing now, and she put the cup and saucer away, emptied the pot, and dried it. There was so much pressure on her back, she wanted to go lie down and put her feet up. She hoped the next week until the baby was due would not be this uncomfortable.

Before she could even get to her bedroom to lie down, another pain forced her to sit down on the couch. That was when she realized the baby would not be waiting a week to make an appearance.

Dr. James had explained to her that it should probably take several hours of contractions before she would have to go to the hospital. He did not want her to wait too long, though, since she needed to travel from Brooklyn to Greenwich Village. But barely two minutes had passed since the last contraction.

As soon as she could walk, she went to the front door and down to Mrs. McGill's. She knocked as hard as she could, hoping her landlady hadn't gone out for the afternoon.

Mrs. McGill opened the door and found Jane bent over and sweating. "The baby's coming?"

Through gritted teeth, Jane said, "Yes. Too fast, I think."

Mrs. McGill helped Jane into the apartment and over to the couch. "Where is Olivia?"

"I sent her out for the afternoon. I don't know where she is."

"We have to get you to the hospital. Did you call Dr. Mann?"

Jane had never told Mrs. McGill that Dr. Mann was not her doctor during the pregnancy. This did not seem like a good time to explain. All she said was, "I have to get to St. Vincent's."

"What? Don't be silly. You'll never get all the way there. This baby would be born in the taxi. You'll have to go to Kings County." She took her coat from the closet. "I'll get Mr. Johnson to drive us. You call Dr. Mann and tell him we're coming." She went out, leaving Jane wondering how she would explain to Dr. James and apologize to Dr. Mann for not seeing him all along.

She was still talking to Dr. Mann, after having to pause several times when she was made breathless by contractions, when Mrs. McGill returned with Mr. Johnson, who was wearing his air-raid uniform, white helmet, and carrying a first-aid kit. The landlady took the phone and told the doctor they were on the way. She listened for a minute and hung up. "He said not to stop for red lights," she told Mr. Johnson. Taking the first-aid kit from him, she added, "And you won't be needing this."

The trip to the hospital seemed to take an hour even though they never stopped and barely slowed down at corners. Dr. Mann was waiting, out of breath, when they arrived. The nurse beside him wrote down the admitting information but seemed to eye Jane as if she didn't believe a word of it. When she asked where her husband was, though, Mrs. McGill came to Jane's defense, chastising the woman for being so insensitive to a young widow. Without another word, the nurse rushed Jane, who had added another dose of guilt about her lies to Mrs. McGill, into the delivery room, barely stopping to remove her clothes. Jane had only a brief glimpse of the anesthesia mask descending on her face before she was blessed with unconsciousness.

When she awoke from the anesthesia, groggy and with the first feelings of pain, Dr. Mann, standing above her, did not greet her in the way she expected. She had gone over the moment in her mind, during the weeks before, imagining what the doctor would say when she awoke. "It's a boy!" Or, "It's a girl!" But he said neither.

The sense that something was radically wrong intensified when she looked over at her sister's tear-stained face. "Is the baby dead?" Jane asked.

Olivia groaned and burst into fresh tears. The doctor motioned the nearby nurse to take her away. As Olivia moved past the bed, she cried out, "Jane, I'm so sorry."

Dr. Mann shook his head. Looking back toward his patient, he pulled out a stool from under the bed and sat down next to her. "The baby is alive. But he is not healthy."

Jane was so happy her baby was alive that she barely listened as he explained. But as the words came through, she began to understand—worse, to realize.

"The baby is mongoloid," said Dr. Mann, his face frozen with grief. "He will never be normal." He coughed. "Indeed, he will be severely retarded." He coughed again. "You'll have to put him into an asylum. In all likelihood, he'll die shortly."

Jane gripped the sheet on which she lay. "No!"

The nurse brought a large needle and gave it to the doctor. "I know this is hard for you to accept," he said, pushing the plunger enough that a small amount of liquid shot out, "but it will be for the best. Children like that," he stabbed Jane's arm with the needle, "are not capable of anything. I'm sorry."

As she drifted off, Jane thought of Lloyd and of his sister who had this terrible affliction. Their parents had felt it best to keep her home, and she had done well, according to Lloyd. As sleep took over, Jane realized something else. This affliction could have come from Lloyd. A last gift of his "love."

****

Jane awoke Sunday afternoon, just in time to see three infants brought into the room she shared with three other women. Each woman was given a tightly wrapped bundle, two of which were crying, small plaintive baby cries that made the mother in Jane nearly wild with anticipation for her own child. She was nervous, afraid of how he'd look, but ready to see him.

Several minutes passed and he still did not appear. A nurse stopped in to see how the other mothers were doing, and Jane asked her where her baby was.

"In the nursery," said the nurse, scowling. "There are orders that he be kept there."

"I want to see him. It must be time for his feeding."

"I'm sorry. You'll have to discuss that with your doctor."

Jane was left languishing, waiting for Dr. Mann. Everywhere she looked she saw the other mothers with their babies, and her heart ached. When Dr. Mann came to examine her, she told him how unhappy she was that her baby did not come to her room.

"I wanted to spare you," he said. "If you don't see him, it will be easier to place him in an institution. It's for the best."

"I want to see him," Jane insisted.

"We'll talk about it tomorrow. Don't worry about him. He is being well taken care of, and he is eating." He picked up his medical bag. "I'm sure when you've thought it over you will see that I'm right."

But after another morning of seeing her roommates with their babies, Jane was more determined than ever. When Dr. Mann came to see her, she gave him an ultimatum. "If you do not have my son brought to me, I will get off this bed and go find him myself."

"You can't do that. You must stay in bed. You just gave birth."

"I feel fine. I could have gotten out of bed yesterday, and I will now if he doesn't come here." She pushed off the blanket and moved her leg to the side of the bed.

"Jane, no." Dr. Mann covered her up again. "He's in the isolation section. I'll have him brought in." He hurried away.

It hurt Jane terribly that her baby had been kept isolated from the other children, as if they could catch his dreadful problem from him if they were close by. But she wiped away her tears and held her breath while the child was wheeled into her room. All the other babies had been carried in—it seemed no one was willing to touch her son. The privacy curtains were drawn around her, leaving her alone. The last glimpse she had of the other women in the room was of their pitying faces.

Jane peered over the top of the bassinette. Inside lay a pink little baby, sleeping peacefully. Jane watched, forgetting for a while all the horrible things the doctor had said, all the sympathetic looks the nurses had given her, even her sister's grieving face. He seemed so sweet, smelling like a baby smelled, at least the ones she had babysat for. The doctor had said he ate well enough. Jane wondered if anyone held him while he drank from his bottle.

After a little while, the baby opened his eyes. They were slate blue in color, but the most noticeable thing about them was their shape. They slanted upward, surrounding his flat nose. His head seemed so small, so much smaller than the head of the baby of the woman in the next bed. His ears were small too, and his hands were stubby. But to Jane, he was the most beautiful baby in the world.

She moved to the edge and reached into the bassinette. The baby was so light, so fragile, when she picked him up, but he looked at her, making a connection she knew instantly could never be broken. She would not put him into an asylum. Never.

Chapter Ten

Olivia came to visit her that evening, after sitting in Jane's office all day. Although they had worried that people would wonder where Jane was, Olivia reported that no one who called questioned her. "When they ask for Miss Baldwin, I say, yes, because I am, and they tell me what they want. I guess I sound enough like you that they can't tell us apart on the phone."

Jane giggled. "Maybe no one will have to know I'm out."

Olivia shrugged. "If someone does, I'll tell him you're sick with the flu."

"Good," Jane said. She leaned back against her pillows and sighed, while the other women's babies were carried in for their feedings.

Biting her lip, Olivia looked nervously at the door. When it did not open again, she looked at Jane, a question in her eyes.

"They didn't want me to see him," Jane said, controlling the distress in her voice. "But I insisted, so I know they'll bring him eventually. It's as if I have to fight the whole world to be allowed to mother him."

Olivia's eyes held tears for her sister. "Maybe you shouldn't. Dr. Mann said—"

"Olivia!" Jane's voice was sharp. "When you declined to go see Lloyd's sister, I let you. But I can't let you give in to your squeamishness when it comes to

Zachary." She had named him Zachary Zebulon Baldwin, after their father.

"How can you call him that? Wouldn't Father have been unhappy to have that poor baby named after him?"

"If you insist, I will change his name. But I will not send him away. When you look at him, you'll realize it's okay that I named him after Father. He is not a defective piece of merchandise to be returned to the manufacturer. I made him. He is my son."

"It's all Lloyd's fault," Olivia exclaimed.

"We don't know that for sure. But we do know he belongs with us. I love him, and you will too."

"I can't. Dr. Mann said babies like that can die."

"You haven't even seen him." She broke off as the door opened and a nurse pushed the baby's bassinette into the room. She had no smiles for Jane as she had for the other mothers, and she took pains to completely enclose them with the curtains as she left, keeping the other women and their visitors from having to see the mongoloid baby. Jane watched as her own sister turned away, but she held her temper. "Come over here," she said softly. "Look at my baby."

Paling even more, Olivia did as she was told. She edged closer toward the bassinette, all the while looking as if she would like nothing more than to run out the door.

"Go on," Jane said.

With her eyes wide, Olivia peered over the top. But Jane could tell she was not looking at Zachary's face. "Look at him. Please."

Olivia's eyes moved up toward the top of the crib. She stood motionless for a moment, then a look of surprise crept over her face. "He's so darling!" she cried. "Oh, Jane. I didn't know."

Jane's heart leaped, and a great weight fell away. "Will you help me?"

With tears running down her face, Olivia looked at Jane, then back at the baby. "Yes."

****

Olivia had a million questions when she visited Jane after work, such as what the term "at the market" meant.

"It means you will take the stock at the lowest price your broker can buy it for you, or sell it for the highest," Jane explained.

"Why can't they just say that? And what in the world is Bessie?"

Jane laughed. "It's shorthand for Bethlehem Steel. Don't worry about it. Just do as I told you, call in the orders, and they will get handled. Then you settle up with the buyers and sellers. Mr. Weaver's clients don't expect you, or actually me, since you're sitting in for me, to advise them."

"But you do sometimes, Jane. You're really smart about the stocks. Didn't Mr. Weaver tell you that?"

"He did. He thinks of me as a kind of protégé. And one of his clients said that if I were a man, I would probably have a future in the field."

Olivia smiled. "I thought you intended to anyway."

"Well, I don't know about having my own seat, as Mr. Weaver will. There has never been a woman member. Although now would be a good time to try to buy one. I hear they're going for under twenty thousand."

"That's out of your price range," said Olivia. "Unless there's something you haven't told me. But I

115

thought you were planning to be a broker."

"Yes, like Mr. Weaver is now. I will, you'll see. Now you had better get home and get some rest. You'll have to fill in for me again tomorrow."

"Have you decided who to put as the baby's father on the birth certificate?" Olivia asked.

"It can't matter now," Jane said sadly. "His father will be unknown. I don't care anymore."

The day she brought the baby home, Mrs. McGill and several of the neighbors crowded in to see him. Mr. Dobbin, who had sent a huge bouquet to the hospital, took a few hours off from work to come greet the new addition.

Olivia had not been able to find the words to tell them all about the baby, it appeared. Mrs. McGill was the first to take a look and she cried out, "Oh, how horrible!" The others strained to see, and Jane turned away, running to her bedroom. Even though the door was closed, she could hear cries of dismay when Mrs. McGill told them what she had seen. Those soon turned into expressions of sympathy with a few suggestions that Jane send the child away.

In her bedroom she looked at her baby, sleeping contentedly in her arms, and wept.

****

Jane saw no one for the rest of the week. But on Saturday she asked Olivia to get Sonia while on her way to the grocery store. Since Sonia's husband was home and could watch the children, Jane wanted to have her meet the baby. She would be returning to work soon, and it was time to arrange for his care.

Sonia came right away. "I can't wait to see the little one," she said. "I just love babies so much."

Her own baby was due in two more months. She went over to the crib and looked inside, her face glowing with anticipation. Jane had just put the baby down and knew he was still awake, and peering over Sonia's shoulder she saw him looking myopically back at her.

Sofia stepped back quickly from the crib. "What's wrong with him?"

"Nothing," said Jane. "He's very healthy."

"No, he isn't. His head is so—he's a monster!" She turned to leave, calling over her shoulder, "I'm not taking care of him. Find someone else."

In shock, Jane watched her go. With no one to watch her little boy, she could not go back to work, and they would have no income. Olivia could not continue to do her job; she was already weary from pretending to be her sister. Jane found herself in tears again, as she had so many times in the past weeks. She hated what she was becoming, an emotional woman incapable of taking care of her family, and she vowed to put an end to it.

"When I go back to work," Jane declared when Olivia returned, her determination never stronger, "I will need your help."

"What do you want me to do?"

"I need you to take care of Zachary. I know it will mean continuing the rest of your semester at night school and giving up working for Mr. Dobbin in the evening, but it can't be helped. We can't wait any longer for me to go back to work."

Olivia nodded. "I understand. I'll do it."

****

Leaving Zachary was much harder than Jane

expected. He had a particularly wakeful night, and Jane was more exhausted that morning than she'd ever been in her life. The baby was finally asleep, though, and she did not dare wake him to say goodbye. She tore herself away when she walked out the door, and her heart felt bruised. It was as if a part of her was missing, the whole way to her office.

When she arrived, she tried to be so busy that the hours she was away from her baby would go faster. But they dragged. Even though she had so much to catch up on, she found her mind wandering and her eyes drifting to the clock, trying to imagine what Olivia and the baby were doing. Was he having a bottle? Taking a nap? Did he need a diaper change? Jane trusted Olivia completely, but it was not the same as being there herself.

At the end of that week, Jane wrote a letter to Mr. Weaver, never letting on she had been away:

Dear Mr. Weaver,

I want to assure you that things are well in the office. Mr. Dobbin's business is getting more orders each day and filling them on time. I don't know what news gets to you, so I will fill you in on the happenings here on the home front and the efforts everyone is making to help out. Just to give you an example, the auto industry stopped making passenger cars, changing over entirely to war production.

For a month or more, there was a parade of uniforms going through our parlor. Olivia's friends each came to say goodbye. There were several naval uniforms, some army, a few marines, and one army air corps—Horace.

I know that his is the uniform Olivia will miss the

most. It was so painful, watching her eyes as they followed him sadly down the steps and out the door. I knew when he was out of sight, because Olivia's head fell forward and her dark brown hair covered her face. Then she looked up, beseeching God to protect him, and her face was wet with tears.

Jane did not mention that after Horace left, Olivia went over to Z.Z., as they had nicknamed the baby, and knelt down beside him, holding him close while she cried.

Her devotion to the little boy was strong. She cooed to him, sang to him, and was often the first to reach him when he cried during the night. Olivia was fiercely protective of him, and when Mrs. McGill's revulsion was apparent, Jane had to hold her sister back in her defense of the baby.

The landlady had been very hard to handle. "You should have listened to your doctor," she said, waving around the polishing rag she used for her beloved brass banister. "He should be sent away. No one will want to see him, and you'll be trapped in this apartment alone with that child."

"That's none of your business," Olivia said. "He is our flesh and blood."

Mrs. McGill's raised eyebrow did not stop Olivia's diatribe. "If you can't bear to look at my nephew, then don't." With that, she picked the baby up and stomped out of the room.

"Your poor departed husband," said Mrs. McGill to Jane, as if assuming she would be more reasonable. "He must be turning in his grave about this."

Jane did not answer, but she managed a sniffle to indicate that her bridegroom might be gone but was not forgotten.

Mr. Dobbin, though, seemed much more accepting of the baby. While he sympathized with Jane, who still grieved for the healthy child she did not have, his quiet strength helped her stand up to the continued opinions that she should institutionalize her baby, given so freely by anyone who knew about his problem. "Jane," he said, "you must do what is in your heart."

"Even if that means defying Dr. Mann and Mrs. McGill and the others?"

"If that is what you want. You're a good woman, and you are a good mother. Don't worry about the others."

In another letter, written to Mr. Weaver two months later, Jane said:

On April 28, the stock market dropped. I was worried I couldn't keep your business open, because people seemed not to want to trade. But then the market turned around and it's been in an up position since. We have more customers than ever, because your clients' relatives all seem to want to invest.

By the end of the year, the worthless stock Jane had been unable to sell finally turned a significant profit. Financially, she was able to take care of them all. Emotionally, though, both she and her sister were nervous wrecks. Their futures were too unclear.

****

Mr. Weaver wrote frequently.

Dear Jane,

I know it has been difficult for you these last few months. Please know I have every confidence in your abilities. You were always very cautious and correct where speculation was concerned and your unerring sense never led to the wrong investments. My clients are in good hands.

I've heard that one in particular, Hugh Canfield, is prospering during the war. His holdings included several key contributors to the war effort. I assume Mrs. Canfield is now covered head to foot in jewels. It's strange, but I don't think she cares much for most of them, unless they are like that cameo she once showed me. It was a lovely thing, something I think you would like.

I wish I could tell you where I've been and what I've seen. Someday we'll sit down and talk about it all. Just know the world is a much bigger place than you would ever have guessed. I suppose if I had followed my father's wishes, I could have had a tour of the continent after high school. But I had more important things to do then, just as I do now.

I was pleased to hear how well Dobbin's factory is doing. I'm sure you are very much responsible for its success. Give my regards to him and Olivia. Until I return, take care of yourself. I miss you. P.

Chapter Eleven

May 14, 1943
Dear Mr. Weaver,

I cannot believe that it is nearly a year and a half since you left. Your letters are so sad, and yet often so full of hope, I never know whether to laugh or cry.

I must tell you the latest. First, the business is having a good month. Many people are investing these days. You will be proud when you read my monthly report.

Mr. Weaver's letters to Jane were friendlier than Jane had expected. At first, when he went into the service, his correspondence was filled with instructions for her on how to handle various situations. He wrote just as if he were there in the office, teaching her as her employer. But the letters had increasingly become more personal, detailing for Jane where he had been, but without being one of those loose lips that could sink ships so many posters warned people about. He also spoke of his family—his mother, whom Jane had met once, on the day she came to visit her son's office, and his sister, whose own husband was conscripted, serving somewhere in the Pacific. He never mentioned his father, but Jane was not surprised.

Jane often wrote about their day-to-day life on the home front.

The most amazing thing happened today. You may

remember my talking about our landlady, Mrs. McGill. Today she made a huge sacrifice for the war effort. I found out about it when I came home, where I ran into her, as usual wearing her American Women's Voluntary Services uniform, polishing the brass rail in the hallway. I know I've told you how much she loves that rail and how she thinks it sets her building above all the others on the street.

She had tears in her eyes.

"What's wrong?" I asked her.

"The men are coming in a half hour to take my banister," she told me. "I've donated it to the war effort." She took her cloth and wiped another fingerprint, which I doubt existed.

I told her how terrific I thought her donation would be and gave her a hug. It's as if the war has changed everyone, mellowed them, somehow. I also told her how proud Olivia would be, even prouder than when Mrs. McGill took on the job of air raid warden for this district.

Through her tears, Mrs. McGill managed a smile. Her regard for Olivia was evident, and she stood a little taller, watching me hold onto the banister, for the last time, on my way upstairs.

When I got there, I found Olivia dancing around.

Jane left out the part that it was with Z.Z. clutched in her arms, giggling. She sighed, knowing she could never share this part of her life with Mr. Weaver.

She was following the steps on paper feet she had cut out. I guess used newspaper must not be on this month's rationing list, or she would never have wasted it.

The feet were numbered so that following them

taught Olivia the newest dances.

"You can't wait for a man to practice with," Olivia told me, seeing me stare. "They're all overseas."

Olivia and Jane worked hard at conserving every possible resource. Olivia kept quoting those ubiquitous posters. "Use it up, wear it out, make it do, or do without," she would say. Olivia wholeheartedly collected the tinfoil wrappers from her chewing gum and made her friends who smoked give her the foil from their cigarette packages. After FDR asked people to gather old tires, rubber raincoats, garden hoses, and bathing caps, Olivia went door to door collecting them. She also packed up Z.Z.'s old clothes the minute he grew out of them and brought them to a collection center for refugees and displaced persons.

Olivia said Z.Z. was a wonderful partner, clutching him to her cheek as she twirled around. He giggled, a sound that sent Jane rushing to cuddle him. She told her sister about the brass rail as she dropped the latest bundle of letters for Olivia from overseas onto the side table.

"Ooh!" Olivia exclaimed. "I'm going to be busy writing back." She shuffled through the mail, as if searching for one letter in particular. A broad smile spread across her face as she pulled an envelope from the pile.

"Horace?" Jane asked.

Tears filled Olivia's eyes, belying her smile. "Yes." She glanced at her watch. "I hope I have time to read it before I go." Without taking her eyes from the thin paper filled with tiny writing, she packed up the footsteps. Since Jane was home to care for Z.Z., it was time for Olivia to go off to roll bandages before she had to be at her factory job, where she now worked six nights a week. She had discontinued her education completely this year because there was such a shortage of workers in the war industries. Everywhere she turned there were posters for Rosie the Riveter, and she had felt she had no choice but to heed their call. She needed to help the nation manufacture the tools of war.

Olivia had to travel all the way to Newark, New Jersey, but she declared that even though she had to go at night, so that she could watch Z.Z. during the day, it was worth it. It was for the boys overseas. She faithfully bought war bonds, and stamps toward war bonds, whenever she got paid. She had more energy than Jane had ever seen, and her eyes held a burning light, all for the war effort. No amount of war news on the radio could kill that light, no amount of hard work could make Olivia tired. "I left your dinner on the stove," Olivia said, while she re-brushed her hair. "It didn't come out exactly as I expected."

"What is it?"

"It was supposed to be beef stew, but I had given most of our meat ration stamps to Mr. Johnson, because he really wanted a steak. He's doing so much to protect our neighborhood, always checking the skies in case of an air raid."

"It's okay," said Jane, "as long as there are eggs and milk for Z.Z."

"Oh, I would never give away anything he needs," said Olivia, her eyes again filling with tears. She tore her eyes away from her letter and stared at Jane.

Jane felt sorry for even suggesting such a thing. She knew Olivia adored the baby, even though he did not do anything the other children his age could do. It was as if he was in some kind of time delay. He had finally learned to roll over and could even sit alone, but he had not mastered crawling. Other children his age could already walk.

Sometimes it seemed as if Olivia was so devoted to Z.Z. she only gave him to Jane begrudgingly. She seemed to think of him constantly, and had made trades for sugar and flour in order to make treats for him.

Jane set Z.Z. on her lap, facing his aunt, and said, "Auntie O. is the best in the world, isn't she, Z.Z.?"

Olivia smiled, grabbed her purse and her already battered fiberboard lunch box, which had replaced her metal one since that was needed for the war. She turned for another look at Z.Z., and Jane waved his little hand at his aunt.

After giving Z.Z. his bath, Jane cuddled her little boy for several minutes before she put him down on a blanket to play with a stuffed toy. He rolled around contentedly, stuffing the toy into his mouth.

She opened the latest letter from Mr. Weaver. As usual, he did not say exactly where he was.

Dear Jane,

I hope this letter finds you and Olivia well. We have been working very hard. I could never have expected this. I'm sure you understand why I can't be more specific.

There was some time this week for quiet thought and speculation. I found my thoughts turning to New York, and I imagined myself back in the office again. You came to my mind, and I realized once more how extraordinary you are. I look forward to the day when I can see you again. There is something I will need to discuss with you at that time.

I look to the future for happiness. There is little for me here but keeping the men in my command focused on the task at hand. They talk of their wives and girlfriends back home and the lives they'll have. I find myself thinking of that too. We are all the same, these men and I. Quite different from the people I so often see in New York. I'm baffled by the cause of people's prejudices sometimes, especially when we face the same enemy. It unites us all.

I must go now. Think of me too. Prescott.

Jane was touched by his confidences. She had never before seen the inner workings of his heart and found them harmonizing with her own. He was such a good and decent man, but it took these extraordinary circumstances for her to discover that.

When Jane put Z.Z. into his crib, she noticed Olivia had left a little story book, one from her own childhood, on the dresser. Jane was touched by her hopefulness, reading to the little boy as if it would help him become more normal, but she was worried. As wonderful as Olivia was for working all night in the factory and slowing down her education so she could care for Z.Z. while Jane worked, she was very emotional about him. Luckily, he was remarkably healthy, given his condition.

They had only called the doctor to the house a few times this year, mostly for colds. But he had warned them several times that Z.Z. should not get overexcited, since there was some weakness in his heart, and they were advised to keep him away from sick children.

That had never been a problem, since Olivia did not like taking Z.Z. to the park. She had, twice, but both times came home in tears.

"The other mothers all stared and made disparaging remarks, not even trying to lower their voices, as if I couldn't understand them any more than Z.Z. can," she had cried. "They treated him as if he was dirty, or diseased, and their children could get sick from him. I told them his problem wasn't contagious, but they turned away. One mother scooped her baby up the second I put Z.Z. into the sandbox. That was when I left. We have our pride, you know."

So Z.Z. did not come into contact with many other children, and therefore had not caught any of the typical childhood ailments. No mumps or measles had sickened her baby, Jane realized with relief. The doctor had warned those could be very dangerous to Z.Z. There was also the ever-present summer danger of polio, a concept that frightened Jane more than anything else.

Z.Z. was growing. He lit up Jane's life, beaming his sunny smiles whenever she came home. But she worried about what the future would bring. She saw herself twenty-five years from now, doing the same thing, working and providing for her son. But she knew she could not ask Olivia to continue. Once the boys were back, she would marry and have a family of her own.

Jane was glad that Horace was Olivia's favorite. Her sister would make a wonderful match with him. He showed promise, worked hard, and possessed a level head, a good sense of humor, and intelligence. He was polite and caring. Several times he had offered to help around the house, doing the heavy chores. For Olivia, the future was bright.

To Jane's relief, Mrs. McGill had mellowed somewhat toward her little boy. One evening in May of

'43 she offered to sit with Z.Z., who slept from seven p.m. until morning. "You girls work so hard," she said, "and you deserve an evening out."

Jane and Olivia went to the movies to see *For Whom the Bell Tolls*, starring Ingrid Bergman and Gary Cooper. Just before the house lights went down, a man wearing his WWI uniform went up onto the stage holding the American flag. Everyone rose and pledged allegiance. Then the theater darkened and *The March of Time* newsreels were run. There was aerial footage of the U. S. capture of Tunisia, and footage of the surrender of the Axis troops in North Africa. Jane thought of Mr. Weaver. His last letter, while as usual not explicit about where he was or what he had done, had sounded as if he had recently been through a very tough time. She wondered if he ever had a moment of enjoyment.

Jane and Olivia thoroughly enjoyed the movie. Walking out into the spring air afterward invigorated them. Sometimes it seemed like there would be an end to the war, and life would resume.

But it never would for Z.Z. or Jane. Her hope of a happy family life was gone. In the back of her mind, Jane had assumed that, after she had Z.Z. and a suitable time had passed, she might meet someone else and marry, for Z.Z.'s sake. It would be good for him, even if it were a marriage lacking passion, as Pearl had once predicted and Jane had resolved never to consider. But with his birth and the circumstances of his affliction, she knew that would never happen. No one would be willing to take on such conditions.

Chapter Twelve

Olivia finished daubing the makeup on her legs. "It really looks like stockings, doesn't it?" she asked, holding the hem of her dressing gown up to show her handiwork. Silk had become a thing of the past, since the war, because nothing from Japan, or the region of the world it controlled, could be imported. Even if they had been able to get nylons, Olivia would have donated them to the cause, since both nylon and silk could be made into parachutes and tow ropes for glider planes.

Jane tore her eyes from Z.Z., who at two was finally beginning to walk, to inspect her sister's handiwork. "Aren't you going to put a seam on?"

Picking up the mascara pencil, Olivia contorted her body for a go at the back of her legs. "Good idea," she said, her voice trailing off as she strained farther and farther. "I can't reach." She giggled. "Would you do it?"

"We sure can, can't we, Z.Z.?" said Jane, putting him into a sitting position on the floor. He chortled.

"Stand on the table," Jane instructed. "I want to be at a better angle." She picked up the pencil and began her work.

"I wish you could go with me," said Olivia, her cheeks pink with excitement. "Tommy Dorsey's band is always so wonderful."

"I just got home from work," said Jane. "Z.Z.

needs me here. I spend far too much time away from him."

"But he'll probably sleep most of the evening. Mrs. McGill could watch him do that. And tomorrow is Saturday and you have off."

"We've imposed on Mrs. McGill too much already," Jane told her, while straining to make a continuous line up her sister's leg. "Besides, she'll enjoy seeing it with you."

Olivia rolled her eyes at Jane.

"I saw that. Why, do you have a better date?"

"Very funny. There isn't a man within three thousand miles."

"Nonsense. There are plenty of men on the home front."

"Yes, married or 4-F, usually both, or…"

"Not your type?"

"That's one way to put it. How are you doing down there?"

"I'm done. But don't look at it until you come down here. You might fall off the table."

Olivia got down to the floor and turned to look at her legs. "They aren't straight," she moaned.

"They look more real that way." Jane giggled. "You never could get them straight."

"That's not tr—" The doorbell interrupted her protests.

Jane opened the door and saw Mrs. McGill, who carried her usual polishing rag, even though it was unnecessary to wipe fingerprints off the wooden banister that had replaced the brass.

"You're early," said Jane. "But come on—" The sight of the person standing with the landlady stopped

Jane cold.

It was a Western Union carrier. And he had a telegram with him.

Mrs. McGill burst into tears. Jane was confused. Why would a war department telegram come there? She glanced over at Olivia, saw the color drain out of her face, and knew who it was.

Horace. He had no family and would have listed Olivia as his next of kin.

Jane took the telegram with shaking hands, and opened it. It said:

THE SECRETARY OF WAR DESIRES TO EXPRESS HIS DEEP REGRET THAT CORPORAL HORACE P. FARNSWORTH WAS KILLED IN ACTION IN DEFENSE OF HIS COUNTRY OVER FRANCE SEPTEMBER 13. LETTER FOLLOWS. It was signed, THE ADJUTANT GENERAL.

The paper floated out of Jane's hands to the floor. Olivia sank to her knees along with it, buried her face in her hands, and wailed, then threw herself prostrate.

Jane rushed to her sister's side, helpless to relieve her pain but wanting nothing more in the world than to be able to comfort her. She stroked her hair uselessly, knowing that Olivia was too deep into her grief to even feel it.

Mrs. McGill, bless her heart, had picked up Z.Z. and taken him into Jane's room, leaving the sisters alone. Jane could hear her singing a little song to the child, to block out Olivia's sobs.

Olivia was inconsolable, then and for weeks after. No words could relieve her agony. She sat in her room, the drapes drawn, eating almost nothing, for the rest of the weekend. Even the baby could not make her smile.

On Monday morning, Mrs. McGill was kind enough to take care of Z.Z. so Jane could go to work, and she promised to take care of Olivia as well. She arrived bright and early, but her mood was somber.

The work day passed slowly while Jane worried about her sister. She left the office as soon as the market closed and rushed home. It seemed to take forever for the subway car to come, and then the trolley rumbled so slowly down Rogers Avenue Jane thought she would scream. When she reached her block, she hurried into the building and ran up the stairs.

A strange silence greeted her when she opened the door. She could tell in an instant that Z.Z. wasn't there. He always greeted her the moment she came in, crying out, "Mama!" and even though she was an hour and a half early, she had expected to see him.

The sound of running water answered her questions. Olivia was probably giving him an early bath. Although Jane usually bathed her son after dinner, if he had become particularly dirty, Olivia would put him right into the tub.

Jane opened the door to the bathroom, expecting to see two surprised faces. But what she saw horrified her. Olivia was alone in the bathroom, sitting on the edge of the tub with a razor blade in her hand, slitting her wrist. A brand new package of blades lay open on the sink.

"Olivia!" Jane shouted, grabbing her sister's arm and pulling it away. Blood dripped from the wound into the tub Olivia held it over. "No!"

"I have to," she wailed. "I can't live without Horace. I love him too much."

Jane bound Olivia's wrist in a towel and held it tightly. She didn't think the wound had cut too deep, but Olivia needed help. Where was Z.Z.? And where was Mrs. McGill, who had promised to watch them both?

She reached over, turned off the water, and wrapped her arms around her sister, waiting until Olivia stopped sobbing so loudly. Then she asked softly, "Where is Z.Z.?"

"I asked Mrs. McGill to take him for a walk, since I didn't want to go out and it was a nice day."

"You mean you sent them away so you could try to harm yourself."

Olivia nodded.

"Do you think this is what Horace would want? For you to kill yourself?"

"I can't go on," Olivia cried. She tried to wipe her face, and the wound opened and bled more. Jane found a clean rag and wrapped it around Olivia's wrist.

Lifting her sister into a standing position, Jane led her out of the bathroom, across the apartment, and to the phone. While still holding onto Olivia, she dialed Dr. Mann's number and told his nurse to send the doctor right away. They sat huddled together in silence, waiting for him to come.

From the first floor she could hear Mrs. McGill shouting a few minutes later. "What's happened?" Carrying Z.Z., she trailed the doctor into the apartment and, seeing them on the couch, stopped and stared open-mouthed.

Dr. Mann ran to Olivia.

Because she was still holding Z.Z., Mrs. McGill quietly said, "Do you think you are the only one going through this? There are hundreds of girls with the same pain."

Dr. Mann looked at the landlady. "Did someone—" He broke off as he realized who it was. Over Olivia's head he mouthed to Jane, "Horace?"

The doctor grew pale.

"I'll go sit with Z.Z.," Mrs. McGill murmured.

Dr. Mann knelt beside Olivia, and took her hand, inspecting the crude bandage Jane had fashioned. No blood leaked through.

"It's just a scratch," said Olivia, her voice sounding dead. "She didn't give me time."

"Thank God," Jane whispered.

"I know you won't understand, but I can't live without Horace."

Jane could not speak. There were no words to ease her sister's pain.

Dr. Mann took Olivia into her bedroom, dressed the wound, and administered a strong sedative. Jane noticed that his hand shook and there were tears in his eyes. He had been Horace's doctor. When the boy's parents were killed in an automobile accident, Dr. Mann had spent hours with the grieving child and spent countless more helping his immigrant grandmother properly raise a young American adolescent.

When they left Olivia sleeping in her bedroom, Jane suddenly felt she should comfort this man who had not only delivered her and her sister but cared for the whole family for so many years. "I'm sorry. I thought you knew. We left a message with your wife."

The doctor pulled a large white handkerchief out of his pocket and wiped his eyes. "She told me there was something she had to tell me, but she said it would keep. I guess she was waiting for the right time." He shook his head. "I don't know why I'm acting like this.

I'm a doctor, after all. I've seen death."

"Horace was like a son to you," Jane said. "We know you checked on him daily after his grandmother died, to make sure he was taking care of himself."

Dr. Mann looked at Jane and smiled weakly. "And you and Olivia gave him dinner four nights a week."

"We wanted him healthy. I always knew he was the one for Ol—" She could not continue. That dream was gone, just like her dream of happiness with Lloyd. For a moment, Jane had a glimpse of the future—with the two of them alone with each other, no men in their lives.

For herself, that was fine. The future would be brighter for her sister, Jane resolved. Someone else would come along, if anyone was left after this terrible war.

She walked Dr. Mann to the door. "She'll sleep for a long time," he said. "When she wakes, I want you to have her take these," he held up some packets of powder, "mixed with water, twice a day. Mrs. McGill will have to watch the baby until the crisis passes. Call me if anything else happens, and I'll stop in on Friday." He reached for the doorknob, and turned, a question on his face. "How is little Z.Z.?"

"Healthy," said Jane.

"That's good. I know I told you that you shouldn't bring Z.Z. home, but I was wrong. He's good for you, and he's good for Olivia. He's even good for that old coot Mrs. McGill." He chuckled, and Jane could see that some of his color was coming back. But his face turned serious again. "It's a lucky thing he didn't get polio. Last summer was very bad. Too many children died."

Jane had heard. Not only had it been in the newspapers, but a woman on the next block had lost her child. Another child was confined to an iron lung. There was panic in the neighborhood for months after that. None of the mothers wanted their children to be around Z.Z., though, which turned out to be a lucky thing. He never had a chance to be exposed. Nevertheless, Jane never let him go near a puddle and never took him to the beach.

"Goodnight," said Doctor Mann. "Take care of them."

To Jane, the instruction was unnecessary. They were her entire reason for living.

Dear Mr. Weaver,

I hope all is well with you. The business totals are favorable.

Thank you for your kind thoughts about Horace's death. Olivia is still despondent. Our family doctor tells me to be patient with her, but I fear she will never be the same.

It had taken weeks for Olivia to regain her color and months before she smiled. The light in her eyes seemed as if it would never return. One day they received a letter from the commander of Horace's unit. He expressed his sorrow and praised Horace, explaining briefly how he had sacrificed himself to save several others. At the end he wrote, "He always spoke of you and of how much he loved you."

Learning about Horace's bravery seemed to help Olivia recover. "He gave his life to protect all of us. It wouldn't be right for us to forget that." She made arrangements for a gold star, and she and Jane put it in the window, signifying for all who saw it that they had lost a family member.

But a week later Olivia received a letter from Horace himself. It had been delayed in the mail, and his words of love and hope for the future sent Olivia back to her bed for days.

Jane continued her letter to Mr. Weaver.

I'm hoping to find things that will interest Olivia in life again. Mr. Dobbin comes to dinner every Sunday. He and Mrs. McGill spend the whole afternoon trying to make this apartment seem like a home with a family.

The afternoons were partial successes. With Z.Z. as the center of attention, there was much laughter and warmth. But naturally, Jane could not mention him to Mr. Weaver.

She concluded her letter, *Please take utmost care. Yours, Jane.*

****

Months later, Olivia was still not the same. She spent many hours with Z.Z. in the victory garden across the street from their block of walk-ups, giving him fresh air while she pulled weeds. She went back to college, with the help of Mrs. McGill as stand-in babysitter. In the evenings, she worked at the factory. Other than her student teaching, which she loved, she had no interest in life, and Jane despaired that she would ever regain her sunny outlook.

As the troops infiltrated Germany and the war effort showed results, worry about postwar economic disruption temporarily put the stock market on the defensive. Nervous and indecisive investors kept Jane busy in the office, and she had to write lengthy explanations to Mr. Weaver overseas. He wrote back that the newly created Office of War Mobilization and

Reconversion intrigued him, and for Jane not to worry. He would be home to see to everything and relieve her of her burdens.

A nagging question haunted Jane when it looked like the war would finally end. In contrast to the propaganda in the earlier war years that encouraged women to work outside their homes, new advertisements and articles in magazines started to remind women that once the war ended their places were in the home. Did Mr. Weaver consider her Rosie the Riveter? Did he think she was only talking to clients as his replacement while he was away but had no future in such an elevated position at his firm once he returned home? She only had the job she did now because of the war, she knew, and because he was away.

Everything she read, however, reminded her that when the boys came home, the women should be willing to give up their jobs and go back to being wives and mothers, tending the family hearth. Jane bristled at the concept. She saw no future for herself in that.

Chapter Thirteen

Jane worked late on April 12, 1945. She had so much paperwork she could not leave her office until six-thirty. She expected to find the street outside empty, but instead she encountered dozens of people, standing in shock. The news was written on every tear-washed face—President Roosevelt was dead.

All the way home she remembered his voice on the radio and the day she and Olivia stood in the pouring rain in October, watching his motorcade go by. It had seemed as if he would be president forever. Now it was nearly unbelievable that he was gone.

The entire country grieved, and Olivia went back to her bed. She ate nothing for days, and Mrs. McGill sat vigil again, watching over her every moment, in case she tried to do herself more harm. At night, Jane was awakened by Olivia shouting for their father, the same way she did after he died. It seemed as if President Roosevelt had somehow become mixed up with him in Olivia's mind.

She had still not recovered when school ended less than a month later. She barely managed to finish her last papers for college, and refused to go to graduation. She had also lost more weight, and her once lustrous deep brown hair hung limp and knotted until Jane came to Olivia's bedroom and picked up her hairbrush.

"Sit up. I want to fix your hair."

"Why bother?" Olivia asked while Jane worked on her tangles. "I'm not going anywhere."

"You'll feel better. You are a college graduate, you know, and you should be proud of that. You had to work very hard to achieve this."

"Maybe tomorrow."

Jane stood up, went to the closet, and took out Olivia's best dress. "Put this on."

"Why?"

"Just do it. And wash your face and put on some lip pomade."

Olivia lay back down on her bed and pulled the covers up. "I can't."

"Would you do it for me? Please?"

She watched as her sister got out of bed and went to the bathroom to wash up. When she returned to her room, Jane went out to the front door and motioned to the people waiting below.

By the time Olivia came out of her room—dressed, Jane was relieved to see—the party was set up. She joined Mrs. McGill, Mr. Dobbin, and Z.Z. in shouting, "Surprise!" Mrs. McGill led Olivia over to the cake she'd spent a whole day—and many ration coupons—decorating with sugar roses. In the center of all the flowers, it said, "Congratulations, Olivia."

Olivia put on a smile, cut the cake, and accepted everyone's best wishes. She thanked them all for coming and thinking of her. But after they left, she went right back to her bed. Even the news of the victory in Europe did not cheer her up for long.

When Olivia's friends began to return from Europe, they rushed to her door. The change in them was striking. When they left, in their immaculate new uniforms, they were attempting to hide the fear they felt. Now, upon their return, their youthful roundness had been replaced by a maturity and self-confidence that would have taken many more years to acquire otherwise.

One young man, Henry, expressed shock upon seeing Olivia so gaunt and pale. Another, Sal, met him descending the steps and was told, "She's not the same girl you dreamed about." Sal seemed to be unwilling to believe it until he saw the truth for himself. Mrs. McGill, who saw the exchange, told Jane about it later. When he raised a hand to the door, he was greeted by the pathetic creature Olivia had become, in Mrs. McGill's words. She said he nearly fled.

Many of the boyfriends had known about Olivia's feelings for Horace but had hoped they would change. In the past, she had truly enjoyed the other boys' company, and there should have been at least one among them who would make her happy. But now, one by one, the potential suitors drifted away and did not return. Jane thought of pleading with them to wait, explaining that Olivia would recover, but she knew it would be futile. No right-thinking individual, long away in a terrible war, would put his life on hold, even for someone like the girl Olivia had been, who now gave no one any reason to hope.

After VJ day, another boy, Martin, whom Jane had not met before, came to see Olivia. Jane watched as he approached her sister, waited for his inevitable shock upon seeing her and subsequent recognition that hope of a future with her was gone. Olivia barely nodded hello, as if she, too, was expecting the visit to be short. She halfheartedly gestured to the couch but made no move toward it herself.

Martin plopped himself down and smiled at Olivia. Without waiting for her to ask, he mopped his brow and said, "It sure is hot out there today. I could use a glass of water, unless you have something stronger."

In her surprise, Olivia fetched him a drink. Where the other boys had immediately become solicitous of her, Martin was oblivious to Olivia's despair. He did not even seem to notice that Olivia had not spoken a word.

"I don't recall meeting you before," Jane said, hoping to fill the void.

"Olivia and I know each other from college," said Martin. "Although I guess she finished her education while I was away." He leaned back and took a deep breath, which puffed out his chest. "Yes, we men made some big sacrifices, but Uncle Sam is going to do right by us now."

"Oh," said Jane, when she realized Olivia was not about to open her mouth, "do you have a job lined up?"

"Not yet. But there are jobs being held for the returning vets, and I'm going to get myself one."

"So you don't plan to continue with your education?"

"I've learned enough and waited long enough. It's time to start my life." He looked over at Olivia. "And find myself a wife. I'm going to make some lucky woman very happy."

Neither Jane nor Olivia said anything. Jane was trying hard not to laugh at this pompous boy, and Olivia did not indicate she had heard.

"Where will you start looking for work?" Jane asked, after a suitable interval had passed and there was no longer a need to respond to the previous statement.

"I'm going straight to the top," said Martin. "I'm going to get a job to suit my qualifications. I'm going to live in a mansion someday, and have a driver and butler and maids. I'll travel to Europe, this time not courtesy of the government, and I'll buy anything I want."

Jane walked him to the door when he was ready to leave. That was about an hour after she was ready, but she had held up one side of the conversation so as not to be rude. "We would like to wish you well," she said. She did not invite him to call again.

But he called every evening, after his day spent job-hunting, and sat with Olivia until nine o'clock, telling her all about his dreams for the future. It did not seem to matter to Olivia that the dreams were pie-in-the-sky; she showed no sign of having heard him. He never seemed to notice.

****

Early one morning in September, Jane sat at her desk, reading a newspaper filled with news of those returning from the Pacific. There had been joy throughout the country since Japan formally surrendered.

The front door of the office opened, and Jane went to see who was there. She had not hired someone to fill her own position when she took over for Mr. Weaver, and so she personally greeted every arrival.

An officer stood in the doorway, straight, lean, muscular, and more handsome than anyone Jane had ever seen. Thunderstruck, she realized it was Mr. Weaver and he was staring straight at her. In all the time she'd worked for him, she had never felt herself so drawn to him. The flame of determination in his eyes,

144

which she had noticed before he left, now burned with passion.

Jane rushed to him. He hugged her close, and seemed unwilling to let her go. "I've missed you," he murmured into her hair. Holding her at arm's length, he stared at her. "You look wonderful."

Self-consciously, Jane pushed back a tendril that had escaped from behind her ear. "I look—" She stopped, seeing a hungry look in Mr. Weaver's eyes that caused her heart to thump and made her stop to catch her breath. "Why didn't you tell me you were home?" she stammered.

"I didn't want to call. I had to come to see you." He smiled. "I'm glad I did."

"It's so strange," said Jane, still trying to believe this man was really here. "I just got a letter from you yesterday. You said it might take a while to get back."

"It did. But I wrote that letter three weeks ago."

Jane bit her lip. Was he back for good? Would she see him every day? The thought thrilled her. "Have you been discharged?" she asked.

"Almost. I'll be back to work in a week. I can't thank you enough for keeping my business going for me. Or maybe I can. I would like to start by inviting you to dinner, in the fanciest restaurant in New York. We'll go tonight."

Jane felt her bubble of joy dissipate. "I can't. I have to go home after work. Olivia—"

"How is your sister?"

"She's been having a very hard time."

"I'm sorry. I know how much Horace meant to both of you. His death must have been hard for you, too."

"It was, but so much worse for Olivia."

"I'd love to see her."

Jane smiled. "I have an idea. Mr. Weaver—"

"Prescott."

"Prescott." The name felt so strange on her lips. "Would you like to come to our—" She broke off, remembering there was someone at home whom he knew nothing about.

But he jumped at her idea. "I'd love to. Seven o'clock?"

Jane had no choice but to agree. After he bounded out of the office, she told herself it was about time to introduce Z.Z. to her boss anyway. He was a good man. He would understand, somehow.

Toward five o'clock, though, doubts began to replace Jane's hopeful attitude. Not only would she probably be demoted back to secretary, she was going to reveal a secret she had kept for over four years. She began to regret calling Olivia and telling her they would have a guest for dinner.

"Who?" Olivia had asked.

"My employer."

"Mr. Weaver is back? Is it really true?" Olivia sounded happy for once.

"Yes." Jane felt the same way, only much more so. Mr. Weaver—Prescott—had become so much more than an employer through his letters. Jane felt very close to him and even a bit embarrassed that she had never told him about Z.Z.

It hit her that she felt emotions she had never thought she would feel again. Feelings of love. How could that be? Shaking her head at her silliness, and knowing full well she was not in his social class, she attributed it to relief at seeing him well, and home.

Now it was time for the truth. She could only hope he would understand, since the circumstances of Z.Z.'s birth, and her blind trust in a person who did not love her, were not something of which she was proud.

But she wondered how she had worked for him all those years and not let herself notice how attractive he was. While she knew the answer was her certainty that she was not of his class, there was no doubting he was attracted to her. Maybe class did not matter to him. She had never felt her heart beat so hard as when she saw him, and the look in his eyes seemed to say the same thing.

"I'm so glad he's coming," said Olivia. "I watched you when you read his letters, and I think you feel something for him."

Jane couldn't contain herself. "I do," she confided. "Mr. Weaver, er, Prescott," she said, trying out the sound of his name on her lips, "means so much to me. I didn't know, myself, until I saw him today."

Olivia smiled. "I'm happy for you." Then she fussed over Jane until she was pleased with the results. "You look beautiful," her sister said, despairing again that Jane had somehow lost their grandmother's cameo.

Prescott arrived at precisely seven, still wearing his uniform. For once, Olivia did not pale when she saw it.

Jane was pleased with the way he looked at her, and she suddenly felt prettier than she ever had. She could barely stop smiling enough to remind Prescott of Olivia.

"You've grown up," he said. "And I understand you got your degree. Congratulations."

He turned to Jane. "There are no words to thank

you for all you've done for me. I know it probably took time away from your sister."

Jane saw Olivia's eyes widen. While it was true, the person who had sacrificed the most was still unknown to Prescott. She bit her lip.

Olivia fluttered around, serving drinks and canapés. She had found the recipes for them in a magazine, and was looking more alive than she had in almost two years.

When everyone was comfortably seated, and dinner was still a half hour from being done, Jane took a deep breath and prepared to introduce her son.

"Mr. Weav—, Prescott, I have someone I would like you to meet. I haven't told you about him before, but I'm sure you two will get along well."

His brows knitted in confusion. Shaking, Jane went to get her child. She wondered if she should have explained more, but what could she say? This is my illegitimate son?

Z.Z. was wearing a new sailor suit. Jane took a moment to straighten his collar and brush his soft, flaxen hair before she led the child into the parlor. "This is Z.Z.," she said. "My son."

Prescott looked up at Jane's words, his face clouded by questions. "Your what?" And then his gaze fell on the child, and he gasped.

He jumped up. "Oh, my God." He stared at the child, then turned away.

Olivia stood up and went to Z.Z. "I'll bet you're hungry. Would you like some bread and butter?"

"Um, good," said Z.Z., as he followed her into the kitchen.

"I'm sorry," said Prescott. "I was just surprised.

You poor thing."

Jane was not sure she liked having him sympathize with her about her child's problems. But she gave him the benefit of the doubt, since he had been so surprised.

"I didn't know you had married," he said huskily, his disappointment evident.

Jane considered telling him the same story she had told so many others, but she could not bring herself to lie to this man. "I'm not. I wasn't. Z.Z. is the product of my own stupidity."

Prescott's forehead vein throbbed, and his face turned red. "When?" he asked, his voice no more than a croak.

He was not asking about the child's birthday, Jane was sure. He wanted to know when she had gotten pregnant. "The spring of 1941."

"Why didn't you tell me?"

Jane had been honest so far, and she did not want to start lying now. "I was afraid you would fire me. I needed to work."

Prescott remained rigid. Turning to look at Olivia, who stood wide-eyed in the kitchen doorway, he said, "I can't believe you hid all of this from me." He picked up his hat. "I can't believe it was all a lie." He took four swift strides, and went out the door.

Jane burst into uncontrollable tears and fell to the sofa, covering her head. Olivia tried to calm her, saying Prescott would get over it. She had seen when he arrived how much he loved Jane.

But Jane had seen the truth when he left. Any love he may have felt was gone. No, it was dead.

****

Prescott went to the nearest bar and drank until he

was numb. The thumps on his back from fellow officers and civilians alike were like blows. He kept hearing Jane's lies, seeing her beauty and knowing it was false, and even feeling her heartbeat when he'd held her that morning. He now knew she had hidden from him its deepest truth.

Later he walked home, over the bridge to Manhattan, stopping at several more bars on the way, whenever he felt he was starting to sober up. He worked his way uptown, where he found a bed in the University Club.

His shattered dreams mocked him while he slept off his drunkenness. He kept seeing Jane's face, and seeing her as he imagined her in bed with another man. He kept seeing himself, naive as a child, all while he had worried about Jane, while she was sick, and then expanding. Filling out, he had thought. And when he left for the war, he had begun to fall in love with the woman whom he did not know carried another man's child.

Self-loathing and revulsion replaced his pain. Anger pushed away his dreams. The family ring he had begun to think she might wear would stay in the vault forever.

****

It did not surprise Jane when a telegram came the next evening saying that her services were no longer needed at the brokerage:

SISTER'S HUSBAND NEEDS JOB STOP YOUR SERVICES NO LONGER REQUIRED STOP. PRESCOTT WEAVER.

Jane wanted to respond, *YOU ARE BREAKING MY HEART STOP AND YOU DON'T EVEN CARE*

WHETHER OR NOT YOU'LL BE PUTTING US OUT ON THE STREET STOP. She held her aching head in her hands. *Please stop.*

****

For two solid weeks Jane beat the pavement searching for a new job. Even with the money she had realized from her formerly worthless stock, plus Olivia's salary, she needed employment. She was told in no uncertain terms that she could not possibly fill a position such as she had held while Mr. Weaver was away, nor were there any related secretarial jobs. In many cases she was not even allowed to leave a résumé. "Those jobs are all reserved for our returning boys," she was told.

Chapter Fourteen

Martin turned away from the window. "There are no jobs out there," he said. "I have pounded the pavement endlessly." His dull, washed-out blue eyes, untidy dishwater hair, and weak chin spoke of a beaten man, and Jane was not surprised he couldn't find work.

She tried not to smile at this melodramatic speech. Martin was convinced it was nothing he did, nor the way he looked, spoke, or carried himself, that kept him from finding work, although if he had ever asked her opinion, she would have been happy to explain to him that no one owed him anything, despite his beliefs. He had managed to avoid distinguishing himself in his service to his country, and had managed not to acquire any skills. Yet the thought of unskilled labor did not appeal to him.

"Martin," said Olivia. "They have to get to know you."

If her sister only knew him, Jane thought. But Olivia was out of other prospects and left with this poor excuse for a suitor. The other boys had pride, and, upon finding Olivia so distraught over Horace's death, had given up trying to win Olivia's love. Not so with Martin. He had no pride, no drive, and no redeeming features. Olivia, who had managed to get her college degree in teaching only one year later than planned, had a job, and she did not mind that Martin had not found one. She never seemed to expect anything from him, or care. Her emotions were dead, as was her free will. She would do as expected, marry and have a family.

Although the ardent light that had been in her eyes before Horace died was gone, a small flame burned when she talked of the children in her class. Jane was so grateful her sister had been allowed to finish her degree even with all her absences. Those children were the best medicine for her. If only she could be content with that and forget about her poor excuse for a fiancé. With time, another young man would come along, someone who would love Olivia more than himself, and someone whom she could love.

"Some people who have jobs to give," Martin said, "are stingy. How am I supposed to deal with that?"

Jane ground her teeth. She knew who Martin meant. Mr. Dobbin had come to her with a problem of his own. "The war is over," he had said, in his quiet way, "and the demand for uniforms is declining. What should I do?"

"There are many people who still wear uniforms," Jane told him. "Maybe you could convert your business to hospital clothing supplies and other kinds of uniforms. Police wear them, and so do bus drivers and many others."

The old man's eyes had gotten that spark that Jane knew meant he was energized. "That's a good idea. I could even expand. But I don't know where to start. And my bookkeeper left when her husband came back from overseas. I know this is asking a lot, Jane, but could you possibly help me out?"

Jane had the sense he was sparing her feelings and avoiding giving her the idea she was a charity case, but she chose to ignore the implication. She swallowed her pride and gave up her idea of working on Wall Street, at least for now, in order to keep the books in Mr. Dobbin's factory and help him in any way possible. He allowed her to work whatever hours were convenient, because of Z.Z.

Martin seemed to think Mr. Dobbin should give him a job too, and the man had offered him a position in inventory, but Martin told him, "It wasn't what I had in mind."

Jane thought he would have agreed if it were not an entry level position. But what else could Mr. Dobbin do? Martin had no business skills. His suits were always rumpled and his shirts yellow and wrinkled. Just because he thought he should start out as president of the firm did not mean he should be given that position. Any reasonable person would realize that, but not Olivia's fiancé.

Martin sighed, loudly and obviously. "If I can't get work, we can't get married."

Jane hoped he would be unemployed for a long time.

"Don't worry," said Olivia. She turned to Jane. "Couldn't we move in here after we're married? Then we would help you pay the rent, and since there is such a housing shortage anyway, wouldn't it make sense?"

She looked hopeful, Jane thought, as she searched for a good excuse to prevent that ever happening. It was puzzling. Maybe Olivia could be happy with Martin. Jane wondered if she was projecting her own feelings onto the relationship, which wouldn't be fair at all.

In considering the idea of them living there after they were married, Jane acknowledged that Olivia was already paying more than half the rent. Jane made much less working for Mr. Dobbin than she had for Mr. Weaver, and if Olivia and Martin did marry and move out, Jane and Z.Z. should probably move to a smaller place. Her new salary was not enough for this apartment, and she refused to dip into her small nest egg. It was for Z.Z.'s future care. Feeling full of defeat, Jane nodded.

Olivia jumped up, more animated than she had been in a while. "Great! Then I can see Z.Z. and you every day."

It occurred to Jane that Martin looked even less happy about the idea than she felt. But he got over it. "I thought we had to wait until I have a job." He frowned, although it seemed to Jane it was an effort for him to keep the corners of his mouth turned downward.

"That's silly," said Olivia. "Now you have to leave. We have a wedding to plan."

****

All through the months before the wedding, Jane had to hide her dread. She told herself it was just because she hated the thought of change, but she knew there was more to it. Martin was not the man for Olivia; he was barely a man at all. Nevertheless, Jane did everything she could to make the event joyful for her sister. Olivia deserved no less. Jane even suggested they switch bedrooms, so that Olivia and her new husband could have more space and a window that faced the street, not just an alley.

"I couldn't do that to you and Z.Z.," Olivia protested.

"I'm sure it would make Martin happy," Jane told her, giving Olivia no choice but to accept the offer.

Jane also found Martin a job. She swallowed her pride and called one of Mr. Weaver's clients. After introducing herself, and evading questions about why she no longer worked for Mr. Weaver, she asked the man if he could find Martin a position in his insurance firm. The man agreed. After a short training program, Martin would be an insurance salesman. For several weeks he was a much more interesting person, less self-centered, and Jane's doubts diminished.

But one afternoon when she was downtown, on a beautiful June Saturday, Jane ran into one of the young men who had been friends with Olivia at college. He had also been, Jane knew, close friends with Horace, but was a year or so older.

"Miss Baldwin?" he said, as if his eyes had deceived him. "Is that you?"

"Sam Roberts," Jane replied enthusiastically, "it certainly is. The last time I saw you was right before you shipped out. How are you?"

"I'm well. I just finished college, finally. How are you?"

"Fine. And congratulations."

Sam blushed. Of all of Olivia's friends, he was the one Jane favored after Horace. He had a gentleness and a sense of humor, with a sparkle in his eyes. But his brow furrowed.

"Thank you, ma'am. I've heard that Olivia is not well, though. We all miss Horace. Please tell her I hope she feels better soon."

Jane saw such sincerity and concern on Sam's face that she felt she should reassure him. "She did have a horrible time after Horace…" Jane bit her lip, trying not to let her emotions interfere. "But she is improving,"

Jane added. "She'll be married shortly, to another young man who returned from the service."

Sam's worried expression diminished. "That's wonderful. Is it anyone I know?"

"His name is Martin Roche," Jane said, wondering if Sam might have met him at Brooklyn College.

"Not—" Sam broke off. "Is he a short guy with dirty blond hair?"

Jane could think of a few more unflattering things to say about Martin, but she just nodded.

"Oh, you can't let her go through with it," Sam said, the sparkle in his eyes gone. "Didn't she tell you how he used to bother her at school? A group of us made sure to stay with her when Horace wasn't around, to keep old Marty from talking to her—he got her so upset."

Even though the sun beat down from above, Jane felt chilled to the bone. She remembered how hard Olivia had taken that boy's rude advances, even to the point of considering leaving college. After saying goodbye to Sam, who told her his new wife, a girl he'd met in Italy, was expecting, she hurried home to confront her sister.

"You know you must call off the wedding," Jane demanded, throwing out her resolve not to interfere.

"I can't."

"Why not? He will hurt you. He has in the past."

"He was only a boy then. He's changed. I know he has. He's grown up now."

Jane found it hard to believe the childish, stubborn, opinionated Martin was an improvement from how he had been as a teenager. And she could not talk her sister out of marrying him.

"All my girlfriends are married already," Olivia told Jane. "Some have children on the way." She did not have to say that the only single woman Olivia knew was Jane, and no one would say she was a happy role model.

"Now that Martin's got his job," Olivia pointed out, "he's really a new man. I know he is. You must believe me. Everything will be wonderful."

****

Prescott Weaver met Regina Marsh, daughter of Mr. and Mrs. Leland Horatio Marsh, at a Sunday afternoon dinner at the home of her uncle, Gil Marsh, a stockbroker. The invitation had been a surprise, since he barely knew the man, but he had accepted gratefully. Mr. Marsh was legendary, and hearing his stories would do a lot to cheer Prescott up. It had been over six months since his dreams of a future with Jane had shattered, and he still felt as if there was a hole in his life.

"I would like to introduce you to my niece, Reggie," Mr. Marsh said, when Prescott arrived. "She's an extraordinary girl."

He led the way through the long foyer to the marble-tiled veranda overlooking his acres of land high above Long Island Sound. Standing alone, looking out on the terraced landscape, stood Regina.

She had the heavy-boned face of her uncle. Her straight brown hair had been styled on Fifth Avenue, and her clothes cut to hide the imperfections of her wide hips. A mink stole covered her shoulders, keeping out the chill of the April afternoon. She smiled when she saw the two men.

"Reggie," said Mr. Marsh, "I'd like to present

Prescott Weaver. He's a young stockbroker, and I'm sure you two will have a lot to talk about."

"I'm pleased to meet you," said Prescott. "Are you interested in the market?"

"Will you both excuse me?" Mr. Marsh asked. "I have to greet my other guests."

"We'll be fine, Uncle Gil," Reggie purred. "Don't worry about us." She linked elbows with Prescott and moved toward the steps. "Wouldn't you like to see the gardens?"

Prescott was unaccustomed to such a forward young woman, but he let himself be led along. They walked past banks of early tulips and blooming azaleas, and Reggie chattered enough for both sides of the conversation. "These will be beautiful white calla lilies," she rhapsodized, pointing to the thin, green leaves just beginning to sprout from the damp earth. "My friend Catherine carried a huge bouquet of them at her wedding." She moved a bit farther. "These rose bushes will be open in a month or so. My uncle has so many varieties. He has some of the newest hybrids, and a large white rose so perfect and lovely that my friend Marian begged him to let her use them for her bridal bouquet."

She chattered on and on, mostly about flowers, especially the varieties her friends used at their weddings.

Prescott began to get the picture that she looked forward to her own wedding. He suddenly felt an urge to get back to the dinner party.

All through dinner, where they were seated together, Regina flattered him, telling him how much she admired his career, and his efforts in the war. She seemed to know far more about him than he would have expected.

At subsequent social gatherings and concerts, he ran into her often. She seemed to be the only single girl in her social circle, and she always sought him out. Soon Prescott realized she did not have much interest in stocks or finances, just what she could spend of her father's money. But she seemed to have a good heart and worked on many charitable committees.

Although sometimes he still longed for Jane and her selfless devotion to all those around her, he turned his mind to Reggie. Possibly, he thought, they could build a life together and have a family. Maybe love would follow.

He proposed one evening, giving her the ring he had long ago stored in the vault, the one he had considered giving to Jane. He hoped to give Reggie his heart as well someday. She accepted immediately.

After the initial announcements, all discussion or talk of the wedding became entirely none of Prescott's business. The date was set, only two months away. All he had to do was plan a honeymoon, and he chose California. One day, he showed Reggie the itinerary in the living room of her parents' home, after the couturier had left.

"I wanted to go to the continent," she whined, when he told her of his plans. "I wanted to show you off on the boulevards of Paris."

"Europe," Prescott said, "was nearly destroyed in the war. There is nothing to visit, and won't be for a while. And I have no desire to see it again, not any time in the near future."

"Oh, Pres," Reggie cooed. "Don't be angry with

me. I understand. But why California?"

"Because it's the farthest place to go in the U.S. And that's where I want to be."

"But," Reggie intoned, "we'll go to Europe someday, right? I haven't been there in sooo long." Lately Prescott had noticed every word that came out of her mouth was over-dramatized. "Daddy said I couldn't go when the difficulty started."

It was just like Lee Marsh to call the spread of Nazism "difficulty."

Reggie moved closer to Prescott, running her fingers through his hair. The sensations that went down his spine made him look forward to their wedding night. Reggie usually kept her distance, saying she wanted to remain pure until they were married. But she seemed to know how to get him to forget his annoyance at some of the things she said, and this was one way. "Our life will be so wonderful. Daddy says the new house will be ready right on schedule."

Prescott caught her hand and pulled it close to his face, feeling the softness of her skin. Looking into her eyes, he said, "I don't understand why he's giving us a house. Isn't he doing enough?" Their wedding promised to rival those of the blue bloods of Park Avenue.

Reggie pulled away and went over to the piano. "He loves me, that's why. That's why he's also going to buy you a seat on the New York Exchange."

Stunned, Prescott grabbed Reggie's hand, turning her toward him.

Her eyes widened, and she frowned. "What's wrong?"

"What do you mean he's going to buy me a seat?

I'll buy my own seat, thank you. I'm not taking a handout."

Reggie laughed, although the sound she made was more insulting than sweet. She pulled her hand away. "You couldn't even afford a seat on the curb."

"I would rather not have a seat on that exchange than have your father buy me one anywhere. And at the rate things are going, it'll take me twice as long to save money, since running that house will cost so much more than I had planned. You'll have to cut back on your wardrobe requirements."

Reggie stared open-mouthed at him. "Father will still buy my clothes, if that's what you want."

"No, he won't. And if you insist, I'll have to call off the wedding."

She did not say anything for a while, and Prescott realized he hoped, at least a little, that she would call if off. He worried, as each day passed, that he was about to make a mistake, since he had not yet fallen in love. But he had given his word.

Reggie smiled. "I wouldn't think of it. We'll get married as scheduled." She came close enough to wrap her arms around him and kissed him lightly on the cheek. "I told Daddy that you'd never accept him buying you a seat, that you were a man of conviction. That's why I love you so much." She was so sincere, he held her close.

"This is just pre-marriage jitters," she assured him, pulling away. "We'll have a wonderful time in California, and a wonderful marriage. You'll see I'm right."

****

A week before Olivia's wedding, Jane made a

feeble attempt to apprise her sister of the particulars of her wedding night. Olivia waved her off, however, saying that while she appreciated Jane's intent, she probably knew more from listening to her married friends than Jane did after her gropings with Lloyd. Olivia was kind about it, and Jane knew she was right.

Olivia and Martin were married the first week of July 1947, in the living room of the apartment Jane and her sister shared. Jane had done her best to make the room look special, bringing in as many white carnations as she could afford.

The bride wore a dress that one of Mr. Dobbin's employees had made for her. The long white fabric was such a contrast to Olivia's black hair, and brought out such a creaminess in Olivia's skin, that several people gasped at her beauty when they saw her. She carried a bouquet of tiny white roses and baby's breath in her lace-gloved hands.

The ceremony by a justice of the peace was simple. It was attended by friends and Olivia and Jane's few relatives, two aged cousins of their father's. Martin's mother, according to him, was unable to make it to the wedding. Olivia had never met the woman and felt terrible, even considering postponing until his mother was available, but Martin would not hear of it. Jane wondered if he had even told her about it. She had never heard him say anything nice about his mother.

Jane acted as Matron of Honor, keeping up the lie of her marriage, and walked up the aisle dressed in a simple blue skirt and matching blouse. She saw Olivia's closest friends and their husbands, smiling and holding hands. Behind her, Z.Z. carried the ring tied to a satin pillow. They were followed by Olivia and Mr. Dobbin, who gave the bride away. Mrs. McGill cried when she saw her. Martin, for once, seemed moved by the event, and Jane crossed her fingers, hoping for the best. As they were pronounced man and wife, with Martin placing on Olivia's finger the ring Vanessa had worn, Jane sent a silent prayer that the union would work out. Her sister deserved happiness.

Afterward, Jane served small sandwiches and punch, while Mrs. McGill passed out pieces of the wedding cake she had spent three days baking and decorating with her elaborate sugar roses and garlands.

Olivia, who had the summer off from her teaching job, had looked forward to a honeymoon trip to Niagara Falls, but Martin thought it was better to stay at home, saving their money. He said he worked on commission, and that his income would improve soon, so they could take a trip in a year or so. His fiscal responsibility might have been considered admirable, but Jane had already decided he was simply cheap.

The wedding night was a nightmare for Jane, since Martin refused to even rent a hotel room for a few days. She covered her ears with a pillow when she realized she could hear the springs in their bed, and she hoped Martin would be gentle with her sister.

The next morning, Olivia got the only wedding trip she ever would. It was a subway ride up to the Bronx, where she finally met Martin's mother. The woman had moved there from Brooklyn during the war to care for her own mother, who had since passed away.

From what Olivia told Jane, the apartment was a tenement in a poor neighborhood, and Mrs. Roche, her new mother-in-law, was less than gracious. She had not known about the wedding and blamed Olivia for not sending her an invitation.

Martin did not correct the mistake.

Chapter Fifteen

The New York Times, the *Herald*, the *Post* and several other papers carried the details of the marriage of Prescott Weaver and Regina Marsh, in the second week of August 1947. Prescott's family seemed pleased, especially his father. "She's from a fine family," said Mr. Weaver. "I'm impressed by your choice."

Their honeymoon trip did not help him fall in love with his wife. Neither did it do anything to change her virginal status. She held back from him, causing him endless frustration. His experience up to that time was limited to women who were not nearly as shy as his wife, and he was afraid of hurting her. So he waited, suffering through endless one-sided discussions of clothes, flowers, and quality families, knowing full well that not one thing he said ever interested his wife.

When they finally consummated their union, several weeks later, Prescott realized there were simply no redeeming aspects to his marriage.

****

Martin was fired from his job a month and a half after he married Olivia. Jane found out a week later when Mr. Weaver's client called to explain. When Jane confronted Martin, he admitted he had been let go but claimed he now spent his days searching for a new place to work.

Although he said he would hunt for a new job every day, he slept until noon, while Olivia brought him breakfast and often lunch in bed. Fortunately, except on weekends, Jane did not have to see it. She had switched her hours at Mr. Dobbin's factory to days while Olivia was off for the summer recess, since her sister had longed to look after Z.Z. "You and Martin will be out all day working," she had said when she first came up with the idea. "Z.Z. will keep me company."

Jane's son was five and a half. He was not as big as the neighbor's son of the same age, but he was a lovely child. His flaxen hair and blueberry-colored eyes, so similar to Jane's father's, and his pleasant disposition, caused even people who were dismayed at his mongoloidism to smile at him. He had learned to catch a ball, but he could not run, because the effort left him winded. The doctor pronounced him fit whenever he saw him, but explained that the boy was not strong.

Olivia had planned to take Z.Z. on outings during that summer, to the zoo and maybe a museum. She had decided she should not care that people said the child should be put away. But she did not have time. She did not think it was right to leave her husband alone, and Martin went nowhere until after dinner, when he got as far as the local bar.

Jane thought about switching back to working at night, so she could be with Z.Z. during the day, but realized that would mean all three of them would be together all day. Besides, Mr. Dobbin needed her during the day shift for as long as she could be there, since much more production was done then. And she had recently suggested he start manufacturing children's clothing, since so many people were starting families. He loved the idea and put her in charge of making it happen, so Jane decided to stick to her day schedule for as long as possible.

One afternoon, shortly after she arrived home, she overheard Martin grumbling to Olivia. "You have to do something about that monster your sister spawned. He should be sent to an institution."

"How could you say that?" Olivia had challenged him, her voice sounding angrier than Jane had ever heard her.

"Aw, he's not so bad," Martin said, backing down. "Just keep him out of my way."

But Jane knew that was not how he felt. She could see his loathing every time he looked Z.Z.'s way.

****

By mid-October, Martin had found another job. He was working for a lawyer, as a clerk-typist. Jane wondered if he was capable of such work, but she kept her mouth shut. She had returned to working late afternoons and evenings, leaving as soon as Olivia got home from teaching school so she could catch the end of the first shift. If she played her cards right, Jane did not have to see her brother-in-law at all.

Following her sister's lead, she took Z.Z. to the park every pleasant morning. One morning she took him all the way to Manhattan, to the Central Park boat basin, as a special outing. He was delighted with riding on the subway and did not notice the pitying faces of the people around him. Jane turned away, though, hiding her tears.

Z.Z. chattered about the train all the way to the park. His speech was rudimentary for a five-year-old, but he got his message across. "Birds," he cried, spotting a flock of pigeons. He trotted after them and was disappointed when they flew away.

It was a beautiful day, with just a mild breeze. They walked over to the boat basin. When the wind picked up, Jane put his cap onto Z.Z.'s blond head and lovingly buttoned up his coat, hoping his knees in his short pants wouldn't get cold.

Out of the corner of her eye, Jane noticed a couple watching her. It took a moment, but she realized it was Mr. and Mrs. Canfield, Prescott's clients. There was no place to hide, and Jane held Z.Z.'s hand tightly, dreading the encounter.

Mr. Canfield waved and guided his wife by the arm closer to Jane. Mrs. Canfield's face under the feathered hat she wore looked pinched in the sunlight, and she wore a Persian lamb coat, even though the day was not that chilly. Underneath, when the front of the coat swung open, Jane saw a New Look dress, long and full in the skirt, with a tight waist, the very height of fashion after the war.

Jane had noticed, on their previous meetings, especially when she sold her the cameo, that there was a reserve about the woman. Her greeting to Jane was cordial, however, and she commented on what a lovely day it was.

Edging closer, Mr. Canfield looked at the little boy, who had squatted down, studying an insect on the sidewalk. "Who have we here?" he asked. "Could this be the reason you can no longer work for Mr. Weaver?"

Jane remained silent. While she did not for a moment believe Mr. Weaver would have mentioned the circumstances, she did not want to discuss her termination. But Z.Z., remembering the manners Auntie

Olivia had taught him, stood up. He turned around slowly, and looked up at the couple, with a big smile on his face.

"Hello," he said. "How do you do?"

Mrs. Canfield's arched eyebrows flew up, and she stared at the child. Mr. Canfield grew pale, and as he mumbled a goodbye to Jane, took his wife by the arm and pulled her away. Z.Z. waved goodbye to them, unaware that anything was wrong, but Jane felt as if she had been slapped. Yet when she looked at the departing couple, she saw Mrs. Canfield's face turned back at her. She looked sad, but not as if she were horrified or even as if she pitied Jane.

The encounter left Jane drained. She bundled Z.Z. up, bought him a bag of chestnuts from a vendor, and took him back to the train. The trip home seemed much less fun than the trip to Manhattan had been.

By the time they got home and Z.Z. was down for a nap, Olivia was back from school. Jane poured out her heart telling her the story, and Olivia held her while she cried. "I can't help wondering if Prescott told Mr. Canfield that I—"

Olivia cut her off. "Of course he didn't. You know he would never do that."

"But I hurt him so badly."

"You must stop dwelling on this. He's married and probably doesn't think about you anymore."

Jane sighed. "You're right." Oddly, though, that did not make her feel better.

She vowed to stay in her own neighborhood from now on. The people around there were used to Z.Z. by now, and Jane did not feel uncomfortable around them and their children. Z.Z. could even play in the sandbox with other children, some of the time, without objections by their mothers.

A week after the incident in Manhattan, when Jane and Z.Z. were in their usual place at the local playground, Jane saw Mrs. Canfield approach. She carried a wrapped package and wore a cloth coat instead of the Persian lamb she'd worn the week before. Without hesitation, she walked up to Z.Z. and greeted him.

"Hello," he said back to her.

"I've brought you a gift, young man," she said, holding it out for him. "I hope you like it." Turning to Jane, she explained, "Your landlady told me where to find you. I hope it's all right."

Z.Z. grinned and looked at Jane for permission to take it. She was so puzzled for a few moments she did not realize he was waiting. When Jane nodded, he opened it happily, pulling a red fire truck from the wrapping.

"Thank you," he said, without prompting. He squatted down and rolled it on the ground, back and forth, inexplicably making little toot-toot noises.

Jane looked at Mrs. Canfield, wondering what to say. But she remained speechless as she saw tears running down the woman's face.

Jane's indecision gave Mrs. Canfield a chance to pull herself together. "I'm sorry," she said, searching her purse and bringing out a handkerchief. "It's just that…you seem so happy together. I thought that wasn't possible."

Jane looked up at her. "Many people think so," she replied, although she was quite surprised. "But Z.Z. is a wonderful companion, aren't you, sweetheart?" She stood up and led him over to the sandbox, where she showed him how to run the fire truck along the edge. When he was settled, she indicated to Mrs. Canfield that they should sit on a nearby bench, somewhat out of earshot of Jane's little boy.

"I could never put him into an institution and let him be treated like an animal," Jane said, sensing concern and sympathy from Mrs. Canfield. She was becoming convinced there was something else, but she could not put her finger on it.

"Even the better ones," she continued, "don't provide the same family life Z.Z. has." She realized she was rambling, just filling the void created by Mrs. Canfield's silence.

The woman had started weeping in earnest. She took the delicate, lace-edged handkerchief and wiped her eyes.

"He's my child, my baby, and I'll keep him with me always," Jane said, as a final defiance of all she had heard for over four years.

The words seemed to hit Mrs. Canfield like blows. She winced, and hunched her shoulders defensively against more of Jane's statements. She caught her breath.

"I'm sorry," Jane said. The woman did not deserve the fallout Jane had heaped upon her.

"No. I understand. I feel the same way you do."

Her statement surprised Jane. She seemed to be so sincere. At the same time, it was puzzling. For a while, they sat side by side on the bench, watching Z.Z. play, with Jane wondering what had brought this woman to Brooklyn.

"I need to talk to you," Mrs. Canfield said after a

few minutes. She seemed about to weep again, and barely managed to get another word out. "Irene."

Jane was not sure she had heard correctly. "Pardon me?"

Mrs. Canfield turned eyes full of misery to Jane. "Irene. My daughter. She is like Z.Z. But I let them take her away from me."

It was as if all the fancy clothing, furs, and jewels the woman usually wore fell away and she stood humbly before Jane.

Embarrassed, Jane stammered, "I-I'm sorry. I didn't know."

"No one knew," said Mrs. Canfield, miserably. "My husband forbade it. We could never talk about our daughter to anyone. And he wouldn't try for another child."

Jane thought about the room she had sat in when she visited Mrs. Canfield to sell her the cameo. It should have been a nursery, but it was a sitting room. Jane had assumed Mrs. Canfield was barren, but this was far worse. She had the capacity to have children and her husband's fears would not allow it. And while Jane knew his opinion was the prevailing one, it was too painful to think about.

"I visit her," said Mrs. Canfield. "I go every Wednesday and dress her up, and comb her pretty hair, and talk with her, and hold her in my lap, even though she is a little big now."

"How old is she?"

"Twelve." Mrs. Canfield smiled. "I tell my husband I am going to a matinee, and off I go to the asylum." She paused, and frowned. "But it is so dismal there, and it smells so. I wish I could bring her home."

New tears welled over.

Jane put her arm around Mrs. Canfield's shoulders. "I'm sure it's hard for Mr. Canfield. But maybe you could try another home for Irene." She told her about the one Lloyd's sister had been in, without telling her how she knew.

"Will you go see it with me?"

Feeling sympathy for all Mrs. Canfield had missed, and an instant bond with the woman as she now knew her, Jane said, "Yes."

Mrs. Canfield stood up, looking suddenly content. "May I say goodbye to Z.Z.?"

"Certainly," Jane said. She went to get her son and his new truck and brought them back to where Mrs. Canfield stood. As they got closer, Z.Z. reached out his pudgy little hand, smiling encouragingly at her to take his so they could all walk together. On the way to the taxi stand, Jane and Mrs. Canfield made plans for their trip to see the possible new place for Irene.

****

Jane told Olivia about her encounter in the park while she finished dressing for work that afternoon. "I know exactly how it feels to be told you must put your child in an institution. Can you imagine how it feels to actually do it?"

Olivia shook her head. "Not everyone is as strong as you are. I wish I had your backbone."

"Nonsense, Olivia. You're doing fine." But that was not as true as Jane would have hoped. Martin's demands of Olivia were annoying and petty, from bringing him his slippers when he got home to cutting his toenails. Jane knew she did not know everything about a wife's duties, but she had never seen her father treat Pearl as Martin treated Olivia.

****

On Saturday, Jane and Mrs. Canfield, who now insisted Jane call her Anne, drove to Brooklyn in Anne's new car, one of the first off the assembly line after the war. Jane was waiting for her, wearing her own New Look dress, but not one from Paris. It was polka-dotted, with a pleated portion from the knees to mid-calf, and the belted waist accentuated Jane's slim figure. She had been able to buy the copy of a Paris designer in Mays for $14.95, only a few weeks earlier, and had been saving it for a special occasion. Her matching hat, pleated and twisted, had a veil with small white balls enmeshed in it, and she pulled the veil down over her face after she put on her gloves. Olivia had convinced her that her outing with Anne would qualify as a reason to dress well no matter where they were going.

They drove to the Garden Acres Insane Asylum. They had a complete tour of the grounds, and Anne thought it was far better and cleaner than the home Irene currently lived in.

The director handed her the papers for Mr. Canfield to sign and asked when he could expect them to be returned.

"I'm not certain when my husband will have time to get to it, but I'm sure it won't take long," Anne said. To Jane, though, she seemed uncertain.

"Do you want more time to think about it?" Jane asked, when they were back in the car.

"What? No. I've changed my mind." Anne smiled. "I'm going to bring her home. You'll help me learn how to care for her, won't you?"

Jane reached out and touched her friend's hand. "Yes."

Anne's conversation turned to her husband. She was most concerned about his reaction to Irene's homecoming. She also spoke of Prescott Weaver and his new wife, Regina. "I once thought he was interested in you," she said. "He was certainly quite fond of you."

Jane was stunned. "Why would you say such a thing?"

"He used to talk about you all the time. Whenever we were at the same function it was always Jane this and Jane that. He didn't seem to care much for the socialites in the room. But I suppose you had someone else at the time and you weren't interested in him."

Jane sat, not blinking in her attempt to avoid spilling the tears that flooded her eyes.

"His marriage isn't a happy one," said Anne, bringing Jane back to the conversation. "He married the daughter of the president of the club." She lowered her voice, even though they were alone in the car. "She was the last of her group to marry, if you get my drift. From what I know of her, she isn't very nice."

Jane had heard nothing about the woman, other than that her father was wealthy. "Since they got married," Anne told her, "her father has become another one on the growing list of Mr. Weaver's rich clients. Prescott is doing so well now, he could probably afford the estate in Long Island that her father gave them as a wedding gift. That is, if his wife didn't visit every couturier in New York on a weekly basis."

Jane tried to skirt the subject. "Has he bought his seat yet?"

"Not so far. I heard his father-in-law offered to

stake him the money, but he refused. I guess he'll do it soon, but I know he won't take that step until he's got everything else covered."

Jane wished she could talk to him again. His enthusiasm was contagious, and she imagined herself sharing his delight at his accomplishments. But she was shut away from that forever.

"They winter in Europe," Anne continued, "when Prescott is able to get away from his office. If he can't, because his brother-in-law—you know, the person who replaced you—isn't up to handling it, his wife goes by herself. I think he seems happier and more relaxed when his wife is away." She paused, but picked up again. "Now that I think about it," Anne said, "he should have fallen in love with you, before you met Z.Z.'s father. You would have made a good couple and probably had a good marriage. Not that I'm wishing Z.Z. hadn't been born, but you know what I mean."

They fell silent for a few minutes. Jane's heart was aching too much to talk, and Anne seemed to have run out of things to say about Mr. Weaver. It was a relief.

Anne sighed. "I wonder…"

"What?"

"What my husband will say." Her fingers squeezing the steering wheel showed white knuckles. Jane could not bring herself to utter any words of encouragement. "I often think that if Irene had been normal, we would have had a houseful of children. How I would have loved that."

Her conversation then turned to her worries about Irene. "How will she feel being out in the world? And how will she learn to love her father? She sees me every week, when I wash her and dress her and read to her and we sing songs, but she has never seen Hugh."

"Never think that children like Irene and Z.Z. can't learn," Jane said. "Whatever I can do to help, I will."

"Thanks," said Anne, as she got out of the car. "Let's go talk to Hugh."

Hugh Canfield jumped up in surprise when Anne told him Jane was there, an angry question on his face.

"Jane has been kind enough to help me with something," Anne said, by way of explanation.

"How are you?" he asked, although his clipped words did not sound warm.

"I'm well," said Jane. She stood straight and proud, not willing to think about this man's opinion of her or of her child.

"Hugh," said Anne. "I have something to tell you."

Turning curious eyes from one woman to another, Hugh Canfield cleared his throat. "It was nice of you to visit, Miss Baldwin, but my wife and I have things to discuss."

"I'd like Jane to stay," said Anne, going to the couch near him. She sat down, patting the cushion next to her for Jane to sit.

"What is it?" said Mr. Canfield.

"Hugh," Anne began, "I have been to see Irene."

"As I recall, we decided that would be too painful for you."

Jane thought she detected an edge behind the statement.

"No, you said it would be. I have seen her many times over the years. It is not difficult for me. What's difficult is saying goodbye to her each time."

"Then you shouldn't go see her."

"You don't understand." Anne reached for Jane's

hand, and, squeezing it, said, "I want to bring her home."

Mr. Canfield's face became purple, and he leapt to his feet. "Here?"

"Yes! This is our home."

"No! Absolutely not."

"Hugh, I am not asking you. I have listened to you for too long on this. Our daughter belongs here with us."

"But she is an idiot. The doctors told you she would never be normal. I won't have her here." He turned to Jane. "Is this your idea? Do you think that just because you brought your little bastard idiot home my wife should bring her mongoloid child into my house? How could you be so selfish?"

Anne stood up. "You may not speak to my friend like that. Jane, please accept my apologies. I'll take you home now."

"No, please," said Jane. "I can find my own way home. You and Mr. Canfield need to talk."

"Good luck," she whispered, when Anne showed her to the door. "Maybe in time he'll accept it."

With tears ready to fall, Anne looked up at Jane. "He's had twelve years."

****

A week later, Jane and Anne went to the institution and picked up Irene. The long ride home was difficult, because Irene had never been in a car before and did not know quite how to sit still while it was moving. As soon as they got off the grounds, she moaned and became ill. They had to stop and clean her up before she was brought up in the elevator to meet her father.

At first he wouldn't look at her. "I told you not to

do this," he told Anne. But his curiosity seemed to get the better of him and he said to Irene, "Come here where I can see you."

Anne led her over to Hugh. He inspected her, scowling the whole while.

A moment later, a small puddle formed on the floor. "She's an animal," he exclaimed. "Just like I told you." He stormed into their bedroom and slammed the door. Minutes afterward, he emerged carrying a small case. "Have the rest of my things sent to the club," he said. "Goodbye."

The child was terrified, both from her expedition into the outside world and by her father's shouting. Anne and Jane changed her clothes and tried to soothe her, but it was very hard on Anne, whose marriage had just shattered.

Anne and Hugh Canfield's sensational divorce was finalized swiftly.

Chapter Sixteen

"Would you like more pot roast?" Jane asked, holding up the platter.

Anne declined but took some for Irene. She carefully cut it into small pieces, allowing Irene to have them only when they were all cut. It had taken months of dinners like these to teach Irene how to eat properly in public. Sometimes she still acted as if she were in the institution, eating her food without consideration for others present.

But she was blossoming from Anne's love. Her light brown hair was clean and well brushed, her teeth had been repaired, and Anne had found stylish clothing to fit the small girl. She sat while her mother cut her food, swinging her patent leather Mary Janes. Her almond-shaped eyes had gone from looking dull the first time Jane saw her, to terrified the day she came home, to content.

Most Sundays, a group gathered for dinner in the home Jane shared with her sister, Martin, and Z.Z. Mr. Dobbin, Mrs. McGill, and Anne and Irene Canfield were always invited, and all of them usually came. It was a warm, happy, extended family.

Irene had become more sociable, and she acted almost as a big sister to Z.Z. The two played together after dinner was over, allowing the adults to enjoy coffee and whatever pie Mrs. McGill had brought.

Although Jane had not gotten around to Martin yet, he grumbled, "Let me have some of that." Jane went over and served him, piling lots of meat and potatoes on his plate. Without thanking her, he hunched over the food and shoveled it into his mouth.

Martin was the only person who did not seem to appreciate the company of the others. As soon as he finished eating, he grunted an excuse to leave so he could buy more cigarettes. When he returned, hours later, his breath smelled of whiskey and his clothing was often rumpled.

Jane knew all was not well with her sister's marriage. Olivia would sit up late most nights, reading in the living room, long after Martin had retired to their bedroom. In the mornings, when Jane was unlucky enough to see him, he seemed restless, with a smoldering anger just beneath the surface. Jane did not confront her sister about what she concluded was a lack of marital intimacy, but she could not ignore it or its ramifications.

After everyone was finished with dinner, the ladies cleared the table and Mr. Dobbin assumed the role of doting grandfather. His business was doing quite well— a line of medical uniforms had been permanently added to the factory, even before Mr. Dobbin's new children's clothing line. It was in great demand, especially since the postwar society was having a baby boom. Everywhere Jane looked, she realized, there was another woman in the family way.

Mrs. McGill, while not quite filling the role of grandmother, became a beloved great aunt. She spent hours knitting sweaters for Irene and Z.Z., and more time in Jane's apartment than in her own, babysitting, cooking, and taking care of most of the people who resided there. She did nothing for Martin, who regarded her as a meddling old woman.

Jane and Anne washed and dried the dishes while Olivia and Mrs. McGill made the coffee and served the pie. The children had theirs first, with large glasses of milk, in the kitchen, so Olivia was kept busy watching them.

"I love Sundays," said Anne. "I feel so warm here, so accepted. Sometimes it can be so lonely for Irene and me, alone at home."

Anne Canfield had changed a great deal in the months since she had reclaimed her daughter. Once a sharp-tongued, impeccably dressed socialite, she spent much less time consumed with herself. Now, she did everything she could for her daughter. The bond she had forged with Jane strengthened, but she spent little time with her old friends. Jane worried about that almost as much as about her sister's relationship with Martin.

"Do you ever go out anymore?" Jane asked.

Anne raised her eyebrows, still elegantly arched. "Why? I am happy with Irene. I don't need those shallow women with their perfect daughters."

"I know, believe me. And maybe it is worse for you because of what else you gave up."

"Do you mean Hugh? Our marriage was close to over before I brought Irene home. Sometimes I wonder if I did it to push him out the door."

"You lost more than Hugh. You haven't done any of the things you used to do. It's as if you divorced yourself from everyone you ever knew and are settling for us."

"How could you say that? I love all of you."

Jane put her hand on Anne's shoulder. "I know. I don't mean you are insincere. You're one of the sweetest people I know. Sometimes I can't believe I thought—"

Anne smiled. "You thought I was a shallow spendthrift socialite."

"I misjudged you. You always did charitable work," Jane argued. "And I know you felt fulfilled by it. But since your divorce you haven't done any of it, or gone to any charity events. You have nothing to be ashamed about, yet you act like you are in hiding."

Anne was quiet for a long time. A tear rolled downward, and she turned to hide it. "I do miss it. I miss the work, and the feeling of worth, and," she smiled, her old self-satisfied smile, "the chance to dress up and put those old biddies to shame."

"I thought so. You have to get back out there."

"Not to the committees I served on before the…"

"No," said Jane. "I wouldn't think so."

As she watched, Jane saw her friend mull over an idea. "I heard there is a need for a chairwoman on the fundraising committee for the new opera house," Anne said.

"You'd be perfect! And before you give me another excuse, we both know you can afford a nurse to watch Irene." Jane did not say another word. She had to give her friend time to think.

Anne put down the dish towel she had been wringing while she tried to decide. A broad smile lit up her face. "I'll do it. Wish me luck."

****

Jane presently found out that her friend was not

one to do things half way. She worked out a schedule so she could be on several committees and not compromise her time with Irene or her friends. The second committee she joined was one raising money for a new institution that would benefit retarded children more severely affected than either Irene or Z.Z. There she met Schuyler Lewis—"Sky" to his many friends. He was a divorced, understanding gentleman whose own child had been born with mongolism. The child had not lived to his first birthday, and the stress of the ordeal had broken up his marriage. "He is a man with a great capacity to love," Anne said, when she told Jane about Schuyler.

"He sounds wonderful. Have you agreed to go out with him?"

Anne blushed. "I feel like a teenager. I'm so nervous."

"If he gets to know you, he will love you," Jane said.

Soon, Schuyler Lewis started coming to the "family dinners" occasionally. He was a wonderful guest.

And three months later, he and Anne were making wedding plans for the following year.

****

"Jane," said Mr. Dobbin. "I can't handle all these orders. What am I going to do?"

"You'll have to put on another shift. You can't turn them away. And I think you'll have to think about expanding. Maybe you could open another factory. I can look into available buildings. Maybe an old army facility."

Mr. Dobbin took off his reading glasses and wiped

them. "I can't believe I was once wondering where my next meal would come from. Now all I wonder about is when I'll have time to eat it."

Jane laughed. "Some people would think this is a good thing."

"I do. But I'm working so many hours, and sometimes I think if you didn't have Z.Z. waiting for you, you would sleep here."

"Don't tempt me."

"Is Martin's drinking worse?"

"I think if it got any worse he wouldn't be able to stand upright. He lost his job, you know."

"I do. He came in here looking for a position as—what did he call it?—'second in command.' That's what it was. I told him the war was over, but if there was a second in command, it was you."

"Why would you say such a thing? I'm just a bookkeeper."

Mr. Dobbin shook his head. "Hardly. And at the rate you're going, you will be second in command of something very big. That new designer you recommended has great ideas about children's clothes. If women keep having babies the way they did this year, we'll be very rich."

"And very tired," said Jane. She was definitely uncomfortable when he spoke of them being rich. The company was his; she was just an employee.

"Maybe you should look for a new factory with a sleeping area," Mr. Dobbin quipped. "When can you start?"

He had never questioned her ability to do what she promised. It felt good that he relied on her, but there was something missing. Well, maybe more than one thing, but the hole in her heart for Prescott Weaver could not be filled. Her chosen career, her goal to trade on the New York Stock Exchange, was not getting any closer, and she was frustrated. Still, she was proud of the job she performed. It had many more satisfying moments than she would have expected, and she was able to be home with Z.Z. during the day.

"On the next school vacation, when Olivia is home, I'll go look. We'll get it up and running as quickly as possible."

"Jane, don't wait. Get that old coot Mrs. McGill to watch Z.Z. We need that factory now."

She studied Mr. Dobbin closely. "Is something wrong?"

He just shook his head. "No. But I'm not getting any younger. I want it established so I can get some time off to see my children and grandchildren, if they'll let me. I love Z.Z. and Irene, but I want to see how my own grandchildren are doing. And I need confidence in my factory's capacity to fill the orders."

Jane could not help wondering if he was worried about something else, although she did not detect any signs of illness, her greatest fear. She would not let this man down. "I'll take care of it."

****

In less than six months, the new factory was up and running. Jane saw to the hiring of most of the people and got an excellent man to manage things when she and Mr. Dobbin were not present. Martin had applied for the position but had no experience whatsoever. Fortunately, he found other employment, although Jane was not quite sure what his exact job title was.

Chapter Seventeen

Olivia woke Jane a little before six one morning in November. It was still dark outside, and Jane blinked, wondering why she had been awakened. Ordinarily, Olivia took care of Z.Z.'s breakfast and did not wake Jane, who worked until well after midnight. The last few weeks she had stayed especially late, converting Mr. Dobbin's factories to the spring production line, and Olivia always took the morning shift with Z.Z. until she was ready to leave for the school where she now taught a second grade class.

"Is something wrong?" Jane asked.

Olivia's eyes were wide and frightened. "It's Z.Z. He has a very high fever. I called the doctor."

Jane jumped out of bed and ran to the alcove where Z.Z. now slept. He was so still, his face so red, and his breathing so labored, that Jane could barely breathe herself. She pulled back the covers, to help cool him off, and opened his pajama top. His chest was covered with a rash. "Oh."

"What? What's wrong with him?"

"I think he has the measles. I remember when you had them."

Olivia frowned but her shoulders relaxed. "I remember hating having them. I got better, though."

The doctor confirmed Jane's diagnosis and mentioned that two other children on the block had measles, too. "The germs must be in the air," he said. But he cautioned them to watch for signs of distress. "With his weak heart, this can be dangerous."

For two days, during which Jane stayed beside Z.Z. constantly, he seemed to be improving and dealing with his discomfort. She moved his cot into her room so she could be close to him at all times, longing to hold him but aware that closeness would cause more distress. With his fever down, though, he seemed more himself, and the sparkle began to return to his eyes.

But at midnight on November 14, 1947, the third day, Z.Z.'s cries woke Jane. "My head," he said, obviously in tremendous pain. Suddenly he lost consciousness and started to convulse.

"Olivia!" Jane shouted, forcing the sound out of her panic-stricken chest. "Come quickly."

Olivia rushed in. "My God, what's wrong with him?"

"Get me some wet towels. He's burning up again."

"Why is he bouncing around like that?"

"I can't explain. Get me the towels!"

Olivia brought them in, and Jane wrapped them around Z.Z. "Call the doctor," she pleaded.

A few minutes later, Mrs. McGill rushed in. "Olivia called me," she explained, taking matters into her own hands. "Put him in the tub. We've got to get his fever down."

"I've already run the water into it," said Olivia. "Doctor Mann said the same thing." She helped Jane carry the boy into the bathroom. "Doctor Mann will be right here," she whispered into Z.Z.'s ear. "You're going to be fine."

Z.Z. showed no sign of having heard his aunt. His

convulsions had stopped, but he lay listless in the tub, after the initial shock of the water. Jane's hands, which supported him, were so cold she wanted to pluck him out right away, but Mrs. McGill said no, not until the fever came down. When it finally did, Jane wrapped him in a dry towel and carried him back to bed, smoothing the covers around his still form.

Soon after, the doctor arrived. He examined Z.Z., spending a lot of time listening to the little boy's heart, not smiling once. Finally he straightened up and put his stethoscope away. "Acute encephalomyelitis," he said. "And his heart has weakened."

Only Mrs. McGill could find her tongue. "Will he get better?"

Z.Z.'s breath came in labored gasps. Jane bit her lip, and Olivia went pale, waiting for the doctor's answer. But in a moment, there was no need for one. Z.Z.'s body arched up again, and his face turned blue. As Jane watched in horror, her son's life seeped out of him.

"No!" she cried, pulling his blanket back to cradle him in her arms. She rocked back and forth, willing him to breathe. "Mama is here," she whispered. "Open your eyes. Please. Don't leave me."

While Z.Z.'s small body became limp on her lap, Jane stroked his blond hair, tenderly smoothing it down, and hummed a lullaby to her little boy.

After a few minutes, with Olivia sobbing on Mrs. McGill's shoulder, Dr. Mann gently pulled Z.Z. away from Jane and placed him back on his cot, tucking in his blanket as if he were asleep.

"He can't be gone," Jane murmured, feeling as if part of her were being ripped away, but knowing in her heart it was true. "I can't believe I've lost him."

The doctor took Jane to the living room, where Mrs. McGill and Olivia sat with her. He made a phone call, whispering, while Jane's tortured mind struggled to make sense of what had happened. She refused to take a sedative, knowing nothing could ever make her sleep peacefully again.

****

At the graveside funeral, Jane, Olivia, Mr. Dobbin, Mrs. McGill, and Anne Canfield with her fiancé and Irene were the only people in attendance. Martin said he had to work and could not attend.

It was a cold, drizzly day, and a shaft of ice formed in Jane's heart that she knew would never thaw. She looked around at the other mourners, knowing they truly loved her child.

Anne gasped as she turned to leave. "What is it?" Jane asked. "Are you afraid for Irene?"

"No," Anne said, shaking her head. "It's nothing." But her gaze turned again to the distance, and Jane's followed. For just a second, she thought a man she saw looked like Prescott Weaver. But it seemed so unlikely she put the thought out of her mind.

****

Prescott wanted more than anything to go over to Jane at the funeral. She stood stoically, staring into the deep hole that had been dug for the little pine coffin, until the coffin was lowered in. Then she shook so, Prescott feared she would fall. He had to will his feet to stay in place, so he would not run to her side.

Her friend Mr. Dobbin held her steady by the elbow on one side, while her sister draped herself across Jane, sobbing loudly enough to hear all the way across the cemetery where Prescott stood.

Jane turned to Olivia, pulling her away from the edge of the grave. Olivia's husband was nowhere in sight. Where was he when his wife needed him?

Prescott knew who all the people gathered by the grave were from his conversation that morning with Anne. She had urged him to greet Jane and express his sorrow, but he had told her point blank he would not intrude. Even her intimations that he was being cowardly did not change his mind. This was simply not the time.

From his vantage point, he had a clear view of Anne, Schuyler, and Irene. They stood together, facing their anguish. Despite their own troubles and sorrows, they were there for their friends, united and strong. All Prescott's good health, and that of his wife, could not compare to the love they shared.

The sadness he felt for Jane included some for himself, Prescott realized. That was all the more reason for him to stay away.

****

Jane could not openly dwell on her grief. But every evening, when she went to bed, she went over to Z.Z.'s cot and cried into his pillow until she fell asleep. Mrs. McGill urged her to take the cot away and give away Z.Z.'s clothes, but Jane would not even allow her to move the books that had been on the little boy's chair so he could sit at the table.

Yet she could never allow her sister to see her suffering, because Olivia had gone into such a deep depression herself, exacerbated by her husband's good cheer following Z.Z.'s death. Martin seemed to have increased his volume in the way he talked and walked and even the way he turned the pages of the newspaper.

"You should be more quiet, Martin," Olivia said, on one of her rare visits to the living room. "You are disturbing us."

"This is my home, just as much as it is Jane's," he said, excluding his wife from any consideration. "And I don't have to worry about Z.Z. sleeping anymore."

Glancing at Jane, who pretended not to see, Olivia started to weep. But that was what she did most of the time anyway.

She had taken to her bed as she had when Horace died, and did not emerge for days, calling in sick to her school each morning but promising to return the next day. Martin spent some time by her side but got weary of playing nursemaid to his wife and told her she had better get over it. One night, after he returned from the bar at the end of the street, he stormed into their bedroom, shouting.

Jane followed him in, fearful for her sister. She tried to quiet him, putting her hand on his arm and reminding him how delicate Olivia was. He pushed Jane aside, nearly knocking her to the floor.

"She's my wife," he roared, drunkenly. "Stay out of it. This is none of your business."

Jane tried again to reason with Martin, but Olivia put up her hand. "Let him be," she said. "He won't hurt me."

But he did. Jane could hear through the bedroom wall, Olivia pleading and Martin insisting. "I've waited long enough," he said, and muffled sounds followed. Jane covered her head with her pillow and cried herself to sleep.

For a while afterward, it seemed Olivia was getting

up the courage to split up with Martin. She went back to work and started each day with a purpose, happily anticipating the students in her class. Jane promised her she would do whatever it took, pay whatever lawyers, to get rid of that man. Olivia seemed pleased but then suddenly stopped her efforts, leaving Jane confused.

By spring, she understood. Olivia had started to wear their father's old sweater, and Jane realized her sister was pregnant. She broached the subject one afternoon.

"How far along are you?"

Olivia sighed. "The baby is due in September."

Although Jane did not believe the baby would have a good father in Martin, she said, "That's wonderful. I'm so happy for you."

Olivia brightened. "Are you really? I've been so afraid to tell you, because of how you feel about Martin."

Jane's eyes filled with remorseful tears. "Oh, I'm so sorry," she said, hugging her sister close. "I don't mean to be so judgmental about him. I just can't stand seeing you hurt."

"I know you love me," said Olivia, with tears in her own eyes. "And he doesn't really hurt me. A man has a right to…" Her brows furrowed for a moment. "But anyway, now with the baby coming, he's been very nice to me."

Jane had not really seen a change in Martin, but she didn't mention it. "He must be so excited."

"Oh, he is. He took me all the way to the Bronx to see his mother and tell her the news."

"Will you be able to finish this school year?" Jane asked.

"I'm hoping to. That's why I got the sweater out. If I'm lucky, no one will notice."

She was not lucky. Two weeks later, the school district asked her to leave because of her pregnancy. The loss of her job proved devastating. The children in her class, who had cheered her up and given her a reason to get up in the morning after Z.Z.'s death, were no longer a part of her day. She fell back into depression, only somewhat lessened by the prospect of her own child.

****

After several months of mourning Z.Z., Jane had decided that life had to go on, and she resumed the practice of Sunday dinners. Mrs. McGill pitched in, filling in for Olivia, who had progressed from morning sickness to all-day sickness. She was unable to keep most food down and was painfully pale and thin, even thinner by far than Jane. With the likelihood of her becoming sick on the street, she was unwilling to set foot outside.

In the evenings, when Martin came home grumbling about his stupid boss, he paid little attention to Olivia's discomfort. He and Jane barely spoke, and the tension in the apartment was too high to bear. Jane had thought about moving out, living in a boarding house if she could not find an apartment, since they were still scarce, but Olivia would not hear of it. "I would be lost without you," she said. "It's lonely enough when you're at work."

Jane had switched to working days after Z.Z.'s death. She took on more and more responsibility, and Mr. Dobbin's business expanded further. She found herself intentionally working late, though, to avoid the scene at home, yet felt guilty leaving her sister alone with that man.

Martin increasingly acted as if Jane were an outsider. Even though the lease on the apartment was in her name, he pretended he was the king of the manor. He paid none of the expenses, did none of the work, even as far as taking out the garbage, but he lorded his presence over the sisters like an emperor.

Mrs. McGill had come in one day, a month after Z.Z. passed away, fully determined to clear things out. She took all of his clothes and bundled them up for charity, pulled his cot into the hall for one of the male neighbors to bring to storage, and returned the books on Z.Z.'s chair to the shelf near the sofa. "We will not forget him," she promised. "But we must go on."

Yet when she set the Sunday dinner table one day, Jane caught Mrs. McGill looking over at that chair. The older woman had been quite affected by Jane's son's death, but she had the uncanny knack of remembering sweet little things about him that helped both Jane and Olivia.

Today she said, "Remember when he mimicked Mr. Dobbin? I thought I was going to burst, laughing so hard."

Jane smiled. It had been so much fun, and Mr. Dobbin had enjoyed it thoroughly. But when Z.Z. mimicked Martin, he had picked up Z.Z. and spanked his bottom before Jane or Olivia could stop him. While it was true Z.Z.'s impersonation of Martin was unflattering, it had been accurate. Another pang of grief caused Jane to freeze momentarily, trying to catch her breath.

Pushing the sad memories out of her mind, Jane

brought the roast beef to the table and announced that dinner was ready. She took a serving for Olivia, and brought it into her bedroom. Mr. Dobbin and Mrs. McGill sent their love along with it. Martin just plowed into his food.

****

Throughout the summer, Olivia and Jane made little sweaters and blankets for the baby and gathered necessities, including purchasing a new crib. Martin had refused to let his child sleep in Z.Z.'s crib, or use any of the things Z.Z. had used. Jane, who had stored it all after Z.Z. grew out of it, had finally allowed Mrs. McGill to give everything away.

Both Mr. Dobbin and Mrs. McGill acted like expectant grandparents. At the weekly dinners, Anne's new husband, Schuyler, spent time with Olivia, who could barely stand, talking about their common interest in art. Sometimes it seemed to Jane he was trying to keep her busy while the others, who could move around a lot more comfortably, did all the work. Olivia's own husband never even bothered to see if she needed a glass of water on those hot summer days.

At the last Sunday dinner in August, Martin spoke to Schuyler, who was a partner in a real estate development company. "I'm trying to put together a partnership," he said, moving closer to the man. "We'll get some venture capital and draft a debenture."

Jane knew why Martin always hovered around Schuyler. The man was very wealthy, but he was down to earth, avoiding the country club life in favor of charitable ventures. Martin had, on several occasions, made big claims to him, as well as appeals, to help him realize his fantastic dreams.

Schuyler was polite about it. "What kind of product will you be selling?"

"Oh, it isn't a product. My money man will discount the capitalization and we'll be making millions. Are you in?"

Jane wondered how Schuyler kept a straight face. It was so obvious Martin had no idea what he was talking about.

"Who are your partners?" Schuyler asked.

"The cream of Wall Street," said Martin. "Although I couldn't get in to speak to Prescott Weaver, our Janie's old flame. Maybe he knows I married Olivia and is holding it against me. Yeah, that's probably it. Otherwise why wouldn't he see me?" He stared at Jane. "It's all your fault. Yours and your idiot spawn."

Jane did not respond. She picked up her plate and brought it to the kitchen. Olivia rose with difficulty and followed her in.

"I'm so sorry, Jane. I never would have told him if I'd thought he would bring it up."

"He didn't just bring it up, he threw it in my face. Why did you tell him?"

"I didn't think it was right not to answer his questions."

"Did you tell him about Lloyd, too?"

Olivia's brown eyes turned to the floor. "I didn't tell him his name."

"Thank goodness. Please don't ever tell him anything personal about me again. He's your husband, so he can know your secrets. But not mine."

"Jane, please." Olivia put her hand on Jane's arm to stop her from leaving the kitchen. When Jane turned, she could see tears in her sister's eyes. "I'm so sorry."

"You should get off your feet," Jane said, softening her voice as she let the anger go. "I'm not angry with you, just Martin. He knew that would hurt me, and he didn't care."

They went back into the dining room. Martin was still talking. "You wouldn't recognize my financier's name," he said, "but he's got the Midas touch. And his partners are all top-notch men."

"I'll look into it," said Schuyler. "Show me the papers."

"Hey, Dobbin," Martin said, turning on the older man, "maybe if Jane loosens some of your company's purse strings, you would like to get in on this deal."

Mr. Dobbin put down his coffee cup. "No, thank you."

Martin tossed his head. "Your loss. But Sky, here, and I are gonna be in like Flynn. I'll have everything I've always wanted and get Olivia and my new baby boy out of this dump. Any day now," he gloated, "he'll be born, and I'll have a son to carry on my name." He turned back to Schuyler. "Too bad you didn't have one."

Jane had to avert her eyes from Anne's shocked face. Schuyler put his arm protectively around her shoulders.

"You guys are too sensitive," Martin said, disgusted. He got up and went to the door. "I gotta get some air."

****

On September 2, 1948, as the first dried leaves skittered up the alleyways and the country basked in the glow of an anticipated landslide for presidential candidate Governor Dewey, Olivia went into labor. No one knew where Martin was, even though it was past dinnertime.

Jane had no time to worry about his whereabouts. She called for a cab and bundled Olivia into it. The taxi driver laughed when he saw Olivia. "You must be the tenth one this week," he said. "I sure hope they make enough diapers."

When they turned the corner, Olivia was having another contraction, but she managed to cry out, "There he is." Jane just had time to see Martin staggering out of a bar. She hoped he was headed home and would get her note directing him to the hospital.

She was sitting in the smoky waiting room with Mr. Dobbin when Martin staggered in. "What are you doing here?" he demanded, pointing his finger at the older man. "She's my wife."

Mr. Dobbin smiled. "And like a daughter to me. I'm waiting to hear she is well."

"She had better not give birth to a monster like her sister did," said Martin. "Or she won't be." He turned to look defiantly at Jane. "Thank God that bastard won't be around to teach my son how to be a moron."

"Please, Jane," whispered Mr. Dobbin. "My arthritis." She realized she was squeezing his poor hand and withdrew her own.

"I'm sorry. It's just—"

"There is no need to explain, dear. I understand. Once again, you have my sympathy. How you can put up with that lout is beyond me."

Jane wiped her eyes. "For Olivia."

Martin sat across the room from them, away from everyone else. All around, men sat nervously awaiting their children's births, talking with their own family members and each other. One by one, nurses came in to reassure them that their wives were all right, and tell them their sons or daughters had entered the world. Back slaps and congratulations rang out, everyone smiled, cigars were lit, and those still waiting turned their attentions back to the door.

Martin just sat there in a drunken stupor, pretending to read a copy of *Life* magazine.

Hours later, Dr. Mann came to tell them about Olivia. Jane jumped to her feet. "How is she?"

"It was a long, difficult labor. Where is Martin?"

Jane pointed to the corner of the room. Martin seemed not to have noticed his wife's doctor standing there. Mr. Dobbin went over to the young father and touched him on the shoulder.

"What do you want?" said Martin. But his gaze followed Mr. Dobbin's and came around to the doctor. "Oh, Doctor? How's my son?"

Dr. Mann smiled. "Your child is a girl, healthy and beautiful."

"And my sister?" asked Jane.

"It was difficult. She needs to rest. Only her husband should see her. The rest of you can wait until tomorrow."

Jane turned to Martin and saw him heading for the door. "Give Olivia my love," she said.

Martin turned and glared at her. "Give it to her yourself. I'm leaving."

"Where are you going? Don't you want to see Olivia and the baby?"

"Why would I?" He pushed open the door, leaving it swinging behind him.

"I think it would be all right if you go see her," the doctor told Jane.

"Whatever will I say about Martin?"

"Tell her he went to buy cigars."

****

Martin did not visit Olivia during the nearly two weeks she spent in the hospital. He would have had to go to Cuba to buy those cigars, Jane thought, in order to explain being gone so long. But Olivia did not seem to mind. She was calmer and smiled readily, especially when Ellen was brought to her side. The little girl was beautiful, with perfectly formed eyes, fingers and toes, and hair as dark as her mother's.

"I'm sorry you had to give away Z.Z.'s crib," said Olivia. "Ellen would have loved it."

"Mrs. McGill's niece is using it," Jane said. "And you said you loved the new set I bought for Ellen."

"Oh, I do. But Martin should have bought it. She's his daughter."

"Well, he would have liked to, I know. He's just short on cash right now." Jane could not believe she was defending that poor excuse of a man, but she felt she had to, for Olivia's sake.

"He's been working so hard, so he can take a little time off when you get home," Jane said, hoping he would at least show up. She had not laid eyes on him since the birth, although she had heard him in his room, late at night, and found used towels on the floor of the bathroom. She'd also seen Martin's dirty dishes left on the table, and noticed that most of the food she bought was disappearing.

Since Olivia was coming home tomorrow, Jane planned to get up early, clean the bedroom she and

Martin shared, and air it out. Not only was the man not interested in his wife or daughter, he was a pig.

****

"Come see your new home, Ellen," said Mrs. McGill, as she opened the door. She stood aside and let Olivia, holding the baby, and Jane, holding the suitcase, step inside.

Jane knew what Olivia saw. It was a huge bouquet of late summer flowers, welcoming Olivia and her baby home, with a card signed by Martin.

"Ooh, how sweet," said Olivia. She looked around, as if expecting to see her husband. Jane had given her another excuse for why he was not there when she was released from the hospital. She couldn't bear for Olivia's happiness to be spoiled by the truth about the poor excuse for a man that was her husband. "Where are you, Martin?" she called out.

"With any luck, Topeka," Mrs. McGill whispered.

He was not in Topeka, as it turned out. Just before dinner time, Martin strolled into the apartment as he always had, and sat down in his favorite chair, the wing-backed chair that had belonged to Olivia and Jane's father, looking around expectantly for his dinner. He seemed surprised when Olivia came out of the bedroom.

"You're home," he said, rising. He didn't even bother to apologize for not visiting her in the hospital.

Olivia smiled. "Come see Ellen. She's so beautiful." She took him by the hand and led him into their bedroom. After a few minutes, Jane heard him cooing at the baby.

She realized she had been holding her breath when it rushed out of her in relief. Maybe it would work out after all.

When Martin called his mother to tell her she had a grandchild, Jane knew they had turned a corner. Now her sister could be happy.

Chapter Eighteen

Ellen became the center of the household overnight. Auntie Jane doted on her, Olivia beamed, and Martin cut short or skipped his trips to the bar almost every night. He bragged to the neighbors several times about his daughter but always told them he would have a son the next time. Jane hoped he would never say that around Ellen once she was old enough to understand.

Olivia still looked worn out, even four weeks after Ellen was born.

"Go to bed," Jane told her sister. "I'll take care of Ellen's next feeding." She had already boiled the nipples and caps and bottles for the baby's formula.

"Thanks," said Olivia.

She still did not look rested in the morning, and Jane worried that Martin had demanded sex, even though the doctor had forbidden it. But, judging by Martin's grumpiness, that was not the case. Jane hurried to dress for work, although she wished she could stay home and take care of the baby so Olivia could rest more.

Even though the baby slept for long stretches at night, and Olivia did little housework, she still looked tired and nervous a week later. She had lost all the weight she had gained while pregnant, and more. She stopped smiling, even at Ellen, and then she would cry, for hours, over nothing.

For once Martin noticed something about his wife. "What's eating her?" he asked one day. "Is she still bawling over Z.Z.? Or is it Horace?" He knew he was second best to Horace, although when he married Olivia he had not seemed to care. But now that she paid no attention to him, Martin brought up that old jealousy.

"I'm worried about her," Jane told Dr. Mann, when he visited several weeks later. "But I suppose this will pass. I had a hard time, too, after Z.Z. was born."

The doctor seemed to take the problem more seriously. "You had good reason," he said. "Olivia doesn't. I want you to keep a close eye on her. Write things down, so you'll remember them."

"Doctor, you're scaring me. Is this serious?"

"It can be. We'll see."

****

Jane picked up the morning newspaper the day after the presidential election. The headlines proclaimed that Dewey beat Truman. Jane was disappointed. She had voted for Truman.

She soon found out the newspapers and magazines had printed their headlines ahead of time, announcing that defeat, but the people of the United States had different ideas. By the time the matter was straightened out and the announcement made that Truman had won, however, Jane's attention was diverted from the subject of the presidency. It had become apparent that Olivia was in deep trouble.

Jane found her the next morning at four o'clock, pacing around the apartment, weeping. She was so agitated Jane could not calm her enough to get her to go back to bed. She kept moaning about not being a good mother, saying she was not taking care of Ellen correctly. Jane tried to reassure Olivia, but it was as though she wasn't heard at all. She sat on the couch in the dark living room with her sister, holding and rocking her, just as she had when Olivia was small.

Jane could remember perching on the edge of her stepmother Vanessa's big bed. Mother's long dark hair was on the fluffed-up white pillows, and she smiled down at Olivia in her arms. She shifted the baby over and with her free hand took Jane's little hand in her own. Jane loved her and her baby sister so much then that she felt as if her chest would burst.

Sometimes, when Olivia was asleep and the baby nurse was watching over her, Mother would take Jane outside as she did before Olivia came. Or she would read stories to her. She smiled a lot and combed Jane's hair, telling her how much fun they would have when Olivia got bigger.

In retrospect, Jane realized Vanessa had been relaxed and rested. Maybe Jane needed to hire a baby nurse to help take care of Ellen, so Olivia could stop worrying so much. She would only need to come during the day, when both Jane and Martin were at work. But Martin refused to hear of it and said terrible things about Olivia being lazy.

"I had hoped this would have passed by now," Dr. Mann told Jane a few weeks later, as he emerged from Olivia's room after examining her. "It seemed enough time had gone by for Olivia to get back to her old self."

Jane, who was exhausted herself from sitting up all night with Olivia, fought back tears. "It's serious, isn't it?"

"You should sit down," said Dr. Mann. "I want to tell you something. Where is Martin? He should hear this too."

"Down at the corner. He's been out drinking every night. He says there is no one to talk to here."

Dr. Mann grimaced. "I don't know how much you remember about Olivia's mother, Vanessa," he began.

Jane looked at the doctor she had known all her life. When she was small he had been the doctor who delivered her and Olivia, and had taken care of both them and their parents where they lived in Larchmont, New York. But when Jane was about eight, Dr. Mann had moved to Brooklyn. She had not understood why at the time, but she knew it was something to do with prejudice against the Jewish man. Jane's father had been so incensed about the way the town treated the doctor that he had put his own home up for sale, and he and Pearl and Jane and Olivia had moved to Central Park West until the crash of the stock market. They had met up with their old doctor again when their circumstances brought them to Brooklyn. Now he was trying to explain something long in the past, and Jane knew it could only be bad news.

"What are you saying?"

He spoke softly, but his intensity frightened Jane. "She had a mental problem after Olivia was born. She was fine for a while, but then she grew despondent, and she never slept. She would cry for hours. Your father was very patient with her, and he tried everything—nights on the town, the theater, dancing—but she never snapped out of her despair. She got sicker and sicker, and one day she cut—" He broke off. "They called me, but I couldn't save her."

"That isn't going to happen to my sister, is it?" she whispered, barely able to get the words out.

Dr. Mann nodded. "I hope not. That's why I'm being so careful with her. But if she doesn't snap out of this soon, it may become permanent."

Jane could not imagine that. And she intended to do everything possible to prevent it.

"How do you feel?" Jane asked, when she went into her sister's room.

"I'm so scared." Olivia picked at the coverlet. Twitching had become second nature to her. "It's as if I dread every day. The hair on my body hurts, as if it's standing on end. I can't sleep, even though I feel that if I don't get some rest I will die."

"The doctor prescribed some sleeping powders for you," said Jane. "I'm going to mix it with some milk so you can get some sleep."

"I don't want to be drugged. What if Ellen needs me?"

"I'll take care of her."

"I'm so lucky you're here," said Olivia. "I know I can't take care of Ellen."

"Of course you can. You were wonderful with Z.Z."

"But he died."

"That wasn't your fault," Jane said, but it was as if Olivia didn't hear her.

"Everyone I know dies, or leaves me. My mother, Pearl, Father, little Z.Z." She burst into tears. "And Horace." She sobbed so loudly Ellen became restless.

When she had finally calmed them both down, Jane went to the kitchen, prepared the sleeping powder and milk and a sandwich, and brought them to her sister on a tray.

But Olivia pushed the sandwich away. "I can't eat. Nothing tastes good."

"Don't worry about it," Jane said, pulling the covers up again, like she had done with Z.Z. "Get some rest now."

Chapter Nineteen

The next morning was much better. After a good night's sleep, Olivia was almost back to her cheerful self.

"I feel wonderful this morning," she said, stretching her neck and turning her head from side to side. "As if I'd slept for a week."

Jane couldn't help noticing the ring of grime on Olivia's neck, and the stale smell of her body. She'd neglected herself lately, not washing nearly as often as she always had. It hurt to see her usually fastidious sister let herself go.

"I'm going to run you a nice hot bath," Jane said. "You can relax for as long as you like."

Olivia smiled. "That sounds good."

While her sister was in the bath, Jane opened the windows in the apartment to air it. It was such a lovely day, more like a day in September than early December, and the breeze and Olivia's lightheartedness lifted Jane's mood.

"Let's go for a walk," she said when Olivia was dressed. "Doctor Mann said that Ellen can go out now, if there is a warm day. We'll take her to the park."

"But you have to go to work," Olivia said. "Mr. Dobbin will miss you."

"It'll be fine," Jane assured her. "He won't be in this morning anyway." He had been very mysterious about where he was going, leaving Jane to wonder what he was up to. She had seen his crow's feet deepen with pleasure, but he could not be persuaded to tell her why.

She gathered up some of the baby's diapers, and a blanket to wrap her in. Olivia went into her bedroom and returned with Ellen dressed in a beautiful pink sweater and hat set that Mrs. McGill had knit for her. They went down to the carriage room in the basement, where they had stored the small buggy that Mr. Dobbin had given as a baby gift.

"I'm so excited about finally using it," said Olivia. Her eyes burned bright. "This is going to be such fun."

They wheeled the baby down the alley and onto the sidewalk. As soon as they reached the street, women stopped them every few feet for a look at the baby.

"Oh," exclaimed one, "isn't she precious? What a beautiful face!"

Another woman came over to peer into the carriage. She looked critically at Olivia, then at the baby. "She is going to look just like you. Such a sweetheart."

It took Jane and Olivia twenty minutes to get two blocks. But with each comment, Jane could see Olivia getting stronger. She herself was bursting with pride that her little niece could garner so much attention. It also brought a tinge of pain, after the averted gazes with Z.Z. Jane pushed that aside and concentrated on the present.

They walked through the park, watching other mothers with tiny children. They, too, came to check the contents of the carriage. The sun shone, the sky was blue, and Ellen slept peacefully, while Jane told Olivia all about the latest plans for Mr. Dobbin's business.

"You would barely recognize the place," Jane said. "It has changed so much from when you worked there."

"Someday I'd like to go see for myself," Olivia told her. "And maybe we'll bring Ellen and show her around."

"The girls will love it." Jane looked at her watch and saw it was nearly eleven. "I've got to go to work soon. Let's walk back."

Olivia appeared to be happy but tired when they got home. "This was fun. I hope the weather stays clear. Maybe we can do it again."

"I'd love to." She watched as Olivia filled a bottle for the baby. Her whole demeanor was so much better than it had been.

As Jane let herself out of the apartment, she realized she was not looking forward to going to her accounting job. It was so mundane, even though the numbers were always good, since Mr. Dobbin's business was booming. He had long ago repaid his original backers double their initial investments. But Jane had no creative part in it, beyond anticipating where the next market would emerge. The actual design of the clothes did not interest her, and she did not arrange financing, or set up lines of credit, Mr. Dobbin did. Jane just kept the books.

Whenever he spoke of reinvesting the capital, meaning using it for more expansion, all she could think of was the stock market. While it was true the business was ready for more expansion, and an overhaul of the equipment, there was not enough capital yet. It would have to wait.

Today, though, when she arrived at work, and after the usual information exchange on Olivia's condition and Ellen's development, Mr. Dobbin told Jane he had made a decision that would delight her.

"What is it?"

"Miss Baldwin," he said formally, "would you please help my lawyers and me to take this company public?"

Responding in kind, Jane said, "Mr. Dobbin, I would be delighted."

She threw herself into meetings with lawyers, auditors, and accountants, everyone working together to prepare Mr. Dobbin's business for the sale of shares of stock. Her long ago dream of being a stockbroker on her own, playing with the movers and shakers and showing them she meant business, resurfaced with a vengeance.

Jane longed to tell Olivia about the progress she was making toward the day when the company would be publicly traded. When she came home one day, full of news of the latest round of meetings, she found Olivia staring at the evening paper.

"Has something happened?" Jane asked.

"What?"

"Olivia, is there something in the newspaper that upset you? You're as white as the tablecloth." When she did not answer, Jane grabbed her by the shoulder. "Is Ellen all right?"

"Ellen?"

Jane did not explain, she just went into Olivia and Martin's room and looked at Ellen lying on her back in her crib. She was giggling and playing with her toes.

"Oh, you little sweetheart," said Jane, picking her up. "I think you need a diaper change."

When the baby was all powdered and changed,

Jane brought her into the kitchen. "She seems hungry," she told Olivia. "When did she have her last bottle?"

Olivia stood up. "I'll get her one." She lit the gas on the stove with a kitchen match and warmed a bottle in a saucepan of water. When it was done, she sprinkled a few drops on her wrist and took Ellen from Jane.

At first, Jane marveled at how second nature feeding the baby had become. But then she realized that while Olivia went through the motions with Ellen, she never smiled at her, or at all. Jane became alarmed. Her sister was going back inside herself.

With her busy schedule, Jane sought out the assistance of Mrs. McGill. The landlady kept her eye on Olivia, going up the stairs with her polishing cloth on the banister as if it were the old brass railing. She made excuses, such as needing to check if there was enough milk, or bread, to gain access to the apartment.

Every evening, when Jane came home, Mrs. McGill filled her in on the day's events. "He hasn't been in yet," she said most times, referring to Martin. Jane's arrival home became later and later, because of the meetings she had to attend, and she still got there before her brother-in-law. "She's pretty good today," Mrs. McGill said, most of the time. Jane felt relieved, since she found herself worrying about Olivia so much when she was away at work. But sometimes Mrs. McGill said, "She's not so good today," which filled Jane with guilt over leaving her sister.

It was late in February of 1949 when the company finally made it to the New York Stock Exchange. There was to be a Champagne reception at Fraunces Tavern.

Olivia insisted on helping Jane dress for the event, reminding her of the date with Lloyd Hammer for which she'd primped and preened. This would be so different, Jane and Olivia agreed, because now she was truly being herself. The royal blue flannel suit dress Jane had purchased for business meetings, a copy of a Paris New Look design, fit her slim figure perfectly, tight at the waist and flaring to the mid-calf hemline. She wore a new hat with it, and small gold earrings.

"Promise me you will tell me everything," Olivia said, looking flushed with happiness for her sister. Her joy added to Jane's, and it seemed that everything from now on would go well.

"I promise."

It was an easy promise to keep. From the wigged doorman at the restaurant, wearing the uniform of a colonial coachman, to the toasts, the evening was magical.

Jane recognized several people from her days on Wall Street, among them Prescott Weaver. He looked more handsome than ever, and he raised his glass in a silent toast. She thought about approaching him to politely say hello, and took a few steps in his direction, but was distracted when someone spoke to her. When she turned back, he was gone. A flush washed over her at the thought that she might have spoken to him.

"Are you feeling overheated?" asked Mr. Smith, one of the lawyers standing nearby.

"No. Although it is a bit warm in here, isn't it?"

"Perhaps," he admitted. "You've done a wonderful job. Mr. Dobbin is lucky to have you with him."

"He's a good man to work for," Jane said. "I'm lucky, too. He was kind enough to tell me to take a vacation. And I am going to do just that."

****

Prescott laughed at the financier's joke. He enjoyed coming to the cocktail parties that were becoming prevalent as businesses expanded and entered the market. This was his third one that week, not counting the appearance he had made at the party for Dobbin's Apparel.

Jane had looked wonderful that evening, flush with her triumph. Prescott admired the way she handled herself, and her accomplishment had been impressive. He had heard several people speak of her with admiration, as if she were a man. If only he could express his own to her.

"Did you see what our Jane did last week?" asked a voice.

Prescott turned and found Anne Canfield Lewis at his elbow, smiling. She had looked so happy ever since her marriage to Sky, and Prescott was reminded once again of what he had missed. "Yes," he said. "She did a wonderful job. I'm not at all surprised."

"I have to admit that I was," said Anne, a scowl forming between her brows. "She had a lot on her mind, what with Olivia's troubles."

"What's wrong with Olivia?"

"She's had a hard time since the baby came. Jane has been very worried."

Prescott felt himself pushed forward as his wife, who had been across the room talking to her old friend and fellow horticulturist Ralph Taggart, came up behind him. Reggie had a way of staking out her property, as if asserting her ownership of him. "Is Prescott boring you with his talk of the ups and downs of the market?" she asked Anne.

Anne smiled at her. "Not at all. I've always found

217

Prescott to be a most interesting conversationalist. But I must not monopolize him. Excuse me." She nodded and turned to walk away.

Reggie frowned at Prescott. "I don't know why she always seeks you out every time you are in the same room. Her husband is as rich as Croesus, yet she never uses you as her stockbroker."

"I don't mind."

"Well, you should. She took so much of Hugh's money he had to cut back on the business he was giving you."

"I think you misunderstood that situation." Prescott did not elaborate. It had been Jane, his former secretary, who caused the whole divorce, at least in Hugh Canfield's mind. The punishment had not been unexpected. It was not so bad, since Prescott thought Hugh had been completely wrong. In the years since he first saw Jane's child, he had made it his business to learn as much as he could about the condition. He had concluded that Hugh was a coward, just as he himself had been in letting Jane's circumstance come between them. He knew he had not left Jane over the child's condition but over the child's existence, but that did not excuse him.

"Prescott," Reggie chided. "Don't look so sad. This is a party, after all." She waved her Champagne glass around and raised her eyebrows at the waiter.

"Actually, it's time to go home. Let me just say goodbye to our hosts." He quickly did that and steered his inebriated wife to the coat room.

Once they were in the lobby, they had to stop again for a young man who came over to thank Prescott for recommending him to another broker as a clerk.

"He was a bright young man but needed a few connections," Prescott explained after the young man walked away.

Reggie sniffed. "Like you were."

"It seems like a long time ago."

"But you didn't give him a place in your firm." Her statement was more like a warning.

"You know I'm saving as much as I can for my seat." Prescott could not get over her lack of trust in him.

"I'm not wearing this dress for a second time because I want to, you know." She frowned, looking embarrassed as Ralph Taggart and his wife Martha, who was wearing the latest evening gown with the pouf Reggie had talked about all week, walked past them to the cloak check room. "I can't bear it."

"Yes, I know." Prescott was fully aware of Reggie's sense of deprivation. He also knew she would never miss a chance to rub it in his face.

****

All Martin seemed to be good for these days was taking time off from work to go to the race track. His latest boss had called that morning, long after Martin left for his job, and asked Jane if he was feeling well enough to come in, since an important client was coming. Jane had not known what to say. When she hung up and Olivia asked about it, Jane just said there was a crossed wire, and the call was not for them. She could not bring herself to let Olivia know just how much her husband lied.

She planned to sit Martin down when she had time to breathe. Her determination built for days, although an opportunity did not readily present itself. So she bided her time, pretending along with Olivia that everything was all right.

On her way home one evening in mid-March, Jane ran into a rainstorm. The streets and subways were flooded, and the conditions caused several delays. By the time she got home, soaked and cranky, Jane was feeling argumentative and ready to take on Martin the minute he came home.

When she entered the apartment building, Mrs. McGill was not there with her update. Mindful of her dripping coat and the slippery steps, Jane went upstairs as quickly as she could.

A crowd of neighbors hovered outside her door. Jane pushed her way through and found her sister huddled on the floor, with her arms and legs drawn up to her chest. Mrs. McGill stood beside her, helplessly looking down while holding Ellen.

"Not a good day," she mumbled to Jane. "Ever since the family on the next block had the measles quarantine, Olivia has refused to take the baby out. I think the two of them are feeling cooped up."

"What happened?"

"She was screaming. Shrieking like a banshee. I ran up to see what was wrong, and so did everyone else in the building. But when we got here, it was just the two of them. Ellen was crying, so I changed her, but Olivia fell on the floor. She's been like that since."

"Get everyone out," said Jane, taking Ellen. "And call the doctor." She put Ellen into her crib and sat down on the floor next to her sister.

She reached out to put her hand on Olivia's shoulder. This close to her, Jane could see that her neck was very dirty, as were her clothes.

"No, go away! I don't deserve you, or Ellen." Olivia sobbed, and then sat up, tearing at her blouse until it ripped. Taking a shred of the fabric, she wiped her nose and eyes, and then tore more. "I can't stand it," she shouted. Standing, she ran straight across the living room and cried, "I have to get out of here!" There was a sickening thud as she hit the wall. She fell back to the floor unconscious. Blood streamed down her face from her broken nose.

Jane stared down at her sister. That was how the doctor found them a moment later.

He shook his head. "I've already called for an ambulance. She'll have to be hospitalized."

"Please don't take her away," Jane cried. "I can take care of her. It's my fault. I was working too hard. I didn't pay enough attention to her." How had she missed so much? Jane wondered. Why hadn't she seen Olivia's illness?

"This sort of thing happens." Dr. Mann motioned for the ambulance attendants to place Olivia on the gurney they had brought. He felt her pulse one more time and told the men to take her out. "I'll be right down," he told them. "It isn't your fault, Jane. Maybe Olivia will recover in the hospital."

Jane grabbed his arm as he was turning to leave. His words had made her blood turn to ice water. "You don't sound like you believe it."

The doctor turned sad eyes toward her. "I don't know what to believe. Maybe with some shock therapy—"

"You can't do that!"

"You must trust us. We'll do what we can. Please, let me go. She needs help immediately." He turned again to go, but stopped. "Tell Martin he will need to take care of Ellen, at least for a while."

It was inconceivable. Was her sister truly gone, leaving Martin responsible for the baby? How would he know what to do? Would he do it?

She had her answers the next day. While she was at work, he came in, packed up the baby, and took her to his mother's apartment in the Bronx.

Chapter Twenty

Jane woke up on Saturday morning and looked around. Something was different. It was past six, and yet Ellen had not cried. Then she remembered. It was the same nightmare she had suffered through for the past several days, one from which she could not awaken. Ellen was gone, as was Olivia.

Tears flowed, even though Jane had thought she had none left. She felt the urge to wallow in them, in self-pity, something she had never before allowed herself to do. She had to take care of this situation, get her sister healthy, and bring both her and Ellen home. Her brief respite from Martin would be over, but this was too high a price to pay for his absence.

Dr. Mann had said it would be a few days before she could see Olivia. But she could go check on Martin and Ellen right away. She bathed and dressed quickly, skipped breakfast, and took the subway to Manhattan and then to the address in the Bronx she found in Olivia's address book.

She had never been to Martin's mother's home before. It was in a walkup, and if it had been overcrowded just after the war, it was teeming now. Every window had a clothesline full of diapers hanging out to dry, and baby carriages crowded the dark narrow hallways.

Jane knocked at the door. Mrs. Roche opened it,

looking far less composed than when Olivia had introduced her to Jane. The woman, a widow, was older than Jane remembered. She wore a frayed housecoat, and her hair was unkempt.

Ellen was crying in the bassinette. Jane rushed to her and picked her up, even before the two women exchanged a word.

Mrs. Roche looked at her myopically and seemed to be searching for her glasses, which were on a table near the telephone. "Are you a visiting nurse? I'm so glad you came. I can't take care of this child myself. I don't know what my son was thinking, bringing her here."

She finally stopped speaking long enough for Jane to respond. "No, Mrs. Roche. I'm Jane Baldwin. Olivia's sister. Where is Martin?"

"He's not here. But he said if you showed up, I shouldn't let you take Ellen. He said he is her father, and she's not your child."

Jane would have thought he could manage to stay home with his daughter, if he felt so strongly, but she did not say it out loud. "Where is he?"

"He hasn't been here in three days," said Mrs. Roche. "He just dumped Ellen here and said I should take care of her since her mother went to the bughouse."

Ellen had quieted in Jane's arms, but she still fidgeted. "She seems hungry."

"She won't drink the milk I gave her."

"She needs formula."

"I can't afford that."

"Didn't Martin give you any money for the baby?"

"No, and who is going to watch her anyway while I

go to the store? I can't drag her around with me. I have arthritis. And how am I supposed to go to work? My husband died a long time ago, and there's no money if I don't go out and earn it. I've already missed three days, and there are plenty of people who'd be glad to fill my position if I get fired."

Stunned, Jane put the baby down, and grabbed her purse. "I'll be right back. Where is the store?"

She filled up two bags of supplies for Ellen and returned to the cramped and not too clean apartment. She found Mrs. Roche attempting to divert Ellen's tears with a gentle rocking motion, while holding her like a sack of potatoes. Jane was amazed that her actions were enough to calm the baby.

After preparing enough formula for several days and putting it into the icebox, she gave the baby a good feeding and bath, then sat down to talk to Mrs. Roche.

"I have no idea where he's stayed for the past two nights," the old woman said, brushing Ellen's hair off her cheek with a gnarled arthritic finger. "He hasn't even called. I'm so tired. The baby seems so fussy. That's why I called the visiting nurses. They said to go to an agency for a baby nurse. But they're so expensive, and Martin told me he doesn't have any money. Said he had spent it all taking care of Olivia and the baby, and you."

Jane felt the sting of her implied accusation. Despite the magnitude of his lie, since he had never contributed a nickel toward the household expenses, including the food he ate, she felt her face flush with embarrassment. The thought of someone else taking care of her, when she prided herself on taking care of herself, overwhelmed her. She clenched her fists, reminding herself that the only thing Martin paid for was the fifteen-dollar hospital bill when Ellen was born, and that had taken several months.

Jane became aware that Mrs. Roche was still speaking. "You have a job, so why don't you pay your own way?" she asked Jane.

"I always have," she said, no longer bothering to hide her indignation. "I paid for everything." She had even dipped into the savings account she had set up for Z.Z. The account had become unnecessary, of course, but she had been planning to save it for Ellen's future.

Mrs. Roche's face fell. "Oh. Then he's been gambling again."

Jane knew she would have to pay Olivia's new hospital bills herself. And now she would also have to pay for Mrs. Roche's baby nurse, and she would have to buy a crib, a bathinette, and several other items Ellen needed while she stayed with her grandmother.

Mrs. Roche stood up, and Jane could tell it was done painfully. "I can't do this. When will your sister be home again?"

It was the first time Mrs. Roche had inquired about Olivia.

"It won't be long," said Jane.

"Did the doctor tell you that?"

"No."

"Did you see her yet?"

"Not yet. They asked me to wait."

"Then you don't know when she'll be home. I could be stuck with this baby for a long time."

"Stuck? How could you think taking care of Ellen is a burden?"

"If you enjoy it so much, why don't you do it?"

"I would love to. I'll take her home with me right now. I know of a good person who would be willing to take care of her during the day." Jane stood up in preparation to gather Ellen's things.

"No." Mrs. Roche shook her head. "Martin is her father, and he brought her here. He said if you tried to take her I should call the police."

"He dumped her here," Jane said. "For all you know, he isn't coming back for a long time. Have you tried to talk to him at work?"

"Oh, yes, I've tried. He won't take my calls anymore. The only time he did, he said, 'Mama, you have a second chance to raise a child. Get it right this time.'"

"Doesn't he want to take care of her himself?"

Mrs. Roche looked at Jane. "A man take care of a baby? Where would you get such an idea?"

"My father took care of my sister and me many times," said Jane angrily. She remembered clearly. He had held Olivia in his arms, rocking her, after Vanessa was gone.

"Well, bully for him. But maybe he should have taken better care of his wives. Maybe they wouldn't have all died."

Jane's face felt hot and she clenched her hands. "Is that what Martin told you?"

"I think you should go now," said Mrs. Roche. "I'm tired and I want to lie down."

"Please, let me take Ellen. Or I could stay here and watch her while you nap."

Mrs. Roche's eyes clouded. "No. Martin said— well, you know what he said. Now I think you should leave."

Joani Ascher

****

Jane paced outside the door of Olivia's hospital room, waiting for the doctor to say she could enter. She had prayed as hard as she could that her sister would recover and be able to bring her baby home again. Mrs. Roche had not allowed Jane to return, and the agency that had sent the nurse had called Jane to tell her they would no longer be servicing the baby, since they had not been paid. She had sent them two checks, but received another call a few days later, telling her the nurses would not work for that woman. They also advised her the baby was not gaining weight at the normal rate, since the woman had not properly made the formula, and had not boiled the nipples correctly, causing them to partially close up. Ellen had suffered two rashes from being left in a wet diaper all night, and her clothing was too small to fit her growing length, even though it was wide enough, since she was so thin. It was all Jane could do to keep herself from rushing up to the Bronx and taking Ellen from Mrs. Roche any way necessary. Instead she called another agency and ordered twenty-four-hour care. She also sent clothes and supplies up to the Bronx in a taxi.

Jane had consulted one of the lawyers who did work for Mr. Dobbin. He told her Martin had all the rights. But after she called him with the information on how Ellen was being improperly cared for, he advised her to request documentation from the agency and hire a detective to watch the home to see if the baby's father ever showed up. If not, they could file for custody on the basis of abandonment, as well as neglect by the grandmother. She had done as he said, paying out more money to get the job done.

Jane's thoughts were interrupted as Dr. Mann finally came out of Olivia's room. "I had hoped she would respond long before this," he said. "But she hasn't. Go see her, and then we'll talk."

With trepidation, Jane pushed the door to the room open. She was startled to find that although it was bright daylight outside, the room within was dark, as if dusk had fallen. It was also stale, with the windows tightly shut. Jane longed to throw open the curtains and raise the windows, but then she saw her sister.

Olivia sat in the middle of her bed with her arms drawn around her, rocking and humming.

"Hello, Olivia," Jane said softly.

Her sister turned to the sound, but did not seem to recognize Jane.

"Olivia, it's me, Jane."

"Jane?" She looked at Jane, really, and smiled. Quickly getting out of bed, she ran over to her and threw her arms around her. "I'm so glad you came. Can I go home now?"

"Do you feel better?"

"I feel good. I want to go home."

Jane smiled. "We can't wait for you to come home," she said.

"We?"

"Ellen misses you too."

Olivia knitted her brows. "Who is Ellen? And where is Father?"

****

When Jane spoke to the doctor afterward, he explained that Olivia fluctuated between thinking she was a child and knowing that her baby needed her. The specialists wanted to try shock treatment on her, in the hopes of jolting her back to reality.

"We've tried to get Martin's permission," said the doctor, "but we can't seem to reach him."

"Did you try his work number?"

"He is no longer employed there," said the doctor. "They don't know where he is, and neither does his mother."

"Can I give permission?"

"You'll have to get power of attorney."

"If that's what she needs, I'll do it."

Jane realized afterward she was not at all sure she wanted Olivia to have the treatment. Everything she had ever heard about those treatments was that they were horrible and painful. But she went through the legal motions, since it was also a good way to document her custody case. She could always deny the treatment later, once the paperwork was done.

Chapter Twenty-One

Anne had invited Jane to her home several times during Olivia's and Ellen's absence. With effort, she was able to attend on two occasions. The love she saw there, for Irene and between Anne and Schuyler, helped repair her own aching heart. For a few hours she could forget how much she missed Olivia and Ellen.

Once, when she and Anne had a few minutes alone in the kitchen, Anne's smiles faded. "You look so pale and thin," she said. "I'm worried about you."

"I'm doing the best I can," said Jane. "It isn't easy."

"You're doing it all alone. That only makes it harder."

Jane shook her head. "I have no choice. But there are people helping me. There's Mr. Dobbin and Mr. Smith, his lawyer, and Mrs. McGill has been very sweet, and so have you. Just knowing you care helps a lot."

Anne frowned. "It seems so unfair that you're alone. It shouldn't be that way." She paused, as if gauging Jane's mood. "I talked to Prescott yesterday."

Jane remained silent. She had to, otherwise she would have let on that her heart still fluttered at the sound of Prescott's name.

"He isn't happy either, you know," Anne continued. "His marriage hasn't worked. His wife is so self-centered, and colder than ice. That's probably why they have no children."

When Jane did not respond, Anne continued. "He asked how you were."

Jane jumped. Keeping her voice carefully neutral, she said, "That was kind of him."

Anne leaned forward and put her hand on Jane's arm. "I know he cares about you. I think he always has."

"As a former employer, maybe," Jane conceded. But her pain and frustration over Olivia made her add, "And as the man who fired me."

"All the women were expected to give up their jobs," Anne reminded her. "And stay home and have children. You would have been wonderful at that."

Jane noted that her friend was painting the facts into a different and not quite accurate picture, but she did not point that out. Instead, she looked straight into Anne's eyes, willing her for once and all to believe her. "I never wanted to stay home. Even if I married, I wanted a career. And I never really expected to find someone I cared about enough to marry."

"You must have expected to get married when you were dating that man," Anne pointed out.

Jane had never told her anything about Z.Z.'s father. Anne did not know it had been Lloyd Hammer, the man Jane had introduced her to that evening so long ago. Jane was not even sure Anne remembered meeting him at the dance club. She imagined it gave him less hold on her if she did not tell anyone his name.

"If I hadn't trusted that would happen," said Jane, "we would never have come to be together."

Anne said, "I didn't mean to imply—"

"I'm sorry. I'm just very upset."

"You're worried about Olivia and Ellen," said Anne. "I understand. But don't worry, it'll all work out."

They went back to the dining room. Jane was not at all convinced things would work out. But at least the discussion of Prescott Weaver was over. She was happy for small blessings.

****

"You have to sign here for the treatments," said Dr. Mann.

Jane had uncontested power of attorney. Now the dreaded decision was before her. "Are you positive it will help?"

"Electro-convulsive therapy may be the only thing that will. And you must understand, she'll need several treatments, three a week over the next few weeks, before we see results."

Jane had heard about amnesia, burns, and other frightening things that could happen. "Isn't it risky?"

"There is some danger. But Olivia has no chance otherwise."

With a sigh, Jane signed her name. Dr. Mann took the paper. Jane waited anxiously for him to return.

It seemed like hours. She kept thinking about Ellen, and Olivia, and even Martin. She was angry with herself for failing to prevent this.

Dr. Mann's return interrupted her thoughts. "It's over," he said. "They're cleaning her up now."

"Is she going to be all right?"

"It's too early to say. She'll be unconscious for hours. Go to work. Come back tonight, and we'll see how she is."

All through the day Jane found it difficult to concentrate. She wandered through the factory, noting the new children's clothing being manufactured for the fall line. Mr. Dobbin's children's wear was being carried by more and more of the finer stores, and Jane had selected several outfits from the spring line for Ellen, including them in the latest package sent to Mrs. Roche. She looked at a few of the fall dresses for Ellen, thinking about the baby's first birthday. With any luck, and the success of the shock treatments, Olivia would have her baby with her by then.

****

Three weeks passed. Olivia seemed to be better after the second week, and by the third she was nearly her normal self. Dr. Mann said that if things continued to improve, Ellen could come to the hospital the next week. It would be a key determining factor in her recovery.

Jane spent hours trying to cajole Mrs. Roche into letting her take Ellen for the day. The old woman was steadfast.

"Martin wouldn't like it if I let you take her."

"I could take the baby nurse with me," Jane suggested.

"No, I don't think that would work. She won't go all the way to the hospital with you."

"Have you talked to Martin?"

"He called me for some money just last week."

"Did he say anything about Ellen?"

"He didn't mention her."

"Then how do you know he wouldn't like it if I took her to see her mother?"

Mrs. Roche frowned. "Ellen is my granddaughter,

and I intend to take the responsibility seriously."

"I was thinking," said Jane. "It would be such a good opportunity for you to have a day to yourself. You could even have your hair done."

"I haven't got money for that. My neighbor has been doing it for me."

Jane had noticed that. "It would be my treat."

"My nails look horrible too," said Mrs. Roche.

Knowing a holdup when she saw one, Jane said, "Have them manicured. You certainly deserve it."

"That wouldn't take all day."

"Why don't you go to Bests? You could spend the day in the city, have the works, even go to Schrafft's for lunch." Jane did not know how she was going to afford it on top of the lawyer's bills, the hospital bills, and the nurses she paid to take care of Ellen's food, clothes, and the area where she slept, but it seemed to be the only way to get Ellen to Olivia.

"Oh, that sounds lovely," said Mrs. Roche. "I think I'll do just that."

****

On June fifth, Jane took three subways up to the Bronx and hailed a cab for Mrs. Roche, instructing the surprised driver to take her to Manhattan. She paid for it in advance and gave the old woman an equal amount for the return trip. She had already paid the salon and told the nursing agency that Ellen would not require a nurse that day.

She saw Mrs. Roche out the door, then bathed Ellen, dressing her in an adorable pink dress, before brushing her tiny, almost-black curls. The baby had Olivia's coloring—pearly skin and dark brown eyes which shone with delight as she rode on Jane's lap in another taxi. She cuddled against her aunt as Jane held her tight and relished the sweet-smelling baby's little coos.

The taxi pulled up to the sanitarium. Holding her breath, Jane alighted onto the sidewalk. A young nurse came down the steps and helped carry the baby's necessities inside.

"Oh, she's darling," the nurse gushed. "I'm sure she's just the medicine for Olivia."

"That's Mrs. Roche," an older nurse corrected her, coldly. "And we'll see how she reacts to her child."

"You don't seem to think she's better," said Jane.

"I have seen cases like this before. Young mothers who have everything going for them suddenly lose all rationality. It's sad, but it's a fact of life."

Her lack of faith did not enhance Jane's optimism, but clutching the baby close, she proceeded to Olivia's room and opened the door.

Sunlight and fresh air streamed in. Olivia was dressed in street clothes that Mrs. McGill had brought, as she put it, "To make her feel more like her old self." Her hair was pinned up neatly, and she even wore a bit of lipstick. She sat in a chair, confident and expectant.

When she saw Jane, she stood up. She had not regained the weight lost while she was so ill, and her clothing hung loosely on her, but she stood steadily and walked the few steps to the door.

"Let me see my baby," she said, opening her arms. "She's grown so much!"

Jane placed the baby in Olivia's arms. They looked wonderful together.

But the baby began to fuss almost immediately. "She's forgotten me," Olivia cried.

"Try holding her a different way," Jane suggested. "From what I've seen, she's used to being held like a sack of potatoes."

Olivia giggled then, although her smiles were mixed with tears. She swung the baby around, following Jane's suggestions, until Ellen hung from her mother's arms the same way she usually hung from her grandmother's. For a moment, she calmed.

"Sit down with her, and she'll get used to you," Jane advised. "She was just as fussy for me, but we're great friends now."

The rest of the visit went smoothly, and Jane left feeling lighthearted. Her sister and niece would be coming home. Over and over she told herself that everything would work out.

****

June twenty-eighth was the big day. Jane and Mr. Dobbin brought Olivia home to the spotlessly clean apartment that Mrs. McGill had worked on for days. The two older people, who had not spent nearly as much time together as they had in the past, seemed to be picking up their usual rhythm together, which Jane was sure would help Olivia feel at home.

Ellen was scheduled to arrive by another prepaid taxi at three o'clock. Mrs. Roche had mellowed somewhat toward her daughter-in-law, even admitting that living with Martin must have sometimes been a strain. That he had not been home once since the whole thing started, nor inquired about his wife, did not improve anyone's opinion of him.

Three o'clock passed, as did four o'clock, and there was no sign of Mrs. Roche or Ellen. Jane called the apartment, but there was no answer. Olivia was becoming more and more agitated with each passing minute, and there seemed to be no way to calm her.

Mr. Dobbin looked at Jane and said, "I must get to that appointment."

She nodded her understanding and gratitude. Mrs. McGill went to stand by the window.

An hour later, the phone rang. Jane answered. It was Mr. Dobbin. "Tell Olivia her baby will be there soon," he said. "But there may be another guest."

As Jane hung up, she thought she heard a man's voice say, "You bet there will."

It was Martin's voice.

Jane did not tell Olivia her husband would be coming home with the baby. She was not even sure herself what it meant. But from the tone of Mr. Dobbin's voice, it did not sound good. If she could only have gone after the baby herself, she could have avoided this problem, but she could not possibly leave Olivia's side. Not yet. That was, after all, why she had arranged to take the next week off.

Another long hour later, they arrived. Martin himself was carrying the baby, who was fussing more than Jane had ever seen her. His mother had opted not to come, claiming it was high time to get on with her life, and the bingo parlor was calling. So it was up to Martin to hold his daughter, and it was evident he did not do it well.

Olivia took the baby from her husband without a word. Ellen calmed a bit but seemed hungry. "It is past her dinner time," Olivia said. "Didn't anyone feed her?"

Both men looked sheepish. Mrs. McGill clucked her disapproval and went to the kitchen to start preparing cereal for the baby. "Someone should check her diaper," she called over her shoulder. "Men!" she concluded.

Jane motioned for Olivia to change the baby. She did not want to leave her alone with Martin for a minute. Mr. Dobbin coughed and went to help Mrs. McGill in the kitchen, where there was nothing but the dried-out remnants of what was supposed to have been a festive homecoming meal.

"I'm surprised to see you," said Jane. "It's been so long since anyone heard from you."

"I've been away."

"You couldn't call to check on your wife?" Jane asked.

"Don't lord yourself over me. I was busy."

"Working?"

"Yes."

"But I heard you lost your job. What were you doing?"

"I got another one."

"Good. Then you can pay Olivia's hospital bills. They were quite expensive. Especially those shock treatments."

"I didn't authorize them. I'm not gonna pay for them."

"She needed them. And there was no way to reach you for authorization."

"I heard you said they could do it. You can pay for them."

Jane opened her mouth to respond, but stopped. This discussion was getting nowhere. "What do you want?" she asked.

"I'm here because this is where my wife and child are. You got a problem with that?"

"A true fair-weather friend, I see. Well, Olivia is in no condition for this. You'll have to leave." She stood, and moved toward him. He was bigger and stronger than she, but she set her shoulders, and he weakened, true to form.

"I'll be back."

"When the time is right, we'll see."

When Olivia returned, holding Ellen, Jane made an excuse about how Martin had to leave but would return. Olivia's face did not change expression, but her shoulders sagged. "When?"

"I'm not sure."

"Not tonight?"

"I don't think so."

"Oh."

"Dinner for Ellen is served," said Mrs. McGill. "And ours will be served presently."

Olivia brightened and kissed the baby's soft hair. "We're ready." Her smile implied she meant they were prepared for much more than dinner.

Chapter Twenty-Two

By the end of the week, Olivia and Ellen had settled into a daily routine that had the apartment humming. Olivia looked better than she had in a while, Jane told herself, and the baby seemed to be thriving on her love.

Martin called several times, but Jane managed to convince him his wife needed more time. "Dr. Mann will check up on her Saturday. We'll know more by then."

Dr. Mann had come by every evening, but Jane did not tell Martin that. At first the doctor seemed to hedge his bets, saying there could be setbacks. But by Friday, he said Olivia's progress was everything they could have hoped for, and there was a general sigh of relief.

"Martin has been calling," Jane confided.

"I expect he wants to move back in."

"I suppose. Isn't there a reason why he shouldn't?"

Dr. Mann looked at Jane with a smile on his lips. "I'm sure there are many, but none of them are physical. See how long you can stall him, though. Olivia needs as much time as she can get."

"I'll see what I can do."

"And Jane," the doctor said, almost as an afterthought, "I understand you will be returning to work next week. I'm not at all sure it would be good for Olivia to be alone yet."

"She won't be. Mrs. McGill will be nearby, and she'll check in often."

"Good."

"Is there something you are worried about?"

Dr. Mann shook his head. "Nothing specific. It's just that you both mean so much to me. And Ellen too. She's a wonderful baby."

"I'll take care of all of us," Jane promised.

****

Jane rushed home that Monday, intent on checking for herself that things had gone well for Olivia and Ellen. And indeed they appeared to be fine. Olivia had even prepared a lovely dinner while Ellen napped.

"You were supposed to have rested yourself, while Ellen slept," Jane protested.

"I wasn't tired. I think I've rested enough to last me a lifetime."

She proudly served the dinner, and beamed with pleasure at Jane's compliments. She was still smiling when she answered the ringing phone a moment later. But after she hung up, she look strained.

"What's wrong?" asked Jane.

"That was Martin. He wants to come see me tonight."

"He doesn't have to if it'll upset you," Jane said. "I can call him and tell him to wait."

"He said he has every right to see his daughter," Olivia said sadly.

Jane did not point out that he had felt no need to see the baby during the entire time Olivia was hospitalized. "I'll be right here," she said. "You won't be alone."

He did not come right away. Ellen went down for

the night at seven, and hours passed, with Olivia checking the street from the window every few minutes. She stopped looking out the window when it got dark outside, although she was still edgy. But at ten o'clock, Olivia's nervousness seemed to dissolve. "I guess he's not coming," she said, her voice sounding hopeful.

The doorbell rang at ten-fifteen. Olivia jumped and the haunted look returned to her face.

"I can send him away," said Jane. "Ellen is asleep anyway."

"We should see what he wants," said Olivia, her voice full of defeat.

Jane went to the door. She only opened it part way, and she quietly told Martin the he wouldn't be able to see Ellen since she was sleeping.

"I want to come in anyway," Martin said loudly. The fumes from the large amount of whiskey he had apparently consumed filled Jane's nostrils, and she could not help wrinkling her nose.

"Don't sneer at me, you old biddy," he said.

Olivia came up behind Jane and pulled open the door. "You have to be quiet," she pleaded. "You'll wake the baby."

Martin did not fail to notice his wife's agitated state.

"Are you cracking up again?" he asked, pushing past Jane. "I knew it wouldn't last."

Olivia shook her head. "I'm fine. It's just that you're so late."

"So what?"

Olivia plucked at her skirt. Jane watched as she struggled to maintain her composure.

"Ellen has already gone to bed," Jane said. "You missed your chance to see her."

Martin started toward the bedroom.

Olivia reached for his arm. "Please don't wake her."

"When are you two going to get it through your heads that she's my daughter?" He shrugged her arm away and stomped forward.

Olivia plucked at her skirt again. "Shhh. Please, don't talk so loudly. You'll wake her."

Flinging the door of the bedroom open so hard it banged against the wall, Martin disappeared inside. Seconds later the baby wailed.

"What are you doing to her?" Olivia asked, shocked out of her immobility.

"I'm not doing anything. I'm just holding her."

"I'm coming, Ellen," said Olivia, and went into the bedroom. The door slammed, and Jane was left outside, feeling a helpless rage.

Someone knocked on the door of the apartment, and before Jane could answer, Mrs. McGill burst in. "What's wrong?"

"Martin is here."

"Is he hurting them?"

"I don't think so. But he isn't helping, either."

Through the closed door, Jane could hear Martin's voice, raised over the baby's screams. She could not make out what he was saying, but she was pretty sure he was "laying down the law," as he called it.

Mrs. McGill, eyes wide, polishing rag limp at her side, frowned. "I'll make some tea. I think we're going to need it."

"That or Scotch," Jane said, under her breath.

"Did you say something?"

"Tea would be lovely," said Jane. As if that were a cure-all.

Several minutes later, Martin emerged from the bedroom. "I'll be back tomorrow. And I want a steak for dinner."

"Then you had better bring it yourself, and cook it too," said Jane. "You're not getting any more free rides."

Martin whirled around and raised a fist to Jane. She stood her ground, and Martin, after glancing over to where Mrs. McGill stood open-mouthed, lowered his arm. Saying nothing, he turned and left the apartment.

Jane raced to Olivia. "Are you all right?"

"I suppose so."

"He doesn't have to live here. Say the word and I'll find a way to keep him out."

"How?"

"You can get a divorce."

Olivia shook her head. "I couldn't do that. I don't want Ellen to come from a broken home. People will talk." She blinked and a tear fell to her cheek. "He's my husband. Please don't make it harder for me. I have to do this."

Martin's homecoming was everything Jane had dreaded. He moved in, more arrogant than ever. It was as if he were king of the castle.

"I'll be having my poker game here on Tuesday nights," he told Olivia, in front of Jane, essentially the way he always communicated his demands to his sister-in-law, by public conversations with his wife.

"That is not possible," said Jane. "It wouldn't be healthy for the baby." Her tone left no room for argument, and Martin didn't make one. He got up and left.

Olivia's bottom lip trembled. "Don't worry," Jane said. "Things will settle down soon." With any luck, he would not come back.

But he did. About midnight, the door opened noisily and slammed shut. Jane, from within her own room, could hear Martin staggering past the couch, colliding with the coffee table, cursing, and moving on into Olivia's room. She shuddered, fearing what would happen, and put her pillow over her ears. Olivia had made it plain she did not want Jane interfering, and Jane had to honor her request, even if the effort to do so killed her.

But she was unable to muffle the noise from the next room. Martin's voice carried, through the walls and through the open windows, increasing in volume by the minute, until the baby began to cry in her crib. When Olivia asked him to be quiet so she could comfort Ellen, Jane could plainly hear Martin say, "Leave her alone! I'm the one who needs attention. And you're gonna give it to me whether you want to or not." The banging of the headboard while Ellen frantically cried would haunt Jane's dreams for weeks.

Olivia was up and in the kitchen feeding Ellen when Jane came in the next morning. She cautioned her sister to move around quietly, since Martin was still asleep. "He got in late," she said, by way of explanation.

"I heard him," said Jane. "Doesn't he have to go to work?"

"He's between jobs right now."

"So how can he afford to go out drinking and

gambling?"

Olivia gasped. "How do you know about the gambling?"

"His mother told me. But I kind of suspected, since he never had a dime, even when he was working."

"He swears it's under control. He only went out last night to say goodbye to the boys."

"So no poker on Tuesdays?"

"He says he won't. He wants me to be happy."

Jane forced a smile of encouragement at her sister. But the truth was too obvious to both of them.

****

Two weeks later, when Jane got home, Martin was where he had been every single day since he moved back in. He sat in his undershirt in the winged chair, reading the newspaper. Jane suspected he never left the apartment, not even to look for work. When she greeted Jane in the evening, Mrs. McGill confirmed that suspicion. But Jane decided to hold her tongue and give it time.

It was difficult, especially since resentment oozed from every pore on Martin's body. He did not bother to ask for money from Jane, and she had seen to it that Olivia did not have access to any. So he sat, dissatisfied, glaring at the door as if he were in a jail cell.

Jane wondered why he stayed. While it was true he was well taken care of, since Olivia tried to give him interesting meals and spent hours washing and ironing everything from his dress shirts to his boxer shorts, he had little to say to her and did not show much interest in Ellen.

****

At night, despite her pillow, Jane could hear Olivia's pain, while her husband assumed his "rightful pleasures." Quite often Ellen awoke during this time, and a stream of curses and admonitions erupted from Martin, who had moved the crib out of the bedroom he shared with Olivia. Jane would hold the baby and rock her, trying to shut out the sound of Martin's voice and the language he used. Her embarrassment was compounded by the disgusted stares of her neighbors in the mornings.

Several times, when Jane went to get a drink of water during the night, she found her sister staring into the crib, or at the kitchen table looking at nothing. Yet every morning, no matter how early Jane arose, Olivia was up before her. Dark circles had come back under her eyes, and she was losing weight again.

"Did you sleep well?" Jane asked one morning, shortly before Ellen's first birthday.

Olivia turned vacant eyes to her sister. "About the same as usual. I'm not very tired these days." She pulled at her housecoat. "Maybe it's because of the sun coming up so early."

That did not make much sense to Jane. The sun was actually coming up later than it had been when Olivia first came home. But she let it go, promising herself to call Dr. Mann and ask him to have a look at Olivia.

"I told her I was calling you because Ellen has the sniffles," Jane said, when she called him.

"Has the baby been sick?"

"No. She's fine, wonderful. A joy."

"Jane, tell me what's been going on."

She told him all she knew. "I think she's stopped

sleeping again, and I know she doesn't eat. She just picks at her dinner, and her clothes."

"She was doing that in the hospital."

"That's what has me so scared."

He came the next evening. For a while he examined little Ellen, and pronounced her healthy, then he quietly asked to speak to Olivia alone.

Jane was left with Martin and nothing to say. She managed to keep him out of his own bedroom by offering him a second slice of cake.

She jumped up when Dr. Mann came out of the room. He nodded at the door, and Jane followed him, making a show of escorting him out.

"You were right to be worried," said the doctor. "She's very thin, and very nervous, and I'm sure she hasn't slept in weeks."

"Why would this be starting again? I thought she was cured."

"There was always a chance there could be a recurrence."

Jane gripped the doorknob. "She can't live through another time like that."

"Pray it isn't so. I've told her to come in for some tests."

****

It was a sweltering hot day in the second week of September, the fourth in a string, with unbearable humidity, and Jane and everyone else felt short tempered. Two women fainted on the platform, waiting for the train, and five men got into a brawl over the last newspaper at the newsstand. The whole building was hushed, as if everyone were asleep, waiting out the heat of the day. Jane went upstairs slowly, since there was so little air, and turned toward her apartment. But when she opened the door and saw a policeman standing next to Mrs. McGill, who was in tears, clutching Ellen close, she knew the worst had happened.

"There's been an accident," the officer said. "At the subway station. Your sister fell off the platform in front of a train. I'm very sorry. She did not survive."

Chapter Twenty-Three

Dr. Mann injected Jane with a strong sedative. "Don't worry about Ellen," he said. "Mrs. McGill will take care of her."

"I don't understand about Olivia," cried Jane. "She was just going to see you. That's three blocks away. Why was she at the subway station?"

"She must have gone there after I saw her."

"What did you tell her?"

"Jane, I think you should know. She was pregnant."

The horror of the situation began to sink in as the medication started to do its work. Jane fell asleep knowing her sister had voluntarily stepped off a subway platform in front of an oncoming train.

****

The funeral was held on a cool, crisp day that gave promise to the coming autumn. Dr. Mann came to check on Jane before she left for the service. He took a look at Ellen too, who sat comfortably on Mrs. Roche's lap, unaware that her mother was dead.

"It was kind of Martin's mother to come all the way down here to take care of Ellen," Dr. Mann whispered at the door.

"Her heart is in the right place," said Jane.

"Maybe Martin's is too, at least a little," said the doctor. "He went to the funeral home before the casket was closed and asked for Olivia's ring. He told the director it meant a lot to him."

Jane looked into the old doctor's eyes. "If you're saying this wasn't all his fault, I'm sorry, but I just don't believe that. He knew how fragile she was. He didn't care." She looked guiltily over at Mrs. Roche, hoping she had not heard.

"You mustn't let yourself become bitter," Dr. Mann warned. "You will only hurt yourself."

Jane sighed. "I've got to go. Thank you for stopping by."

The doctor kissed her on the forehead and walked her downstairs. She knew his arm was around her shoulders, but she was too numb to feel it.

An hour later Jane stoically watched as the coffin was lowered into the ground, then murmured responses to the other mourners. She felt as if she, too, were being buried, standing there holding both Anne's and Mr. Dobbin's hands. Mrs. McGill stood a few feet away, sobbing, and a few of the neighbors clustered around her trying to offer comfort. Standing alone, on the other side of the grave, was Martin, looking bewildered, who left as soon as the first shovelful of dirt was put onto the coffin.

That evening, Jane sat rocking Ellen to sleep. Martin had done his disappearing act again, not even bothering to try to take the baby with him. He did take the two silver picture frames Mr. Dobbin had given him and Olivia. One had a picture of the baby and the other had their wedding photo in it. Jane was touched but mystified by his sentimentality, because it was in such contrast to his behavior.

He put the frames, all his clothes, and any of the

small, valuable gifts he and Olivia had received at their wedding into the good suitcase that had belonged to Jane and Olivia's father. When he slammed the door on the way out, it was clear he would not be back.

The minute she could, Jane resolved she would sue for custody on the grounds of abandonment by the baby's father. Martin's mother, who had witnessed his departure, agreed with her, calling him several names. These included many pertaining to the debt he owed her, since he had never paid her one cent to defray the loss of her wages while she cared for Ellen.

****

Jane did not see Martin again until the hearing, when he swaggered into court looking more disheveled than ever and stated to the judge that he did not want Jane to have custody.

"Your honor," said Jane's lawyer, Mr. Smith, "this man has twice abandoned his baby daughter, and since the child's mother is dead, we ask you to grant the petition to award custody to Miss Baldwin."

"Did she tell you her own freak baby died?" Martin asked the judge. "Now she wants mine. You can't let her take Ellen. Uh, your honor."

The judge pounded his gavel. "Order. Are you contesting this lady's right or ability to take care of the child?"

"I am, your honor."

"I'll hear motions on this, with full documentation, by Friday. Adjourned."

Mr. Smith took Jane's arm and escorted her out of the courtroom. "Let me take you to lunch," he said. "We can talk there."

"Can he really block custody?" Jane asked, when

they were seated. She felt as if the world was coming to an end.

"He is the baby's father."

"He keeps abandoning her."

"Yes. But he can contest your right to gain custody."

"What if I tell the judge about his drinking and gambling?"

"You can't do that. He'll deny it, and he might bring up things about you that would be more damaging."

Jane had told Mr. Smith about Z.Z. and the circumstances of his birth. "Martin is not making a good impression on the judge. If he finds against you, Ellen could end up in an orphanage."

The room began to swim. Mr. Smith patted Jane's hand solicitously. "In your favor, though," Mr. Smith continued, "is the fact that you have a good paying job and a reliable babysitter. If we don't sling stones at Martin, maybe he won't have an opportunity to impugn you."

Jane struggled to calm down. "What are we going to do?"

"My guess is Martin wants something. We're going to find out what it is."

It did not take long. Martin called and told Jane he wanted money. A lot of it. And he promised to sign whatever he had to, if he got it.

"Can't we tell the judge?" Jane asked Mr. Smith. She had called him right away. "It's extortion. He's asking me to buy the baby."

"It won't help you. Do you have the money?"

"Me? No! I spent everything I had, plus some, on

Olivia's hospital bills and her funeral. I still owe a lot of money."

"Then I don't know what we're going to do. See what you can do. I'll check things on my end. We only have until Friday."

Jane looked dismally at her bank book. There was not nearly enough money there to meet Martin's demands. She swallowed her pride and called Anne.

"Schuyler is out of the country," Anne reminded her. "His ship sailed right after the funeral. I don't have access to that much money, at least not right away. All I have in the household account is five hundred dollars. Can't you stall him until Sky comes back or I can sell some stock?"

"We only have until Friday. Can you sell it by then?"

"I don't think so, but I can try."

Jane talked to Mr. Dobbin, although she knew he had no ready cash. "If only you had asked before I bought that material and the new machines," he said.

Jane became desperate. She ransacked her apartment, looking for anything she might be able to sell. All she found was her father's pocket watch. She knew she would not get much for it, but maybe Martin would take the money over a period of time and the watch would be enough for a down payment. She had to try.

She straightened the veil on her hat with her gloved hand as she stepped into the pawn shop on Rodgers Avenue. It was dark inside, and Jane felt the sadness of all the people who had sold their property out of hopelessness. Her eyes roamed the shelves while the pawnbroker inspected the watch.

Then she saw them. The two picture frames Martin had taken from the apartment, side by side, with the pictures still in them. She did not hear the pawnbroker state his price.

"I'm sorry if that is too low," he said quietly. "But it is the best I can do."

"Where did you get those?" Jane asked, pointing to the frames.

"Oh, that is a sad story. A young man came in a few weeks ago and sold them to me, along with a wedding ring. He said he needed the money for medicine for his little daughter. I gave him a good price for them. I know it wasn't good business, but look how cute that little girl is."

Jane looked at the picture of Ellen, then back at the pawnbroker. She could see he had not believed a word Martin had said. Who would, when he had not bothered to keep the pictures?

"I'll give you the watch for the ring and the frames," Jane said, knowing she had lost whatever money she might have made on the watch.

"You have a deal. Let me just take the pictures out."

"No! Leave them just the way they are."

****

Prescott Weaver sat behind the desk in his office, but his mind was far away. It was in Europe, and Northern Africa, with war all around him. He pictured himself at the Kasserine Pass, in that disaster, amid all the casualties. But even then, when he had a moment, he had contrived to place himself in the peaceful oasis of a letter from Jane. Her words then, when he still imagined her becoming his wife, had carried him through the worst days.

He knew she had thought herself plain. She had not seen herself the way he saw her, as the picture of love. He knew that. Maybe he should have told her. Certainly he should have told her the way he felt about her. His hindsight was perfect, and his life was ruined. He had let someone else take her right out from under his nose, and she had been hurt.

Now someone else was trying to hurt her again. As if she had not been through enough with her poor son. He remembered her face at her child's funeral. She was devastated, but she had held onto Olivia, easing her sister's pain. After all that, Jane now had to bear the pain of what had happened to her sister. The man Olivia had married was the lowest form of life, according to Anne, his lifeline into Jane's world. If only she had come to him for help. But she would not. Besides her pride, he was a married man. She could not know it was in name only.

But what she did not know could help her. That was why he had sent that note to Martin Roche.

A knock on his office door told him the bait had been taken. Martin Roche was on time.

Prescott answered it himself, since he had set this appointment for after his secretary left. He did not need anyone else seeing the man.

Martin came in carrying his hat, looking around as if he were in a museum. "This sure is a fancy office," he said. "I could get used to working here."

Prescott motioned for him to sit in the studded leather chair facing the mahogany desk. "Where do you work, Mr. Roche?"

"I'm between jobs right now. Would you have an

opening?"

"Do you know anything about trading stocks?"

"Nah. I leave that to my know-it-all sister-in-law. But I don't have to tell you about her. Isn't that why you called me here?"

Prescott fanned out his hands on his desk. "You know what I want?"

"I have an idea. You want me to lay off my claim to Ellen. You have a lot of nerve, trying to get me to give your ex-girlfriend my baby."

"You seem to have your facts mixed up."

"Nah, I got it straight. Olivia, my crazy late wife, told me."

"Told you what?"

"About how you were in love with Jane, although I don't know why. You should try living with her. She's no picnic, let me tell you." He smiled, or actually, leered. "But you seem to have done all right for yourself, even with your, uh, broken heart. I hear you married some rich daddy's girl who gives her everything she wants." He stopped, showing his teeth in an evil grin. "Oh, yes. I've been poring over the society pages for years, ever since Olivia told me, reading all about you. Too bad your wife hasn't given you any kids yet. Or maybe there's something wrong with you. Is that it? Are you in the market for my kid? Well, well, maybe I should think about this. How much do you want her? I'll tell you, she's cute, and healthy. Make me an offer."

Prescott was around the desk by this time and had Martin by the throat. Martin put his hands up, trying to release the grip. When Prescott finally let go, Martin sank back into his chair and straightened his collar.

"You listen to me," Prescott growled, "you worthless excuse for a man. There obviously isn't a shred of honor or decency in you. I can only hope your child never finds that out." Prescott returned to his chair and pulled his checkbook out from his top desk drawer. "I'll ignore your offer to sell me your baby. My wife and I are not interested. But based on what I've heard, and certainly from today's demonstration, you shouldn't be allowed within ten miles of Ellen. I understand Jane wants to adopt her. You will not stand in the way of that adoption."

"Oh, yeah? And what's going to stop me?"

"Your big bank account. I'll give you twenty thousand dollars to sign away your rights and never see Jane or the child again."

"Ha. I only asked her for ten thousand."

"I know. You see, I know everything I need to about you. I know you are deeply in debt for bad bets on the horses, and that you haven't got a prayer of getting a decent job in New York. Too many people have too many bad things to say about you." He wrote out the check and started to hand it over to Martin.

Martin made a grab at it but Prescott pulled it away. "This check has strings attached. One is that you will move out of town." His voice had taken on a tone he had never used before. It was cold and threatening, and he meant every word he said. "Seek your fortune elsewhere."

"I've thought about it," Martin said, his fingers twitching at the check held so close. "I thought I would give Florida a try."

"Good idea. And you will never try to see Ellen again."

"But she's my daughter."

Prescott pulled the check farther out of Martin's reach.

"Okay," Martin squeaked, "I'll stay away."

"And the last caveat is," Prescott continued, "you will never tell Jane about our meeting. Ever. If you do, your future anywhere in this country will be without a job." He moved the check closer, holding it between two fingers.

Martin lunged for it, caught it, and held it close, reading the numbers. "This is only five grand. Do you think I'm some kind of chump?"

"You'll get the other fifteen after you sign with the courts."

"You've got a deal." Martin extended his hand to shake Prescott's, but there was no reciprocation.

The stock broker stood with his back to Martin, looking out the window. "Get out of my office."

****

By Friday, Jane was desperate. She had not been able to come up with anything close to what Martin wanted, even after asking all her friends for a loan. As it was, Mrs. McGill was babysitting for free, and her lawyer was doing the case pro bono, out of respect for Mr. Dobbin. But when she arrived in court, the lawyer was smiling.

"I don't know how you did it, Jane," he said.

"What do you mean?"

"Martin signed away all his parental rights five minutes ago. He said there were no strings attached."

"Are you saying he has completely given up any claim to Ellen?"

"Yes."

Jane took a moment to process that information. She felt as if a huge burden had been lifted from her shoulders. "Why?"

"Martin didn't say. And I don't think we should ask, at this point. We don't want to look at this too closely, or it might become a problem." He took Jane's arm. "The judge wants to see us. Remember what I told you. You need not feel worried that he will think less of you because of Z.Z. Let's go."

The meeting was longer than Jane expected, considering that Martin had signed the documents. But the judge wanted to be sure Jane would be a good person to raise Ellen.

"I understand you work outside the home, Miss Baldwin, yet you have petitioned to be Ellen Roche's mother."

Jane had prepared her answer. "Your honor, there are other women who must go out into the business world. Many did during the war, when their husbands were overseas. We could not have won the war without them. They were able to manage, and I will be able to as well."

"What arrangements have you made for her while you are at work?"

"My neighbor, Mrs. McGill, who is like family, will take care of Ellen."

"And what would happen if you were to die?"

"My dearest friend, Anne Lewis, will adopt her."

"What if you should marry?"

Jane wanted to laugh at that ludicrous question, but she remembered Mr. Smith's admonition to take every question seriously. "Ellen is my first consideration. Whatever happens in the future will be entirely dependent on her needs."

"I'd like the child brought in," said the judge. The bailiff left to get Mrs. McGill and the baby from where they sat in the hallway.

They came in, with Mrs. McGill looking very shy. When Ellen saw Jane, her face split with a smile and she reached out her arms for her. Jane took the baby and snuggled her close.

The judge banged his gavel. "Good luck to both of you."

Chapter Twenty-Four

Mr. Dobbin's voice could be heard across the whole first floor of the factory. "I said, 'Go home,' Henderson. I don't want you here. If you don't leave now, you're fired."

Sylvia and Frances, Jane's assistants, stared wide-eyed in the direction of the noise. "What's going on?" Frances asked. "I've never heard Mr. Dobbin talk that way."

That was certainly true. In the almost ten years since he opened the factory, Mr. Dobbin had never once raised his voice to an employee. Now he was shouting at a man whose wife was in the hospital, dying of cancer. Jane rose and went to find her friend.

On the way, she found Henderson, a thin, graying, forty-year-old man, standing near the time clock with his hat in his hand and his lunch box by his side, hesitantly fingering his time card. "Am I fired, Miss Jane?"

"Don't do anything yet," she said. "I'm going to speak to Mr. Dobbin. Just stay right here."

"What's wrong?" she asked, when she found Mr. Dobbin with his head in his hands leaning on his desk. "You just told our foreman to leave or be fired."

He turned red-rimmed eyes to her. "I couldn't let him stay here. His wife—his family needs him now. He should be with them, not here. We don't need him as much as they do."

Mr. Dobbin's voice was filled with grief, puzzling Jane. She pulled over a chair and sat next to him.

"The hospital visiting hours don't start until one o'clock," she pointed out. "Surely he can stay until then?"

"No. Henderson's children will be home for lunch at noon. He should be there for them, and see them back to school on his way to the hospital. They have enough to deal with without coming home to an empty house every day at lunchtime."

"The eldest child is fourteen," Jane said. "She's capable of handling a few sandwiches."

Mr. Dobbin's face became red. "But should she have to? Her mother is dying. Why must she be without her father too? Why should Caroline have to wash the baby's face and hands and answer all of Harry's questions?"

Jane looked closely at Mr. Dobbin. "Henderson's children's names are not Caroline and Harry, and his youngest is eight. There is no baby." She patted his hand. "You're talking about your own children, and when their mother died, aren't you?"

He brushed a tear away and hung his head. "I wasn't there for them. I had to work to put food on the table, or so I told myself. But couldn't I have managed to be with them a little more? That was the hardest thing they ever had to do in their lives, and I let them do it alone."

"Henderson needs the money," Jane said.

"Cut him a check. We'll pay him for the whole month, and if he needs more time, we'll pay him for another. I want him with his family. If I have to do his job myself, I will."

Jane went out to tell Henderson what Mr. Dobbin had said, and the man nearly wept with gratitude. "Ask him if I can work in the morning, at least. He has a big order coming due, and I can't just leave him to fill it alone."

"I'll talk to him. But for now, you should go home. Give me your time card. I'll see that everything is taken care of. Come in tomorrow morning, and we'll talk about the details."

"Thank you, Miss Jane. And thank him for me." He put his hat on his head and went out.

Jane went back into Mr. Dobbin's office. He still sat at his desk, staring into space. "That's taken care of," she said. "But I think you have something else you must do."

He turned his watery blue eyes to her. "What?"

She picked up the phone receiver and held it out to him. "You have to make a few phone calls." She took a deep breath. "To Caroline, Harry, and Peter."

Mr. Dobbin nodded, and Jane left him to it.

She was still thinking about the look of relief and reconciliation on his face after his round of phone calls while she was on her way to see Anne. Unfortunately, Anne's world had recently collapsed.

"They treat me as if I'm a fragile piece of crystal, without a brain in my head," Anne complained over a cup of tea in her Park Avenue apartment. Her clear gray eyes, still shrouded by grief, held a determination Jane had never expected when she first met the woman so many years before. With Hugh Canfield, she had played the socialite, carefree and occasionally nasty, although Jane had found out she was only covering up her pain.

But with Schuyler, she had been herself, loving, caring, and a wonderful wife and mother. Irene had blossomed with her mother's love, and Schuyler had achieved many of his goals, not only financially but also philanthropically and philosophically. But now a sudden heart attack had ended his life, leaving Anne a widow only five years after her marriage.

Anne was not only alone, she was the head of a corporation, unusual for a woman in 1952. Schuyler's will had been specific on that point, and no one dared question it. Jane's heart was breaking for her friend.

"As if you didn't know to the penny what you're worth," Jane said. "Why don't you go to another firm?"

"I've talked to several. These men seem to believe I can think of nothing but jewelry and furs."

"What about Prescott?" Jane hated to bring it up, but she knew he wouldn't treat Anne that way. "Couldn't he handle your investments for you?"

"No. I assume Hugh got custody of him in the divorce. I'm sure he'd be willing, but I know Hugh would hate that and take it out on Pres. I couldn't do that to him."

"But he was at the funeral," Jane pointed out. She had gone breathless at the sight of him. He had changed. There were frown lines around his mouth and between his eyebrows which had never been there when she worked for him. But he was just as handsome as when he'd returned from the war.

"He came as a friend," said Anne, "and he is a good one. But I use another firm entirely. That is, Schuyler did, and they were competent. It's just that I don't feel all that comfortable with them. They seem to think the whole concept of investment is over my head." She put down her tea cup when Irene called out to her from the bedroom.

Jane went with Anne to visit Irene in her frilly pink bedroom. Anne and Irene had picked everything out together when they moved to the new apartment after the wedding, and if the wallpaper was a bit childish for someone of Irene's age, it was exactly what she wanted.

But she looked so sad now, lying on her bed with her cheeks swollen.

"Does it hurt again?" Anne asked.

Irene nodded.

"Okay, sweetheart. I'll get you some more aspirin. Aunt Jane will stay with you while I'm gone."

Jane sat on the bed next to the girl. "I told Ellen you've been to the dentist," she said, knowing that this latest round of dental care had been extensive. Irene had terrible trouble with her teeth, a not uncommon situation among children with her affliction. "She hopes you feel better soon."

Anne returned with a small bowl of applesauce. "Here you are." She spooned some up for Irene, and Jane saw the chopped-up aspirin in it. "The pain will go away in a little while. Try to get some sleep." She turned off the light and shut the door on the way out with Jane. "I wish this was all over for her, but since her medical problems never seem to end, some other problem will crop up once this is done."

"Sooner or later everything will be fixed," Jane said, hoping it would be true.

Anne looked very worried. "She's just not bouncing back the way she used to." She listened at the door, and motioned Jane to follow her.

"How is the bomb shelter coming along?" Anne

asked, when they were back in the living room.

"Mrs. McGill is very busy filling it up now." Jane was not sure the room in the basement would actually protect anyone from atomic fallout, but people all across the country were building their own shelters, and Mrs. McGill had been using any spare time she could find to gather a Geiger counter, containers of water, first aid kits, and canned goods.

"She would do better to invest in the stock market," Anne said. "Then she could get a return on her investment."

"You don't believe in bomb shelters?"

"Not really. I know it's all the rage to worry, but there always seem to be more immediate problems around me."

The pain from Schuyler's death and Irene's ill health was etched clearly on Anne's face. Jane tried to divert her. "Maybe you should try to find a woman broker. Someone who would give credit for your intelligence where it is due."

"I was thinking the same thing," Anne said, a small smile creeping onto her lips. "I know of someone who is not even in the field yet but who gives advice to many people, both her friends and several people where she works, and they do quite well. I was thinking of someone like her."

Jane shook her head. "I'm not licensed."

"Then I want you to get licensed."

"I can't just go out and get a license. I would need an affiliation with someone who has a seat, and I can't possibly afford it."

Anne scowled. "I didn't realize… Well, you'll just have to find a way. Maybe Pres—"

"No."

"Why? Because he broke your heart?"

"He did not. We were never in love."

"But you might have been, if things had turned out differently."

It was uncanny how Anne had always seen that possibility. But Jane had lost any chance she might once have had with Prescott. She still remembered the look on his face when she would not hug him goodbye when he left for the war, and the feel of his lean, muscular body when he returned. But the look of betrayal on his face when he found out about Z.Z. still appeared in her mind like a nightmare, one of her own making. "It was my fault. I wasn't honest with him. If I had been, things might have been different." If only, Jane thought for about the millionth time.

"Yes, you and he could be old marrieds by now, with several children. As it is, neither of you has any."

Bristling at that, Jane put her empty tea cup and saucer down on the coffee table. "Ellen is my child. She couldn't be closer to my heart if I had borne her myself." She glanced over at the picture on Anne's piano, of herself and Ellen, smiling at Ellen's sixth birthday party only a month before.

Although it did not show in the picture, there had been ten of Ellen's playmates at the party, even with all the polio scares. Naturally they had held it outside, to minimize any danger, and the plans for a wading pool had been scrapped. They had set up a pin-the-tail-on-the-donkey game, which had the children both bewildered and delighted. The pool would have been, as Mrs. McGill said, "just asking for trouble." Every morning, she told Ellen not to get too tired, stay away from puddles, and inform her immediately if she had a headache. Ellen was not too clear on the concept of a headache, but she always assured Mrs. McGill she would tell her when she got one.

Anne nodded. "That's true, and I'm sorry. But you have to admit, Pres has no children. And from the looks of things every time I see them, no love for his wife."

For once, Jane did not change the subject immediately. Even though talking about him hurt, she felt the need to satisfy her curiosity, just this time. Hearing anything about him brought her a tiny bit closer, somehow. "So tell me," she said, leaning back into the sofa cushions, "why does he stay with her?"

"Because he is nearly as stubborn as you. Pride is a terrible thing in a person, when it keeps him from happiness, and pride is what makes him keep his promise to be married to that witch. But at least he respects it in others."

"What are you talking about?"

"He understands your pride. That's why he never told anyone he was the one who paid Martin off. But his business partner blurted it out the other day, after I said something unkind about Prescott's treatment of you."

Jane was on her feet. "What are you saying?"

Anne sucked in her breath. "I think I said too much."

"You can't stop now. Did you just tell me Prescott Weaver paid Martin to agree to drop his parental rights?"

"Yes."

Feeling as if the floor had just dropped out from underneath her, Jane sat back down. For years now she had wondered what made Martin come to his senses and realize that Ellen belonged with Jane, and the truth was he had been paid off to agree to give up his child. And it was all done behind Jane's back, by a man who had— She could not believe it.

"You've known this for a few days?"

"Yes. I should have told you immediately. But I promised I wouldn't."

Jane tried to digest the information, but it made little sense. "What right did Prescott have to do that?"

"If he hadn't, you could have lost Ellen."

"Never! I would have found a way."

"Oh, really? You, who refused to take gifts, who only wanted to borrow what she could hope to someday repay? Wasn't your happiness and Ellen's worth more than that? Or was your pride worth the most?" Anne stopped for a moment as tears filled her eyes. "Life is too short. You shouldn't waste it standing on principles. I thank God I never wasted a minute, not a precious second, with Schuyler."

"That's different," Jane said. The look in Anne's eyes told her that conceding the point would be charitable. "But I'll take it under advisement." She had more than enough to think about. How could she repay Prescott Weaver? How could she face him? And how much had he paid Martin?

Her head whirled, but she would not let on to her friend how upset she was.

Anne scowled. "I can see you're still unwilling to discuss this."

"What would be the point?" It wasn't as if there was any hope for a future.

"Fine," said Anne. "Have it your way. Will you try

to find a way to get affiliated with the stock exchange? Both the Big Board and the Curb would be useful."

Jane was impressed by Anne's knowledge of the distinction. Stalling for time, she said, "I heard they are changing the name of the Curb to The American Stock Exchange."

"Oh? That sounds better, somehow, for a woman. 'The Curb' makes one think of the gutter." She paused for a moment but went right back to her quest. "So, can you do it?"

"I'll see what I can do."

"Thanks," said Anne. "Oh, and please don't tell Prescott what I told you."

"I'm not likely to be talking to him anytime soon."

****

Ellen smiled when Jane came home. "Let me show you the picture I made, Mommy." She put a piece of paper on the table.

Two stick figures were drawn on it, one tall and one short, with triangle skirts. The small one had black straight hair, and the tall one had yellow curly hair. Another figure, lying down, floated over their heads. "That's my first mommy," Ellen explained, pointing to the floating person. "And here we are. You," she pointed to the tall figure, "and me. Isn't it good?"

"It's wonderful. Where should we hang it?"

"Grandma said we should put it in a place of honor. What's honor?"

Jane laughed. Mrs. McGill, whom Ellen called Grandma, talked a lot about honor. The woman was a model of honor and decency. If not for her, Ellen's early years would have been much more complicated. As it was, they were almost as natural as those of the other children in the neighborhood. It was true Ellen's mother worked, unlike most of the other moms, but her family life was as normal as anyone's.

Looking deep into her daughter's chocolate brown eyes, so like Olivia's, Jane said, "Honor means someone who did something very respectable or something special. And your picture is very special, so we'll put it right on the wall over the sofa."

Ellen beamed. "Why were you so late coming home, Mommy?"

"I stopped off at Anne's."

"How is Irene? She must be so sad that her daddy is gone."

Jane wrapped her arms around Ellen. The child, as young as she was, understood about Schuyler's death. And she regarded Irene as an equal, a rather large six-year-old. "She's sad, honey," said Jane. "But they'll be all right. We'll make sure they are."

"Is Schuyler with my first mommy?"

"I hope so. They were great friends." The thought was a comfort to Jane, who missed her sister terribly. She still felt guilty that she had been so busy while Olivia was caught in the grip of her madness. If only she had gone with her to the doctor's office. But as everyone had told her since, no one could have predicted that Olivia would do what she did.

Jane squeezed her eyes shut to blot out the waking nightmare. It must never touch this precious child. But someday, Jane knew, she would figure out that she was supposed to have a father too.

Ellen had never really asked about her father, Martin, but when she did, Jane had to have a story prepared. What it would be, short of saying he was dead too, eluded her. She only hoped that day of reckoning was far off.

The thought of that brought back the knowledge of who had paid him to disappear. Jane sat rigidly on the sofa, trying not to think about it.

"I'm going to draw a picture for Irene," Ellen said. "I'll make it happy so she can be happy."

"That's a good idea, sweetheart," Jane told her. "I'll sit right here next to you."

Ellen was well into her drawing when Mrs. McGill came out of the kitchen and picked up her house keys. "What happened to you?" she asked.

"Why do you ask?"

"You have a look on your face that I haven't seen since, well, let's say for a very long time. What happened?"

Jane knew when she had seen that look. It was the day Prescott Weaver came to dinner, only to rush out and never come back. "I don't know what you're talking about."

"Then just tell me who you were thinking about. Be honest."

"Yes, Mommy. That's what you always tell me."

"Okay. I was thinking about Prescott Weaver. Anne told me about something he did."

Mrs. McGill's mouth formed an O. "There isn't much point thinking about him, is there?"

"No, there isn't."

"I'm going now," Mrs. McGill said. "Your dinner is almost ready." She looked at Ellen, who had gone back to drawing. "Our girl is quite an artist, isn't she?"

"She draws from the heart," said Jane. "That's the best crayon."

"I'll draw a picture for you tomorrow, Grandma," said Ellen. She went over and hugged the woman. "Would you like that?"

Mrs. McGill smiled. "Yes. I'm going to go downstairs right now to find a place of honor for your drawing." She turned to Jane. "Don't waste time on things that can't be."

"I won't."

But long after Mrs. McGill had left, Jane was deep in thought.

Chapter Twenty-Five

Regina slammed down her powder puff. Prescott saw her do it through the connecting door between their bedrooms. He had seen that move before, and gritted his teeth. The emphatic way she thrust it back into its container made powder fly, dusting the mirrored table. It meant she was more angry than usual. She had become so bitter these last few years. All his efforts to cheer her up only made her more vindictive, to the point where he had given up altogether.

"We'll miss the first act of the opera," Prescott said, hoping to head off another tirade. Of late, they had been frequent. Reggie complained about everything, from the maids to the cut of meat the butcher had sent. The chauffeur was the latest victim of her ire.

"You didn't seem to care about missing your golf game with my father," Reggie said sarcastically. In the six years of their marriage she had not learned to talk in moderate tones. "And he had several prospective clients set up for you to meet."

"You've already criticized me for that. I explained that I had to go to a funeral. And I had told your father to cancel the game."

"He told you the game was important. It's not like you're willing to spend time with me. You could at least spend time with my father." She paused, letting her resentfulness seep into Prescott's guilty conscience.

But she did not stay quiet for long. "Who was Schuyler Lewis anyway? He wasn't even a client."

"He was the husband of a dear friend of mine, as you well know."

"You care more about Anne Canfield than me," Reggie whined. "Maybe now she's single again, you should marry her."

Prescott found his mind turning immediately to the prospect of marriage not to Anne but to the woman who had stood at her side during the funeral. Jane. She had looked more beautiful than ever, even in grief. Her eyes, so caring and full of love for her friend, had only met his briefly, and when they had, the light in them had died. He knew he was the one who had killed it. But at least she had Ellen. That sacrifice, which had set him back a year on his plan to buy a seat, had been worth every penny. Thank goodness she would never know he had been the one to get rid of that leech Martin Roche. The only other person in the world who knew was his business partner, the one who had carried him for several months after the disbursement. He would forever be grateful to the man.

Reggie had screamed when she heard he still did not have the money for his own seat. The fact that he would not explain why infuriated her. But she had actually managed to cut back on her spending, out of embarrassment, she said, so he was able to buy the seat in 1950. For all of three months, she had been proud of him, but then she had just gone back to her usual nit-picking, criticizing, complaining ways. And now she was complaining again, this time about him.

"I don't know why I put up with you," she said, crossing her room and coming into his. "You haven't even given me a child."

"There is only one way to do that," Prescott said evenly, fighting his frustration and rage. All the years he had spent trying to figure out how to please Reggie, to make her want to have a family, threatened to spill over. But as usual, he fought the urge to tell her what he felt, and how hard it was for him seeing those other men with their children and their smiling wives. She never seemed to care anyway. Instead, he said, "You don't seem willing to do your part."

"I'm not willing? You act like you're fulfilling an obligation, not like a man in love."

What man would not? Prescott wondered. She held him at arm's length, acting as if the feel of his body close to hers was repulsive, and lay in bed like a stone. His images of what a husband and wife would be like together never seemed to coincide with the reality of his wife and himself.

He had experienced more excitement just looking at Jane.

"Maybe I should divorce you for being unable to father a child," said Reggie, derisively.

Prescott thought about it. Reggie's reason was not grounds for divorce, but they both knew how easy it would be to provide them. He knew what that would mean, all the pain, the trumped-up adultery photos to satisfy the courts, such as those Anne and Hugh Canfield had submitted, and the notoriety. But maybe it would be worth it. "If that's what you want."

She looked at him, wide-eyed, and burst into tears. "I can't believe you don't care."

He wondered if she meant that he did not care about losing her. It didn't matter, really, and he was not about to be drawn into comforting her. She had never once comforted him, not when his mother died, nor when his father had a stroke and was left paralyzed. "I'm sure I love you as much as you love me," he said.

Reggie turned off the waterworks. "It would cost you, buster. I would get as much as Anne Canfield got from Hugh."

"Percentage-wise, maybe," said Prescott. "But I don't think you would be as well off. Don't worry, though. I'm sure your father would provide for you, until you found someone else." He was amazed at the turn in the conversation, and excited. Whatever the cost, if he could get free of her, it would be worth it.

She came close to him. "You won't get off that easily. I'm not ready to dump you yet. You promised 'till death do us part.' And you're so damned honorable, you'll keep that promise."

Prescott took a drink after his wife went out of the room. "Damned" was a good word for it.

****

Jane's hand shook as she raised it to knock on the door. She could not believe she was standing in front of Prescott Weaver's office, about to talk to him. No words had passed between them in years.

Something hard inside her kept her from taking normal breaths. It was as if a piece of steel had lodged itself in her chest. She wondered how she would get through the next few minutes.

In answer to her knock, Prescott himself opened the door. He looked at her in astonishment. "C-come in."

"I'm sorry to come without calling first," said Jane. She had tried to call, several times, but got no farther

279

than the third number each time, actually stopping the rotary dial on its return to position on her last attempt.

She looked at Prescott, searching for some sign that he would listen to what she had to say. While he was still undeniably attractive, almost like Cary Grant, she also saw that he was a sadder man. Not sad in the sense of grieving for a friend's husband, as he had been at Sky's funeral, but almost as if he was sad about life in general. Even though she knew his business was successful, as evidenced by his paneled office, finely crafted desk, and Persian carpets, she saw a man who was missing something.

"You don't need to apologize," he said. He motioned her to follow him to his inner office, a much better appointed one than when she'd worked for him. He had moved several years earlier, according to Anne, into this building. "My secretary has gone home or I would offer you some coffee or tea." He took his seat and motioned for her to sit down.

"Prescott," Jane began, hoping she could find the words. Ever since Anne had told her about Prescott's gift, she had looked for the right way to thank him. But no inspiration came. She would just have to say it. "I just learned of what you did for my daughter and me."

"How?"

"It doesn't matter. I had to come and try to tell you how grateful I am."

"It was nothing," said Prescott. He stood up and started pacing. "You would have found a way if I hadn't stepped in. I have faith in you."

Jane had trouble telling what he was thinking, especially since he kept moving around. She went to him and touched his shoulder. "Please. You don't understand. You probably saved our lives by doing what you did. And I didn't even wonder why Martin backed down. What was I thinking?" She shook her head at her own naiveté. "How could I not see that someone must have intervened? Or was I just so desperate I didn't want to see the truth?"

The hard thing that had been in her chest, constricting her breathing, suddenly vanished, and Jane dissolved in tears. "How can I possibly pay you back?"

"Jane," said Prescott, handing her his handkerchief, "don't do this to yourself." He lifted her chin, forcing her to look into his eyes. "It's one of the few things I've done in the past few years that made me proud of myself." He turned away, and when he spoke again, his voice sounded strangely husky. "Please don't diminish it by trying to repay me. It wasn't about money."

"Oh," Jane gasped, putting her hand to her mouth. "Now I've insulted you. I'm only making it worse." She stood up. "I have to go."

"Wait," he said, turning back and taking her arm. He looked right into her eyes, and then at his hand, and let go abruptly. His voice was without emotion when he said, "Don't go while you're upset."

"Prescott," Jane said, barely able to look at him. "Please let me leave. Let me try to keep some of my dignity. God knows I have little enough left."

He turned away again, not even saying goodbye. She slipped out the door.

Not until she was outside in the stairwell did she let her tears flow again. Biting the handkerchief to keep from crying out, she stayed there for a half hour, hoping no one would come by.

When she heard the doorknob rattle and thought

Prescott would be leaving for the day, she darted away, down the stairs and out into the darkened street.

****

"I'm not taking any handouts," said Jane.

Anne shook her head. "That's the same song you've been singing since I've known you. If you don't let someone help you, it will take years to get established. It's already been four months since I asked you to handle my investments."

"I can work for someone, if it means that much to you."

"Prescott?"

"No! There are other brokerage houses."

"Which one will hire a woman? Besides, I thought you wanted your own firm."

"I do. I did. I don't know. I had given up this idea a long time ago. There's Ellen to consider. With my job now, I can spend much more time with her than if I were totally dependent on myself to make my business successful. How would you feel leaving Irene alone all the time? And she's almost an adult."

"Only chronologically," Anne reminded her. Her eyes clouded, and it was as if her thoughts were far away. "I used to dream of her teenage years, before she was born, and I saw…" She looked at Jane and smiled halfheartedly. "But she's happy. What more can I ask for? Not every dream comes true."

Jane knew many other women would have caved in under the mountains of grief Anne had experienced. She had truly loved Hugh Canfield, and his abandonment of her, little by little over the years and finally for good when she insisted she had to bring their daughter home against his wishes, had left a huge hole in her heart. And she had loved Schuyler, whose warmth and love had healed most of the deepest wounds. Now Anne was dealing again with the loss of her long-repressed dreams of bringing her daughter out into society, but it explained why she did not want her friend to abandon her own.

As if for emphasis, Anne added, "And Ellen will be proud of you, when she's old enough to understand."

Jane did not tell Anne she had figured out a way to do it. She did not want to get her hopes up until all the details were worked out. It would mean a lot of juggling, but since she would be starting with just Anne as a client, she could manage. If she could set up an affiliation with a seated broker, she could still keep up with her work for Mr. Dobbin.

"I'll let you know," Jane said. She could not hide the smile on her face.

Her friend did not miss it. "Good."

Chapter Twenty-Six

"Jane," said Mr. Dobbin, stepping into the small cubicle that was her office, "there is something we must discuss."

Jane looked up from her double-entry ledger. She could tell by his tone that whatever he wanted to say was serious. A knot of fear about what it might be gnawed at her all the way to his office.

"Sit down," he said, seating himself behind his desk. He looked sad, and his eyes were watery.

Jane leaned forward. "What's wrong?"

"I want to talk to you about getting a replacement. It's time for you to move on."

She leaped to her feet. "What are you talking about? Why do you want me to leave?"

"Please, Jane," said Mr. Dobbin, holding up his hand. "Don't think I want you to leave. But you must pursue your dream."

Jane took a moment to try to calm herself. "Don't you know that my dreams are not as important as my family? You are part of my family. I couldn't leave you."

"I'm not asking you to forget about me," said Mr. Dobbin with a weak smile. "Please. This is so hard. I don't know how I'm going to stand not seeing you every day, not having your ideas and opinions. Without them this place would have closed a year after the war.

But you have always wanted to be in the market, and now it's time."

Shaking her head and forcing a smile, Jane said, "I am doing just that. I've been doing it for a while. You know all about it, it was the only topic at last Sunday's dinner."

"That's what I mean. You should have seen your face. You were more than fascinated. It all made perfect sense to you, the rhythms of the market, far more than it did to me. You will make a lot of money when you have your own business, and so will your happy clients."

"I don't need that," said Jane. "Not if it means leaving you."

Mr. Dobbin pulled out a handkerchief and wiped his eyes. "We'll still see each other. And you don't have to leave right away. First you'll train someone, and hopefully make a smooth transition to being a stock broker full time. And you can expand, following up on your idea of getting middle-class people involved. You said yourself that it seems unfair only the rich can get richer."

"All of that is true," said Jane, thinking about the many people afraid of losing their savings the way their parents had. To help them overcome their fears and enter the market, they needed someone who had gone through the same things, someone like her, so they could invest for their futures.

She realized she'd felt pulled away, bit by bit, from Mr. Dobbin and his business. "Have you forgotten my fiasco with investments when I was trying to build a nest egg for Z.Z. and his father?" She swallowed, feeling as if a bad taste had gotten into her mouth.

Mr. Dobbin smiled. "No, honey, I haven't."

"Then why are you pushing this?"

"I know I can't replace your father," he said, "but I must act just as responsibly. This is hurting me more than it will you. It's for the best."

Jane turned to leave, knowing he was right. It was a risk, but one she had to take, now or never.

"Jane," he said, stopping her in her tracks. "There is something I want you to do as your first official deal."

Something about the way he said it put Jane back on her guard. "What is it?"

"I want you to arrange for me to buy back the outstanding stock in this company."

"You already have a controlling share. Why do you want to stretch your resources and buy it all?"

His sheepish smile told her as much as his words. "I never really wanted it to be publicly held. The company is financially able to stand on its own, with a nice cushion for further expansion. I don't like having to answer to the shareholders."

Jane had only heard the first part of his statement. "You went through all of that just so I could take it public?"

"Yes and no. It was necessary for our expansion to raise capital. I just picked the way that would give you the most pleasure."

Jane's tears were ready to fall. "You've given me so much—too much."

Mr. Dobbin shook his head. "No more than you've given me, tenfold."

****

Anne put down the dividend statement Jane had

given her. "I knew I made the right choice," she said. "You've done very well with my investments. And from what I hear, you're doing well for a lot of people."

Jane nodded, modestly keeping quiet.

"I remember Hugh saying it was too bad you weren't a man."

"It might have been easier," Jane said.

"Maybe. A man wouldn't have needed to hold down a full-time job while starting a second one. And that's all on top of being both mother and father to Ellen."

With a shrug, Jane looked for a way to change the subject. She did not want to think of Ellen's father.

"I can't believe she's almost eight already," Anne said. "She'll be in high school before you know it."

"Not exactly."

"So what are your plans for her birthday?"

"We'll have the same five or six children," said Jane. "And this year, we'll have a three-foot-deep pool where the victory garden used to be. I've arranged to have a swim party."

"But what about the polio?"

"Everyone has been vaccinated," Jane reminded her. "We don't have to worry about it anymore. But there is a problem."

"What?"

"I got a letter. From Martin."

Anne's mouth dropped open. "What did he say?"

"That he wants to see Ellen."

"No! He gave up all his rights to her."

Nodding, Jane said, "I told him that."

"You talked to him?"

"I called to tell him he can't see her. And he told

me that if I refused, he would tell her I had my boyfriend buy her for me."

"That's a lie!"

Jane sighed. "Of course it's a lie. I told you no good would come of it."

"Does he want her back? Why aren't you panicking?"

"No. He doesn't want her back. It seems he will be passing through New York, and he just wants to see her. I told him he could come by one morning as she is leaving for school."

"Who will you say he is?"

"I won't say. I don't even think she'll notice him passing on the street."

"Did he say where he's been?"

"No. And I didn't ask. I really don't care. He hasn't once sent her a note or anything. Or even asked me about her. Maybe he's just curious."

"School doesn't start for weeks," said Anne.

"Right." She let down the strong front she had been struggling to maintain and wrung her hands together. "I hope he changes his mind."

****

But he did not. Martin showed up on the first morning of school. Jane stayed home to take Ellen herself, something she did every year on the first day of school, and as they walked out the front door, she spotted him.

He had changed. All the swagger seemed to be gone, and he looked pale. His clothes were worn, seedy. It seemed he had not had a new suit since the ones Olivia bought him.

He did not live up to the agreement. "Hello, Ellen,"

he said, as they passed him.

Her dark brown hair, in long braids on either side of her head, hung down the sides of her puffy dress sleeves as she looked up. Puzzled but still polite, she responded, "Hello." Then she looked at Jane, for explanation.

Jane opened her mouth, but no words came out. Her hands balled into ineffective fists. Who would she say this was?

"I'm a friend of your father," said Martin.

Ellen cocked her head. "You look like a picture I have of him, but different."

Biting her lip, Jane waited.

Martin smiled. "You are a smart little girl."

"We have to go," said Jane. "Ellen, you don't want to be late for school."

"But I want to talk to—to my father's friend. Please, Mommy."

Shooting him a hateful stare, Jane repeated, "We have to go to school, Ellen. You don't want to be late."

Ellen held back. Jane had little choice but to relent. "He can come by after dinner. You can talk to him then."

****

Jane fretted all day about Martin. She called her lawyer, who said he had no legal claim to Ellen. But that did not stop Jane from worrying. And by seven o'clock, when Martin came to their apartment, she was so tense her teeth hurt. In anticipation of his visit, Ellen had gone through a box in the back of her closet, in the room that used to be Olivia's, and found the picture Jane had saved from the pawnbroker, of Olivia and Martin at their wedding. Ellen was beaming with pride when she showed it to him.

She looked at it and then him. Cocking her head, she said, "Why did you go away, Father?"

"I couldn't take care of you."

You wanted the money more, Jane thought.

"Mommy could, so she took me?"

Martin looked puzzled. "Mommy died."

"No, that was my first mommy. My second mommy is her sister. She became my mommy."

Martin raised his eyebrows. "Is that how she explained it? What did she say about me?"

Ellen furrowed her brows. "What did you tell me, Mommy?"

Jane had never really told Ellen anything. The child had not asked. She had always thought that one day, when Ellen was much older, she would explain about how some people should not be parents. But that time had not come yet. How could she tell this eight-year-old that her father had not loved her enough to do whatever it took to take care of her? Or that if he could not, he could at least have found a way to stay in her life?

"I think you should hear it from his own lips," Jane said, unable to even say "your father" in front of Ellen.

Martin narrowed his eyes, the way he used to when he had to explain to Olivia why he had not found a job, or did not have his paycheck, or did not show up until four in the morning. Jane knew a lie was coming, but she was helpless to prevent it.

"I had to go away. I missed you terribly, but it couldn't be avoided."

Ellen stared at him for a long moment but remained silent. Jane wished she could know what the child was thinking.

Furrowing her brows, Ellen said, "Will you be leaving again?"

"No. Well, maybe, but I'll come and see you again. If that's all right with your mother."

He looked at Jane, as if challenging her to say, in front of Ellen, that he could not see her.

What could she say? Did she want the responsibility of sending Ellen's father away?

"Let us know when you'll be in town again," Jane said, moving toward the door. Martin stood up himself, patted Ellen on the head, and said good night. He even gave Jane a peck on the cheek. She fought the urge to wipe it away, mindful she was in front of the child.

After he left, Ellen made no move to get into her pajamas, even though it was past her bedtime. Jane did not know what to say to her. She felt an explanation was in order, but the truth would contradict Martin, and this was not the time.

"Why didn't he ever send me a letter, Mommy?"

Jane shook her head. The child truly was bright.

"I don't know."

"Did you tell him he couldn't?"

"No."

Ellen bit her lip. But she didn't say anything, and she went to her room.

Jane was left to wonder where this would all lead.

****

Two months later, after an especially good run on the market, Jane was in a position to establish her own independent firm. She swore she would never again take a risk with her money, and taking a risk with someone else's was naturally out of the question. She depended on word of mouth, when she opened her office, and it took quite some time to build a client base.

One of her first clients was Frances, her assistant at Mr. Dobbin's company. The forty-five-year-old woman, who had never married, came into the little office Jane had rented, clutching her bank book.

"I've never done this before," she said nervously. "My father always told me it was a big mistake."

Jane knew that Frances had cared for her elderly parents for years, giving up her own opportunities to marry. Now that they were gone, she was alone in the world.

"But I decided I would take the chance, as long as it was with you," she added.

"We'll be very conservative," Jane told her. "I wouldn't do anything that will risk your savings."

"You have to do something, though," Frances said. "With what I have saved, I won't have to worry, but I'll never get to take a cruise or see Paris, either. I want to be able to do that someday."

She and Jane discussed various types of stocks for an hour, and when Frances left she promised to tell her friends about Jane's new business. Within a few weeks, five of them came in, and in turn, they sent more people.

As promised, Jane was very conservative with her clients, most of whom were housewives investing the tiny amounts of money they had managed to save from their husbands' household expense allotments. Her conservatism was a good choice, because right after that the stock market, which had been booming for years, developed a nine-month case of jitters. Jane nervously scanned the ticker tape hourly, fretting whenever a stock she had recommended dropped a fraction of a point, but her clients were confident enough to follow her recommendation not to sell hastily. And when it was over, her business was on a steady upward course.

She had repaid all her debts, and her investment of the one hundred dollars the teachers' pension fund had sent when Olivia died had grown substantially. Although it was in her name, since Olivia had forgotten to change the beneficiary's name to Martin's, it was entirely earmarked for Ellen's college fund. Since she did not do high-risk investments, or urge her clients to buy and sell frequently, she did not earn as much as her counterparts with Wall Street addresses. Yet her penny pinching enabled her to accumulate a bit of a nest egg.

But with all she had, she felt something was unfinished, someone not repaid, and it troubled her for weeks.

At the same time, life moved along smoothly. Mrs. McGill took excellent care of Ellen, filling in for Jane whenever necessary. Jane paid her a handsome salary, even though she tried to refuse it.

"I love taking care of Ellen," she would say. "It's like having a grandchild of my own."

Jane knew it was one of Mrs. McGill's big disappointments that her own son had not lived to marry and have a family. That was why she took care of the Baldwin girls, as she used to call them. No one mentioned that she did not start doing that until she got over disapproving of them. "Two girls living on their own like that," she had said to some of the older neighbors. "It isn't right."

Jane had come to love the older woman, whom she

could not visualize without her perpetual polishing rag for the banister. And it finally hit her—that was the debt she had not repaid.

It took some doing but she got it accomplished. On a sunny Saturday in May 1957, Jane called Mrs. McGill and invited her to lunch. They spent hours afterward, shopping and talking, even going to a museum, before they got home. Ellen had returned from her friend's house, and she greeted them outside the apartment building, smiling reassurance that the mission was complete.

"Mommy has a surprise for you," said Ellen.

Mrs. McGill wiped her face with her handkerchief. "I'm so tired, I can't take anything more."

"Don't worry, Grandma, you'll like this." Ellen opened the front door and stepped aside for Mrs. McGill to look within.

All the neighbors were standing there, many of whom had lived there since before the war. The others, relative newcomers, had already heard the tale. And all of them wore huge smiles.

It took Mrs. McGill a moment before she realized what they were smiling about. There, in the place where the wooden banister had been, was a new brass one, almost identical to the one Mrs. McGill had given up for the war effort. A string with a new polishing rag attached hung from the rail.

Mrs. McGill clapped her hands to her face. "I never thought—" Then she burst into happy tears and hugged Jane and Ellen. In the end, she had hugged everyone in the building, including several dogs.

Chapter Twenty-Seven

Before she knew it, Ellen was finished with sixth grade, having skipped third. She was growing up way too fast.

Ellen had seen her father once a year since her meeting with him. He seemed to remember her around the time of her birthday, although he was hazy on the date, and he would send a note saying he would stop by during the second week of September. It was the same every time. He asked Jane if he could take Ellen out alone, and Jane refused. They often just sat in the living room talking, with Jane hovering in the kitchen nearby. Many times it seemed to Jane that Martin sounded as if he were whining, or complaining, but she could not hear his words, nor did she wish to. At those times, Ellen seemed impatient to go out, and Jane went with them. It was very awkward, especially when people looked at them and smiled as if they were a family.

Before Ellen's tenth birthday, Martin came to Jane's office. "I want to take Ellen to see my mother. She's her granddaughter, you know."

Jane ignored his defiant attitude. "I've made it a point to take Ellen to visit your mother every year at least twice. But if you like, I'll invite Mrs. Roche to come see us this time."

"That's asking a lot. She'd have to take so many trains."

"I'll pay for a cab, if she likes. I'll talk to her about it when I ask her to come."

Martin seemed about to say something, but he stopped. He cleared his throat. "I asked Ellen what she wants for her birthday. It's a real expensive porcelain doll, and I'd really like to give it to her. She should have a pretty doll."

Jane did not comment. It struck her as odd that Ellen would have asked for such an expensive gift.

"But it is real pricey," Martin continued, "and I don't have the cash right now, what with the hard times and all. I don't want to disappoint her."

The whole country was experiencing prosperity, but Martin seemed unaware. "I'd pay you back," he said. "Just think of Ellen's face when she opens it." Jane knew she would never see it again, but she gave him the money. Ellen's happiness was the only thing that mattered.

When it was time to open the presents, the porcelain doll he'd promised was a poor rubber-faced substitute. Jane vowed that if Martin asked her to fund a gift in the future, she would buy the present and wrap it herself.

Ellen looked puzzled at the gift but did not say anything. "Tell your grandmother about how well you did in school last year," Martin prompted Ellen, by way of diverting attention from the doll.

"She told me all about it, Marty," said Mrs. Roche. "We can't wait around for you to show up to see each other, you know."

Mrs. Roche had turned out to be quite fond of Ellen, and the child enjoyed her. Their relationship was not close like the one Ellen and Mrs. McGill shared, but it was solid. She had even come to respect Jane, and allowed her to invest some of her meager savings so that she would have an easier time in her old age.

The weakest link between them was Martin. After he and his mother left, Jane commented on the lovely sweater Mrs. Roche had knitted for Ellen.

She did not mention the doll, but Jane could tell she was not happy with it. Jane took Ellen in her arms and said, "If you really want the porcelain doll, I'll get it for you as soon as I can manage it."

Ellen stood back and looked up at her mother. "What porcelain doll?"

"Martin said you told him about one." She did not mention that he had asked her to pay for it.

"I'm really not interested at all in dolls," Ellen confided. "But don't tell Martin that. I don't want to hurt his feelings."

Mrs. Roche suffered a stroke six months later and complained because her son never came to see her in the hospital. Jane brought Ellen to visit the old woman in the convalescent home in the Bronx as often as possible, but neither Ellen nor her grandmother ever talked about Martin to each other again.

On Ellen's eleventh birthday, Martin visited, although he had not even called since her last birthday, and asked what his little girl would like for a present.

They were standing in Jane's living room. All the windows were open, letting in the lovely September air. Jane was about to go to the kitchen so they could have some privacy, but Ellen said, "Please stay, Mommy."

Jane returned to the couch and sat down. She watched Martin's face. He never seemed comfortable with Ellen, and never showed her any affection.

"I heard the girls are playing with hula hoops," Martin said. "Would you like one?"

Ellen, by now nearly as tall as Olivia had been, sighed. "What I'd really like from you is..." She paused. Then she straightened up, and said in a shaky voice, "To never see you again."

Martin opened his mouth and closed it several times, as if expecting words to come out. Finally he was able to ask, "Why?"

"Because you say mean things about my mommy," Ellen said, "and you never care about me more than once a year."

Ellen took Jane's hand and faced her mother. "My mommy loves me and takes care of me, and she made her ship come in. Not only that, she invested the money Mother Olivia left when she died, so that I can go to college."

She turned back to her father. "Everybody loves Mommy. All you've ever done is say nasty things to me about her. And I don't want to hear it ever again. Goodbye, Martin."

She went into her bedroom and shut the door.

"This is your fault," Martin growled. "You've turned her against me."

"She is speaking her own mind."

"She's a child. She doesn't have opinions of her own."

Jane shook her head. "You don't know a thing about Ellen."

"I'm not going away," Martin said defiantly. But in a less confident tone, he added, "I can't. I have to stay in town."

The way he said that convinced Jane there was

something coming. In hopes of deflecting it, she said, "You don't have to come around here, though, do you? You have no legal rights with Ellen, you know."

"Yeah, I know. Listen, I wouldn't stay in this slum of a city if I could pay off some of my bills. Then I could go away, maybe California or someplace like that."

"You could probably pay off your debts if you got a job," Jane said.

"Nah. No one is hiring. I don't need that much, just a coupla thousand." Then, as if a light bulb went off in his head, he stood up straighter and looked Jane in the eye.

"That money Olivia left shoulda gone to me."

Jane caught her breath. "That's Ellen's money."

"Nah. It should be mine. I was the one married to that crazy bitch. I deserve it, after what I hadda put up with." He narrowed his eyes. "I could take you to court. They'd give it to me. I was her legal husband when she died."

"There isn't that much," Jane said. "She only left a hundred dollars." Which, Jane knew, Martin would have gambled away in a month.

"But you're a whiz at making money for the little people," Martin said. "I got ears, and I heard all about it. So you must've turned it into a coupla thousand dollars by now."

"It's tied up in the stock market. If I sell it now, it will lose a lot of its future value."

"Too bad."

Jane sighed. "If I give you two thousand dollars, will you honor Ellen's wishes and not contact her again, as well as give up claims to Olivia's legacy?"

Jane could not be certain, but it looked like Martin was salivating. "Yes."

She wrote him a check with a limited endorsement. Not surprisingly, she had to explain to him that signing it made it a legal document giving up all future claims.

After he left, Jane realized two things. Not only had Ellen gotten rid of her father, she was not a little child anymore. It was a shock for Jane, who had not realized how grown up her daughter had become.

When Ellen began to talk of accepting the scholarship she had been offered to an exclusive girls' boarding school the following year, Jane had to consider it seriously. She was so bright and so mature. The thought made Jane's heart ache, but she owed it to Ellen to think about it.

****

There were several other rocks in the road around that time. Jane's business was successful, but some of her friends needed her.

Mr. Dobbin was ill. He was over seventy-five, and his health had been failing. Every breath he drew was difficult, but he insisted on going to work each day. His doctor warned him that he needed to rest, but he could not let go.

Jane suggested he sell the business. She had struggled to find the words to help him let it go. "Your children don't want it, and you can't do it anymore. If you sell it, you can relax, and maybe go visit them. They've invited you several times." The relationship between Mr. Dobbin and his children had healed a bit since he'd called and begged their forgiveness for not being there when they needed him. "We'll find a new owner who will keep your staff together."

"Would you like to come back and take it over? It should be yours, after all. Without you it would be nothing."

Jane hugged him. "I can't. I have my own business now."

It took a lot of persuasion, but he finally sold it, realizing an enormous profit. After signing the final papers, he shook his head in amazement. "All those years ago," he marveled, "when I was nearly penniless, I never imagined I would end up with millions. And it's all because of you, Jane."

"No, it isn't," she said. "It was your hard work."

Mr. Dobbin's eyes, which watered so easily, filled. "Janie," he said, "for once in your life could you accept responsibility for something good without trying to credit someone else? You never hesitate to take responsibility when something goes wrong."

Jane clung to him, wishing she did not have to ever let him go. "Don't forget you have other family here," she reminded him.

"I won't."

****

One day in late November, Jane's heart was ready to break again.

Anne arrived fifteen minutes late at the restaurant where Jane was waiting, but she did not apologize. That was unusual, to say the least, since Anne was one of the most punctual people Jane knew.

She had aged beautifully, Jane thought, watching her approach. She was nearly fifty, yet she had the smoothest, most wrinkle-free skin. Even her worry lines and her smile lines were invisible. Yet she seemed distracted.

Jane realized all her small talk was falling on deaf ears. She switched to a more pertinent subject. "How's Irene?"

At the mention of her daughter, Anne's face clouded.

Jane's heart jumped. "What's the matter?"

"She's been different lately. At first I thought it was because she had all that trouble with her teeth."

Irene still suffered terribly from gum disease. Most of her teeth had been removed. At twenty-five, she looked like a much older woman, her skin deeply wrinkled.

"How is she different?" Jane asked.

"She's lost her zest. Nothing seems to interest her. I took her to the doctor, and he thinks it's her heart." Tears spilled over onto Anne's cheeks. "He doesn't think she'll live much more than a year. I'm losing her, and there isn't anything I can do about it."

Jane took the news as if she had received a blow to her stomach. "I'm so sorry."

Anne looked across the table at her. She was clear-eyed and determined, even though Jane could see, now that she looked at her closely, that Anne had been crying. "I've made a decision. I'm giving up all my charity work and my place on the opera board. I have to spend every minute I have left with my child."

"You aren't facing this alone," Jane promised. "We'll be with you."

Anne reached over and took Jane's hand. "I couldn't do this without you." She seemed for a moment to be about to say something, but then a sly smile crossed her face. "I won't be able to keep tabs on Prescott, though."

Jane shook her head in exasperation. For so many years she had listened to Anne telling her what she had missed, and how Prescott was doing. "For the last time, I don't care."

"He still misses you. He always asks how you are. And his wife is such a bitch—"

"Anne! Such language."

Anne leaned closer. "I wouldn't be surprised if he hadn't slept with her since their honeymoon. It's no wonder they don't have children."

Jane felt her heart tighten in her chest at the thought. "So why does he stay with her?"

"Rumor has it that she's always sick. I'm sure it isn't serious, because she's never been in the hospital, as far as I know. And her garden, which she keeps herself, is always glorious. You'd think a sick person wouldn't have time to weed. More likely, though, he's too proud to admit he made a mistake."

Jane hated this painful topic, but it seemed to take Anne's mind off Irene, so she stuck with it. "Why would you think I would still be interested in him after all these years? And why do you think he's still wondering about me?"

"I'll answer the second question first. Because he asks about you all the time. And why do I think you're interested in him? Because of your face whenever we talk about him." She looked away, over Jane's shoulder. "I think we can cut some of the speculation," she said.

Jane thought she had lost the thread of the conversation. "What?"

Anne did not answer. She was on her feet.

Jane turned to see why, and she found Prescott

Weaver standing next to her.

He had changed since she last saw him that day at his office. Gray hair showed at his temples, and his face had deepening frown lines. But at just past forty, he was still lean, strong-looking, and his eyes still pulled Jane in the way they had on his first day back after the war.

"It's good to see you, Jane," he said, his voice resonating off the crystal chandeliers. Or at least that was the way Jane perceived it. The sound seemed to envelop her.

"H-Hello, Prescott," she stammered. "How are you?"

"Why don't we sit down?" Anne asked.

Jane was speechless, so she let Anne talk with Prescott. He told them he had just finished lunch with a client and had noticed them on his way out. But all the while he talked, he looked directly at Jane.

She could not deny her heart was racing. But when he asked about Ellen, it felt as if it had stopped cold. The memory of her poor expression of gratitude embarrassed her still. The two of them sat silent, as if unable to say a word to each other.

Anne's clenched fist smacked the table. "I'm going to freshen up. Work this out between yourselves."

Prescott smiled. "I think she's losing patience."

"She's been through an awful lot. Irene is..."

"I know," he replied, staring at the tablecloth. He gritted his teeth, making his cheeks stand out. Then he looked up at her. "Would you have dinner with me some evening?"

"Will your wife be joining us?"

"No. She doesn't do anything with me, unless it's for show." He sounded more than bitter, and Jane thought his lips had taken on the slightest curl.

But Jane did not think it would be proper for her to see Prescott, as much as she wanted to. "I don't think I can do that," she said.

He looked so sad she had to turn away.

When Anne returned just after that, Jane stood up to leave. "Take care, Anne. I'll call you soon. And Prescott"—she looked in his direction—"it was nice to see you."

Chapter Twenty-Eight

Prescott turned the key, willing himself to open the door. This door, this house, had never seemed like home, certainly not a place to go to when he was feeling sick.

And he was feeling awful. Not only was he feverish, but his throat hurt and his head ached. He had no time for this. There was an important conference coming up, and he had been asked to speak. He needed to get some hot tea and a lot of aspirin and blast those germs out of himself.

Pushing open the door, he got a whiff of the polish the maid used to buff the woodwork. Reggie always insisted that it be shined to a high gloss, even though the teak was supposed to have an oiled finish. She was very particular, and harsh on the people she employed to take care of the house. She had seemingly never found one who worked hard enough. "They're all just waiting for a handout," she often said. Prescott had tried to explain that there were better ways of getting work done, but Reggie would never listen.

She never listened at all. In fact, lately, Prescott felt as if he had no one to talk to.

Dragging his feet, he mounted the steps to his bedroom. The past few months, with the ups and downs of the market, would have been filled with pleasure, if he could have been with Jane. Reggie did not care about the stocks at all, except for finding out how many people had come to trade at his post so she could spend his commission. It was hard to believe, but she had become even more self-centered lately, caring little about his opinion on anything. She probably would not even wonder what he was doing home so early. At least he would not have to waste his breath and strain his sore throat trying to explain it to her. In the past year, and certainly since their last big argument, she had become very distant, often turning on her heels if she came into a room and found him there.

A noise from the direction of Reggie's bedroom made him turn toward it instead of his own. He had thought she would be out this afternoon, at the garden club.

He knocked on her door, to tell her he was home, so she would not be frightened. The maid was off this afternoon, it being a Thursday, and Reggie had complained lately of burglaries in the neighborhood.

He opened the door. "Reggie, I'm h—" He broke off. Reggie was in bed with Ralph Taggart. Their startled faces turned to look in his direction, and what Prescott could only describe as rapture on Reggie's face turned to shock.

"I'll be in my room," he said, suddenly understanding so much, the trips to Longwood Gardens that she had supposedly taken on her own and come back so happy from, the phone conversations she broke off when he came into the room, and the lack of feeling for him or willingness to get close. "I'll be packing." He walked into the bathroom they shared, locked the door at her side of the room, swallowed a handful of aspirin, and passed through into his bedroom.

A few minutes later he heard knocking on her bathroom door. "Prescott, you idiot," she shouted. "You've locked the door again."

Ignoring her, he folded several shirts and laid them atop the slacks he had already packed. His suits would have to be packed in a separate case, one that was in storage in the hall closet. He would get that after he finished packing the rest of his things.

A knock on the bedroom door told him Reggie had gone around to the hall. "Prescott, let me in," she said. "Let me explain."

"There is nothing to explain," said Prescott. "You've finally made it possible for me to get out of this god-forsaken marriage."

"You mean a divorce?"

Prescott opened the door to get a look at her face and see the defeat he knew would be there. "Yes, darling, a divorce." He went to the hall closet and pulled out the suitcase he needed. Turning back to his room, he saw his wife's blanched face. "You've finally committed the only act this state considers grounds for it—adultery."

Reggie began to cry. "You wouldn't."

Knowing it was not true, that even in his rage he would never expose her like that, Prescott said, "Oh, but I would. I wouldn't hesitate to accuse you of adultery. How would you like to see that in the papers? How do you think your daddy would feel? And what about Ralph's wife and children?"

Reggie sank down on a leather chair in the corner of the bedroom. "Please. I made a mistake. I can admit that. But you have to give me another chance." She took a step closer to him and put out her hand, as if reaching for him.

He moved away. The aspirins were beginning to ease the pain in his throat, but he was not about to continue talking about this. "I think the best thing for both of us, right now, would be for me to move to my club. We can both think more rationally in the morning."

"I'm not going to let you g—" she was saying as he slammed out the door

He was feeling better, he realized as he carried his cases downstairs. Even with what was probably a case of influenza. His sham of a marriage was nearly over.

****

Mrs. McGill was out of sorts in July of 1960. "She'll be off to boarding school in two months. I'll have nothing to do."

"You've earned a rest."

"I don't want a rest."

"Maybe you should travel. You've been talking for four years about going to visit your sister."

Suddenly it seemed like the most important thing to the landlady. "I should do that. But who will take care of the building?"

Jane smiled. "I will. It seems little enough after all you've done for us." She saw Mrs. McGill's hand, the one that held her polishing rag, twitch. "I'll make sure to polish the banister every day."

Mrs. McGill protested, but only for a moment. In less than a week, she was ready to go.

Anne was visiting the day Mrs. McGill left. She had not been the same since Irene died. She had gotten so thin that Jane was worried about her.

"You could use a trip yourself," Mrs. McGill told

Anne. Jane had already heard the landlady's opinion that Anne could snap out of it if she got out of her apartment, but she was surprised to hear the woman say it to her face.

Mrs. McGill continued, "You're a pretty woman. You should take a cruise." As if by way of explanation, she looked at Jane. "All the gentlemen will flock to her."

Embarrassed, Jane turned to Anne, expecting to find her even more pale and teary-eyed. Instead, she saw a spark of life. "I just might do that," Anne said.

A few weeks later, Anne was set to go. "But I hate leaving all my work behind," she said, looking Jane in the eye. "Could you help me out?"

Jane had never realized how many volunteer positions Anne held. While she had farmed out most of them to her other friends long ago, before Irene died, there were still a few key seats that required what Anne called, "A sensitive, intelligent hand."

"Surely there are people who can fill those positions," said Jane. "I have so much work. Shouldn't someone who doesn't have a job be there?"

"Are you saying it should be someone who was born with a silver spoon in her mouth and has a husband to take care of her?"

Jane was puzzled by Anne's strident tone. She had not heard it before.

"You really shouldn't put yourself down," Anne continued, more softly, but clearly exasperated.

"I'm not. What are you talking about?"

"It's the same thing as always. You don't want to be on the board because the other people went to the best schools, live in the biggest mansions, and belong to the finest clubs. So poor little Janie, standing on her principles, won't associate with them. That's why you let Prescott go."

"It is not! I never let him go. I never had him."

"You would have, if you'd had enough confidence in yourself to notice anything about him other than his pedigree."

Jane could not dispute that. She had not realized how fine a man Prescott was until it was too late. But that fine man had walked out on her when he learned of her promiscuity. And he had never returned. She could not fool herself. Their meeting at the restaurant had proved that. He still considered her a loose woman. Why else would he ask her out without his wife being present? Suddenly the absurdity of the situation got to her.

"Why are you laughing?" Anne asked.

"This is such a ridiculous conversation."

"Look," said Anne, as she packed the last of her trunks, "there is only one committee on which I'd like you to serve."

"What is that?"

"A retarded children's organization. They need your help. If we're ever going to change how people think of children like Z.Z. and Irene, we're going to have to work for it."

That seemed reasonable. Besides, Jane felt she could hold her own, even among a bunch of snooty committee members. In addition, she figured anyone who would have a problem with children like Z.Z. and Irene would not be on such a panel.

"Okay."

"Good, it's all settled. Now we have to talk about

Ellen's clothing for school."

Jane noticed that Anne had a fire in her eyes long missing. "Do you want to go with us to shop?" she asked.

"I want to do more than that. I want to buy everything Ellen needs. She may be going on scholarship, but she will be well dressed."

By the time Anne and Jane finished buying everything on Ellen's school list, from her uniforms to her party dresses, her Lanz nightgowns and bathrobe to her penny loafers and Papagallos, and had packed her trunks lovingly, there was little left to do. They had a farewell lunch at Schrafft's and prepared to go their separate ways.

On September 2, 1960, when Ellen was exactly twelve, she left for boarding school in upstate New York. Anne left for Europe. Mr. Dobbin had moved permanently to Kansas, near his son.

Jane was alone.

Chapter Twenty-Nine

Jane's first committee meeting was two days after Anne sailed for Europe. It was set for five-thirty, so she went over after work.

There were women there from many walks of life, some even bringing their affected children. Jane thought her heart would break, especially when she saw a child of about six who could have been Z.Z.'s brother. He had colorful smudges on the side of his right hand and all the way up his elbow.

"He's so adorable," she said to his mother, who looked to be about Jane's own age. Then she squatted down and smiled into the boy's face. "Do you like to draw?"

The child beamed at her. "Yes!"

"What is your name?" Jane asked, standing back up.

"Tommy."

"Tommy, my name is Jane. It's nice to meet you."

His mother shook Jane's hand. "My name is Marie. It's so nice to meet someone who thinks of my son as a person." She looked around. "Or maybe everyone does, here. It's my first time, and I don't know what to expect."

"It's my first time too," Jane admitted.

"Do you have a child like Tommy?"

Jane bit her lip. "I did," she said, when the danger

of tears had passed. "But he passed away."

"I'm so sorry," said Marie.

They were interrupted by the entrance of another person. The arrival caused the rest of the people in the room to take seats, and Marie, Tommy, and Jane followed suit. It was not until they were seated that she looked at the person facing them in front of the room.

He had aged over the years, and his hair had gone totally gray, but the fire in his eyes that she had seen the first time she met him remained stoked. Lloyd Hammer, still a motivating speaker at almost fifty, addressed the group.

"First of all," he said, "I'd like to welcome the newest members of our group and thank them in advance for all their help. We hope to have a productive year and get the message out. Too many of our loved ones have been relegated to institutions out of ignorance. We've made progress, but there is more to do."

A polite round of applause followed. Jane realized she had just sat, dumbfounded, throughout, only when she noticed Marie staring at her.

"Are you all right?" she whispered.

"Um, yes. It's hot in here, isn't it?"

Marie looked puzzled, but nodded.

When she turned back to the speaker, Jane allowed her mind to wander again. She was furious at Anne. How could she ask her to join a committee, no matter how important, that had Lloyd Hammer as its leader? But she had to suppress that anger, since she was almost positive Anne never knew who it was Jane had been involved with, who had left her alone and pregnant with Z.Z. She berated herself now for not telling Anne it was the man she had met that night they were dancing, so this moment could be avoided.

Leaning close to Marie, she said, "I'm sorry. I've got to leave." Then she moved toward the door, keeping her head averted, so Lloyd could not see her face.

She made it out of the room and rang for the elevator. She put on her coat, even though she was so hot, and wondered how she would tell Anne she could not keep her promise. Maybe she could join another committee.

Her buttons done, she waited for the elevator. If it took another moment, she promised herself, she would go to the stairs. She had to get outside, fast.

"Jane?"

She squeezed her eyes shut. It couldn't be. He was addressing the committee only a minute ago. Would he have just walked out on them?

"Jane." He came to stand beside her. "It's so good to see you. Why did you leave?"

"I have an appointment."

He put his hand on her shoulder and started to turn her toward him. She shrugged it off, and turned, all her anger spilling out.

"How dare you touch me?"

"I'm sorry. But I wanted to talk to you."

"I see things haven't changed. You still think it's all about what you want. It isn't. I'm leaving."

She turned back to the elevator, which had finally arrived, and got on, pushing the button for the ground floor. As the door started to close, Lloyd jumped inside.

"I know about Z.Z.," he said.

Her insides turned to stone—or were they ripping apart? She was not sure, but she knew she could barely breathe. "How?"

"Your landlady. Mrs. McGill. I came by one day to see you, and she told me, or should I say berated me, all about my son. He had died only a few weeks before. I guess she never told you."

Jane was stunned. "She never wanted to hurt me." Her implication was clear, at least in her mind, but Lloyd seemed to miss her point.

"I wish you had let me see him."

"You had no rights," Jane said, feeling her anger build nearly to the breaking point. "You forfeited them all when you married someone else."

"That was a mistake. I did it for my sister."

The elevator had arrived on the ground floor. Jane got off, and turned back to Lloyd, who was still on it. "I know you love your sister—"

He interrupted her. "She died last year."

"I'm sorry," Jane said. "But I loved our son. And you missed the joy of him."

As the door closed, taking Lloyd back upstairs to his meeting, Jane thought she heard him say something about regret. That, Jane thought, about summed it up.

****

The telephone connection from Denmark was scratchy, and Jane had difficulty making out what Anne was saying because of the constant echoes and delays while their voices traveled. "I'm so sorry," came out loud and clear. As did, "I didn't know, I swear. I honestly didn't remember meeting him that night."

That night at the Rainbow Room seemed like centuries ago to Jane, and she wondered how she could have been so blind and gullible with Lloyd.

"I forgive you," Jane said. "Do you forgive me for

quitting that committee?"

"I understand, let's put it that way. Will you consider another one? It really needs your touch."

"Are you sure it won't involve any more nasty surprises?"

"Do you have any more secret paramours?"

Jane laughed. "No. My life is too boring."

"That's why you should work on this other committee. There are really nice people there, trust me."

****

Jane surprised herself by enjoying her work on Anne's second committee. She made several acquaintances and found herself more at ease with the rich and, as she had formerly considered them, indolent. They worked tirelessly to help set up financing and educate people on business, helping them to improve their prospects.

It turned out that many of the women with whom Jane volunteered admired her for the career she had pursued. She also discovered mutual interests with some of them, something she had never dreamed would exist. To her surprise, several of her preconceived prejudices had disappeared.

She was no longer alone. While she missed Ellen terribly, as well as Anne, Mrs. McGill, and Mr. Dobbin, there were so many other people to talk to she had little time to dwell on it. Her weekends, which she had expected to be her loneliest times while her loved ones were away, were still filled with lunches, shopping trips, museums, the theater, opera, and symphony, and the occasional date. And she enjoyed it.

****

In late October, Constance Merriam invited Jane to be her guest at a charity ball, promising she would have a wonderful time. Jane had helped Anne prepare to attend several, but this would be her first. She chose her gown with great care, had her hair and nails done, and got ready to go. It would have been more fun if Ellen or Anne had been there while she got ready, but she called each of them and told them about her dress, shoes, and purse. They both requested calls afterward.

Jane had chosen an ice blue gown with a jewel neck. Instead of the way she usually had it styled, her light brown hair was swept up in a chignon, and, since the hairdresser had put a rinse into it, the few silver strands she had found no longer showed. She put her stepmother's pearls, "real Pearl's fake pearls" as Olivia used to call them, around her throat and wore the long matching earrings.

Anne had long ago begged Jane to "fix yourself up, so the outside matches the inside, and stop saying Olivia was the pretty one." When a saleswoman at Saks suggested a lipstick color, Jane dutifully bought it, along with her first mascara and a new rouge. She had watched Anne often enough to know the blending methods for her new makeup.

Amazingly, Jane's face, which she had always thought of as mottled with freckles, looked smooth and even, once she had applied the foundation and powder. The end result pleased her.

The event was held at the Plaza Hotel, and when Jane arrived, the ballroom was full of tuxedoed gentlemen and jeweled women. She met with the group from her committee and their spouses. Several mouths fell open when she greeted them.

"You look marvelous," Constance whispered. She wore a lace dress in a shade of lavender that Jane adored. "Look, everyone's eyes are riveted on you."

"Would you like a glass of Champagne?" someone asked.

"Why, yes," said Jane, knowing she was blushing. She found herself looking at Douglas, a man she had met through her clients the Madisons. "Thank you."

"You are the prettiest woman here," he said, leaning close to her ear.

Douglas was a nice person, and Jane had enjoyed the time they'd spent seeing *The Sound of Music*. He seemed very interested in her, and while she did not return his ardor, and she had made that clear, they still enjoyed talking with one another. The cocktail hour sped by. Soon it was time to be seated for dinner.

"You're sitting with us, Jane," said Constance as they all walked into the dining room. "We made up almost three tables with just our committee. There will only be one or two outsiders."

Jane had consumed so much Champagne she did not even think about who the outsiders might be. Douglas took her by the elbow and escorted her to her table. But when she was seated, the person next to her was none other than Prescott Weaver. He looked at her, then at the departing Douglas, and stood up.

"I'm sorry," he said, to Constance, his hostess at the table. "I've just realized that I have to leave."

Jane looked at his face and then his hand, which was next to hers on the table as he pushed away and stood. She put hers on top of his and murmured, "Please stay."

He looked down at his hand covered by hers and

then up, deep into her eyes, making her so uncomfortable she almost wished she had not stopped him from leaving. But he sat back down, smiled at the others and said, "Perhaps I can stay, after all."

When the others had resumed their conversations, he leaned close to her. "I have to thank our friend Anne. She arranged this." He sounded somewhat unsure about the outcome of her interference.

Jane had suspected as much. "From Istanbul?" she said, struggling to keep her voice from quavering.

"Is that where she is now?" He smiled. "I think she was in Italy at the time the seating arrangements were made."

"She never said a word to me," Jane said, wondering how she felt about her friend's action. If she had known about it, Jane would not have allowed Douglas to accompany her into the dining room. She suddenly wanted nothing to intrude upon her sitting there, at that moment, with Prescott.

Once Jane had the time to look at Prescott, really look at him, she noticed how remarkably handsome he still was. More so, in a way. His frown lines were still noticeable, but his eyes had a determination in them she had not seen when they met that day in the restaurant. He looked sad.

She felt her heart go out to him. She might have been without a husband all these years, but she had many people to love and who loved her. Prescott did not seem to have had the same good fortune. "Is something wrong?" she asked.

Prescott lowered his head. But he brought it right back up, and looked at her hopefully. "Would you like to dance?"

Putting her hand into his outstretched one, she stood up and smiled. "I would love to."

They danced several waltzes, with Jane becoming more comfortable in his arms as each song progressed. When the music stopped, Jane clung to him, wishing it would continue.

"I think dinner is being served," he said, into her ear. His voice sounded tight. "We should go sit down."

Constance beamed as they rejoined the table. "I see you've met Mr. Weaver," she said. "He has been so wonderful on our committee's board of directors."

Jane was impressed as Constance continued, outlining some of Prescott's activities on the committee's behalf. None of that would do a thing for his business, yet he had done it wholeheartedly. There was so much she did not know about this man.

"Anne told me you had agreed to join the retarded children's committee," he said when they were alone together again. They strolled through the lobby of the hotel, past the jewelry and clothing shops, past the florist and tobacconist, seeking a breath of fresh air on the sidewalk.

"There was a problem, a conflict," said Jane.

"A different philosophy?"

"You might say that."

"I went to a meeting this month. What exactly is it you don't agree with?"

Jane decided to avoid his question as long as possible. "Why would you go to those meetings?" she asked.

"Because it is something that concerns me. I know how difficult it was for Anne, and for you."

Jane did not say anything. She was trying too hard

to fight her tears.

"I realized, too late," said Prescott, "what a mistake I had made. I could have been a good husband to you, and a good father." He turned Jane to face him. "I have chastised myself for my hotheadedness every day for the past ten years." He laughed, but it was harsh and humorless. "First it took me nearly five years to grow up enough to realize my foolish pride," he added, to explain the passage of over fifteen years since he'd walked out of her apartment in a rage.

"I made my share of mistakes, too," said Jane.

"Don't berate yourself. It's happened to many people. You trusted the wrong person. If I ever get my hands on him, I'll make him see—" He broke off. "What's the matter?"

Jane was thinking about Prescott attending the retarded children's committee meetings. If he knew Lloyd Hammer had contributed to their separation for all these years, Jane was afraid of what he might do. "I don't need you to defend my honor. Please, forget about it." She looked up into his eyes. "Can we start over?"

Prescott took her hand. His voice was husky when he said, "I think we had better go back inside."

Maybe she had presumed too much about what he was saying. Maybe he just wanted to establish a friendship. But Jane didn't want to go inside and have to make conversation. She wanted to be alone with Prescott. The thought sent shivers down her spine.

"Are you cold?" he asked. He took off his dinner jacket and draped it over her shoulders. As he did, his hand brushed against her exposed collarbone, and she felt weak in the knees.

Chapter Thirty

Anne's promise to have Prescott seated with Jane had let him spend hours fantasizing about this evening. Tonight, his dreams had materialized. When he held Jane while they were dancing, he was the closest to bliss he had been since his return from the war.

Now, alone with her for the first time in decades, it was nearly torture having her here next to him. Those soft curls escaping from her hairstyle caused a long-forgotten itch to touch them, even after so much time and so much history. The years seemed to drop away, and he remembered how he'd felt when he came back from Europe, how she had looked and how she had felt when he held her close then. If only she wanted him. But it was so late for that.

She stood beside him looking quite small in his coat, and vulnerable in the dim light of the hotel lobby. He had to find a way to keep her close to him.

"Let's take a hansom ride," he said. "We'll go through the park."

"Prescott, how will we explain our absence to our hosts?"

"Don't worry," he said. "Leave it to me. Come inside to get your coat, and I'll go make our excuses."

He knew he was nearly babbling when he said good night to their table, where the main course had just been served, and hoped Jane would not be annoyed that he had said she was coming down with a virus.

They snuggled down beneath wool blankets in the cab. For several minutes neither spoke, and the only sound was the clopping of the horse's hooves in the dark park. Prescott could feel Jane beside him, and he wanted so much to kiss her it hurt. But he was afraid.

"We've let so much time pass," he said, thinking out loud. "Why were we so stubborn?"

****

"Stubborn?" Jane asked, wondering why he sounded so miserable. Until then she had been experiencing profound joy, encircled as she was in his arms. She wished more than anything she could make this moment last forever.

"You know what I mean," he said. He tilted her chin up to his, and she could feel his breath. "I've never stopped having feelings for you."

She caught her breath at his admission. Maybe it was time for her to be honest too. She had always loved him. But so much time had gone by.

The ride was over too quickly. Prescott helped her from the carriage but held her tight even after her feet were on the ground. "I'm sorry," he said, as if embarrassed. "Let me take you home."

He hailed a cab, and they drove to Brooklyn. Telling the cabby to wait, he walked her up to her apartment and took her hands in his. "Will you join me for dinner?"

Jane was grateful for the dark hallway, because she knew she was blushing. "I already have."

"No, I mean tomorrow, and the next day and every day after that. Will you?"

****

In just a few weeks, Jane realized he was completely part of her very soul. At that moment, she stopped cold.

"What's wrong?" Prescott asked. They had been walking through Central Park, enjoying the mid-November sunshine streaming through the leafless trees.

Jane stared at him. He was hatless, like John Kennedy, the president-elect, and the sun shone on his face. "Prescott, I—"

He stopped her and led her to a bench. They sat down, but he immediately moved off the bench and knelt on one knee in front of her. Pulling a Tiffany box from his top coat pocket, he said, "I never dared hope I would find my way back to you, but miraculously, I have. Will you make me the luckiest man in the world and marry me?"

"Yes!" She took his face in her hands and kissed him. A small group of bystanders began to clap.

Pulling him back up onto the bench, Jane buried her burning face in his shoulder.

She waited until the crowd moved away. Swallowing hard, she said, "But I'm too old—"

"To have children? I don't need children. I want you. Besides, Ellen is a wonderful girl. Anne always says so."

Jane laughed. She had only been worried that she was too set in her ways to marry, but his words caused tears of relief and hope to run from her eyes.

****

"Ellen," Jane said, "I would like you to meet Prescott Weaver."

She was adorable. Prescott recognized her

similarity to Olivia, whom he'd first met when she was not much older than Ellen was now. Her long dark hair shone in the sunlight. But the way she looked at him, with those large, dark brown eyes, was more like the way Jane assessed people, forthright and open.

Ellen looked up at him and then at her mother. "Welcome to our family, Mr. Weaver."

"Please call me Prescott. If that's all right with your mother."

"Of course," said Jane. "Whatever is comfortable."

Ellen scowled, wrinkling her dark eyebrows. "How about Uncle Prescott? That sounds more related."

"That's a deal."

Prescott realized Jane had been holding her breath when it came out in a relieved rush. He put out his hand and Ellen shook it, sealing the agreement.

It seemed as if fifty young girls came to say goodbye to Ellen while she and Prescott were packing up the car. Ellen proudly introduced each one to her Uncle Prescott. It took much longer to leave than he had expected, but he didn't have the heart to rush her along.

Throughout the Thanksgiving weekend, Prescott saw Jane and Ellen almost continuously during waking hours. Their conversations ranged from discussion of the recent election to the Cold War to questions about countries Prescott had visited and places Anne was scheduled to see. They also spoke of pets and horses. Ellen was a charming child, very intelligent and interested in the world around her. The school she attended was obviously doing an excellent job.

Unlike some children Prescott had met, Ellen neither shied away from talking to adults nor monopolized a conversation. She was very grateful when he took her to her first basketball game at Madison Square Garden. He was able to get seats close to the floor, and Ellen sat, in her hat and gloves, transfixed, watching as Ray Felix made foul shots. And on the way home, she reached out her hand and put it into his. He could not speak for five minutes.

****

Ellen confided to Jane before going back to school, "I like him a lot. I can barely wait for the wedding."

Jane hugged her daughter. "Me too."

****

Jane walked up and down the corridor outside the judge's office in the Newark, New Jersey courthouse. New York State refused to recognize divorces such as the one Prescott's ex-wife had obtained in Florida, forcing them to go out of state for their wedding. All during the ferry ride, Jane had become more worried.

The shoes she wore, vanilla to go with her silk suit, clicked on the tile as she paced, sending echoes. She touched her kid gloves to her matching pillbox hat, just like the ones Jackie Kennedy wore, and straightened its little veil.

"Why are you so nervous, Mom?" Ellen asked. For the occasion, she wore a new dress, deep crimson velvet with white ribbons, with black patent leather shoes that sounded solid compared to Jane's as they walked. "Aunt Anne and Grandma say you've loved Uncle Prescott for years."

Jane stopped and smiled, feeling as though a fog had lifted. "I really have. I'm just nervous about being someone's wife."

Ellen blushed.

"I wasn't talking about that, young lady, and get it out of your mind. I meant sharing a home. I'm so set in my ways after all these years."

"Oh," said Ellen. "Hold on a minute. I have a note here from Aunt Anne. She said to give it to you if the subject came up."

Jane took the note and read it. "Dear Jane," it said. "If you are reading this, you've told Ellen you are afraid Prescott will be displeased by your set ways. I can only remind you that I was worried about that with Schuyler, and it turned out not to be a problem." She had signed it, "Your more rational friend, Anne."

"Did she send you any more letters to give me?"

"Three. They are in case you worry about giving up your career, which she says don't, changing your politics, for which she advises agreeing with whatever Uncle Prescott says and then voting your conscience, or postponing the wedding until she comes home. She's emphatically against that."

"Your vocabulary is improving," Jane noted. "Is that it?"

"There was one I wasn't supposed to open." She held an envelope out.

Jane took it and opened the flap. It read, "I wish more than anything that I could be with you today, to see your face full of the love I know you have for Prescott. All my love, Anne."

A man came out of the judge's chambers. "We're ready."

Jane moved forward, but Ellen stopped her. "There is one more thing from Aunt Anne." She took a small box out of her coat pocket.

Opening it, Jane found another note from Anne. "I

can't be there to attend you, but I wanted to be sure you were prepared. I had the store include a blue bow on your slip with your outfit, as you probably noticed, and this will fulfill the other requirements." Jane opened the felt pouch attached to the note. Inside was her grandmother's cameo, the one she had sold to Anne so many years ago.

Ellen and Jane held hands as they went inside. Then Ellen stepped back, linking Jane's hand with Prescott's. With her twelve-year-old daughter giving her away, and Mr. Dobbin, Mrs. McGill, and Prescott's sister and brother-in-law standing as witnesses, and all that had led to this point, Jane was nearly overwhelmed. But when she looked into Pres's eyes and saw the happiness there, she felt her own heart expanding to envelop her whole family.

Well-wishers met them back in Manhattan, where there was a small luncheon at the Union League Club. As the Champagne was poured, Mr. Dobbin stood and held up his glass.

"Jane, you are like a daughter to me," he said, his blue eyes watering once again. "And yet in some ways, you have always taken care of me. Prescott is a lucky man." He smiled at both of them and directed his gaze to Jane's new husband. His voice nearly broke when he added, "Take care of her."

Prescott rose and shook the old man's hand. "I give you my word, sir, I will."

Mrs. McGill wiped the tears from her eyes and hugged Jane and Prescott when it was time to leave. When their friend Constance Merriam came to take Ellen and her own daughter back to their boarding school, Jane held Ellen close before she left. "I'm going to miss you so much," she said.

"Oh, Mom, you always say that," Ellen teased. "Besides, you and Uncle Prescott will be coming to see me during the winter games. They're only weeks away." Putting her hand up, she touched the cameo pinned to Jane's suit. "Now that you are married, I'm supposed to tell you that is one of the gifts from Aunt Anne. It's no longer borrowed, it's yours."

Jane missed Anne more than ever, as she hugged Ellen. "Your aunt is a wonderful woman."

Prescott held Jane close on one side, with Ellen on the other. Then Ellen blew a kiss to the married couple and ran outside to catch her ride.

Jane and Prescott were finally alone.

They went to the suite in the Waldorf that Prescott had reserved for the night before they left on their honeymoon trip. He carried her over the threshold into a room filled with yellow roses and illuminated by dozens of candles.

"The roses," she said, remembering her reaction all those years ago.

"I'm hoping they'll make you happy this time."

"They do. You do." She wrapped her arms around his neck and held him close. He leaned down and kissed her until she was lightheaded, then picked her up and placed her on the bed, where they continued their exploration of one another.

Contrary to what Jane's stepmother, Pearl, had predicted, Jane's marriage never lacked for passion.

Chapter Thirty-One

The New Year and John F. Kennedy's new administration brought a resurgence in the economy. Both Jane and Prescott were kept busy. They had agreed to keep their businesses separate, and each blossomed.

But they had time to set up their new apartment on Fifth Avenue, overlooking Central Park. It had four bedrooms, a study, a large formal living room, a dining room, and three fireplaces. Jane had never before allowed herself to care about her surroundings beyond being clean and tidy. Now she threw herself into decorating. By sacrificing some of her lunch hours, she was able to select fabric, dusky pinks and dark greens, to go with the blond wood of the Danish Modern furniture she chose for the apartment.

She found a schoolgirlish excitement in getting mail with her new name on it. Mrs. Prescott Weaver. It was silly to be so enamored of it, but she could not deny her feelings.

That is, until one day when she got a letter with no return address. It was postmarked Manhattan. She had hurried home to dress for the opera but took the time to open the envelope:

Dear Jane,

Let me be among the first to congratulate you on your marriage. I read about it in The New York Times.

I, too, have good news. There is a wonderful investment opportunity coming up which will finally enable me to fulfill my potential. I can assure you, it's strictly legit. Unfortunately I am a little short on capital. It would be a pity if I missed out on this. I'm hoping you can help bridge the gap.

I will only need five thousand dollars. At present I am between residences, but I will call on you in a week. At that time I am sure you'll be generous enough to lend me the money I need. After all, we are bound by a mutual love for Ellen. Sincerely, Martin.

Jane's hand shook as she read the letter. Prescott was not home yet, and she did not want to spoil their evening with such a nasty reminder of the past. She tore the letter up and threw it into the fire, intending to put the entire thing out of her mind.

But she found herself worrying all week about what to do when Martin called on her. She thought about telling Prescott, but she wanted more than anything not to trouble him with this remnant of her past life. She finally decided the best way to handle it was to send him away without seeing her. She left instructions with the doorman that when a Mr. Martin Roche came he was to be turned away, firmly and finally.

****

A few weeks later, she received another letter from Martin:

Jane,

I don't think you understand how important my investment is. I must have that money. There is no more time to wait or play games. If you don't pay the money, all five grand, I will find a way to make you give it to me. Or I'll make you wish you had.

His signature, under an underlined "Sincerely," looked like the writing of an extremely angry man. Jane knew it was time to tell her husband about the threats.

"There's something I must tell you." As calmly as she could, she explained about the letters she had received.

Prescott tilted Jane's chin up and looked deeply into her eyes. "Don't worry. I'll take care of it."

"What are you going to do?"

"If we don't put a stop to it, we'll never be free. He has no power over us. I'll just point that out to him."

****

Jane and Ellen had barely stepped out of their car in front of their apartment building when they were set upon by reporters.

"Is it true what they're saying about Prescott Weaver?" asked one.

Jane's heart felt as if it were lodged in her throat. "What do you mean?"

"A man attacked him. When he was arrested he made allegations that Mr. Weaver had purchased a baby. That's a federal offense. If it's true, Mr. Weaver could be in serious trouble."

Ellen stepped toward the man. "My stepfather never did any such thing."

The man held his pencil poised over his pad. "Any comment, Mrs. Weaver?"

Jane looked from him to her daughter. Ellen had never been told about the money her father took to give up custody. She did not want her to find out now. "Come inside, Ellen." Pulling her by the arm, she led her into the building, with the doorman bringing in her bags behind them.

He shut the door in the reporter's face. "I'm sorry, Mrs. Weaver. I didn't know he was going to say those nasty things."

"I'd just like to get Ellen upstairs," said Jane, looking in frustration at the empty elevator. The operator was apparently on break. "Would you take us right up?"

"Yes, ma'am."

Once they were in their home, Ellen turned to Jane. "What was that all about? Is Uncle Prescott in trouble?"

What could Jane say? How could she tell her child what had happened so many years ago? But Ellen had a right to know. At the same time, Jane was terrified of what it might mean to Prescott, and she had to talk to him right away.

"Jane, is that you?" Prescott's voice came from the kitchen. He pushed open the door and came into the living room.

"How did you get here?" asked Ellen. "We didn't see you downstairs."

"I came through the servants' entrance. I can't believe I had to do that in my own home." He came around the corner into the living room, and Jane saw that he had a blackened eye.

"Prescott," said Jane, "what happened to you?"

"I, uh—"

"Who did that to you, Uncle Pres?"

He came over to Ellen and hugged her. Over her shoulder he looked at Jane, leading her to believe it was Martin. And from what the reporter said, she knew it had been bad, and public.

"We'll talk about it soon, darling. But I'm

expecting a call from my attorney."

Jane barely noticed when he helped her off with her coat. She had a terrible sense of foreboding. "There was a reporter," she said.

Prescott nodded. "Outside. I saw. That was why I came around the back. If I had known you would be coming in then, I'd have run interference. I'm so sorry."

"It isn't that," said Jane. She turned to Ellen.

Ellen looked at each of them. "I think I'd better unpack."

When she was gone, Jane took Prescott by the arm and led him to the couch. "Let me get you something for that eye."

"It's fine. Don't worry about it."

"Just wait a moment." She went into the kitchen and took out the thick steak she'd planned for dinner. Suddenly her knees felt very weak, and she had to lean against the counter to regain her strength.

"Pull yourself together," she murmured to herself. Taking a deep breath, she brought the steak to her husband and helped position it on his swollen eyelid. "I have to talk to you," she whispered. "The reporter said something about buying a baby."

Prescott's face had drained of all color. "Martin must have told the police."

"Tell me what happened."

"He came to my office," said Prescott. "I told him he would never get another penny out of this family. He said he would make us wish we'd never heard of him."

"I already wish that," said Jane, "except for Ellen."

Prescott nodded. "He said he would ruin us."

"He doesn't have any way to do that," said Jane.

"I guess he figured one out. He told the police

about the arrangement."

"When did he go to the police?"

"They came to him. Actually, my secretary called them. Martin got very angry, and he came around my desk and punched me in the face. My secretary came in when she heard me fall against the bookcase, and she screamed. She called the police even though I had the situation under control."

Jane worried about his fall. "Are you hurt somewhere else?"

"Mostly in my pride. But I think it's going to take a much bigger beating now that Martin has publicized my part in Ellen's adoption."

"We have to tell Ellen."

"Maybe not. Let's just wait."

When the phone rang, Prescott handed the steak back to Jane and took the call in the study.

"What's going on?" Ellen demanded when she came back to the living room.

"We're not sure. We have to wait."

****

Half an hour later, Prescott emerged. "It's time for a family meeting," he announced, trying to hide the worry in his voice. It had been a tough phone call, but nothing compared to what they were up against.

They sat together at the dining room table. The cook had asked if dinner was to be served yet, but Jane, whose face still looked unnaturally pale to Prescott, asked her to wait a little longer.

"I talked to my attorney," Prescott said, feeling extremely tired. "He explained there were reporters at the police station when Martin was brought in. They overheard him and jumped on the story. Because of the publicity, the district attorney feels he must prosecute."

"Uncle Pres, what happened?"

He looked from Jane to her child, suddenly noticing how much she had changed, how much more beautiful she had become. No man, he knew, could feel more blessed than he did having Ellen and her mother in his life. If it cost him his seat, or even his career, it had been worth it to rescue Jane's child.

But if that was true, why was he having so much trouble explaining it to her?

"Ellen," he began, then stopped to clear his throat. His voice sounded foreign to his own ears. "There is something I have to tell you, about something I did."

"No, Prescott," said Jane. "It's my fault. Don't take this on yourself."

He put his hand on top of hers. "Don't, sweetheart. You didn't do it. I did." Turning to Ellen, he said, "Your mother didn't even know about it."

Wide-eyed, Ellen said, "What did you do? Was it something illegal?"

"I never thought so. It's true I did it secretly, but that was because..." He could not say that he wanted to protect Jane from finding out because he knew she would insist on paying him back and there was no way she could. "Because it was no one's business but mine."

"I don't understand," said Ellen. She turned to Jane, who was crying. "What's wrong, Mother?"

Prescott realized he could not explain without telling Ellen what her father had been like. That's why Jane was crying. As mature as her daughter was, it was going to crush her to learn her father had given up his rights not because it was best for her but because he wanted money.

"When you were very small, when Olivia died…" He could not even finish a sentence, let alone explain.

Ellen's eyebrows were furrowed. She blinked her eyes and gripped the arm of her chair.

He had to put her out of her misery. "When Olivia died," he began again, "your mother, Jane, wanted to adopt you. But Martin—"

"I don't want to talk about him," said Ellen angrily.

Taking a deep breath, Prescott tried again. "We have to, sweetheart. You see, he wouldn't give up custody. Not without money."

Ellen jumped up. "The baby they said you bought? It was me?"

Spent, Prescott hung his head. "Yes."

Jane stood up and went to Ellen. "Prescott did it for us. He and I weren't even in contact with each other then."

"Martin didn't want to give me up but he needed money? Is that why it happened?"

Neither Jane nor Prescott answered. If the child wanted to believe her father gave her away because he had to, Prescott was willing to let her. It was better than telling her the truth—that her father wanted to get rid of her—to the highest bidder.

But she seemed to guess. Turning eyes full of misery on her mother, Ellen asked, "How much? How much did he make Uncle Pres pay for me?"

"It isn't important," said Jane, hugging Ellen close. The girl shook her off and moved back. "But you have to understand," said Jane, her grief-filled voice breaking, "it was so much more than I had. If not for Prescott, I might have lost you."

"I wouldn't have let that happen," said Prescott. He

moved closer, trying to somehow pull his shattering family together.

Ellen clenched her fists and railed at Jane. "So you let him pay for me?"

"She didn't know anything about it."

"How could he hate me so much?" Ellen cried. She ran out of the room, and a moment later they heard the door of her bedroom slam shut.

Prescott held Jane tight.

She sobbed on his shoulders. "How can she ever understand?"

"I don't know. It's more than a child can comprehend."

"No," said Jane. "I think she understands Martin's side of this perfectly. That's why she's so upset. Was I wrong to keep the truth from her?"

"You did it to spare her."

"But what are we going to do?"

Ellen came back a few minutes later. She had stopped crying, but her eyes were puffy and her nose was red. "Did something happen with Martin today? Is he the one who did that to your eye?"

"Yes." Prescott recalled it vividly. Martin had swaggered in, unsteadily, as if he'd been drinking. It was immediately evident the man had aged badly. Although it had been over eleven years since he had laid eyes on Martin, and everyone got older, this was more. His hair was gray, but so was his skin, and his hands shook. But that hadn't stopped him from throwing a punch, only made it less painful.

"Did you hit him back?"

"No." He had simply grabbed him by the throat and forced him into a chair to await the police. If he had known Martin was going to tell them about Ellen, he would have thrown him out the window. Or at least considered it.

"The police came, and he told them that I paid for you to be adopted by Jane and that I threatened him if he didn't give you up. All of which is a crime, and my attorney told me we will have to go to court."

Jane looked faint, and Prescott settled her into her chair.

"Prescott," said Jane, "What are we going to do?"

He wished he knew.

Chapter Thirty-Two

The trial began soon after Ellen was finished with school for the summer. Crowds of reporters swarmed around the Weaver family as they made their way into a courtroom at the New York Supreme Court. Jane held Ellen's hand tight in her own kid-gloved hand, but she was terrified for her husband.

The lawyers had not made the prospects sound good. What they faced today was even more humiliating than the lurid newspaper reports about the incident. Not only was their private life now open to the public, but Prescott also faced the loss of his stock exchange seat—his very livelihood. The board had issued a temporary suspension pending the outcome of the investigation. The possibility of his going to jail loomed, as well.

But that all paled in comparison to the threat to Jane's custody of Ellen.

"Good morning, Mr. and Mrs. Weaver," said Clark Atherton, Prescott's chosen attorney. The lawyer was a name partner at one of the most prestigious criminal law firms in the city. He nodded in Ellen's direction. "Miss Baldwin."

She wore a more youthful version of the navy suit Jane wore. "Modest and sincere," Mr. Atherton had advised, when telling them how to present themselves. He had spent several days in his office counseling his clients about the trial, discussing the witnesses they had chosen to call, and reviewing documents in Jane's possession pertaining to the circumstances of Ellen's adoption. The papers lay in a pile on the conference table while the Weavers and their attorney talked, speaking of all the things Martin had done long ago.

Atherton had been pleased when he learned that Prescott had not officially adopted Ellen. "It shows that you weren't concerned for your own personal gain." They had also rehearsed testifying, with Mr. Atherton advising them not to volunteer any information, simply to respond yes or no to the questions.

Jane was upset that both Anne and Mrs. McGill were scheduled to testify. "It isn't right to drag them through this with us," she had protested.

Prescott admitted that he agreed with Jane, but Mr. Atherton left them no choice. "You need character and factual witnesses. Who better than they to speak for you?"

When Jane had continued to demur, Mr. Atherton had lost patience. "Do you realize there is a possibility Ellen's adoption might be overturned? Do you know what that would mean?"

Horrified, Jane had a flash of Ellen, in torn clothes and lacking sleep and proper nutrition, living in some rundown room over a bar somewhere with Martin. She swallowed, and agreed to keep her friends' names on the witness list.

Mr. Atherton looked over another list that his secretary had placed on the table. "The prosecution has not put anyone on its witness list but Martin and his mother, and Regina Taggart."

Jane felt the blood drain from her face and looked

over to see Prescott's face had turned red with rage. "Why would they call her?" he growled.

"What could she say about this case?" Mr. Atherton asked.

"Nothing. She knew nothing about it at the time. In fact, she'd never have known if it hadn't been in every paper in the city."

"It's not definite she'll be called," Mr. Atherton said. "And in all likelihood, it would only be as a character witness."

Jane wondered what Prescott's ex-wife would have to say about him. Yet her mind raced ahead. "Did you talk to Mrs. Roche?" she asked. She had seen the woman during Ellen's spring vacation, but not since, and it was very difficult for Mrs. Roche to get to a telephone. Jane had sent cards for the woman's birthday, and Ellen had gotten a letter from her, but there had not been time for another visit.

"Both the prosecution and I thought it best to leave her alone," said the attorney. "But since she might have information, her name was included. I think it unlikely they'll call her."

Jane felt a sense of relief. She couldn't imagine anyone more likely to be hurt by being called to testify, with the single exception of Ellen.

"Promise me, Atherton," Prescott said, "that you will not try to call Ellen to the stand."

Jane sighed. "He might have to. She could tell them what kind of stepfather you are."

"This isn't about now," Prescott said angrily. "This is about then, and she couldn't possibly remember."

"But she can remember how Martin was. It was only last year that she sent him away for good."

Prescott slapped his hand down on the conference table. "I won't allow it!"

They had been arguing about this for a week. Jane agreed it would be very hard on her daughter, but she felt Ellen would be a strong argument toward discounting Martin's allegations. Furthermore, Ellen had specifically said she wanted to testify.

"She's twelve years old," Prescott exclaimed. "She has no idea what that will mean."

Mr. Atherton agreed with Prescott. "It would be too easy for her to say something she didn't intend to say. How would she forgive herself?"

Finally Jane conceded. But the attorney was not done with his advice.

"You must remember that it is difficult to predict what a jury will do," he warned Prescott. "It is imperative that you control your temper. An outburst like the one you just had could cost you." He grimaced. "The prosecutor is hoping to make a name for himself on this case. I don't want you to help him."

That last conference had made Jane extremely uneasy, and now, in the courtroom on the first day of the trial, she was so absorbed in thought she barely noticed when the bailiff shouted, "All rise." It was only the echoes on the marble walls of the courtroom of wooden chairs scraping on the floor as the people at the defense and prosecution tables stood up that jolted her back to reality. She stood also.

The judge took his seat on the bench, and the bailiff called the court to order. It was time for the opening statements.

The prosecutor, looking dapper in a well-cut suit, with a pocket square that matched his tie, rose and faced the jury.

"Ladies and gentlemen," he said. "We are here today in the matter of the State of New York versus Prescott Weaver. He is charged with violating the New York State Penal Code by paying money to Mr. Martin Roche to relinquish his parental rights to the minor child now known as Ellen Baldwin.

"These are very serious crimes, ladies and gentlemen. Make no mistake about that. If people could buy and sell children, it would tear apart the fabric of society.

"The State will show, with documents and witnesses, that Mr. Weaver intentionally intimidated Mr. Roche and extorted the release of his rights to his child. Without his interference, Mr. Roche could have enjoyed a relationship with his daughter. This is about a basic human right, that of a father to be a parent to his child, and about another man's disruption of that right, in violation of the laws of this state. Thank you."

Mr. Atherton stood, his somber gray suit and tie matching his serious demeanor, and walked over to the jurors. Their faces registered ill regard for Prescott, intensifying Jane's fears for her husband.

"Ladies and gentlemen. The prosecutor has outlined the charges in this case, but he did not tell you they are erroneous. I will show that the situation was entirely different from that characterized by him, that Mr. Roche relinquished his rights voluntarily, purely for monetary gain, of his own volition. In fact, I will show that the best interests of the child were served by those involved."

At the conclusion of his statements, the district attorney was asked to call his first witness.

"The state calls Mr. Martin Roche."

With shivers running down her spine, Jane turned to see Martin enter the courtroom.

****

Ellen gasped. "Why does he look like that?"

"Prison pallor," said Atherton.

Prescott turned and saw Jane bite her lip.

"What did you say?" Ellen asked. "Has he been in jail?"

"Yes," said Atherton. "He was sentenced to serve a year for fraud, and he has other charges pending against him. The encounter with Mr. Weaver happened when he was out on parole." He shook his head. "This should never have happened. The man is a hardened cr—"

"That's enough," Prescott growled at his attorney. He turned to Jane. "Maybe you and Ellen should wait outside." He did not want the child to hear any more horrible things about the man who had fathered her. And he certainly did not want her to hear any bad things about himself. They had argued about it again only that morning, with Jane saying Ellen was old enough to face this.

Jane seemed uncertain and began to stand.

"No!" said Ellen, in a loud whisper. "I'm not leaving."

The judge looked at them and frowned, pounding his gavel. "I will not allow any outbursts."

Ellen leaned back against her chair, and Jane, looking hopelessly at Prescott, sat down. Prescott turned back to face the judge.

Martin was sworn in, and instead of looking at Ellen, he spent the time on the witness stand, when he was not actively answering questions, scowling at Jane.

Prescott could hear Ellen and Jane whispering behind him. "He doesn't even look at me," Ellen said. "Do you think he forgot what I look like?"

Jane whispered, "I don't know." Although she had matured since he last saw her and wore her hair in a more grown-up style, Prescott knew Ellen had not changed drastically. Martin just was not interested in his daughter.

Atherton nudged Prescott. "Pay close attention and let me know if what he says is an exaggeration or is, in any way, inaccurate."

Trying his best to focus on something other than Ellen and Jane and all their pain, Prescott listened closely to the questioning.

"Mr. Roche," said the prosecutor. "You claim Mr. Weaver offered you money to give up rights to your child."

Martin squared his shoulders and sat up straight. "Yes, sir, he did."

"How much money?"

"Twenty gr-, er, thousand dollars."

"And what were his conditions?"

"That I never try to see my child, my own flesh and blood, or the woman who was adopting her, again."

"Are you saying he just handed you twenty thousand dollars?"

"Not exactly. He gave me five grand up front, to reel me in, and another fifteen after I signed away my rights to my baby." He took out a handkerchief and blew his nose loudly, displaying a face full of sorrow.

"Did he say anything that would ensure you kept that promise not to see them again?"

"He threatened me."

A gasp rippled through the spectators, and two of the jurors glanced at Prescott. He sucked in his breath.

The judge banged his gavel and nodded toward the prosecutor to continue.

"In what way?"

"He said if I told anyone about it, or tried to see my baby, he would make sure I never got work in New York again."

"Did you believe him?"

Martin looked over at Prescott and made a big show of cringing. The prosecutor had obviously prepared him well for this testimony. "Yes, sir, I did."

"No further questions," said the prosecutor.

The judge ordered a short recess, and Prescott and his attorney went into a small room, leaving Jane and Ellen. Prescott felt ripped away from them when he needed them most.

****

Jane had always tried so hard to make Ellen strong, so she would not have problems like Olivia had. Part of her efforts included protecting her from details of her past that could hurt her. No one could provide such protection for her now.

Was it really less than two years since Martin had last come to see Ellen? At that time he had at least managed to pull himself together enough to appear respectable. Now he wore an oversized jacket that Jane suspected was provided for him by the prosecutor. And the shoes he wore were so scuffed, and with such dilapidated heels, that Jane wondered how long he had owned them.

"I shouldn't have sent him away," said Ellen. "This is all my fault. He's doing it because he's angry at me."

"No," said Jane. She took her daughter's hand. "This has nothing to do with you. I don't really think it has to do with Prescott, either. Martin has always hated me."

Ellen scowled. She opened her mouth but did not say anything, because Prescott and his attorney had returned. The court was called back to order. Martin came in again, walking self-righteously back to the witness chair.

"Your witness, Mr. Atherton," said the judge.

Mr. Atherton quickly rose, buttoning his jacket, and approached the witness. "Mr. Roche," he said, "you have testified here that Mr. Weaver paid you to relinquish your parental rights. Is that correct?"

"Yes."

"And you stated that he offered you twenty thousand dollars for the baby."

"Yes."

"But you didn't mention that you had previously asked Mrs. Weaver, who at that time was Miss Baldwin—"

"Yeah," Martin interjected, "by then she had stopped using that phony married name she took so people wouldn't know her monster kid was a bastard."

Jane felt her face burn as people in the courtroom started talking to each other. The lady in the first row of the jury box stared right at her.

The judge banged his gavel. "Order."

Mr. Atherton sent a warning look to Prescott to keep calm. From her viewpoint behind him, Jane could see her husband's shoulders hunched in that way he had when he was angry. Beyond him, at the prosecution table, the prosecutor was glaring at Martin, and shaking his head slightly. Martin swallowed, and looked back at Mr. Atherton.

"Mr. Roche," Mr. Atherton continued. "Please let me finish. Isn't it true that you had previously demanded ten thousand dollars from Jane Baldwin to give up your rights to Ellen Roche, now Baldwin?"

Martin slipped lower in his chair. "Yeah."

"So you had asked Miss Baldwin for money to give up the baby. Did you think she had that much money?"

"She could get it. She had that rich boss."

Mr. Atherton consulted his notes. "Would that be Mr. Jerome Dobbin?"

At the mention of his name, Jane's eyes filled with tears. The man had recently passed away.

"Yeah, that's him."

"Did you think he would give her the money?"

"I bet he would, but she didn't ask him."

"How do you know that?"

"Because I asked him for it. But he said he would do whatever Jane wanted."

"So where did you expect her to get the money?"

"I don't know. She had rich friends."

Jane felt her stomach knot. Her worries about Anne being called to the stand increased. It was asking so much to put her through this.

"Did you approach her friends?"

"Nah. I figured Jane would find a way to pay. She had a good job and all."

"But didn't she have to pay for the hospitalization of her sister, your wife Olivia, and for Olivia's funeral, as well as the custodial expenses while Ellen was being cared for by your mother?"

Martin held his hands with the palms turned up and

shrugged his shoulders. "How much could that have cost?"

Mr. Atherton shook his head. "I would like to leave this line of questioning." He picked up some papers that had been on the defense table and walked toward Martin. "This is a copy of the judgment against you. The one for which you recently served time."

"Objection," shouted the prosecutor. "That has no relevance."

"He tried to use the story of the baby sale as his psychological defense for the crime, your honor," said Mr. Atherton, stepping closer to the bench. "I think that makes it relevant."

"Overruled."

"Mr. Roche," said Mr. Atherton, as he walked back toward the witness stand. "Did you testify under oath, and I quote, 'I fell into a life of crime because I was forced to sell my child to some big shot's former mistress?'"

"Yes. I would never have been involved in anything illegal if I hadn't been overwhelmed with grief."

"But wasn't that many years before you committed the crime for which you were on trial?"

Martin paused before answering and seemed to be thinking. "Yeah. For that one." He looked at the jury. "It's been like an animal sucking at my guts."

Mr. Atherton followed up. "Was that when you were convicted of running a pyramid scheme?"

Very quietly, Martin said, "Yes." He turned to the jury. "But I would never have done that if I wasn't so upset."

Mr. Atherton looked at Martin. He waited a

moment, causing Jane to worry that he had run out of questions to clear Prescott. Just when she was about to panic, though, Mr. Atherton turned the sheaf of papers he held over to the last page. "The jury didn't buy your defense, did it, Mr. Roche?"

"No."

"And you didn't give the court the name of the person whom you claimed made you sell your baby, did you?"

"No. They didn't believe me anyway."

"Why did you think Mr. Weaver called you to his office on October fifth of 1949?"

"I thought he was going to offer me a job or something."

"Did he?"

"No. He started talking about Ellen." Martin turned earnestly to the jury. "I offered her to him. I knew that he and his wife—his first wife—didn't have any kids. I thought it would be nice if my little girl grew up in luxury." He looked sadly at the jury. "But as it turned out, she didn't get that from Jane."

"So Mrs. Weaver, at the time Miss Baldwin, didn't have a lot of money, correct?"

"Yeah. That's why I only asked her for ten thousand."

"That was very understanding of you."

Martin looked puzzled. The prosecutor rose to his feet and objected.

"I'll withdraw my comment, your honor," Mr. Atherton said. He looked at Martin. "You had only asked for ten but Mr. Weaver offered you twenty?"

"Well, it had all those conditions. They were worth another ten thousand, weren't they?"

"I don't know, Mr. Roche. I've never thought about offering to sell one of my children."

"Objection," shouted the prosecutor.

"He certainly is objectionable," said Mr. Atherton. He started pacing back and forth in front of Martin as the judge sustained the objection.

Ellen gasped. Jane put her arm around her shoulder. She wished there was some way to protect her.

The judge banged his gavel and admonished the attorney.

"Sorry, your honor." Mr. Atherton turned back to Martin. "Did you keep up your end of the deal?"

"What do you mean?"

"Did you stay away from Ellen and Jane?"

"Of course."

Atherton looked surprised. "Would your honor please remind this witness that he is under oath?" He stared at Martin.

Martin coughed. "Well, a few years later I decided I should go see my daughter, and make sure she was all right."

Mr. Atherton stopped pacing and looked at Martin. "And was she?"

He blinked twice. "She seemed okay."

"How often did you see her?"

"A lot of times. I used to take her out for her birthday."

Flipping through his legal pad, Mr. Atherton ran his finger down one of the pages.

"When you say a lot of times, you mean once a year, around her birthday, isn't that true?"

"Uh, yes."

"And you only did this for about four years, correct?"

"Yeah."

"Then you stopped doing that, right?"

"She asked me to."

"Miss Baldwin?"

Martin looked at Jane and shook his head. "Not her. Ellen."

Mr. Atherton stood stock still. "Your daughter asked you not to come see her?"

"She was brainwashed."

"So you stopped seeing her, didn't you?"

"That's right."

"After Ellen asked you to stop seeing her, didn't you ask her mother for more money, money you needed to help pay your debts?"

"It was only a coupla thousand. And it shoulda been mine. It was from an insurance policy that my wife left."

"She left you two thousand dollars?"

"Not exactly. She left about a hundred dollars, but there was interest."

Mr. Atherton stopped walking and stared first at the jury and then back at Martin. "What bank pays such a good interest rate? I'm sure everyone here would want to know."

"Er, it wasn't a bank. Jane invested the money, and it turned into two thousand."

"So you were only entitled to one hundred dollars, correct?"

"Who says?"

Mr. Atherton turned to the jury and back to Martin. "You sold your child twice, didn't you?"

"Objection."

"Withdrawn," said Mr. Atherton. He cleared his throat. "Did you contact her mother again, after her marriage to Mr. Weaver?"

"She wouldn't give me nothin'. She had all that dough and she wouldn't give me any."

"Did you think she should?"

"Yeah! She got to be with my kid and I didn't get anything."

"Did you want to be with your daughter?"

"Sure. I miss her." He made a sad face, showing it to the jury. "I'd love to see her."

"Some time has passed. Would you even recognize her?"

"Of course. I'd know her in a minute."

"Did you know she's been sitting in this courtroom all day?"

Martin craned his neck and looked around. "Where?" After a moment, his gaze came to rest on Jane, and moved sideways to Ellen. His mouth dropped open. "That's my baby, over there," he said.

Ellen looked back at him. Then she covered her mouth and ran out of the courtroom.

Chapter Thirty-Three

Jane found Ellen sobbing in the washroom. "He didn't love me at all. You never told me."

"I didn't want to hurt you."

"Why couldn't Uncle Prescott be my father?"

Jane had no answer for that.

Ellen wiped her eyes on the rolled cloth toweling near the sink. "I thought he loved me."

Jane shook her head. "I don't think Martin ever loved anyone."

"No," said Ellen, shaking her own head. "I don't mean him. I thought Uncle Prescott loved me."

"He does."

"Then why hasn't he adopted me?"

Jane blinked. "Would you like him to?"

Ellen nodded, her eyes brimming with tears.

Jane wondered how Prescott would feel about that. Would he want, as his own, another man's child, especially a man who was so despicable?

But there was no time to find out. They had to get back to the courtroom.

When they opened the courtroom door, Jane saw that the prosecutor was back, asking Martin more questions on redirect.

"Am I to understand that you initially signed away your rights to Ellen out of concern for her well-being and not for the money?"

"Objection," said Mr. Atherton. "He is leading the witness."

"Sustained."

"Let me rephrase that question. Mr. Roche, why did you give up your parental rights?"

"Because I knew that at that time I could not be a good father to my child. My mother could not help me, either. So I said Jane could have her." He looked at the jury. "But I never did it for the money, and it has been weighing on my mind ever since."

"That's all, your honor."

"I have a few questions, your honor," said Mr. Atherton. At the judge's nod he went to stand in front of Martin again. "You said you could not be a good father to your child and that was why you gave her up for adoption. Am I stating that fairly?"

"At the time," said Martin, stressing the word time.

"Then why did you ask Miss Baldwin for money to give up your rights if you agreed that you should do so?"

"It was only fair. She was getting Ellen."

"No more questions."

Martin got up and stepped off the stand. His smirk, as he walked past Jane and Ellen, was almost too much to bear. Jane gripped the armrest on her seat, willing herself not to get up and run, screaming, after him.

****

"The state calls Mrs. Regina Taggart."

As Reggie walked down the aisle to the witness stand, Prescott turned and had a view of both Jane and his ex-wife, who was wearing a pink suit—undoubtedly Chanel, given her love of the designer—and lacy gloves. Was it his imagination that Jane looked slightly ill? She turned her eyes to him, managing a weak smile, and nodded reassuringly.

After Reggie was sworn in, the prosecutor established that their marriage had commenced prior to the time of Ellen's adoption and had lasted until well afterward. "Mrs. Taggart," he said, "did Mr. Weaver tell you of his participation in the adoption of Ellen Baldwin?"

"No," she intoned. Her dramatic way of speaking, Prescott noted, had not changed.

"Then he did not inform you that he was spending twenty thousand dollars to pay off Martin Roche?"

"No, he did not tell me anything about the money."

"In fact, you knew nothing about the situation until recently?"

"Correct," she pronounced.

"And what would you have said if he had asked your opinion back then?"

"I would have told him not to do it."

"Why?"

"Because it was none of his business. He was married to me and he was saving for his seat on the stock exchange. Now I understand why it took him so long to buy the seat."

"And did that pose a hardship to you?"

"Yes, it did. I had to live practically like a pauper while he saved for that seat, and it lasted far longer than I ever expected." She looked at Prescott. "Now I know why." She turned to the jury, adding dramatically, "And he didn't care at all how much I suffered."

"No more questions."

Prescott was seething when Atherton took his place to question Reggie, but he kept his temper in check.

"I'd like to know, Mrs. Taggart," said Atherton, "if the money Mr. Weaver used to give Mr. Roche was from your joint account."

"No. He took it from the account he had set aside for his seat."

"Did you ever take money from that account?"

"No. I had to get by with the money in my savings account."

"Did it cause you to stop purchasing clothes?"

"No," Reggie declared, looking pained. "But out of concern for my husband's goals, I only bought fifteen new dresses and four ball gowns one autumn, far fewer than usual."

"Did you have to give up vacations?"

"No, but we had to manage with only two weeks in Florida, instead of two months in Europe."

"So you did not go to Europe when you were married to Mr. Weaver?"

"I did. But he didn't go with me, because he said he had to stay and take care of his business. If he hadn't wasted that money on that child, he could have gone with me."

"No more questions," said Mr. Atherton.

The prosecutor lost no time getting to redirect. "Did the payment to Mr. Roche cause you suffering?"

"Yes it did." She looked sadly at the jury. "It hurt my pride to take money from my father for my necessities. That money should have come from my husband."

The word necessities grated on Prescott's ears. She made it sound as if she would have been walking around in rags if not for her father's money. Prescott had never missed making Reggie a more than adequate monthly allowance for household and personal needs. Reggie's tastes and requirements were what had been out of bounds, although he had only belatedly understood her need to impress Ralph Taggart.

"So Mr. Weaver showed reckless indifference to your needs when he purchased Ellen Baldwin for Jane Baldwin, correct?"

Reggie's eyes took on a triumphant look. "Yes, he did. He's a dreadful man."

The prosecutor nodded toward Atherton, but before he could rise for re-cross, Prescott stopped him. "No more," he said, fighting to keep his voice to a whisper. Atherton reserved his opportunity to reexamine the witness at a later time.

"At this time, your honor," said the prosecutor, "the state rests."

With a bang of his gavel, the judge said, "The court will recess for lunch."

****

Anne and Mrs. McGill, who wore a new hat with artificial cherries draped around the brim, had been sitting in the hall right outside the courtroom all morning. When they saw Jane and her family come out, they took Ellen to a restaurant down the street from the courthouse. Jane and Prescott went to a luncheonette with Mr. Atherton.

"Yours, Anne's, and Mrs. McGill's testimony," the attorney said, "will turn Martin's allegations around."

"You sound confident," Jane said. She was anything but.

"I must be honest with you. This case is quite serious. If the court finds that Martin's relinquishment of his child was coerced, it could be overturned."

"You've said that before," said Prescott, looking very tired.

"I want to be sure you understand."

"I do. I just want this to be over with."

"We have a way to go," said the attorney, picking up his hat. "And court will reconvene soon. Let's go."

Anne, wearing a pale gray suit with a light blue flowered scarf around her throat, looked poised, calm, and like a million dollars on the stand. "I met Jane in 1940, when she worked for Mr. Weaver. She took over his business when he went overseas, so that he wouldn't have to give it up. She was always very competent."

"Did you become friends?"

"Not then. But we became good friends a few years later, around 1948. She is a wonderful woman, loyal, caring, and considerate. She is also a wonderful mother."

"Did you know Martin at the time of his wife's death, Mrs. Lewis?"

"I did. He was not much of a father. And I knew, after Olivia, uh, died, that he had abandoned his child again."

"No more questions."

The prosecutor got eagerly to his feet. Jane saw Anne sit up a little straighter as if preparing herself.

"You said you knew Miss Baldwin when she worked for Mr. Weaver. Was that when you and your first husband had business at his office?"

"Yes."

"And later, after you became friends with Miss Baldwin, your husband left you, isn't that true?"

Anne looked shocked. In a quietly indignant voice, she said, "It certainly was not Jane's fault."

"But it had to do with her son, correct?"

"No, it had to do with my—our daughter."

"But you knew Miss Baldwin's son, didn't you?"

"Yes."

"And there was something wrong with him, wasn't there?"

Anne didn't speak right away. The prosecutor looked at her sadly. "I'm sorry to have to ask you such difficult questions, but it is important. Was there something wrong with little—" He checked the papers in his hand. "Zachary?"

"Some people might have thought so."

"He was a mongoloid idiot, wasn't he?"

Anne sat straighter and was obviously gritting her teeth. "He had what is now called Down syndrome."

"So he wasn't normal, correct?"

"He was a wonderful child," Anne cried. "He was sweet, thoughtful, and kind." She gulped. "My daughter was the same way."

The faces on the jurors showed pity and in some cases, revulsion. Jane trembled.

The prosecutor seemed to have no regard for Anne's feelings. "The little boy passed away, right?" he said, in an accusing tone.

Anne's face became pinched, and Jane saw tears in her eyes. "Yes."

"So she wanted to replace her baby with Ellen Roche."

"No! Certainly not. She wanted to take care of her sister's child."

"Please just answer the questions," said the prosecutor. "Did her grief over losing her child, and then her sister, lead her to want to adopt Ellen?"

"You're twisting everything."

"I'm not twisting anything. She wanted a baby and Prescott Weaver bought her one. Isn't that the truth?"

"She didn't know anything about his gift."

"Oh, so the baby was a present?"

"No! You're changing everything I say to make it sound bad."

"Do you think people should be allowed to buy and sell babies?"

"No. Martin sold his baby, but Jane did not buy her."

The prosecutor looked at the jury. "She couldn't afford to, so Mr. Weaver did it for her." As Mr. Atherton rose to his feet to object, the prosecutor turned to the judge, a disgusted look on his face. "I have no more questions for this witness." He went back to the prosecution table and sat down, looking satisfied.

Mr. Atherton rose for redirect. "Don't," said Prescott. "Prove it some other way. Just let her get off that stand."

"Nothing at this time, your honor."

Anne stood, shaking, and Mr. Atherton helped her off the stand. She did not stop when she passed Jane; she just went out of the courtroom. Jane wanted more than anything to go after her, to tell her it was all right, but she could not leave. Not now, when Mrs. McGill was taking her place on the stand.

Mr. Atherton strode purposefully to Mrs. McGill. "You have known Mrs. Weaver for a long time, haven't you?"

She tugged at the bow at the neck of her polka-dot dress. "She and her sister moved into my building in the late thirties."

"And you were close with them?"

"Yes, I felt I had to watch over them, since they were both so young. But Jane did a wonderful job with Olivia and saw that she was properly cared for."

"And you saw how Mr. Roche treated his wife?"

"I not only saw how he hurt her, I could hear it. All the neighbors could." She dropped her voice. "At night…"

Mr. Atherton let the significance of what Mrs. McGill could not say settle on the courtroom. He coughed, then he continued. "Was he around much after the baby was born?"

"He disappeared when he found out she was a girl, and he didn't come home for a week."

"Objection."

"Sustained." The judge admonished Mrs. McGill to confine her answers to the questions.

"Miss Baldwin saw that her sister was ill after the baby was born, correct?"

"Yes. She was very worried. So was the doctor."

"And you tried to help out, correct?"

"Yes. I knew how sick she was, because I checked on her many times a day."

"And when Mrs. Olivia Roche died, Mr. Roche left without saying where he was going?"

"Yes. I wasn't surprised. He's a nogoodnik."

"Your witness," said Atherton.

The prosecutor approached Mrs. McGill slowly, as if conceding what she had said. "It sounds like you took good care of the Baldwin sisters. They were lucky to have you, weren't they?"

Mrs. McGill swelled with pride. "They were good girls."

"Would you consider a young lady who got pregnant out of wedlock to be a good girl?"

Shock at such a question registered on Mrs. McGill's face. "Jane told me she was married."

"But you learned since that it was not true, correct?"

With an apologetic look at Jane, Mrs. McGill said, "I understand how it happened. She was naive. I met that scoundrel who got her pregnant, and I can understand how she was lured in."

"So she wasn't the paragon of virtue that her lawyer wants us to believe she was, was she?"

Mrs. McGill fixed him with a withering look. "You are mistaken. She is a wonderful woman. I was close to her for years, taking care of Ellen while she worked, until she married Mr. Weaver, and she never did one single thing wrong."

"Oh, so once she got married, she no longer needed your help and she fired you?" The prosecutor looked at the jury as if to invite their understanding of how this poor woman was used and tossed away.

"No, she did not. Jane didn't need me to be there for Ellen anymore."

"She got married and sent her beloved daughter away to boarding school?" said the prosecutor, sending another knowing look at the jury. "Was she trying to get her out of the picture so she could be alone with her new husband, the one who bought her Ellen in the first place, to replace the child she had lost?"

Mrs. McGill burst into tears. "You have it all wrong."

"I don't think so." The prosecutor walked away from the witness box. "I think I understand perfectly."

Jane leaned forward and whispered to Mr. Atherton. "I insisted on paying her—she didn't want the money."

Mr. Atherton returned to Mrs. McGill's side and handed her his handkerchief. "Were you employed by Jane Baldwin?"

"No, of course not. I helped her out. But she insisted on giving me money for taking care of Ellen, because she felt it was such a big favor. I would have done it for free. I love that child as if she were my own granddaughter."

"She calls you Grandma, doesn't she?"

"Yes."

Mr. Atherton turned to stare at the prosecutor. "The state brought up the subject of Miss Baldwin's son. You knew him?"

"Yes. And I admired her for her strength, for the way she loved him, despite what was wrong with him. No mother could have been more devoted than Jane to her children. And I mean both of them. Ellen is hers as much as little Z.Z. was."

"Thank you, Mrs. McGill. No more questions."

Mrs. McGill smiled at Jane as she went past. Jane smiled back as best she could, because it was now her turn to take the stand.

****

Jane had never felt so nervous in all her life. She stared out at the gallery, where Anne and Mrs. McGill now sat in front of a row of stone-faced reporters. But the most important people in the room, Ellen and Prescott, gave her reassuring smiles.

"Mrs. Weaver," said Mr. Atherton. "A lot has been said in this courtroom today. Would you tell us, in your own words, about the circumstances surrounding your attempts to adopt Ellen?"

Jane explained as best she could, carefully selecting her words and remembering how Mr. Atherton had said to present it. "Mr. Roche asked me for money. I didn't have it."

"And what did you think when you found out that Mr. Weaver had given the money to Mr. Roche?"

"It was years before I learned of it. At first I was shocked that he even knew about the circumstances, and then at his generosity. He never told me about it, and certainly he did not expect anything in return. But when I did find out, accidentally, I went to thank him."

"Did he ask you for anything at that time?"

"No. He did not."

Mr. Atherton looked at his notes. "Mrs. Weaver, did a physician attend your sister when she was ill?"

"Yes. Dr. Mann took care of her."

"And did he tell you to keep Martin away from his wife while she was recovering, during the time after her hospitalization?"

"Objection, your honor. That calls for hearsay evidence."

"Sustained."

"Exception to the rule, please, your honor. Dr. Mann is deceased," said Mr. Atherton. "He cannot testify."

"You will have to make your case another way then," said the judge.

Mr. Atherton shook his head. "No more questions of this witness."

The prosecutor approached. "Mrs. Weaver, your husband was married to another woman at that time, wasn't he?"

"Yes."

"Didn't you think he owed his loyalty to her?"

"Of course. He had no relationship with me at that time."

"This court has already heard that you were not above having a relationship out of wedlock. Did you expect to have one with Mr. Weaver, for whom you had worked, saving his business for him, once you found out about his payment? Or did you think he bought Ellen for you out of gratitude for your work during the war?"

"Objection."

"Sustained. Withdrawn." The prosecutor came over to Jane and apologized. "We're all tense," he said. "There is a lot at stake."

Jane did not comment.

"Your reputation is not what is in question here," the prosecutor continued. "Mr. Weaver's actions are on trial. Did you think what he did was legal?"

"I didn't know about it at first," Jane reminded the prosecutor. "And he did not buy Ellen. He merely gave Martin the money he requested."

"He gave him more than what was asked from you. So that he would leave you alone. What did you think about that?"

"To be honest, I thought it was a blessing. You do not know what kind of man Martin Roche is."

"He is not on trial," the prosecutor said coldly. "No more questions."

****

"Mr. Weaver," said Atherton, when Prescott had taken the stand. "Would you please tell the court, in your own words, what transpired between you and Mr. Roche?"

Prescott took a deep breath. He had seen how upset his wife and stepdaughter had become over Martin's testimony. He did not want them to be hurt any further. As carefully as he could, he explained about his meeting with Martin.

Atherton did not interrupt. When he was finished, he asked, "And why did you offer him the money?"

"Because I knew Jane couldn't pay him what he wanted, and even if she could, I thought he would be back for more. That was why I stipulated that if he wanted the money, he would have to stay away from Jane and Ellen."

"I understand that, but what I want to know is why did you intervene in the first place?"

"Because I knew what a terrible situation it was. Jane's sister had died and Mr. Roche had abandoned the baby a second time—"

"Did you say a second time?"

"Yes. When his wife, Olivia, was hospitalized, he took the baby to his mother. But he gave no support and never visited. So when Olivia died, Jane wanted to adopt Ellen and give her a stable home."

"Were you having a relationship with Jane at that time?"

"No. I was married to another woman. I had no contact with Jane at all."

"So how did you know about this?"

"Her friend, Anne Lewis, told me. I kept up with Jane's welfare through her friend."

"You said you were married to someone else at the time. Why did you want to know about Jane?"

Prescott turned his head away from the attorney. He looked directly at Jane. "Because I loved her. I was only fooling myself when I thought I could marry someone else and forget her. I spent years watching over her, and then Ellen, from afar. I've always, only, wanted what was best for them."

Jane bit her lip.

Atherton turned to the judge. "No more questions, your honor."

The prosecutor rose and took his place in front of the witness stand. Prescott felt such resentment for the man he wondered how he could contain his temper. But a look at his attorney reminded him of the extreme importance of doing so.

"Mr. Weaver," said the prosecutor, "you've admitted to this court that you paid Mr. Roche twenty thousand dollars to give up his parental rights." He held up photostatic copies of the checks Martin had accepted. "And is there a written stipulation on each that he must never see his child again?"

"Yes."

"Didn't you realize your threats were against the law?"

"I never threatened to harm him. It was best for the child. He just wanted the money."

Martin stood up and shouted, "He said he'd make it so I could never get a job in this town. It's no wonder I had to turn to crime."

The judge banged his gavel. "Order!"

Banging his gavel again, the judge admonished the spectators who were noisily talking among themselves to remain quiet. He looked at the prosecutor. "Do you have any more questions?"

"Nothing further, your honor."

Atherton stood at the defense table. "Did Mr. Roche ask you and your wife for more money recently?"

"Objection, your honor," said the prosecutor. "Mr. Roche's behavior is not the issue here."

"Your honor," said Atherton, "the accuser in this case should not be above having his actions questioned."

"Overruled," said the judge. He looked at Prescott. "You may respond."

"Yes. He told both of us that he would ruin us if we didn't give it to him. I refused. I will not let him threaten my family."

Prescott was dismissed and resumed his seat in front of Jane. "It being four-thirty," said the judge, "this court is adjourned. I'll listen to closing statements on Monday morning at nine o'clock sharp."

Chapter Thirty-Four

"I'm sorry," said Mr. Atherton, when they met at his office on Saturday morning. "But we may have a problem."

Prescott turned a tired face to his attorney. "You think we're going to lose, don't you?"

"I think some of the testimony was damaging. The district attorney made it look like it substantiated at least some of Martin's claims."

"Aren't there any other witnesses we can bring in to clear up the confusion?" Jane asked.

"The only other witness on either list was Mrs. Roche. I don't think it's likely she'd help our case."

Jane looked from one face to another. "What should we do?"

"I'm going to have to write a terrific closing statement," said Mr. Atherton. "And I will be meeting with several of my colleagues to get that done. We'll have the best legal minds in New York working on this."

"Let's go home," Prescott said, standing. "If this is our last weekend together before I go to jail, I want it to be special."

"You go home," said Jane, once they were outside in the corridor. "I have something I must do." She put her hand on her beloved husband's forehead, smoothing his furrowed brow. "I'll try to get home quickly."

"Do you want me to go with you?"

"No. Go home to Ellen. She's isolated herself from all her friends. Talk about what we'll be doing out on Long Island as soon as this mess is over." She did not have to say, "If."

Prescott put his arms around Jane. "I'm going to miss you so."

"If I can help it, you won't get a chance to." She gave him a peck on the cheek and disentangled herself. "Let me get going, so I can come home faster."

As soon as she was outside, she hailed a cab and had it take her to the Bronx.

****

Mrs. Roche appeared to have shrunk since Jane last saw her, but the nurses gave assurances that she was improving. "It's good of you to come see me," the elderly woman said, sitting up in her hospital bed. "But where is Ellen? Is she still at school?"

"No, she's home for the summer. She'll come to see you soon. But I had something I wanted to talk to you about, and I didn't want her to hear it."

"It must be Martin, then. What has he done now?"

"He accused Prescott of buying Ellen from him for me."

Mrs. Roche narrowed her eyes. "So he did take money for her. He always swore to me that he didn't."

"Prescott is on trial," Jane explained. "He may have to go to prison, and the court may reverse the adoption. Ellen could go back to her father's custody."

"I see."

"She'd have to live with Martin and rely on him to take care of her. And Prescott could be ruined." She tried not to cry again, but the tears just welled up anyway. "He didn't do anything wrong."

"I assume you're talking about your husband," said Mrs. Roche in a cold voice.

Jane looked at her, worried about the tone of her comment. She stood up and looked sadly at her daughter's grandmother. "You can't help me, can you?"

Mrs. Roche smoothed the light blanket that lay across her legs. "I don't think you need me. Besides, Martin is my son." She reached out a withered arm toward Jane. "Don't worry. I'm sure nothing will happen."

****

Jane let herself into the apartment, relieved to find no one else at home. They'd left a note saying they were going to see a movie. She knew she had only been grasping at straws, but she could not just let the inevitable happen without at least trying to help. Now her profound sense of defeat, bordering on despair, was not something she wanted her family to see.

When they got home a few hours later, Jane put on her best optimistic face and cheered them up. But when the morning papers came, bearing headlines such as, "The wisdom of Solomon needed to choose," and editorials including, "Children come from God, not as presents from married boyfriends," the family was plunged into despair.

****

"This court will now resume session," said the bailiff. Jane and the rest of the people there stood while the judge took his place on the bench.

Mr. Atherton had explained that the prosecutor would make his summation first, and then, depending on how long those statements had run, there would either be a recess or Mr. Atherton would present his closing remarks. But instead of the prosecutor taking his place at the podium, he handed a note to the judge. Both attorneys were called forward to speak with the judge.

"Step back to your places," he said, banging his gavel. Turning to the court, he said, "There is another witness."

The courtroom was instantly filled with the sound of murmuring, as people asked each other who would be coming forward.

"I know this is unusual, and I wouldn't ordinarily allow it, but this witness has gone to a considerable amount of effort to be here today, and the prosecution feels we should hear her." To the bailiff he said, "Please bring her in."

Jane stood up in surprise as she saw Mrs. Roche being wheeled by a nurse to the front of the courtroom. Ellen pulled on her arm to get her to sit back down.

"I thought she wouldn't be coming here," Ellen whispered.

"That's what I thought too."

"Can I talk to her? Afterward, I mean. I haven't seen her in so long."

"I hope so, honey." But Jane worried about whether she would still want to, after the testimony. And she worried about what the old lady would say.

The prosecutor had the look of a man assured of winning as he approached Mrs. Roche, who had been helped onto the witness stand. "I want to thank you for your extraordinary effort to come here today. I understand you have something you want to say to the court."

"Well, aren't you going to ask me any questions?" said Mrs. Roche, seemingly put out that the prosecutor was going to have her do his work for him.

"Oh, yes, ma'am," he said, obviously taken aback. "Are you Martin Roche's mother?"

"Yes. I thought you knew that."

"Ahem. Yes, I did. Then you are Ellen Baldwin's grandmother, am I correct?"

"Yes."

"And as such, you also suffered the loss of your grandchild when her father was forced to give her up for adoption to Miss Baldwin, correct?"

"Objection, your honor. He is leading the witness."

"Sustained."

"Let me rephrase. Did you experience a loss when Ellen was given up for adoption?"

Mrs. Roche shook her head. "No. I did not suffer at all. I saw her just as often. She was still my granddaughter."

The prosecutor's grin slipped a bit. He furrowed his brows, and paused. But then he asked another question. "Your son was forced to give up his child by Mr. Prescott Weaver, is that correct?"

Mrs. Roche widened her eyes. "Have you ever tried to get Martin to do anything? It's impossible. No one could force him to do something if he didn't want to."

"But in the face of all that money, he decided to give his child up, didn't he?"

"I never heard about the money until recently. He sure didn't use any of it to pay me back for taking care of his baby when he left her with me for such a long time. And he never once asked about her when I had her, or came to see her." She scowled. "He didn't care at all about that child, not for a minute."

The prosecutor's smile was entirely gone, and his face looked pinched. "I have no further questions, your honor. I'm sorry for troubling you, ma'am. Let me help you get back into your chair."

"Your honor," said Mr. Atherton, jumping to his feet. "I'd like to cross-examine the witness."

The prosecutor opened his mouth to protest to the judge, but the judge's nod at Mr. Atherton made him close it again. He sat back down, nervously tapping his pencil.

"You told this court that you were not aware your son had received money at the time he gave the baby up for adoption, is that correct?"

"Yes. All I know is that he went away right after that, and he didn't come to see me again until years later, after he got out of jail."

A murmur filled the courtroom. Ellen's face got very pale, and she clutched Jane's hand.

"Mrs. Roche," said Mr. Atherton, after the judge had banged his gavel to quiet the courtroom. "From your earlier testimony, it sounds as if you were not opposed to the adoption of your granddaughter by Miss Baldwin. Is that true?"

"I was not. I was worried, at first, that I might not get to see the baby any more, but Jane has always kept in touch. I've spent a lot of time with Ellen over the years."

"More than your son did?"

"As I said before, he never cared about her. And it was probably good, so that sweet little girl didn't have to listen to him bad mouth her mother. He really hates

Jane."

"No further questions."

As Mr. Atherton sat down, the prosecutor got up. "Redirect, your honor?"

"Go ahead."

"You said that Martin changed his mind about not seeing his daughter. Correct?"

"You could say that."

"He went to see her, when she was eight, didn't he?"

"Yes. He wanted me to give him money, as usual, after he got out of prison. Not that I have much, but that didn't stop him from wanting it. I told him he would never get one red cent out of me again, since he had disappointed me so much, not giving so much as a fig for his little girl, his own flesh and blood. That was why he went to see Ellen. To try to get back on my good side. He said he'd show me how much he cares about his kid."

Jane gasped. So it had not even been Martin's idea to come and see Ellen in the first place. She felt as if she were going to faint.

Mrs. Roche sighed. "All I wanted him to do was ask me about her, but he never seemed to think of it."

The prosecutor looked shaken, but continued. "So your comments got him to think about how his daughter was and how much he missed her and wanted to see her?"

"If that's how you want to look at it. It was probably just more of Martin being Martin. When I offered to take him and say he was a friend of mine, so he could see her, but not tell her who he was, he said, 'I don't need you to go, Ma. You never did anything for me.' That was when he wrote to Jane and said he was coming."

Mrs. Roche looked across the courtroom directly at Jane. "I'm so sorry. I should have warned you when he told me he would go see Ellen. I never believed he'd really do it."

The prosecutor tried to get Mrs. Roche to stop talking. "Your honor," he said, several times.

The judge banged his gavel repeatedly. "Madame, please confine your testimony to the questions asked."

But Mrs. Roche continued. "I felt so guilty, for years afterward, that I couldn't tell you what I'd done." She was crying now. "I'm so sorry I raised such a poor excuse for a human being. And after I saw yesterday's newspapers, I knew I had to come and tell the truth."

Ellen ran to the front of the room and threw herself into Mrs. Roche's lap. "It's okay, Grandma."

The judge banged his gavel until the court got quiet, and Ellen went back to her seat.

The prosecutor, looking angry, said, "Did someone tell you to say this, Mrs. Roche?"

"No."

"No one came to see you at your nursing home, pertaining to this case?"

"Jane came to see me. On Saturday, but she didn't tell me what to say. She wouldn't. She's the most honest, reputable woman I know."

"Any more questions?" asked the judge.

The prosecutor hung his head. "No, your honor."

****

There was a short recess, allowing for order to be restored and for Mrs. Roche to visit with her granddaughter before she went back to her nursing home. Jane went to thank her for her honesty.

"I didn't think you would come," she said.

"I had to. It wouldn't have been fair for me not to tell the truth. What your husband did, so you could adopt Ellen and take care of her, was the nicest thing I ever heard of. Martin had no business starting trouble, and if he tries to get custody of her, I'll fight it with every breath in my body. He'd be no better now as a father than he was back when she was a baby." She took a deep breath and smiled. "Now you go back in there and help your husband win this case."

"We'll see you soon," Jane promised.

After summations, Prescott, Jane, and Ellen waited in the hall for the jury's decision. The time dragged endlessly, and Ellen offered to go find them some coffee.

****

"I'm sorry, Jane," Prescott said. "I wish this had never come into the open. Ellen keeps looking at me as if I'm a stranger."

"She'll learn to deal with this," Jane assured him. "But I think she feels such a sense of loss. She wondered why you never asked to adopt her."

"Did she say she wanted that?"

"Of course she does. Both of us do. But you didn't ask."

"I felt I had no right. How could I ask for such a gift?"

Jane shook her head as if to clear it. "Are you saying you wanted to, but thought the idea should come from us? But how could we ask you to do such a thing?"

"I felt the same way. How could I ask for her to let

me adopt her?"

Ellen returned, carefully balancing the coffee cups. "I hope you like it with milk," she said.

Prescott took them from her and handed one to Jane. "This wouldn't be a good time, would it?"

Jane shrugged. "There's so much going on, but I think it's important to clear the air." She turned to Ellen. "It seems we all wanted the same thing, but each of us thought it would be too much to ask. I guess that means we'll all appreciate it more."

"What do you mean?"

Prescott took Ellen's hand. "It would make me so happy if you let me adopt you."

Instead of smiling, Ellen pulled away and frowned. "You told him that was what I wanted, and he said he would do it...out of pity?"

"Of course not," said Jane.

Prescott understood. "I've always wanted to. Ever since I first asked Jane to marry me. But I didn't think I had any right to ask."

Ellen considered his statement for a few minutes. She had a serious look on her face, almost an angry look, but then she giggled and looked up at him.

"I'd love it if you would adopt me."

Prescott felt he was being given the best gift of his life, second only to Jane's hand in marriage. Now he would have Ellen as his own daughter, a girl he could not love more if he had sat with a box of cigars in the fathers' waiting room, anticipating her arrival.

"Do you mean it?" he stammered. "You'll let me adopt you?"

Ellen's eyes brimmed with tears as she nodded.

Extending his elbow for Ellen to interlock with her

own, he said, "It will complete my life's wishes. Then no one can ever come between us again."

****

His wide smile suddenly faded. "But I will not do it if I have to go to jail."

Jane felt her own bubble of happiness burst. That possibility was too awful to consider, almost as bad as the thought of losing Ellen.

Mr. Atherton came out of the courtroom. "The jury has asked to review some of the testimony and then recessed until tomorrow. Go home and get some rest." He looked extremely tired himself, and his usual look of confidence seemed strained. He declined to speculate on what the jury was looking for.

There was little said between Jane and Prescott when they got home, although they tried to keep their spirits up for Ellen. But it didn't work, as Jane discovered when she found Ellen, already in her nightgown, packing her suitcase.

"What are you doing?" Jane asked, with her heart breaking from the grief-stricken look on her daughter's face.

"I don't want to have to pack tomorrow," she said. "It would be too hard."

"Where are you going?"

Ellen kept her head down as she spoke. Jane saw teardrops falling onto the light blue bedspread. "They're going to make me go to Martin's."

For a moment, Jane was confused. "Is that what you want?"

"Of course not!" Ellen turned to her. "I never want to leave you and Uncle Prescott. I want him to be my father. But they don't care what a little girl has to say."

"This jury won't be making any decision on that," Jane reassured her. "This is only about what Prescott did."

"He did it for us! And I'm glad he did. I don't want to go to Martin's. I don't ever want to see or hear him again."

Jane wished she could tell Ellen she would not have to and have it be true, but she could not be sure. A hearing was a possibility—a probability, according to Mr. Atherton—if Prescott were to be convicted.

She gently took Ellen's suitcase off the bed and took her daughter's hands in her own. "Listen to me. I will not let you go anywhere without the fight of my life." She brushed a tear from Ellen's cheek, seeing that her eyes were filled with more tears. "You are mine forever. As long as you want me."

Ellen threw her arms around Jane and held her tight. "Forever," she said. "And longer."

Jane pulled back the covers and helped Ellen into bed as if she were a small child. "Get some sleep," she said. "And don't worry. I won't let you go."

She was able to get all the way out of Ellen's room and even close the door behind her before she collapsed in tears in the hallway. Prescott found her there.

He lifted her to her feet, and then off her feet, and carried her to their bedroom. "It will be all right," he said, placing her on the bed. "But it might not be all right soon enough."

Jane was frightened by his tone. "What do you mean?"

"If I am convicted, I want you to divorce me."

"Never! We'll file an appeal."

He turned tortured eyes to her. "Please. You must

listen. It's the same as I told Ellen. You must be free of me if the jury finds me guilty. Otherwise you might lose your daughter, and I can never let that happen."

She opened her mouth to protest, but he put his finger on her lips. "You can't let Martin have her," he said. "It was wrong twelve years ago, and it's more wrong now." He took his finger away. "Promise me."

Jane could barely speak. "How can I let you go?" she whispered.

"I can survive. Ellen can't."

Jane shook her head and squeezed her eyes shut. She could not bear to think about it. Prescott took her in his arms and held her tight.

****

"They're coming back," said Mr. Atherton, when they arrived at the courthouse at eleven the next morning. "They wanted to review Martin's testimony, and Prescott's." He looked at his client. "It's your word against his, when you come right down to it." He held the door open for them. "Let's go see what they decided."

Knees shaking, Jane took Ellen's hand and followed her husband back into the courtroom. They took their places behind Prescott, who stood facing the judge.

As the jury filed in, Mr. Atherton motioned for Prescott to remain standing.

"Has the jury reached a verdict?" asked the judge.

The foreman rose. "We have your honor." He handed a paper to the bailiff, who gave it to the judge.

"Please state your verdict," the judge directed the foreman.

"In the matter of the State versus Prescott Weaver,

on the first count, intimidation, we find the defendant not guilty."

A murmur rippled across the courtroom. Jane clutched the arm of her chair and held her breath for the next verdict.

"On the second count, extortion, we find the defendant not guilty." The crowd started talking at once, and people congratulated Prescott.

The judge banged his gavel to restore order. "The jury is to be thanked for the care and consideration they displayed." He turned to Prescott. "You are free to go." He banged his gavel one more time. "This court is adjourned." Reporters ran out of the courtroom to get their stories into the evening papers.

Jane, with Ellen, pushed through the people surrounding her husband and went to stand beside him. All three turned to face the cameras, and several pictures were taken of Jane and Prescott and his soon-to-be daughter.

Anne and Mrs. McGill stood smiling just outside the courtroom doors. Jane brought her family over to join them, pausing while Prescott shook hands with the many well-wishers who had gathered. She briefly imagined they included all those people she had loved in her past before she hugged the people who were her present, her future, and her whole world.

A word about the author...

Joani Ascher is the author of the Wally Morris mystery series, published by Thomas and Mercer. She lives in New Jersey with her husband, works in the children's room of a local library, and just finished raising her fifteenth Seeing Eye® puppy, something she wanted to do ever since she was a girl in Brooklyn, New York.

Find her at:

joaniascher.com